MW01275264

Fat Virgins,
Fast Cars
and Asian Values

Singapore Press Holdings

tHEATREwORKs

Photography by Albert Lim KS
Typewriter for cover kindly supplied by Tong Mern Sern
Antiques & Crafts

Published by Times Books International
an imprint of Times Editions Pte Ltd
Times Centre, 1 New Industrial Road
Singapore 1953

Times Subang
Lot 46, Subang Hi-Tech Industrial Park
Batu Tiga, 40000 Shah Alam
Selangor Darul Ehsan, Malaysia

Reprinted 1995

Printed in Singapore

ISBN 981 204 407 8

Fat Virgins, Fast Cars and Asian Values

A COLLECTION OF PLAYS
FROM THEATREWORKS WRITERS' LAB

SPONSORED BY SINGAPORE PRESS HOLDINGS

TIMES BOOKS INTERNATIONAL
Singapore • Kuala Lumpur

Foreword

While Singaporean book-writers have achieved much in recent years, local playwrights haven't enjoyed quite the same measure of success. Only a few locally written and produced plays can be said to be memorable. Many simply didn't pull, which can be disconcerting, considering the amount of time Singaporeans now give to the arts. The fact is, local audiences today enjoy good acting and are willing to pay for it. But where are our plays?

Local talent, as the Theatreworks Writers' Laboratory discovered, is in no small supply. There are writers in our community with marvellous ideas for excellent plays. Unfortunately, many lack the courage to begin. Most don't even know how.

In that regard, the Laboratory has been a terrific success. It has fanned creative sparks into flames, which we hope will continue to burn in the bellies of those who can now call themselves playwrights.

When Singapore Press Holdings sponsored the Laboratory, we didn't imagine the magnitude of the impact it would create on the local stage scene. But the result has been most pleasing. In this compendium of plays, the nine writers of the first Theatreworks Writers' Laboratory present the fruits of their labour.

May this book be an inspiration and an entertainment to all those Singaporeans who enjoy drama.

Denis Tay Koon Tek

Chief Operating Officer
Singapore Press Holdings

Contents

Introduction

Sponsorship for developing and nurturing projects in the arts has traditionally been difficult to secure. We are fortunate that the Theatreworks Writers' Laboratory is sponsored by Singapore Press Holdings. A theatre culture would ultimately suffer if theatre practitioners, the National Arts Council and critics do not project ahead and invest in the future. If we do not, no one else will. Plays do not grow out of thin air. Playwrights have to be nurtured: this is a slow process of evolution. It involves them first finding a personal voice of expression and then expanding this voice till it speaks universally.

This, as in all evolutionary processes, will take time. We are only at the beginning. As an older theatre company, we realise that we have to share a greater responsibility in pushing boundaries. With more plays to select from, the better plays will be produced while the weaker plays will fall by the wayside. Our theatre should reach the point where a Singaporean play is produced because of its quality rather than because it is one of a rare breed.

These nine plays have emerged from the first year of the Laboratory. They are diverse in theme and style, reflecting both Western and Asian influences. *Blood and Snow* by Desmond Sim is greatly influenced by Western verse, Shakespeare, and even the basic content itself is Western, that is, the subversion of the Snow White fairy tale. Tan Tarn How's *Home* is a naturalistic piece written in the tradition of American realism, though the situations and characters are intrinsically Singaporean. *Three Fat Virgins Unassembled* by Ovidia Yu demonstrates the flexibility, muscularity and transformational quality of Asian theatre, though its content is essentially Western notions of sexual politics. Robin Loon's *Absence Makes the Heart Grow Fonder* is a fusion of Western naturalism and Chinese melodrama with its warm sentimentality.

Dana Lam's play often reads like a film script with its quick cuts: short but tight, it explores explosively male-female tensions. Russell Heng and Theresa Tan deal with the sexuality theme in their intimate monologues very differently; the former with a gut-wrenching, confrontational approach befitting the material, the latter with a lighter, more feminine and whimsical touch. The third monologue, *Good Asian Values* by Chng Suan Tze, is a short but telling monologue of some of the schizophrenia in Singapore: Asian roots with a Western cosmopolitan shell and the inevitable inherent contradictions. *Fast Cars*, with a Brechtian base, may appear trite on first encounter but it reflects very Singaporean attitudes. It poses the question of how far one is willing to sell one's soul in an increasingly materialistic society, a modern morality tale with the inevitable melodramatic overtones.

In our search for a Singaporean voice, it is important that plays are published as well as produced. One of the crippling factors in the theatre scene thus far has been the lack of documentation and printing of scripts. As our theatre grows, it is important that a library of Singaporean plays is established and slowly built up. This will encourage critical thought, study and analysis of the Singaporean theatre.

Ong Keng Sen
Artistic Director
Theatreworks

Bernard's Story

A ONE ACT PLAY

by Dana Lam

BERNARD'S STORY is not about rape. It is about the oppression of an unfortunate young man by a callous middle class.

CHARACTERS:

BERNARD CHAN, 38. On the surface, a normal, not unusual, young man. Clean-cut. Well built. Speaks reasonably good English. Ordinarily bashful until provoked. Given to sudden flare-up of temper.

DENISE LEE, 35. On the surface, a modern, brassy young woman.

SUSIE, 28. A pretty prostitute.

LUCY. A coarse prostitute.

SIM EE. Bernard's aged maiden aunt.

LAM SOH. A neighbour.

FATHER. Bernard's father.

BERNARD'S STORY premiered at the Black Box on 15 April 1992. It was produced by Theatreworks, directed by Lim Yu Beng, and featured Casey Lim as BERNARD, and Rina Ong.

It was given a rehearsed reading by Theatreworks on 8 June 1991. It was directed by Ong Keng Sen and featured Lim Kay Siu as BERNARD, and Neo Swee Lin.

The Scene: *A small room in a police station in Singapore.*

Time: *The play opens in the pre-dawn hours, one Christmas Day. Events in the play occur over a time frame that includes the night before and the protagonists' past. Several time-shifts are necessary.*

(At rise – the room is lit by a faulty fluorescent tube light that blinks and flickers, threatening to blow any time.
BERNARD CHAN is discernible in conventional security guard's uniform, sitting on a plain wooden chair, rapt in thought.)

Time: Present.
(BERNARD speaks suddenly.)

> DON'T TOUCH ME! DON'T! NO! PLEASE, NO! LEAVE ME ALONE. LEAVE ME ALONE, PLEEEESE!

BLACKOUT

LIGHTS

Time: Present.
(The fluorescent tube is off. Light from street lamps outside filters in through a window.
BERNARD is answering police questions with regard to a rape earlier on in the same evening.)

BERNARD: Sir? Yes sir. I believe I did, Sir – raped her, Sir. Lee Sau Mui? Oh, you mean Denise Lee, Sir. Yes, sure it was Denise. *(As afterthought)* She likes to be called Dee, Sir.

How did I do it, Sir? The same way as anybody, I guess. Just like you would, in fact – sorry, I don't think it's funny too but you wanted to know – *(becoming agitated)* Just HOW DO YOU THINK I SHOULD DO IT, but just like you? Or you. OR YOU? I am also a man, right? You take off your pants, don't you? Huh? Well, so do I. Then you *(awkwardness)* take hers off, right? And you...well...you...

BLACKOUT

Time-shift. Sometime on Christmas Eve.

DENISE *(voice only)*: Bernie, BERNIE! WHAT ar–NO! BERNIE NO!

LIGHTS

Present.

BERNARD: I made sure she didn't laugh this time. *(Softer, to himself)* Made sure she couldn't. She was too, what you call – what? No, Sir, never. I've never done it to anyone before.

Sure I'm sure, Sir. Why? You don't believe me? *(Mood changes)* I know, I know... a man like me... *(short laugh).* You know what the Lam Soon *towkay soh* always used to say?

Time-shift. Sometime in the past.

LAM SOH *(voice only)*: AHH, Handsome! Come to collect your Ah Mah's soap powder ah? Good, good. My, my, you're growing up fast, you are. *(calls behind her)* Eh Lam ah, look at Chan Ma's boy, going to be taller than our Ah Bee. Eh, you're going to have a fine time with the women, handsome!

Present.

BERNARD: Yes, I'm 38, Sir. A Taurus. The sign of the bull – look at me, look. I'll show you.

(Stands, pushing back his chair. Pulls open his shirt, showing off.)

Look, Look, what do these look like, eh? Durian, right? Look, you can count them one by one – it's called definition. Comes from hard work, OK? Training – one hundred and fifty sit-ups, three times a day. Once, when I wake up, once before lunch and once more before going to bed. That's not all; in between, I pump iron, ha. I got my own set, not too heavy mind you, don't want to look like a beefcake *(short laugh)* don't want to look like the Incredible Hulk *(laughs convulsively).*

(Sudden shift in thought.)

BERNARD: What did you get for "A" levels, huh? How well did you do? How well? *(To himself, tinge of regret)* I was too busy doing my sit-ups. *(Aloud)* Making a man of myself, see? See? See?

NO, DON'T! DON'T TOUCH ME! I can report you to higher authorities, you know that? Don't think just because I don't have 'A' levels I don't know my rights. I'm –

Are you threatening me, Sir? ARE YOU THREATENING ME!

Time-shift. Sometime in the past.

SIM EE *(at the top of her voice)*: I'm counting to ten. If you don't come out of there, I'm going to nail this door, Meng, I swear. One, Two...

BLACKOUT

LIGHTS

Present.

BERNARD: The rape, Sir? Yes, yes. The rape. *(Seems to think for a while)* It was Christmas Eve. Yes, I was on duty – yes, at Greendale Condominium. I was on graveyard shift, they always put me on graveyard shift as if I don't know what they're trying to do. *(Confidentially)* They're trying to get me out of the job, Sir. They always do. But they can't, Sir, not this time, Sir.

Time-shift. Sometime on Christmas Eve.

BERNARD *(to DENISE)*: I always do a good job; makes it a point you know? That's why it hurt so bad when they told me to go.

DENISE: Aw, it was just bad luck, that's all...

BERNARD *(in officious tones)*: We're sorry we have to ask you to go, Bernard. *(Quietly, as if to himself)* Go, Bernard. We don't want you. Vamoose. Get lost. That's what you get for looking after your employers.

DENISE: You've got a good job now, Bernie. Don't think about all that any more.

BERNARD *(continuing)*: Do you know, no other sales staff came anywhere near to what I was? I cared about that company. I looked after its interests, that's what I did.

DENISE: Good for you, too!

BERNARD: How many people you know do that? You tell me. Every night, even when I was tired, so tired, I'd clean out the briefcase. I'd polish it inside-out – keep it ready for new stock. EVERYTHING. Everything goes into the bin – antibiotics, hormone capsules, creams for women's insides, creams for women's outsides *(pause)*, killer jellies – "we shouldn't be pushing old stock," I told the manager. "It affects our reputation."

Time-shift. Sometime in the past.

SIM EE *(gossiping in hushed tones)*: She went to the Sin Seh again, you know? Saw her sneaking about the kitchen myself. Her face like a white sheet. I said to my brother, something's very wrong when a married woman doesn't want her babies. My brother? He wouldn't listen, would he? He had to wait for the woman to open his eyes herself.

Present.

BERNARD: Denise? Yes, Sir, of course I know Denise. She's on the sixth storey – new girl on the block. She's the only one who bothers to talk to me *(short laugh)* – the lowly security guard – like in a friendly way. *(Laughs at the thought)* Even told me to call her Dee, Sir. Ya, she's Singaporean – just come back from LA. Lived there for three years, she told me. With a boyfriend.

BLACKOUT

Time-shift. Sometime early on the same night.

DENISE: Hiiiiiiiiie! Season's greetings, Bernie! What a beautiful evening huh, look at the stars! Hey! Why the sulk, Bernie?

LIGHTS

Present.

BERNARD: She insists on calling me Bernie, even though I told her my name is BERNARD, as in Bernard Salosa *(does a Bernard Salosa imitation)* – Bernard Chan in my case.

Time-shift. Sometime in the past. BERNARD is a teenager.

BERNARD: Susie, Aunty Susie, my friends call me Bernard.

SUSIE *(teasing)*: Do you mean you want me to call you Bernard, Bernard? OK, I'll call you Bernard provided you call me Susie, OK, Bernard? Just Susie. "Aunty" makes me sound so old. I'm not old yet. Only twenty-eight. How old are you now, Bernard? Fifteen?

Present.

BERNARD: Sim Ee said she was a BAD woman. But she was so – *beautiful.*

Time-shift. Sometime in the past.

SUSIE: What do you think you're looking at, young man?

BERNARD: Noth-nothing.

SUSIE *(giggling)*: I know, you're growing up, aren't you? You naughty boy? Are the old hags – your Sim Ee and Granma – are they around?

BERNARD: Yes.

SUSIE: Oh-oh, too bad. But you can come see me any time you can get away, OK? Standing invitation, OK, Bernard?

Present.

BERNARD: Do I like women, Sir? Nooono. Oh, sometimes I do. Sometimes I don't, Sir. But Susie was special, you know. I've known her a long time. I've always liked Susie.

Time-shift. Sometime in the past. BERNARD is 7 or 8 years old.

BERNARD: Sim Ee, Sim Ee, look what I got. Twenty cents.

SIM EE: Who gave it to you?

BERNARD: The pretty aunty next door.

SIM EE *(hysterical)*: Aiya, Meng, I told you never to go near the kind next door. Look also bring bad luck, that type. All chickens. Bad chickens, I tell you. Painted top to toe. The kind that paint their toe-nails, that's the worst. No good ever came from a woman who paints her toenails. For nothing why give you twenty cents?

BERNARD: She said I was a good boy, Ee.

SIM EE: Aiya, Heavens. Good boy, good boy. What did she make you do, tell me, quickly!

BLACKOUT

(DENISE's screams in the dark.)

LIGHTS

Sometime in the past.

SIM EE *(in a put-on voice)*: "You like sweets, boy? Come and get some, come. Aunty has plenty of sweets for you." THAT'S how she will get you, Meng. You mark my word. That's how the chickens get their cockerels, always. That's how your mother got your father alright.

BLACKOUT

LIGHTS

Present.

BERNARD *(talking to himself)*: She was so NAKED. So STARK NAKED! Everything on her shook *(pause)* and jumped about like... I wanted to laugh, she was – so funny, so...ugly. But I, I was afraid—

No, no, don't touch me. Please, don't touch me. I ca-can't. I want Aunty Susie, Susie, WHERE'S SUSIE?

BLACKOUT

LIGHTS

Time shift.

(BERNARD is a boy of 6 or 7 years old. He is playing with a row of empty coke or other bottles, hitting them with a metal spoon in rhythm.)

BERNARD: One, two, three, four, five
Better button your fly
Six, seven, eight, nine, ten
Them chicks are at it again
A-cheep, a-cheep, a-cheeping
A-cheat, a-cheat, a-cheating
A-peck, a-peck, a-pecking
A-pecking at your bottom

(He laughs, innocently, sweeping all his bottles to the ground as he finishes.)

BLACKOUT

LIGHTS

Present.

BERNARD: I'M NOT A CRIMINAL, Sir. Don't go calling me a criminal. Hey, hey, I got an education OK? I got P1 for art and literature in GCE, OK? *(Pause.)* So I failed all the other subjects, so? A P1 is a P1 OK?

(To himself) Of course, nobody cares what I'm good at. All they remember is what I'm bad at. *(Aloud)* OK, so I'm bad at maths, I'm bad at science, OK, OK, I'm bad at everything, alright? I'm Useless, alright? You're happy, are you? ARE YOU? *(He is restrained by invisible police.)*

Time-shift. Sometime in the past.

SIM EE: Your father is a proud man, Meng. You should know that by now. You should know better than to disgrace him!

Time-shift. Sometime on Christmas Eve.

BERNARD *(to DENISE)*: Father sat at one end of the dining table. Mah-Mah was on his left, Sim Ee on his right. I was alone at my end of the table. I felt I was going to throw up any time but I kept forcing the rice into my mouth. I was so afraid, waiting for father to say something.

(As FATHER) What CAN I do with him now? He's good for nothing. I should have let him go with his rotten mother.

Time-shift. BERNARD is 17.

BERNARD: I don't know why the sheets are wet, Sim Ee. I DON'T know. Please, just leave me alone and DON'T EVER come in my room again! NO! Ee? Ee don't ever come in my room again!

SIM EE *(to anyone)*: He takes all the bottles in the house and hides them under his bed. And that's not enough, you know? He pees in them. No wonder he never gets out of his room! Rows and rows – F & N bottles, brandy bottles, beer bottles, even my soya-sauce bottles! Aiya, what has come over the boy!

Time-shift. Earlier on, evening of Christmas Eve.

BERNARD *(to DENISE)*: I don't know why I did it, really. I guess I just wanted to – do something radical. Mind you, when I was doing it, it didn't seem like anything unthinkable. Not anything like what Ee and all the others make it out to be. It was just a bit of challenge to myself. You know, it takes skill to aim that way. You miss the first time, you try again. You miss again and you try again. I got pretty good at it.

DENISE *(disbelieving)*: No!

BERNARD: I filled up every bottle, OK? Without spilling a drop.

DENISE *(giggling)*: No!

BERNARD: What, you want me to show you?

DENISE *(still laughing)*: No, I don't, oh come on.

BERNARD: I'll show you. *(Grabs an imaginary bottle, unzips his fly, fumbles with the bottle.)* Oh shit! I've lost touch! (*Sound of bottle being thrown.*)

BLACKOUT

DENISE: Bernie, BERNARD, BERNARD, YOU'RE HURT-ING ME!

LIGHTS

Present.

BERNARD: But I have to give you all the details, Sir. So that you can have a PROPER statement, Sir.

Time-shift to sometime in the past.

A WOMAN: Aiya, Sim, what's the matter with your Kok Meng,

huh? Such a waste, you know, so tall and strong, and good-looking some more. Still trying to re-do his GCE ah? Isn't it too late? How old alleady? 26 ah? Tsk. Tsk. Could be somebody's father alleady! How is it the father never talks to him ah? Very unusual, isn't it, father not talking to his own son?

SIM EE *(speaking in hushed tones)*: You HAVE to do something, brother, you are his Fa—

FATHER *(in an outburst)*: I am NOT his father – How do you know I'm his father? I don't!

SIM EE: He – but…

FATHER: Don't say any more. I don't want to hear any more. I wash my hands of that boy a long time ago. I should have sent him off with his so-called mother.

Present.

BERNARD: Did I say I am Chan Kok Meng, Sir? Actually, I'm not sure if I am. But it's in my IC right? Right. *(Perks up)* It also says MALE for sex, right?

Time-shift. Sometime in the past.

(BERNARD labours with his weights.)

SIM EE *(aside)*: Look at him, huffing and puffing with those weights. Always looking in the mirror; always locked up in his room or the bathroom. What kind of man is that? *(She spits.)*

Time-shift. Sometime in the past.

PROSTITUTE: My, you're a good-looking man, mister. Susie, Daisy, what does it matter? We're all the same. Not that much different. My name is Lucy, rhymes with Susie, got chance or not?

BERNARD *(hesitant and in fear)*: No, No, Don't. Don't Touch Me. I've, I've changed my mind. I don't want to do it. Don't, Don't,

Get off, Get off, Get off me!

Time-shift. Present.

BERNARD *(to himself)* She was so naked. So STARK NAKED.
She fell on top of me. She said it wasn't the usual position but
some clients like it – "maybe it will help you," she said.

(To an imaginary person) Get, get off me, Get OFF!

(To himself again) She pushed herself against me. I could hardly
breathe. I could feel the sweat on her body. She was laughing,
her mouth was opened. I could see stains and lipstick on her
front teeth. Then she raised herself and her breasts swung at me
– left, right, left, right – LEAVE ME ALONE, leave me alone.
Please. Don't touch me. Don't touch me.

(BERNARD breathes rapidly.)

(To police officers) I AM talking about the rape. YES, SIR,
THE RAPE.

Huh? Lee Sau – Denise Lee? Oh yes, of course, Denise.

BLACKOUT

*(A dim light on DENISE and BERNARD, sometime on Christmas
Eve.)*

DENISE *(in an intimate whisper)*: It's the loneliest night of the year,
isn't it, Bernie, Christmas Eve? Don't you hate Christmas Eve?
I HATE Christmas Eve. Nobody cares about me on Christmas
Eve, Bernie, nobody. If I killed myself tonight, they'd still be
celebrating tomorrow.

BERNARD: Who'd be celebrating tomorrow?

DENISE *(tipsy)*: You. Maybe. Cos, I'm killing myself tonight, remember?

BERNARD *(also tipsy)*: I'll also be dead then.

(The two of them laugh.)

DENISE: Do you like me, Bernie?

(BERNARD does not answer.)

DENISE *(repeating herself slowly)*: DO YOU LIKE ME, Bernie?

BERNARD *(quietly)*: Yes.

DENISE *(elated)*: Really? Reallyreallyreally? *(Directly)* Why?

(BERNARD does not answer.)

DENISE *(in a tantrum)*: I want to know why, Bernard.

BERNARD: You talk to me. Nobody really talks to me.

DENISE *(disappointed)*: Oh. And if I don't talk to you, won't you like me any more?

BERNARD: I guess not.

DENISE *(simply)*: You're a shit-hole, Bernard.

BERNARD *(flaring up a little)*: Don't call me names! I won't take that from anyone. Not even you.

(Silence.)

BERNARD: What are you doing?

DENISE: Taking off my clothes. *(Stands with her clothes off, look-ing at BERNARD).*

It's hot.

(BERNARD looks away. Sinks to his haunches. DENISE, too, sinks down to her heap of clothes. They sit in silence, she with her head tilted toward the ceiling, he with his head turned away. After a stretch of time, she speaks without moving.)

DENISE *(head still tilted to ceiling)*: I need somebody.

(BERNARD does not respond. After a moment's hesitation, DENISE laughs, an embarrassed laugh, still with her face to the ceiling. Imperceptibly at first, BERNARD begins to move, almost furtively, towards her. When he is close enough, he makes a tentative move to touch her. She reaches down to him. They embrace in a kneeling position.)

DENISE: Oh, Bernard. *(She tries to kiss him.)*

BERNARD: Don't laugh at me, Dee.

DENISE *(protesting)*: I wasn't.

BERNARD: Don't laugh at me.

(They kiss; a long kiss. She guides his hands along her body. They move to the floor, she over him, then he over her. Lights out. Silence except for their breathing and murmurs from DENISE.)

DENISE: Bernie...Bernie, I want you.

(Silence.)

DENISE *(urgently)*: Bernie, I'm ready.

(Silence.)

DENISE *(puzzled)*: Bernie, what?

BERNARD *(urgently)*: Don't worry Dee, I can do it.

DENISE *(puzzled)*: Wha-What?

BERNARD: Don't worry Dee, I can do it, I can.

DENISE: Bernard, you're hurting me. Bernard?

(Sounds of fumbling and tumbling in the dark.)

DENISE: Bernard? Bern... what are you up to? The bottle's broken, Bernie – Noooo! no! No! Bernie, Nooooo!

(DENISE screams.)

Time-shift. Present.

(BERNARD takes his hands from his ears, a strange glint in his eyes.)

BERNARD *(to police officers)*: I did it, you know? I did it.

-END-

Lest The Demons Get To Me

by Russell Heng Hiang Khng

Transvestite KC has problems: family rejection, a lover who is a married man, and the closure of Bugis Street. He decides on a sex change in the belief that this will resolve the dilemmas in his life. After his operation, his father passes away, and he is asked to perform funeral rites, being the only son. But 'he' is now a 'she', and so a big dilemma remains: should KC go dressed as a man out of filial duty and for the sake of family decorum, or as a woman to be true to himself as he is now? Where does the honest path lie?

CHARACTERS:

KIM CHOON, a Bugis Street transvestite

CHUCK

LANDLADY

MOTHER

SISTER

LEST THE DEMONS GET TO ME premiered at the Black Box on 15 April 1992. It was produced by Theatreworks and featured Jeremiah Choy as KIM CHOON. It was directed and designed by William Teo, with lights by Tracie Howitt.

It was given a rehearsed reading by Theatreworks on 20 Sept. 1991. It was directed by Ong Keng Sen and read by Koh Boon Pin as KIM CHOON.

KIM CHOON is the only character to be seen on stage. The other characters are voices from off stage. All LANDLADY and MOTHER's lines are spoken in any Chinese dialect which the cast can manage. English translations of the Chinese lines are provided in parentheses and are not to be said aloud.

ACT ONE
SCENE ONE

(The scene is a rented room in an apartment probably somewhere in Geylang, and furnished in a way typical of a flat in that neighbourhood. The essential props would be a bed with all kinds of clothing strewn on it, a wardrobe, a screen for the character to change costumes on stage, a telephone, a writing table with a little mirror on it which doubles as a dressing table, a stand-up body-length mirror and an armchair. Kim Choon, the Bugis Street transvestite, stumbles in all dolled up and singing the last few lines of the theme song from "The Final Night Of Madame Chin.")

KC *(sings)*: 曲终人散，回头一瞥…最后一夜 *(Speaks)* My Malay friend Anita Sarawak loves this song, can sing every Chinese word of it but doesn't know the meaning. Not Anita, *the* singer, but Anita, my best friend, who works with me on Bugis Street.

最后一夜 – it means "the final night" in English, I explained to Anita. Well, we have come to *the* final night; the final night of Bugis Street! God, what a party it was! You should have seen the people who turned up and the things we did.

(Pause.)

But no, I don't want to talk about it. My friend, or sister, as we call each other on Bugis Street; my sister, Anita Sarawak, she said to me, "KC, we are going to make the most of this night and after that, we will not talk about it any more. There's no point looking back for we are never going to get another place like this street again, ever! Not in Singapore. Not in the whole world." Damn right she is! So I am not going to talk about it. What's over is over!

(Sits at dressing table facing audience and looks into mirror.)

Time to get out of all these too.

(Removes wig and starts to remove make-up.)

He was there tonight with a group of his friends. You know, he looked at everybody and everything but not me as if just by letting his eyes rest on me for a moment would let out that he and I are having a whatchamacalit. Well, I don't suppose I should be surprised or angry. He did write to me *(picks up an envelope from the table and waves it)* announcing his intention to be there with some of his friends to witness the passing of Bugis Street *(takes out letter from envelope and reads it).*

Dear Kim, *(pause)* that's what he calls me; by my middle name Kim, as in Kim Choon. All the men call me Kim. Suitably androgynous, I suppose. But all the sisters in Bugis Street call me by my initials "KC." *(Turns back to letter and reads)* Dear Kim, I am going to be there for the final night of Bugis Street with some friends. Shall see you next week, same time, same place. Look forward to it. Capital "C."

(Puts down letter.)

"C" stands for Chuck. Chuck! What kind of name is that for a Singaporean, you tell me. You know, all these four years I have been having this whatchamacalit with him, I always suspected that Chuck is not his real name. Can you imagine that?! Four years and I may not even have his real name. I know bits and pieces about Chuck, gathered here and there through our conversations. The onus has always been on me to find something to talk about. He just sat there on the bed screening the topics I raised. If it was taboo, like his job or his family, he kept silent.

If he approved, I got monosyllabic answers or, if he was in the right mood, an entire sentence.

Fortunately a seasoned old pro like me knows enough tricks of the trade to handle a difficult customer like that. And so over the years, you can say something has been worked out between us. He visits me regularly. At least once a week. Brings me little presents now and then; always something extra nice on the anniversary of the day that he first came back with me to this room. Which goes to show he can be sentimental about us. But there has never been any gifts on my birthday because he has never bothered to ask me when it is. He used to pay me every time he visited, like all the others. Then he started to pay me by the month. Somewhere along the line, he stopped paying altogether. I don't think I mind, at least not about not being paid. Honestly, I can't even remember when exactly he stopped being a paying customer and became a, a, a... Yes, that's the part I mind. I don't know what he has become to me. He is not a client but he is also not a lover.

"Then why do you put up with him?" asked the sisters. "Well, I like that," I said to them. "Don't most of you have creeps like him in your lives too?!" And we would all laugh at this thing we have in common: a taste for self-punishment. I guess we put up with the likes of Chuck because they are one of the few things that are constant in our lives *(lights cigarette)*.

Initially he used to say, after answering my questions in the shortest of sentences, "You are quite boring!" I could have throttled him but a poor girl has to earn a living. So I worked at it. I prepared long lists of harmless topics and nowadays we actually talk quite a lot. He has quite wide-ranging interests, that man. Books, the theatre, music, both pop and classical, and politics. A rare breed in this country. He said the same of me too. "If I did not know you personally, I would not think there could possibly be someone like you," he said when I debated

him to a standstill on economic sanctions against South Africa.
It was his polite way of saying, "I never knew a Bugis Street ah
qua can be so well informed." I did not tell him that this ah qua
had three years at the London School of Economics. *(Pause.)*
Although I never did finish my degree.

But I did find out that he studied in the US, and that could have
given him the name Chuck. But don't ask me which university
he went to. He wouldn't tell. And, of course, he wouldn't say
what he read for fear that I may guess his occupation. The sisters
and I used to joke about what Chuck did for a living. Since he
carries a pager, they thought he could be a doctor. But the few
times the pager sounded while he was here, he did not rush off
to check it out, which was what you would expect of a doctor
with a patient waiting. It did cross my mind that he could be a
lawyer because he speaks rather well. But all the sisters thought
he was too well-built and suntanned to be doing a desk-bound
job. They reckoned he was more likely to be an architect or
engineer, somebody who had to go out and survey a work site in
the sun. Since Chuck was so secretive, he could well be a senior
civil servant. God forbid! And somebody suggested that he
could be a Rhodes scholar since he is built like a rugby player.
Can you imagine that?! One of Singapore's four Rhodes schol-
ars is fooling around with me! To that, my friend Anita would
say, "This country is not as well behaved as we would like to
think it is, KC. It is just full of hypocrites. People like us who
parade on Bugis Street for all to see are some of the very few
honest people there are."

(At this point, takes off bra and removes tissue paper padding.)

Well, perhaps not all that honest. Sure, all of us get secretive
customers. But Chuck's behaviour is just too extreme. You
know, all these years and I still have no means of getting in
touch with him if I need to urgently. Or if I miss him, which I do
sometimes. He doesn't give me a telephone number or an ad-

dress. I can send him a note but only to a PO box. He rings me
only from public phones as if he is afraid I would get Telecoms
to trace his calls. I know because we are always interrupted by
the beeping tone warning us that time is running out and Chuck
would fumble for another coin to feed the machine.

Most of the time, he writes short notes like this. As if that is not
bad enough, he types them. I suspect he fears handwriting can
give him away. Once I teased him that the capital "C" for Chuck
in his letters always looks chipped in the middle and, what do
you know, he went out and bought himself a new typewriter. So
now the "C"s are perfectly anonymous.

(Radio clock goes off.)

Shit, what time is it? 9 am. Why on earth would I want to set the
alarm so early for? What day is it today?

(Rummages among things on table and produces a diary.)

Oh dear, it is visiting day. I need something strong for that.

(Walks to corner to fix a drink.)

I don't like these chirpy Sunday morning songs. There is nothing
to be chirpy about on visiting day!

*(Turns off the radio and turns on the tape recorder. Chinese opera
is heard. Takes up a pair of pyjama trousers and starts to do opera
movements with them.)*

LANDLADY *(baritone voice offstage in dialect)*: 金姐，你不想睡，
我想！关小声点！ ("Sister Kim, you may not want to sleep but I
do. Turn down that thing.")

KC: That is my landlady. Used to be my landlord; until he had his
operation. One of the early pioneers of Bugis Street. Saved up
enough for a sex change, was kept as a mistress by this old
Indonesian businessman who gave him, er, I mean her, a few
houses. She can afford to stop working and live comfortably on

rents. Oh, well! It won't be long before I become a real woman myself. *(Waves a bank account book)* Finally saved enough for a sex change operation. But having the money for it is not the biggest problem. The most agonising part is being sure yourself that you want this final irreversible crossover from one sex to another.

They say it is painful, very painful. So you start asking yourself, is it necessary? What do you get for cutting yourself up to look like a woman? Greater acceptance? Heck, when I came to work on Bugis Street, I more or less decided that acceptance was not important any more. We just had to be ourselves to be happy. And Bugis Street is where we can be at our campy best and people leave you alone because it is expected of you.

But Anita warned me about staying too long on the beat. In this business, forty is old, she said. Accepting yourself is one thing but making enough to pay the rent is another. Look at those old sisters, KC! They don't make the money we make. But what is there in this country for a retired ah qua to do? Take my advice, KC, go get that operation. It doesn't make you a better person but it sure gives you more options. That Indonesian business-man would not have bought your landlady all those houses if she had remained a man in drag. I don't understand the psychology behind it but I sure know how to get around it, said Anita. She is getting her operation next month. Only tonight, she was say-ing to me: "Some men can accept you as a transvestite but their country will not. If I want my immigration papers, I've got to be a woman to marry my Aussie lover properly. And don't forget there is Jeff unless you are prepared to be saddled with Chuck for the rest of your life."

Yes, Jeff. Jeff Slater, my American pen pal. Anita registered me with this scheme where European men are paired up with Asian brides. That was how she found her Australian. I corresponded with six guys from three continents but this *(fishes out a photo of a mature rugged looking American man from his drawer)* lasted the longest. Ah, I almost forgot... *(fumbles in handbag and fishes out an envelope)* Jeff's latest letter. I was too busy to open it yesterday. Hm... rather a big envelope *(tears open envelope)*. Well, I'll be damned. A birthday card. How on earth does he know next Tuesday is my birthday? I don't think I ever told him. *(Reads letter enclosed in card)* ...As usual, it's all about snooker. Now, let's see, one, two, three... six grammatical errors.

Well, at least I get a card. And Anita will remind me that Chuck does not even know when my birthday is. She is quite determined to get me to dump Chuck and go for Jeff. And Jeff wants a woman, KC... And KC wants a man whose passion is more than just snooker and who writes good English, even if it is American English.

(Telephone rings and she walks over and picks up the receiver.)

Hello. Oh, it's you, Sis. Yes, Sis, tell Mother I haven't forgotten. I shall be back today. Oh, the usual time. Well, perhaps a bit later. I haven't taken my shower yet. How is Father? Is he still under medication for his blood pressure? Oh, c'mon, Sis. Not you too. Even if I come home today with a blushing bride by my side, Father will still need to be treated for blood pressure, diabetes and whatever else he is suffering from. My marriage will make him a happier person, not necessarily a healthier person. Yes, I know, I know. I will be careful with my words. I don't want to aggravate his condition. Look, if we continue talking I am going to be real late. Yes, bye bye.

(Hangs up receiver.)

God, all these years, my family never let me forget that what I am can kill my Father if he finds out.

(Takes off last bit of dress leaving only a pair of briefs on and stares at himself in mirror. He then wraps towel round waist but then

decides to wrap it round his chest. Hums "Final Night" as he leaves the room.)

LANDLADY: 生意好吗, KC? ("How's business, KC?")

KC: 差不多啦. ("So so.")

LANDLADY: 昨晚很晚才回来? ("Back very late last night?")

KC: 是啊! 有个 party. 黑街的最后一夜。你忘了吗? ("Yes, there was a party. Have you forgotten? It was the last night of Bugis Street.")

LANDLADY: 是吗? 好快啊! 那你以后有什么打算? ("Really, so fast. And what are you going to do from now onwards?")

KC: 学你啦! 找个有钱丈夫。 ("Emulate you, find a rich husband.")

LANDLADY: 啋! ("Choi." – *A Cantonese expletive.*)

SCENE TWO

(KC walks into room after his shower with towel round his chest and another wrapped round his head. Phone rings.)

KC: Hello. Oh, it's you again. Tell Mother I won't forget to come back dressed as a man. No, I won't forget the things I am supposed to have bought from Thailand. No, I haven't bought them yet. I shall get them on my way home from the fruit shop. No, it won't be a problem. Tell Mother she can even have a choice. Does she prefer Thai durians or mangos? Both are in season. Yes, see you all later, Sis *(hangs up)*.

People who do not know my family would never believe what I have been doing. When I left my family to work on Bugis Street, Mother knew as mothers tend to have a knack for knowing such things. But my father! He would have killed me or himself or both if he had found out. So we kept it from him. He is rather frail and I don't want to be responsible for causing his death. Mother tells him that I am running my company's Bangkok office and can only come back once a month. And so once a month on visiting day, like today, I take out my suitcase *(drags out little suitcase from under the bed)* and go home like I have just gotten off a plane from Bangkok.

(Starts to dress as an executive looking man.)

To improve the deception, I buy Thai fruits in season. It will be mangos this time. Thank God for the excellent merchants of Singapore, I can buy the freshest Thai fruits even at the little shop round the corner. Then I would put them into this suitcase which is always ready-packed to be used as a prop for this monthly farce. I have even got a Bangkok Airport baggage tag on it. As Anita would say, "You can't beat an ah qua for getting the little details right!"

But then I have always wondered; maybe Father knows after all. He just does not want to be told directly. When I was in primary school he did not like me watching Chinese operas. So Mother said to me, "Your Father says you should not be watching too many Chinese operas because you are always moving like you are one of the heroines on stage. You don't walk, you glide!" And she stopped taking me to the opera, and for a while I hated Father for that. Mother also stopped playing her opera records. But it did not really work. The neighbours on either side of our house were avid opera fans and they played their records through the day and I would sing along silently beneath my breath. Sometimes when Father wasn't looking, I would even mime to the music. It didn't fool him, of course, but there was nothing he could do about it. And so today, I can sing ten complete Chinese operas. I think Father knows. He is resigned to it.

Then there was the time when I tried putting on Mother's black bra for size. It was my last year at secondary school and coming back one afternoon, I saw Mother's black bra lying around in a pile of laundry. Nobody was at home and so I slipped into it, stood in front of the mirror and started to do what had always come naturally to me: play at being a woman. Boy, did I want a pair of tits. That afternoon, I was in my element, swaying my hips, stroking myself all over, when suddenly, I saw in the mirror Father standing at the doorway. I expected all hell to break loose, but he only shook his head and walked away. We never talked about it.

Well, whether fooled or not, Father certainly sounds very earnest every time he warns me against Thai women. "Be careful, Choon," he would say, "I hear that women in Thailand are quite good at snaring men with black magic." Which is also his way of telling me I should start thinking about getting a wife. That's parents for you. They never give up hope.

There were times when I felt so tempted to go home in full drag and let the truth out. And once or twice, I left a faint trace of lipstick on to test the waters. Father did not notice but Mother flipped. Which is why she or my sister would now ring up every visiting day to tell me to dress properly. She allows me one concession though. I may wear a little earring if I want to. She, after all, was the one who put it on me when I was a child. My parents had five daughters in a row before having me, a son. As a child I was often ill. When Mother consulted a fortune teller, he had this to say: "Mrs Lee, you are not supposed to have a son at all. The demons are jealous of you for cheating destiny and they will be out to get your baby boy. One of the ways to fool them is to make them think he is just another daughter. Put an earring on him. During festivals or on the first and the fifteenth days of each lunar month, be especially careful. I suggest you dress him up as a girl." Now you know why I like cross-dressing. I have had lots of practice. The boys at school used to tease me but I dare not take the earring off because I was frightened of the demons. Later on in life, I ran into other boys who were wearing a single earring for the same reason.

(Clips on one earring.)

Then, of course, it became fashionable and single earrings were legion in the streets. Poor demons, it must be getting impossible for them to track down their targets now.

(Takes off his earring and looks at it.)

Lest the demons get to me. Lest the demons get to me. Mother used to remind me on the phone, "Don't forget to come home dressed like a man. Wash off all your make-up but wear your earring." I have stopped wearing it for quite some time now and she has not said anything. I don't think it is because she has not noticed. Nothing like this could escape her. Nope, she has probably given up on me and wouldn't mind letting the demons have me.

I wonder what my parents will say when I have my sex change. In a way, this worry has kind of held me back all these years. Anita keeps telling me: KC, don't be a fool. One day they will be dead and you will be alive. Your old man will be upset but he will get over it. Just like mine.

(Telephone rings.)

Hello. Oh! it's you, Chuck. Yes, what can I do for you? Yes, I saw you with your friends last night. Do I mind you not coming up to say hello? Let's put it this way, Chuck: I do not mind minding. No, I am not angry. No, I cannot see you today. No, of course, I am not angry. Today is visiting day, have you forgotten? Oh, sorry, I take that back. You can't forget something which you are not aware of in the first place, can you?! Oh, you are aware that I visit my family once a month. I thought it would be like so many other things about me that you have no interest to know. No, Chuck, for the third and last time, I am not angry with you. No, we can't talk because I am already rather late for my home visit. Would next Sunday afternoon be alright? Yes, I guess so, unless you cancel by mail. No, Chuck, for the fourth and last plus one time, I am not angry. Why am I shouting? I am not shouting. It is a poor line. I hear you very faintly so I automatically raise my voice thinking you will have the same problem. This phone has been like that for the past week or so. Perhaps somebody is bugging it, Chuck. You better not say anything self-incriminating even though you are using a public phone. For the fifth and last plus two time, I am not angry with you. Besides, you are using a public phone, aren't you? There you are, I hear the beeping tone now. Your time is almost up, Chuck, and I really must go. Bye bye.

(Hangs up, picks up suitcase and exits.)

ACT TWO

SCENE ONE

(A year later. Same room but decorated with roses, some of which must have been there for a few days because they are already wilting. KC sits at writing table looking tired. She is a real woman now having had her sex change. She should be dressed simply like an ordinary woman. Telephone rings.)

KC *(picks up phone)*: Hello. Oh! Hello, Sis. Yes, I have eaten. I feel reasonably well. Pain? Not much now. The funeral? I told you I will come if I don't have to dress as a man. Sis, it says here in my new IC, in the blank space for sex, capital "F" for female. Tell Mother I am no longer her only son. The surgeon changed that last week. I am now her sixth daughter, your new younger sister. Sis, you have always been a fair person. Don't you think I'll look absurd in a man's wig and a very loose shirt to hide my breasts. You know my tits are really bigger than yours now?!

Do it for Father! That's a very familiar line. Do it for Father! Do it for Father! All these years I have been doing it for Father.

Father is dead now. Do I need to go on duping a dead man? Isn't it a lot more civilised if you all carry on with Father's funeral without me? When it is all over, I shall visit his grave quietly on my own and I won't be embarrassing the family. Yes, of course I know there are funeral rites which should be performed by a son. But I am no longer a son, dammit! That's what I have been trying to explain to you all this while! Are you stupid or are you just plain stubborn?! I AM NOT MY FATHER'S SON. I AM HIS DAUGHTER LIKE YOU! GODDAMMIT! *(Slams down receiver and flops onto table sobbing.)*

(Knocking on the door) Who is it?

LANDLADY: 你男朋友又送你一蓝花。 ("It is another basket of flowers from your boyfriend.")

KC *(runs over to door, opens it a little and stretches out her hand to bring in a basket of flowers)*: 谢谢。 ("Thank you.")

LANDLADY: 哗! 每天送你玫瑰，一定很爱你。几时可以喝你的喜酒? ("Wow, he must really be in love with you to send you roses every day. When are we going to be treated to a wedding banquet?")

KC: 没有你那么好命! ("I am not as lucky as you are!")

(Slams the door.)

On the morning that I came back from hospital, Mother called me on the phone to tell me that Father died suddenly of a heart attack in the middle of the night. Well, she can't say I caused it because he did not know I was in hospital. She never once asked me how I felt after the surgery. All she wanted was for me to go back and perform the funeral rites as a son. I did not argue with her. I just hung up and did nothing but weep. Both Chuck and Anita came and put their arms around me. Anita wasted no time in telling me that I should be firm and not go back if I didn't feel like it.

But Chuck said, "You better go, Kim, since you are the only son." Anita beat me to an answer. "Chuck, KC is no longer the only son. She is the additional daughter, just in case you have been too busy to notice." Chuck snapped back, "For you and I, Kim is now a woman. But for her father, Kim is still his son." "But her father is dead and KC is alive." They both sat there sulking until I broke the silence and told them about the strange dream I had round about the time Father must have passed away. It seemed like a dream but there was a point when it was as if he was standing there by my hospital bed, smiling in the most reassuring manner like he wanted to tell me that he understood why I did what I did and that it was alright.

Anita busied herself by unpacking for me but Chuck was really absorbed by the story. Then he changed the subject and said, "I bought you these roses. Your favourite flower." Anita cut in again before I could say anything, "Roses in full bloom, KC, pretty to look at but they won't last long." I guess she is right, some are wilting already.

Then Anita fished a letter out of her handbag and handed it to me. "Letter from Jeff; I hope it is the one you are waiting for." It was! It was a letter proposing marriage but I can't say I was wild with joy. Instead I handed it to Chuck as if that was the most natural thing to do and even before he could finish reading it, I explained how I knew Jeff as if I owed him an explanation. Chuck looked up from the letter and asked, "What does he look like?"

I handed him this picture of Jeff *(produces framed picture from drawer of table)*. Chuck studied Jeff's photo, looking ill at ease because Jeff isn't bad looking. In fact I would say Jeff scores higher points in the looks department with that firm Caucasian angular jawline and the greenish hint of unshaven stubble.

Chuck's next question, "Are you going to marry him?" "Are you going to marry KC, Chuck?" Anita beat me to an answer again. Chuck sat there very quiet and I got more and more impatient. Finally I said, "Yes, Chuck, I am going to marry Jeff." He said, "I see. You know this guy only through his letters. You think that is enough?" "Well, Chuck, I know his full name, his home address. I can call him on the phone. That's far more than anything I know about you." "What does he do for a living?" Chuck continued. "He cooks," I replied. Chuck asked, "He is a chef?" I said, "I wouldn't say that. He cooks at this hamburger joint." Chuck smiled at this and it sure as hell bothered me. So I screamed at him, "At least he tells me what he is doing. That makes him one of the very very few honest people I know! And honestly, I am sick and tired of you and your dishonesty. The biggest favour you can do me will be to get out of my life!"

He has not been back since. In the past, whenever we quarrelled, he would phone later to apologise. But no calls this time. Only the flowers keep coming. One bouquet a day. Anita, of course, isn't impressed. "You are better off rid of him," she said.

(Pauses in deep reflection.)

I wonder why he was so firm about getting me to attend father's funeral. Didn't know he was big on fathers. He never talked about his parents. "Oh, get wise, KC. He never tells you anything. So why should he discuss his old man with you. Remember, Jeff is the one who sends you Valentine cards and birthday cards. Not your balding secretive Chuck." But there are these flowers and Chuck does not know when my birthday is. "Oh, yes. Chuck knows when your birthday is," says Anita. "I told both of them. It was an experiment I conducted to see who cares more for you, KC. How do you think Jeff found out the date. I even suggested to Chuck that it would be nice if he sends a card and offered to buy one for him. But he just mumbled something about not being the sort who are into cards. God knows what he is into, KC." Yes, trust Anita to do something like that.

(Goes over to airpot to make coffee while humming "Final Night.")

Chuck asked me once, "You are always humming this song from the movie. Are you moved by the sentimentality? About everything being so mutable, the party that must end, the music that must be stopped on the final night?" See what I mean? The guy can talk. Oh, God, I do miss that man. I wish he would call or send me a letter. And damn it, Chuck, why don't you even give me your pager number?

(Phone rings.)

Hello. Where the hell have you been this whole week? Like hell, I am not angry. No, no, no, I can talk. Oh, you want to come over later. OK, we will talk then. See ya, Chuck.

(Hangs up as light fades out.)

SCENE TWO

(Sound of heavy rain before light fades in. Chuck is behind the screen changing. KC leans against the wall beside it, smoking a cigarette.)

KC: Chuck, why do you have to strip behind the screen? There is no part of your body that I have not already seen!

CHUCK: I am shy.

KC: That much I figured out, thank you. Here, pass me your wet things. I guess you parked three streets away as usual so that nobody will see your car; even in this rain.

CHUCK: I'm sorry, Kim.

KC: Nah, it's alright. After all these years, what is there left to be sorry about? Or to be sorry for.

CHUCK: So are you going to the States?

KC: You think I shouldn't?

CHUCK: It is your decision.

KC: God, Chuck, don't you ever say outright what you feel?

CHUCK: I did last time I was here. You did not like it.

KC: No, I suppose I didn't. What would you do after I am gone? Find another drag queen to have a similar arrangement with?

CHUCK: I haven't thought of it. All I know is I'm going to miss you.

KC: Oh, thank you very much. Heh, why are you standing behind the screen talking to me?

CHUCK: Because you have not given me something to put on.

KC: Oh sorry, I forgot I am only allowed to see you naked beneath the blanket. I'll get you a bathrobe.

(Goes over to wardrobe where a black dress and a black shirt cum trouser set hang from door. Removes them to open wardrobe.)

Do you really think I should go to my old man's funeral?

CHUCK: Yes.

KC: Why?

CHUCK: Because he is your father and you will regret it one day if you don't.

KC: No, I don't mean that sort of why. I mean why are you so intent on making me go to the funeral? It is the latest mystery about you that Anita and I cannot figure out.

(Long pause.)

Well, I am waiting for an answer.

CHUCK: Because I was not at my father's funeral and I have regretted it to this day.

KC: Tell me more about it. Heh, why are you still standing behind the screen? Oops! Sorry. I haven't given you the bathrobe.

CHUCK: And it is getting cold.

KC: Sorry, sorry (*reaches into wardrobe and brings out a bathing robe*).

(Knocking on the door.)

Who is it?

SISTER: Choon, it's me.

KC: God, what on earth are you doing here, Sis?

SISTER: I want you to come back with me to the funeral.

KC (*rushes over to screen to speak to CHUCK but does not pass the robe to him*): My sister is at the door. Keep still. I will try and get rid of her.

SISTER (*knocks persistently on door*): Hurry up, what's taking you so long?

MOTHER: 阿春，快开门！? ("Open the door, Choon. Hurry up.")

KC: God! Mother is here too. Oh no! It's not going to work like that. You are not coming in.

SISTER: Listen, Choon. Taoist priests will perform the final rites tonight. Mother says if you are not there to do it, Father won't rest in peace.

KC: No, Mother! This has got to stop! You have made one too many demands of me. Exploit! That's the word! You exploit my fear of hurting you. Mother, this has got to stop. It is not fair.

MOTHER: 阿春，他在讲什么? ("What is Choon talking about?")

KC: Sis, you tell her what I just said. My dialect has never been that good and I am out of practice.

SISTER: It's no easier for me and I doubt she will ever understand. *(In halting dialect to MOTHER)* 妈，阿春说你不该迫他回去。他说那样很不讲道理。你就是不讲道理。("Mother, Choon says you should not force him to come back. It is very unreasonable. You have always been unreasonable!")

KC: That's not all I say, Sis. I didn't just say she was unreasonable. Tell her why I think she is unreasonable.

MOTHER: 不讲道理？我怎么不讲道理。你爸跟我辛辛苦苦把他养大，他却让我们伤心难过。送他到英国念大学，他也没有把书念完。("Unreasonable. How have I been unreasonable? Your father and I, we have done our best for him. But he only made us very sad and ashamed. We sent him to England to study and he didn't even finish his degree.")

KC: Oh, I like that, Mother. So I did nothing worthwhile but made Father and you sad and ashamed. But look what you have done to me!

MOTHER: 他在讲什么？("What is he saying now?")

SISTER: 他说他今天这样是你害的！("He said you are the cause of what he is today.")

MOTHER: 我害他！我怎么害他？难道我叫他跟男人睡觉！("I am the cause?! I am the cause?! How am I the cause?! Don't tell me I forced him to earn a living by sleeping with men!")

KC: 不是你，是谁害的？("If you are not the cause, who is?!") Sis, ask her who first taught me I should dress like a girl even before I could talk? Who made me wear an earring?

SISTER: You know the reasons for all that. They were trying to protect you.

KC: Oh, yes! Protect me! Lest the demons get to me! Well, Mother, you have succeeded brilliantly. I no longer need to be disguised as a girl to fool the demons. I am a real woman. They wouldn't want me any more.

MOTHER: 阿春在喊什么? ("What is Choon shouting about?")

SISTER: 他说你不该迫他戴耳环。就是因为那样他才想做女人。("He says you should not have forced him to wear an earring. He says it is because of that that he wants to be a woman today.")

MOTHER: 好，怨我，怨父母! 你阿明叔的儿子也是戴耳环。人家结婚 生子三个孩子。("Oh yes, blame me. Blame the parents. Your Uncle Beng's son was also made to wear an earring. He is now married with three kids.")

KC: Yes, I know, I know! Uncle Beng's exemplary son! He wears an earring too and it did not stop him marrying and having three children. So I shouldn't make an issue of wearing an earring, is that it? Ha! Sis, ask Mother how many times have all the relatives tittered behind his back. "Oh, what does his wife see in him. What a girlish man! He gayleks more than his wife! Who would have thought that he was capable of giving her three children?!"

Uncle Beng's son only deceives himself. He fools nobody and the contempt that all of you have for an outrageous ah qua like me is also what he gets. So what difference does it make! No, Sis, I don't believe in self deception. I see no need for dishonesty. Not after what I have gone through to be what I want to be. "To thine own self be true." That is what it is all about, Sis. Honesty! Do you understand? Honesty!

SISTER: What about other things which are also just as important in life? Like not hurting your parents unnecessarily when all it takes is to attend your own father's funeral. Alright, Choon, if you so insist on honesty, let's be honest about what you are doing. You just want to get even with Mother and Father, isn't it? You blame them for all this and so you want to make them pay!

KC: And why shouldn't I blame them! If my life is a mess, they have a lot to answer for!

SISTER: Did they cause you not to finish your degree in London? It took a great chunk of Father's savings to send you there. And did they force you to be a whore? Even if you didn't finish your degree, you don't have to work on Bugis Street. Choon, we can't blame our parents for everything that goes wrong in our lives!

KC: Alright! Alright! I shall go back to pay my respects together with you and our four sisters, all the filial daughters of our father. I have this black mourning dress here.

(Drops the bathrobe he has been holding all this while and grabs the black mourning dress hanging on the wardrobe door.)

Very respectable. No plunging necklines.

SISTER: Oh, don't be ridiculous!

KC: Why is it ridiculous?! If the old folks cannot accept me as I am then they have no business demanding that I have a duty to them!

MOTHER:你们还在争什么? 没时间了。阿春，快开门呀! 我们被雨淋湿了。("What are you two arguing about? We don't have much time. Choon, will you open the door and let us in. We are drenched by the rain.")

KC: Mother, the rain has stopped. Sis, you can drive her home to change into something dry. It won't take 15 minutes.

SISTER: 妈，回去吧! 没用的。("Mother, let's go back. It's useless.")

MOTHER:春，我真是白养了你! ("Choon, it was a waste of time bringing you up.")

KC: Mother, wait! *(Flings dress on bed, rushes over to desk, rummages about for a piece of paper)* Here is my birth certificate *(shreds it)*. Mother, you can tell yourself you have never given birth to me.

(Opens door a slit and flings the torn birth certificate out while screaming in dialect) 报生纸还给你, 算你没生我啦! 算你没生我啦! ("Take back this birth certificate and consider that you have never given birth to me.")

(Then slams the door, picks up the bathrobe lying on the floor and rushes behind the screen, sobbing. Lights fade out and fade in quickly for Scene Three.)

SCENE THREE

(A few hours later. It is night. KC is lying on her bed smoking a cigarette. Chuck has left.)

KC *(hums "Final Night")*: Chuck and I had another row. Last night, he told me for the first time he was married. No, that was not what the row was about. After all, it didn't surprise me. I suspected all along. No, I wasn't angry until he said, "Now, you know why I lead life so furtively. I am scared of what exposure can do to me and my family. I cannot afford to strike a posture on this thing called honesty."

Strike a posture! Me! I said to him, "You have a choice. You don't have to mess about with me. Stay home. Be a good husband and father. Then there will be no question about exposure. If you want to lead a dishonest life, don't make me pay for it."

"But is it really all about honesty, Kim?" "What do you mean, Chuck?" He then asked in a cold deliberate voice: "Does Jeff know you were once a man?" I said, "Well, no." "Why not?" He pressed, "Shouldn't you be honest with him seeing that honesty is getting to be such a big thing with you?" I didn't like that line of questioning and retorted, "I am not being dishonest. If he asks, I shall tell him. As he has not asked, it is no more relevant than for me to tell him that... that... I had my appendix removed at the age of eight." To that, Chuck laughed and said, "Do you HONESTLY believe what you just said?" Something snapped at that moment and I screamed at him, "Get out! Get out of my life!"

He walked to the door in his usual lazy manner and said, "I can go, but it wouldn't change anything because deep down you know that you are no more honest than any one of us. You sneer at us for our lack of courage. I don't deny that, Kim; that we lead lives of secrecy because we fear the consequences of others knowing about our secret. I respect you for your greater courage. But you should not sneer at us and now you understand why; because, at last, you also know what it is like to count the cost of somebody knowing your secret. Face it, Kim, the reason why you have not told Mr. Jeff Slater that you were once a man is that you fear you might lose him should he find out the truth!" Then Chuck left.

(Telephone rings.)

Hello. Hi, Chuck. There is no need to apologise. You had angry words. So had I. What! You still think I have taught you a few valuable lessons about honesty. That's encouraging. Never in my wildest dreams would I have thought I can teach anybody moral lessons. And you are going to be more honest with me in the future! Well, what about telling me what you do for a living? You what!? No, you are kidding me! Oh! I don't believe this. Wait till I tell Anita about this. Oh, I'm sorry, I take that back. You wouldn't want me to tell Anita, would you? This is just between you and me. Another exception to the rule of total honesty. It is sometimes to be limited to a select circle.

Next question: your wife. Is she beautiful? Career woman? Do you love her? No, no, I don't mind. It's not my prerogative to mind. It's the most natural thing that you should love your wife. I'm glad for both of you. Do I sound hurt?! No, I am not hurt, Chuck. Envious, perhaps, but not hurt. Look, let's change the subject. Tell me, where do you live? District 10. How fashionable! But where exactly, I mean, which house and on what road? Oh, you are not ready to tell me that much yet. No, no, I don't mind. The third exception to the rule of total honesty. There are areas it does not extend to.

Then tell me what is your real name. It can't be Chuck. It is! You were given it at birth! Your parents must have loved American names. It is not an American name! It is a Chinese name! Oh, it is spelt C.H.A.K. and not C.H.U.C.K.; well, I'll be damned! Yes, yes, I guess I jumped to conclusions too quickly. The fourth exception to honesty: It is not always apparent. Now, you want to ask me some questions. Alright, fair's fair. Your turn now.

Do I love Jeff Slater?

(Pause.)

In the sense that I love my parents, my friend Anita, and the good moments you and I had together, I guess I love Jeff. Or I can learn to love him. And I think it is worth trying and I think I have more than an even chance of succeeding.

Next question. If I don't learn to love him, will I at least be happy with him?

(Pause.)

Honestly, Chak, I don't know. There you are, that would be the fifth exception to the rule of total honesty: sometimes it is beyond our means to know enough about something to be honest about it. Yes, yes, I know, I know. I'm being my usual smart-ass self.

Look, Chak, I must ask the questions again. Just what the hell does it matter to you whether or not I am going to be happy?!

You wouldn't do anything differently, would you?! *(Listens on the line for a while and shows signs of getting irritable.)* It has been a long conversation, Chak. You must be running out of ten cent pieces to feed the phone. What? You are calling me from home. Well, it is indeed a day of surprises. Yes, I shall write to you from America. At your PO box number until such time as you give me a proper address.

Heh, aren't you going to press me about going to my old man's funeral? You think I will definitely be there? What makes you so sure? Well, how observant. You saw the black shirt and trousers hanging in the wardrobe. But I have also prepared a black dress to wear. We will see, Chack, we will see. Maybe I will toss a coin. Heads, go as a man; tails, go as a woman.

Did I like what you left on the table for me? Oh, I have not seen it. Ah ha! here it is.

(Picks up from the desk an envelope and opens it.)

Well, well, well, a birthday card. Anita, you should be here to see this. And what else have we here? A first class return air ticket to America. I have no complaints about travelling first class but I doubt I will use the return portion of the ticket. Still it is nice to know that somebody wants you back. Even in his own peculiar way. Thank you, Chack. I will miss you. Bye bye *(hangs up)*.

Now, for the funeral.

(Music from "Final Night" begins and gradually gets louder. KC collects men's clothes from the wardrobe and changes in front of a standing mirror. Then she changes into the black dress. Still unhappy, she changes into men's clothes again. Lights fade out as she is changing, leaving the audience guessing as to her final decision.)

-END-

Fast Cars and Fancy Women

by Kwuan Loh

Psst... you there! Yes, you! You wanna buy a fast car? You want Life in the Fast Lane? – That's Life with a capital 'L'! You need a fast car to crrruissse in. Just imagine where that fast car will take you... Come with us, join us on our joyride through the fast lane. See the sights. Smell the flowers. Let us take you to the Ultimate Destination where you will find the answer to all your dreams. You have the choice to make it happen. Anyone there wanna buy a car? Anyone wanna buy a dream?

Boy meets girl and falls in love in this simple story. But no. Life is not really so simple. She does not want boy. He doesn't drive a big enough car. He only drives a Mini. She wants a man with a fast car who can give her everything she wants. He only wants her and he will try everything to get her. In the end, they both get what they always wanted, with a little price, just a little price.

This little modern morality play is concerned with the dreams and desires of a naive materialistic people.

CHARACTERS:

STELLA LEE HUI LING

CHEONG HOCK BENG

EDDIE GOODTIME

ENSEMBLE: Mother
            Classmates
            Colleagues
            People at a party
            Wedding guests
            Friends of the family

FAST CARS AND FANCY WOMEN premiered at the Black Box on 15 April 1992. It was produced by Theatreworks, directed by Lee Seng Lynn and featured the following cast:

STELLA	Nora Othman
CHEONG	James Tan
EDDIE GOODTIME	Christian Huber
ENSEMBLE	Sol Foo, Cheryl Lee, Ivan Oh, Jeffrey Tan, Celine Teo, Richard Tsen

It was given a rehearsed reading by Theatreworks on 21 Sept. 1991. The reading featured Tan Kheng Hwa as STELLA, Andrew Koh as CHEONG, and Remesh Panicker as EDDIE GOODTIME. It was directed by Ong Keng Sen.

PROLOGUE

(The stage is darkened. Light goes on. Spotlight on a dazzling gold car of any make. Fanfare-type music. EDDIE GOODTIME appears, microphone in hand. He tests it by tapping a few times and then beams at the audience.)

EDDIE: Ladies and gentlemen, you are privileged tonight to be among the elite, to see unveiled, for the very first time in Singapore – The Car of the Century...
(Fanfare) The ultimate in driving luxury – the Ultimobilo.

The exterior – curves that will really move you. Note the sleek lines, aerodynamically designed, specially created to make this baby cruise along at top speed.

And under the hood beats the animal heart of a power machine that is designed to give maximum performance at top economy. All the push and the power you'll ever want.

The interiors. Seductive bucket seats that invite you to just sink into them. The lap of Luxury... pure Luxury. Everything built purely for pleasure... your driving pleasure.

Sheer Style with a capital "S." The man with the Ultimo is a man of good sense and sound judgement. The Ultimobilo – The Car of the Century – The single most luxurious car you can buy. Can you afford not to get it?

But... I'm not here to sell you a car. Sure, the car's for sale. You can pick up a flyer downstairs in the lobby.

I'm here to sell you a dream. You there... you want a fast car – you want LIFE in a fast lane. Life – That's Life with a capital "L." And you, you want a fast car to cruise in. Just imagine where that fast car will take you. Just think of all those fancy women looking at you as you drive by in that fancy fast car. Fancy women... and you just cruising along. *(Gets caught up in the fantasy. Then comes back.)*

Oh, yes of course, nothing comes for free. The dream has a little price-tag. Affordable, not too high, don't worry about it! Don't worry about it! Because it will be worth it. Hey, I know these things – I'm Eddie Goodtime, your personal guide to the Good Life.

You have the choice to make it happen. Anybody out there wanna buy a fast car?

ACT ONE

SCENE: WE ARE HERE AT THE STARTING POINT OF THE RATRACE.

(Stage is bare. EDDIE GOODTIME appears.)

EDDIE: Looks like a good place to start. The University... Matriculation Day – the start of a new life. Isn't this exciting? For the guys, release from their national obligations and the girls, a brave new world. Tell me, young lady, what are you here for?

GIRL 1: I'm here to get an education.

EDDIE: Ooo... An education... That's nice, but is that all?

BOY 1: Hey, check out those chicks! Look at that one with the tight T-shirt!

EDDIE: Now we're talking...

BOY 2: Excuse me, but can you tell me how to get to the R.B.R.? My tutor has set me two assignments already. I better do my reading before everyone else...

EDDIE: Get out of here!

BOY 2: But you haven't told me where...

EDDIE: OUT!

GIRL 2: My mother says that I should marry a graduate after I graduate. So I come to the university-lor.

EDDIE: It may not be a good time looking but it sure is a good idea. Here, check out the SRC after 4.30 pm. That's where the sports jocks hang out. You'll meet real men there.

BOY 3: I want a degree so that I can get a good job and earn lots of money, pots of money.

BOY 4: My, aren't some of us a little confused. The aim of education is not and cannot be the attainment of a piece of paper that states that three years of your life were spent in this institution and the course entitles you to higher pay. We should instead seek to broaden our minds and develop our talents to their full potential so that we may become more able, more equipped leaders of tomorrow. It's only our responsibility.

EDDIE: My God, he sounds like a potential PAP member.

GIRL 3: Look, cut the crap. All I want to do is get through the university with minimum effort and then get on with the rest of my life.

GIRL 4: I'm scared, I'm really scared. I know I won't make the grade. I can't make it, I just know it.

EDDIE: Don't worry. It's a cinch. Yes, yes, get the degree, get on with your life. The paper's just a passport and you'll go really far. It's just a first hurdle. It's a snap. It's a breeze. It's not that hard, just take it slow. Are you ready? Get set. Go!

(There is a kind of conveyor belt where they are all standing in line. It's a kind of vogue, with them posing, reading, writing, eating, opening locker etc. All chant.)

CHANT 1   LECTURE. LUNCH. LIBRARY. LOCKER. LOO.

CHANT 2   COPY NOTES. BORROW NOTES. PHOTO-
STAT. WORK AND WORK.

CHANT 3   HI. HELLO. HOW ARE YOU? WHAT'S YOUR
NAME?

EDDIE: And the wheels start spinning round and round.

(STELLA comes in and joins the end of the line.)

STELLA: Hi, my name is Stella. Stella Lee Hui Ling, and I'm from
NJC. I'm majoring in Economics and Stats and Maths. I would
like to work in a bank or in any kind of financial institution.

(CHEONG comes in and joins the end, next to STELLA.)

CHEONG: I'm a Malaysian from B.M. That's Bukit Mertajam.
Cheong Hock Beng is my name and I live in a rented flat in
Tiong Bahru because the hostel is very expensive. It's quite far
but I've got my own transport. I drive a second-hand Mini which
I bought with the money I saved from giving tuition.

CHANT 4   STRESS. STRESS. MORE DISTRESS.
EXAMINATIONS.

*(During this chant STELLA tends to miss the momentum and gets
more and more out of sync.)*

EDDIE: You there keep in line… keep in line…

STELLA: Where is this all leading? *(Getting out of sync.)* One
tutorial after another tutorial.

Why am I here?

What am I doing this for?

*(Chants repeat themselves into a kind of cacophony. STELLA is
now getting hopelessly out of sync. CHEONG steps out of the line.
Picks up imaginary phone.)*

CHEONG *(on telephone)*: Hello, ma. I'm alright. Just a bit tired. No, I'm not taking on too much tuition. Yah, the work is getting a bit hard. I'm eating well. Making friends, yah, a few. Studying hard more than anything... I'll come back and see you in May, OK. Bye... miss you.

(CHEONG rejoins the line.)

EDDIE: Spin, wheels, spin...

STELLA *(helpless)*: I can't do this by myself... God, what am I doing?

CHEONG: Let me help you... *(gives her notes).*

STELLA: Thanks. Er... I'm Stella.

CHEONG: Cheong. Here, these were last week's notes on Marketing and these are the references. And...

STELLA: Oh, thank you. *(Gets back into sync.)*

CHEONG: If you need anything, anything at all...

STELLA: Thank you.

(She smiles at him and then turns away. At that moment, he looks at her intently. They carry on in conveyor-style. All this while, the chant continues.)

EDDIE: Hey, if you made it here, you made it for life. Sure, there'll be a few dropouts, people who don't make the grade. Oh, hard cheese... what does it matter? Just means there'll be fewer people sharing the pie. And that means larger slices of the Good Life.

ALL: The Good Life...

EDDIE: The Good Life is not a dream. It begins here. It is now. Reach out and grasp it with your hands. Embrace it, draw it into your soul, believe it with your heart.

ALL: The unspoken dream, a reality.

EDDIE: Speak to me of your dreams.

ALL: One wife, two or three children, four wheels, a five-figure salary, sixty thousand a year or more.

EDDIE: Speak to me...

ALL: Towards love, liberty and the pursuit of individual happiness.

EDDIE: This is only the beginning.

SCENE: MOTHER VALUES

MOTHER: Why so late come back?

STELLA: Studying in the library.

MOTHER: Studying until so late?

STELLA: Ya-ma, tomorrow got test.

MOTHER: Then who send you back?

STELLA: Cheong.

MOTHER: Who's this Cheong?

STELLA: Classmate only, ma.

MOTHER: Classmate? Take bus?

STELLA: Car.

MOTHER: What kind of car?

STELLA: Second-hand Mini.

MOTHER *(resolutely)*: Classmate only.

SCENE: DADDY'S GIRL GOES DRIVING.

STELLA: When I was young, Daddy used to take me driving.

First he'd dust the seats so they were clean and then he'd place this sheet of towelling on the white covered seat of the car, and then he'd put two cushions so I could sit on them and look at the shiny lady with wings standing on the hood of the beautiful silver car. Then Daddy would get in and start the engine. The engine would purr like a cat. Daddy'd move the gear stick and down the long driveway we would go, from the garage to the end of the driveway and then back again.

Sometimes, if I was really good, Daddy would let me help him wash the car and polish the lady with the silver wings. Daddy only let me do this if Uncle was not around. Uncle lived in the big house and we lived in the little one behind it and Mummy would wash and clean and serve in that big house.

Sometimes I would see all these beautiful women at Uncle's big house. Women dressed in pretty dresses with stars in their ears and voices that seemed to tinkle from a music box. They would whirl and twirl around and around, spinning, spinning... Then their cars would roll up the long driveway and take them home. Mummy would take me home and I would fall asleep dreaming.

(Pause.)

When Daddy died, I never went for rides again in that big silver car. And I never saw those fancy women again and sometimes I wonder if I had dreamt it all, the cars, the women, the winged angel on the bonnet of an old car... dreamt it all.

SCENE: DREAMS

(EDDIE is seen on the stage and he is orchestrating this almost, egging them on.)

EDDIE: Second year at the university. Systems smoothly running. Wheels well-oiled. Time to relax and take stock of things. Once again, tell me what is important.

MAN 1: Imagine being able to walk into any designer shop and just walk out with anything paid with cold, hard cash. And it isn't even a sale.

MAN 2: You need to be a billionaire to do that. Do you know "Lifestyles of the Rich and Famous" lists only two billionaires in Singapore?

WOMAN 2: I wonder if one of them has an eligible son. They are probably old and balding already.

WOMAN 1: Ooo... dressed by Chanel, Ferragammo or Gucci.

WOMAN 2: Well, at least by Marusho, Mitsumine rather than BB, AA, Top Ten or even Metro.

MAN 2: Hi-fi Stereos. Anything – State of the Art. Top of the line and the latest in technology.

WOMAN 3: To succeed where no woman has done. To make it in a man's world...

MAN 3: Successful women – Ha!

WOMAN 2: To walk into any posh restaurant and be recognised and given your usual place, the one by the window.

MAN 3: To walk into any car showroom and tell the dealer, "I'll take that. Deliver it to my house immediately."

WOMAN 1: A luxurious condo in district 9, 10 or 11.

WOMAN 2: A room with a very large view.

MAN 1: Not just the money but the high profile. So what if you're a millionaire before thirty-five?

MAN 3: Featured in Accent, Vantage, Her World, Go, Beverly Hot Nouveau, Man, and Singapore Business.

WOMAN 2: Oh, yes, I want it... I want it all.

(MAN 4 and WOMAN 4 look puzzled. They talk to each other.)

WOMAN 4: Is that what you want?

MAN 4: Not really. *(Pause.)* And you?

WOMAN 4: I don't know.

MAN 4: I don't think that is what I want.

WOMAN 4: What is it then?

MAN 4: I don't know but all we want is... to be happy.

WOMAN 4: Enough money to be comfortable? Maybe a little more.

MAN 4: I really don't mind living in a HDB flat. What's wrong? After all, more than half of Singapore's population live in HDB flats. Anyway at today's property prices...

WOMAN 4: Maybe a small car. Just to get around in...

MAN 4: I don't really mind taking the MRT. Especially when parking is so expensive in town.

WOMAN 4: I think I would really like a job... that gives me time for myself. I want to work and do well but not so hard that I can't relax and enjoy the people around me and the things that life has to offer.

MAN 4: I don't want to spend my life chasing after things... things that don't seem to last very long.

(They pause, look at the others who are still comparing their material possessions.)

WOMAN 4: Is there something wrong with us?

MAN 4: I think in my older brother's generation, they would call us hippies.

(They look at the others who are still talking brand-labels, image and sales.)

WOMAN 4: It's like a vortex, isn't it? Sucked in and under?

MAN 4: Uh-huh, and I don't think I want to be sucked in.

WOMAN 4: Do we have any choice?

MAN 4: Maybe not...

(Pause.)

EDDIE: Why so glum? Don't be afraid to dream. Hey, if you've got to dream, dream big. After all, dreams are free...

(To STELLA) And you, pretty lady, what would your dream be?

STELLA: A dream? Hmm... let's see. If I have to dream... I think it'd be fun if I married a man... with a fast car. The faster the better... And live happily ever after. *(Giggles because she thinks it's funny.)* Wouldn't that be a really wonderful dream?

EDDIE: Good, good, my kind of girl, my kind of girl...

(He crosses over to CHEONG on other side of the stage.)

 And what would make you happy, Cheong?

CHEONG: I don't know.

EDDIE: Really, now. You work really hard all the time. It's got to be for a reason. Tell me about your secret desires.

CHEONG: I don't have any.

EDDIE: Really? You've got to be joking. Young man like you, I'm sure you have dreams. Come on, tell me, tell old Eddie Goodtime.

CHEONG: I want someone I can talk to. OK, this sounds stupid but I want someone to love, someone who loves me. I want to be able to hold her in my arms and to be able to give her the best... my love and the best of everything. It would make me happy if she were happy.

EDDIE: Cheong, I don't understand you. Who's this "she?"

CHEONG: Hey, look, there's Stella.

EDDIE: You like her, don't you? You're entitled to your dreams but where Stella's concerned, you're wasting your time. She doesn't know her own mind. Let me introduce you to some other sweet young things here in the University.

If you want Stella, I might as well introduce you to Mimi, Lucy and Fifi, just a few acquaintances of mine domiciled in Geylang. At least for the money, they might provide more satisfaction...

(CHEONG grabs Eddie by the collar and pulls him up.)

CHEONG: Don't you ever talk about Stella like that!

EDDIE: Hey, I was only joking alright... I didn't mean to compare Stella to my friends in Geylang, but these women are...

CHEONG: I'm not interested.

EDDIE: What about the boys then?

CHEONG: I'm not that kind of guy.

EDDIE: Hey, I wasn't suggesting that kind of thing. I mean, go out with the guys, a few beers, a game of tennis or squash, just a bit of male bonding. Just a bit of fun with friends instead of work, work, work all the time...

CHEONG: Look, I promised my mother that I would do well. I know the girl I love will want it too. I've got to work really hard.

EDDIE: Hey, suit yourself. The choice is yours... *(To audience)* Dreams can come true, you know. You can make them happen. All you've got to do is want it badly enough... really badly enough.

SCENE: CONNECTING

(CHEONG is sitting by himself reading. STELLA comes along.)

STELLA: Oh, hi, Cheong...

CHEONG: Hi, Stella...

STELLA: Here, here are your notes. Thanks so much. You know yours are the neatest notes in the whole class.

CHEONG: These... I thought I had the ugliest handwriting actually.

STELLA: What are you reading?

CHEONG: Just some old book I decided to pick up again. No, it's not a textbook.

STELLA: Can I have a look? *(Takes the book from him.)* Oh, Saint-Exupéry's *The Little Prince.* I read this when I was a child and I loved it.

CHEONG: Really?

STELLA: It's my all-time favourite book.

CHEONG: It's mine as well. Once in a while, I pick it up to read it all over again and every time, I find new things in it.

STELLA: I haven't read it in years.

CHEONG: Really? Do you want to borrow it?

STELLA: Only if you've finished with it?

CHEONG: Take it... I can read it again any time.

STELLA: Oh, thanks... *(Flips through the book, pauses and looks up.)* You know my very favourite part?

CHEONG: Which one?

STELLA: It's the part when the prince is talking about his rose. How vain and silly the rose was and how much the prince loved the rose that he was willing to go to such great lengths to protect her and give her everything, all the security *(pauses)*. It also happens to be the saddest part.

CHEONG: Yes, when you love somebody or something, you'll have to love them till the very end, isn't it?

(There is a moment of silence as each reflects in his own private world.)

STELLA: Cheong, you never fail to surprise me. It's nice to know that there is something more in common between the two of us... Hey, I've got to go now. I'll see you at the lecture... *(Gets up to leave.)*

CHEONG: Enjoy the book... *(Watches her as she walks away. To himself)* To the end... the very end...

SCENE: MOTHER VALUES II

(Stage is bare. MOTHER comes in with a basket of clothes which she is sorting out. STELLA comes in.)

STELLA: Ma...

(MOTHER doesn't acknowledge her. STELLA goes and puts her books down. MOTHER continues to fold clothes. After a while...)

STELLA: Ma, I need to get some more money from you. I have to buy some books.

MOTHER: What, that day I give you, not enough?

STELLA: No, that was because of some fees I had to pay.

(There is an uncomfortable pause.)

MOTHER: You sure you buying books?

STELLA: What do you mean?

MOTHER: Where you get this? *(She takes a blouse from the pile.)* This is new. I never see before.

STELLA: Yes, ma, I bought it at a factory outlet.

MOTHER: Why you spending so much money on clothes? You think we print money is it?

STELLA: Ma, it's a budget shop. It's very very cheap stuff.

MOTHER: The problem with you young people is you all don't know the value of money. Something like this still costs money, right and every time you see something "cheap" you want to buy. We all not rich like your friends you know.

STELLA: Ma... It's one bloody blouse. I paid for it out of my own savings. If you want to see the books I bought and the price tag, I will show you.

(STELLA is unprepared for her mother's resounding slap.)

MOTHER: How dare you be rude to your mother. Waaah, now you go to the university, already talk big, know how to answer your mother. Your mother slave day and night so you can talk back is it? You never work one day in your life and you dare... you dare...

STELLA: It's money... It's always money. Every time you hit me, it's because you think I'm spending your precious hard-earned money. Do you ever think what I have to go through? I can't join my friends for teas because I can't pay. I have to make them presents for their birthday and lucky, lucky for me they think I'm trying to personalise their gifts. I never complain, Ma, I try to spend as little as I can. I hate being poor and you don't have to remind me all the time that we are poor.

MOTHER: You remember, hah, you remember, OK.

STELLA: I will remember... I will remember.

SCENE: REVELATIONS

(CHEONG is holding a little box and a bouquet of red roses.)

EDDIE: So what are you going to do?

CHEONG: I'm going to give her this for her birthday.

EDDIE: Expensive... A bouquet of roses... out of your precious hard-earned tuition money? And what's this... what's this?

CHEONG: It's a jewellery box. Listen...

(Music tinkles out.)

EDDIE: Beautiful... just like Stella. But are you sure she's worth it? *(Sees CHEONG'S face)* I'll take that back.

CHEONG: Stella's my friend and I'm giving this to her as a token of my friendship.

EDDIE: Who do you think you're fooling?

CHEONG: What do you mean?

(CHEONG makes an attempt to go over where STELLA is sitting at a table in a kind of study area. A group of five troop in, singing "Happy Birthday." They crowd around her.)

FRIEND 1: Here's your present. Open it! I want to know if you like it.

(STELLA opens it, squeals with delight and takes out a bottle of very expensive perfume.)

STELLA: A bottle of Eternity. Ooh... how did you know I wanted this perfume...

FRIEND 2: We guessed.

FRIEND 3: What about this one?

(STELLA opens it and pulls out a beautiful long scarf.)

STELLA: Oh, it's beautiful.

FRIEND 3: It's from Mondi. Check it out.

STELLA: Thanks so much... I really love these. I'll wear the scarf tonight but I'll save the perfume for a special occasion.

FRIEND 4: All set for the party tonight?

STELLA: Fred's made all the arrangements. It's going to be at a chalet in Ponggol. I don't know... he's doing everything.

FRIEND 2: So, the whole gang's going to be there, huh?

STELLA: That's what Fred told me.

FRIEND 5: What about Cheong?

FRIEND 3: Are you asking Cheong?

FRIEND 1: I thought I saw him hanging around just now.

FRIEND 4: Cheong, the nerd? The one with the second-hand Mini?

FRIEND 2: Shh... Cheong is Stella's friend. They study together.

FRIEND 4: Oh, is it? That kind of friend?

STELLA: He's just a friend!

FRIEND 5: I don't think you should ask him. He'll spoil the party.

He's not one of us. He probably doesn't drink or dance and he's just going to sit there like a blooming wallflower.

STELLA: You really think I shouldn't ask him? He *is* my friend, you know and he's been a real help...

FRIEND 2: Why shouldn't Stella invite him if she wants to?

STELLA: It's my birthday.

FRIEND 2: It's her birthday.

FRIEND 4: Studies are one thing but fun is another. OK... OK, it's your birthday. Do what you like.

FRIEND: Just don't say we didn't warn you.

STELLA *(pause)*: OK, I won't ask him. But don't you all dare say anything in front of him?

(FRIEND 4 looks at watch.)

FRIEND 4: Die, late for lecture. Gotta go.

FRIEND 3: Me, too. See you tonight, huh...

FRIEND 5: Bye, Stell!

(The three of them move off, leaving FRIEND 1 and FRIEND 2 behind.)

FRIEND 1: Hey, look... there's Cheong again.

STELLA: Yeah, yeah *(she doesn't look up)*.

FRIEND 2: Oh, no, he's coming this way.

STELLA: Don't forget. You promised not to say anything about tonight's party.

FRIEND 1: Make sure you don't...

CHEONG: Hi, Stella! *(awkwardly)* Hi, Susan and... er, May. Stella, can I speak to you for a minute?

STELLA: Sure...

CHEONG: I wanted to wish you Happy Birthday and give you this. *(Hands her the presents and the bouquet and sticks out his hand to shake hers. She takes it gingerly.)* Er... happy birthday.

STELLA: Thank you but you shouldn't have...

CHEONG: No, no, it's my pleasure. After all, we're friends and study partners right?

STELLA: These roses are very nice.

CHEONG: Why don't you open the present?

STELLA: I'll do it later.

CHEONG: I was just wondering if you might be celebrating your birthday in any way...

(There is a pause. Friends look meaningfully at her.)

STELLA: No, I'm staying home with my mother tonight.

CHEONG: Oh, I see... family dinner, is it?

STELLA *(avoids his eyes)*: Sort of...

CHEONG: Maybe we could go for a cup of coffee or something?

STELLA: No... There's next week's test and I still haven't gotten round to the readings...

CHEONG: Maybe we could do that together.

STELLA: No, I've been depending on you to help me a little too much and I feel a bit bad about...

CHEONG: No, we're studying together. You help me too, you know...

STELLA: Anyway, I'd like to spend a quiet evening by myself if you don't mind. It's just the thought of another year passing, you know...

CHEONG: OK, I understand...

STELLA: But I'll take a raincheck, though.

CHEONG (*cheered by this*): OK.

(*Fade out. CHEONG is on the phone. Mrs Lee is on the other end.*)

MOTHER: Hello?

CHEONG: Hello, may I speak to Stella, please?

MOTHER: Stella not at home.

CHEONG: You mean she's stepped out for a while?

MOTHER: Stella not at home.

CHEONG: When will she be coming back?

MOTHER: Don't know. Stella go stay in chalet with friends. Celebrate birthday.

CHEONG: Chalet? Aunty, she left after dinner with you?

MOTHER: No, early, early, already go. You are who?

CHEONG: My name is Cheong.

MOTHER: Oh, the classmate.

CHEONG: You mean, Stella has ever mentioned me?

MOTHER: She say you drive second-hand Mini.

SCENE: HEY, THERE LONELY BOY...

EDDIE: Cheong, Cheong, will you take your nose out of your

books for a minute? Listen to me.

CHEONG: I can't... I've got a test coming up.

EDDIE: I swear, Cheong. Don't you know how to ever enjoy yourself? Don't you have any friends?

CHEONG: I thought I did.

EDDIE: Stella, your friend? She's just a stupid fickle girl. Why waste your time mooning over someone who will never love you? You're in love with a dream, an illusion.

CHEONG: I'm not asking for love...

EDDIE: Who do you think you are fooling, boy? Look at you. So she lied to you. And so you shut yourself up in this little room in your rented Tiong Bahru flat and study. You think she knows? You think she cares. C'mon, if you really like her, then do something about her. Carpe diem or something like that... Whatever it is, get a hold of your life...

(There is a pause here.)

CHEONG: Someday... I'll make her feel something for me.

EDDIE: Now, Cheong, now...

SCENE: HOW DOES IT FEEL TO HAVE THE KNIFE TWISTING IN YOUR BACK?

(Stage is empty, save for STELLA reading a poem. EDDIE stands there but she is not really speaking to him. He is like an echo.)

STELLA *(reads)*:

The More Loving One by W.H. Auden

Looking up at the stars, I know quite well
That, for all they care, I can go to hell,

But on earth indifference is the least
We have to dread from man or beast.

How should we like it were stars to burn
With a passion for us we could not return
If equal affections cannot be,
Let the more loving one be me.

Admirer as I think I am
Of stars that do not give a damn
I cannot, now I see them, say
I missed one terribly one day.

Were all the stars to disappear or die,
I should learn to look at an empty sky
And feel its total dark sublime,
Though this might take me a little time.

(Repeats) If equal affections cannot be, let the more loving one be me... *(Pause.)* Oh, shit. I hope this doesn't mean that Cheong's in love with me.

EDDIE: Cheong's in love with you?

STELLA: Cheong left a note on my locker and it had this poem stuck on it. I used to dream of guys sending me poems and that it would be so romantic. But Cheong? It must be someone's idea of a practical joke.

EDDIE: Joke?

STELLA: It *is* Cheong's handwriting. It's not a joke. This is serious.

EDDIE: Serious? I thought he was your friend?

STELLA: He's my friend. But I'm not in love with him and I don't want to hurt him. *(Pause)* If he's really my friend then I should be able to go to him and tell him... Clear this stupid matter up or something. But...

EDDIE: But what?

STELLA: I don't want to hurt him. What am I going to do?

EDDIE: What are you going to do?

STELLA: I don't know...

(Fade. EDDIE goes over to the other side where CHEONG is standing.)

EDDIE *(puts his arm over CHEONG'S shoulder)*: So, m'boy, how's it going?

CHEONG: I don't understand. What is she doing? She's avoiding me, isn't she? What have I done? I don't understand. Why is she so cold all of a sudden? *(Pause.)* It's the poem. She doesn't like me. She hates me. She's trying to say that.

EDDIE: Hates you.

CHEONG: But I will always be her friend.

EDDIE: A friend? For always?

(Fade. EDDIE recrosses over to the other side to STELLA.)

STELLA: Cheong is so persistent. I've given him the cold treatment but he won't leave me alone. He still hangs about with his stupid nerdy face and it is getting very irritating. I can't stand his attentions. Can't he see? I don't like him and I'm beginning to like him less and less each day.

EDDIE: Like him less each day?

STELLA: He's not my type. He doesn't have what I want.

EDDIE: What you want?

STELLA: Look at him. He has no friends. He's socially inept. He doesn't dress well or talk knowledgeably about anything outside his studies. He has to support himself by giving tuition all the time. He's a small town Malaysian boy with a middle-class background who will never be able to give me what I want.

EDDIE: What you want.

(Fade. EDDIE crosses over again to CHEONG.)

CHEONG: She persists in making my life miserable. What have I asked except for friendship and a little space in her heart.

EDDIE: A little space.

CHEONG: I was just asking that she allow me to love her? She won't even allow me that.

EDDIE: So now you admit it is love?

CHEONG *(pause)*: Yes...

EDDIE: Do you love her, really love her?

CHEONG: I think I must, or my heart wouldn't break this way.

(EDDIE points at far side. CHEONG turns to see STELLA. She is crushing the flowers he gave her.)

EDDIE: Do you still love her?

CHEONG: I... I don't know. *(He is confused.)*

(Again, EDDIE directs CHEONG to see STELLA breaking the delicate jewellery box into pieces and stamping on it.)

EDDIE: Do you still love her?

CHEONG: I don't know. *(Growing and hardening resolution)* I don't think I can love any other woman now.

EDDIE: Cheong, don't be stupid.

CHEONG: Stella will always be the only woman in my life. Forever. Always. Until the very end.

ACT TWO

SCENE: LIFE IN THE FAST LANE I

EDDIE: So, Uni's over. We get to the race proper... The next lap, so to speak.

WOMAN 1: I got a BA Honours, Second Upper.

MAN 1: I'm going to work for EDB. It'll be my stepping stone to bigger and better things.

WOMAN 2: I just got all my credit cards – all three, Visa, Mastercard and of course, American Express. I won't leave home without it.

MAN 2: I just bought my first car – a Honda Civic.

MAN 3: I just got my first feature as the youngest General Manager in Singapore in no less than Singapore Business.

WOMAN 3: I just made my first killing on the stockmarket. I'm into big bucks.

MAN & WOMAN 4: We've just joined the teaching profession. We are doing something worthwhile with our lives.

MAN 4: I think.

EDDIE: Work hard. Play hard. Meanwhile in New York... guess who's got a new image... Bring in the man.

(CHEONG comes in dressed as in the previous scene as a ordinary university student dressed in jeans and a polo t-shirt.)

EDDIE: Time for a little change here.

(Enter clothiers. They remove his jeans and polo t-shirt and exchange it for a smart suit, ties and shoes. They brush his hair and exchange his plastic frames for a pair of Armanis.)

EDDIE: Voila, look at the miracles a good tailor can do! The image is slick. The West has brought out the Best.

(CHEONG is no longer nerdy but quiet and suave-looking, totally transformed.)

EDDIE: Welcome to the new-improved you. Do you like it?

CHEONG: I don't care for it one way or another.

EDDIE: So how's New York? Isn't this place exciting? The shows, the nightlife, the muggers – met any lately?

CHEONG: The streets are empty and the nights are cold. It's far from home, very far.

EDDIE: Look, Cheong, you've come this far to New York. You are the envy of your year. You've successfully completed your MBA scholarship and passed with flying colours as usual. You are now employed by one of the most reputable consultancy companies, earning pots of money and living in an expensive apartment on the upper east side, Manhattan.

CHEONG: It's not enough.

EDDIE: Not enough?

CHEONG: No.

EDDIE: What is it now that drives you to success?

CHEONG: A rose… a little vain rose. Or perhaps a star…

EDDIE: A star…?

CHEONG: A distant indifferent star.

EDDIE: A cold star. A star in the East perhaps…*(He laughs.)*

CHEONG: A star that will lead me home again. A distant indifferent star.

(Silence.)

EDDIE: Still in love with Stella.

CHEONG: Love? I'm not quite sure I can call it that.

EDDIE: Then?

CHEONG: Love... or Hate? I don't know. When I was young, I told myself that if I love something, it has to be forever. It's a naive belief. *(Pause.)* But wanting is an acquired habit. You always want what you can't really get, anyway.

EDDIE: So you still want her?

CHEONG: Yes... And this time, I know how I'll win her. *(Pause)* You're going to help me, aren't you?

(There is a brief pause.)

EDDIE: But you despise me, don't you?

CHEONG: Let's just say that I recognise you for what you are. So are you going to help me?

EDDIE: Ah, yes... but what will you give me in return?

CHEONG: My time.

EDDIE: Time! It's a deal! We all could use a little time here and there.

CHEONG: Sold!

SCENE: SO TELL ME, ARE YOU HAPPY?

WOMAN 1: And so, I heard...

WOMAN 2: Really-ah?

WOMAN 3: I knew it. I always knew it. That girl...

WOMAN 2: Three promotions in four years. There's something fishy about this.

WOMAN 1: And there is no smoke without fire.

WOMAN 3: But what's the problem? So what if the manager likes her?

WOMAN 1: And the MD? And the GM? I swear the woman's got margarine legs and uses them to climb her way up the corporate ladder.

WOMAN 3: Margarine Legs?

WOMAN 1: You know, those that spread easily...

(Fanfare. SBC "It's Your Move" type music. EDDIE is the game show host.)

EDDIE: Welcome to the world of unlimited options. Welcome to "It's Your Choice," the game show that everyone wants to play and stands to win COMPLETE HAPPINESS and SUCCESS. In our studio today we have a completely new contestant, Miss Stella Lee Hui Ling. Stella, what do you do for a living?

STELLA: I work in Standard Chartered Bank as an Assistant Manager. I...

EDDIE: That's enough of personal detail. Let's go into the game itself.

Today's options for the young woman are:

1. Career Woman.

(Applause. Lights up on Woman seated at desk with Filofax and juggling phones and directing people around. Newspapers flash her picture: "Business Woman of the Year.")

2. Housewife.

(Applause. Lights up on Woman in an apron and a big smile with tray of cookies or something. Husband comes in with briefcase and gives her a peck on the cheek. Two little cherubic children complete

the family. Freeze.)

3. Working wife.

(Applause. Lights up on smart looking professional woman stirring a pot of food while reading cookbook on Cordon Bleu and systematically ticking away at a list.)

4. Lady of leisure.

(Applause. Lights up on lady in lounging clothes eating strawberries or chocolates. French maid type comes in with pot of tea on a silver tray.)

These are just some of the choices you have...

So, Stella, which will it be?

STELLA: Er... I don't know... Maybe working wife... But the working wives I know are so stressed out because their husbands don't help...

EDDIE: Housewife, perhaps?

STELLA: No. *(Pause.)* I'll be bored after a while... The Lady of Leisure, but that's unreal, isn't it?

EDDIE: Is it?

STELLA: You've got to be joking...

EDDIE: Hey, Stella, everything is a possibility if you want it enough. You still want your fast car, don't you? Tell me what you want. It's your choice, remember? You can be a fancy woman if you want to.

(Four men in a line, each representing a different kind of car. They are in shadow and gradually emerge one by one to dance with STELLA.)

EDDIE: Stella, you haven't tasted the Good Life yet.

STELLA: We don't live in a three-room HDB flat any more.

EDDIE: And...?

STELLA: I have a career I can be proud of. I am competent enough at my job for people to bitch about it... But no, not yet, not enough...

EDDIE: You still want your fast car, don't you?

STELLA: Yes...

EDDIE: You can afford one of your own.

STELLA: It's not the same.

EDDIE: You want one with a man attached.

STELLA: Yes...

EDDIE: If that's what you really want...

(MAN 1 steps forward. They dance together in an almost mechanical fashion.)

MAN 1: Tell me what's a nice girl like you doing in a place like this.

STELLA: My name is Stella. What kind of car do you drive?

MAN 1: I'm Hugh. I drive a Honda.

STELLA: A Honda.

EDDIE: Aspiring yuppie with the potential to upgrade to a better make. Willing to pay a lot for the name and precision parts.

STELLA: Honda – not fast enough.

(MAN 2 steps forward. Similar choreography.)

MAN 2: Haven't I seen you some place before?

STELLA: My name is Stella. What kind of car do you drive?

MAN 2: I'm Alfred. I drive an Alfa 33.

STELLA: An Alfa 33.

EDDIE: Alfa owners are a little like their cars – High performance but low in reliability. When they run, they really run. When they don't, they're in the workshop.

STELLA: Alfa 33 - Faster than a Honda but not fast enough.

(MAN 3 comes forward and begins to dance with STELLA.)

MAN 3: Hello, is this place taken?

STELLA: My name is Stella. What kind of car do you drive?

MAN 3: I'm Benedict. I drive a Beemer. A BMW.

STELLA: A BMW.

EDDIE: BM owners are reliable. They are dependable and they are usually up-scale family men. They are...

STELLA: I don't want dependable. I don't want reliable. I want a fast car and a Beemer is not fast enough. Besides, I just found out that Ben's father paid for his car.

EDDIE: So? Are you finished? Are you tired? I'm waiting...

(STELLA moves on to MAN 4. She interrupts him before he begins to speak.)

STELLA: Don't give me any lines. Just tell me what kind of car you drive.

MAN 4: I'm Lawrence and I drive a Lamborgini.

EDDIE: Man, that's faster than any car you've seen so far.

STELLA: Excuse me, Lawrence sells Lamborginis. That's why he drives them. He doesn't own them.

EDDIE: Picky, picky. You wanted a man who drove a fast car and on some good days even taxis go very fast.

(After a while, the others begin to interrupt, each taking turns to tap the other on the shoulder until it gets ridiculously manic.)

STELLA: I'm bored. I'm tired of this game. These men... they are all so shallow.

EDDIE: Don't forget. You're looking for a man with a fast car. Not depth. Anyway, don't generalise. Get your priorities right.

STELLA: Can't I find someone who...

(MOTHER appears with pile of clothes, folding silently in the corner.)

EDDIE: Give it up, then, Stella. Give it up...

(STELLA sees MOTHER as she dances with these men.)

STELLA: I... I can't.

EDDIE: But aren't we having fun? Look at all those women standing on the sidelines green with envy. One day, one man and a different kind of car. Isn't this what you always wanted – to be the envy of everyone?

(The women stand, gaping at her as she dances.)

WOMAN 1: Look at her. She's using men like Kleenex. Finish already, throw away.

WOMAN 4: No, Stella should stop all this. This is no good for her.

WOMAN 2: But she's having so much fun.

STELLA: I'm having so much fun. I could, like, just die!

EDDIE: Believe me, darling, the right man will come along. The knight in shining armour in maybe a white Porsche and he will sweep you off your feet into his arms and carry you into the sunset and you will live happily ever after.

(To audience) If she believes this, she'll believe anything…

STELLA: Who? What? When? When?

EDDIE: And the lady dances on, waltzing in the dark, spinning…

STELLA: When? I'm bored. I'm tired. I want something more…

(CHEONG appears.)

STELLA: Cheong…

EDDIE: Ah, Cheong…

SCENE: THE TEMPTATION – THE PROPOSAL

(The stage is bare. Just the two of them, standing facing each other.)

STELLA: Cheong.

CHEONG: Stella, still as beautiful as before.

STELLA: It's been a long time.

CHEONG: Six years to be exact.

STELLA: When did you get back?

CHEONG: About four months ago.

STELLA: And you haven't contacted the others?

CHEONG: No, I have been busy.

STELLA: What with?

CHEONG: Setting up the regional company here. A branch of the business consultancy company based in America.

STELLA: I heard about that.

CHEONG: You have?

STELLA: I heard you were doing well. I didn't think you were coming back.

CHEONG: May I have this dance?

STELLA: I thought you didn't...

CHEONG: Didn't?

STELLA: Never mind, some stupid ghost in the past.

(They dance in silence.)

STELLA: You've changed a lot, Cheong. You look different. You talk different. You've changed.

CHEONG: Yes, I have. I don't drive a second-hand Mini any more.

STELLA: I don't suppose you do.

CHEONG: I drive a Corvette. The only Corvette in Singapore.

STELLA: A Corvette.

(Silence.)

CHEONG: Stella, I want to marry you. Say yes.

STELLA: I'm not trying to be coy, but this is so sudden.

CHEONG: You've been a lot on my mind these past six years. Say yes.

STELLA: I don't know.

(EDDIE appears, slightly exasperated.)

EDDIE: Come on, girl. This is the big fish you've been waiting for. He's a big man in his company. He's suave, good-looking and he even can dance now. He drives a Corvette and he wants to marry you. Don't let it be said that he was the one that got away.

STELLA: But I don't feel anything for him. Isn't there supposed to be racing pulses and fireworks when we kiss or something?

EDDIE: Go ahead. Kiss the man! Romantics!

(They kiss.)

EDDIE: Well? Well?

Stella: Nothing.

EDDIE: What does it matter? Love is for the pitiful anyway. Forget all that Barbara Cartland, Mills & Boon stuff. You can't
have everything. This is reality. The man can give you anything
and everything you ever wanted. Say yes. *(She hesitates.)* Don't
ask so many questions. Say yes.

CHEONG: Say yes.

STELLA *(pause)*: Yes.

(They kiss again.)

EDDIE: Yes, embrace the reality… your dreams, you've both got
your dreams now. *(Laughs.)* Now we shall see where your fast
car and your fancy woman take you…

SCENE: THE WEDDING

(People mingling at a party. There is laughter and merriment.)

WOMAN 1: Oh, oh, will you just look at this?

WOMAN 2: Look at all the wedding decorations. Pink, white and
purple. It's so beautiful.

WOMAN 1: Look, so cute – got heart-shaped balloons too. I swear
the man's spared no expense.

MAN: I heard that he booked this place completely for the party.
He's got three suites to accommodate his family from Penang or

BM or what...

WOMAN 2: Stella is so lucky.

WOMAN 1: Aiyah, Stella is not lucky – she is smart. Look at how before Cheong came back, she was going around with so many different men. All of them were rich and drove big cars. Stella just pulled up the biggest one, the one with the gold coin in its mouth.

MAN: Don't be such a bitch, can or not? Look at her. She looks happy and she looks very in love with her husband.

WOMAN 1: Looks can deceive, you know. Did you look at that ring of hers? I wonder how she is able to hold her hand up even. Cheong must love her a lot. I don't think I want to be slapped by her. The rock is big enough to kill.

WOMAN 2: I wonder what's her secret. Does anybody know if Cheong has a brother or something?

MAN: Sorry, dear, but Cheong is the only son and he worked his way to the top. You should have seen him when he was in the Uni – such a nerd, OK?

EDDIE: Is everybody having a good time here? Help yourself. Plenty of wine. Plenty of food. Plenty of envy.

(WOMAN 4 takes STELLA aside.)

WOMAN 4: Stella, are you sure?

STELLA: Sure about what?

WOMAN 4: Stell, I've been your friend since school days. Is this what you really want?

STELLA: I don't know...

WOMAN 4: Do you love Cheong?

STELLA: Cheong is a nice person. He is kind and considerate and makes no demands upon me whatsoever. He gives me what I want. He'll make a good husband. And he loves me. That's enough.

WOMAN 4: He treats you like a prized object of art... Look, why don't you...?

STELLA: It's too late. Anyway, I don't want to love Cheong. If he treats me like a possession, so be it. We're both being practical.

(Sounds of Bridal March. CHEONG and STELLA move forward to take their vows.)

CHEONG: I, Cheong Hock Beng, take you Stella Lee Hui Ling to be my lawfully wedded wife, to have and to hold, for richer or for poorer, in sickness and in health, till death do us part.

EDDIE *(to audience)*: Strange things these wedding vows. How they seem to be the apex of the relationship between a woman and a man. How glorious the words sound! How, for every young girl and young man, this would be the nadir of the greatest of human experiences!

But notice, wedding vows preclude love. You may marry a person but you do not need to love him. It is not required in the terms of the contract.

STELLA: I, Stella Lee Hui Ling, take you Cheong Hock Beng to be my lawfully wedded husband, to have and to hold, for richer or for poorer, in sickness and in health, till death do us part.

EDDIE: Happy, Cheong? I helped you get her, didn't I?

CHEONG: Yes, and I'll have to work to repay my debt to you, I suppose.

EDDIE: But this is what you wanted. The Good Life is about getting what you want, isn't it?

CHEONG: Yes, it is but don't keep asking me if I'm happy. I think it's immaterial. Yes, I have her and that's all that counts...

(Applause. Bridal fanfare. Blackout. EDDIE's laughter.)

SCENE: LIFE IN THE FAST LANE II

MAN 1: I've been promoted... again.

WOMAN 2: So what! We've all been promoted. It's either vertically or laterally. Who cares?

MAN 2: What's the use of promotions? They are just convenient names. What counts are the big bucks. I'm a dealer – that's just a name. But I bring home the moolah every month.

WOMAN 1: Who cares if you're bringing home the big moolah? You're losing your hair.

WOMAN 3: These days, you can tell the successful man by the amount of hair he has lost.

MAN 2: Bitch!

MAN 3: It's the stress, the damned stress.

WOMAN 2: The pressure of deadlines.

WOMAN 3: Expectations.

MAN 2: Projections.

MAN 3: Achievement and more achievement.

MAN 1: Those bitch lady bosses with their eternal PMT.

WOMAN 3: Fuck off! What about unreasonable male chauvinist bosses with a low testosterone level?

WOMAN 2: Sexual harassment in the office.

MAN 1: Who's on my side?

MAN 2: Who's on mine?

WOMAN 1: Office politics.

MAN 3: But we are only getting ahead.

WOMAN 2: By stepping over the heads of others?

MAN 3: That may be the only way of doing it.

WOMAN 3: Problems and more problems.

WOMAN 1: The sexism.

MAN 1: Trust the women to raise an unimportant issue.

MAN 3: Too much work.

WOMAN 2: Not enough pay...

EDDIE: Excuse me, but isn't this what we always wanted? Some challenges in our work place. *(Pause. To audience)* Pardon these people. They are still very naive. Working life is not all that bad. And there are always a lot of perks in the corporate world. But Life isn't just work, remember? There are sales...

(Huge sign descends. "When the going gets tough, the tough go shopping.")

WOMAN 1: Let's go shopping.

WOMAN 2: Eh, you know, Galeries Lafayette got sale, Daimaru got sale, Tangs got sale, Isetan got sale and Metro got sale...

MAN: Let's face it. The whole of Singapore is on sale.

WOMAN 1: Want to take leave or not?

MAN: What? To go shopping?

WOMAN 1: Then? How are we going to get the real bargains if we don't get there first?

WOMAN 2: That's true. OK, I'm going to shop until I drop...

WOMAN 4: I don't need another dress or another pair of shoes.

WOMEN 3: But you feel good when you have shopped. It's... it's cathartic.

WOMAN 2: Who says money can't buy happiness? They just don't know where to shop!

(Huge sign: "I shop, therefore I am.")

EDDIE: That's better.

WOMAN 2: Eh, after that go for afternoon buffet tea, OK? I know where we can eat 40 different dishes for only $9.90 ++.

MAN: Is it the Nonya tea at Goodwood Park?

WOMAN 1: Or that very sinful chocolate tea at Pan Pacific? Yah, everything from chocolate. It's so sinful can die.

MAN: I just want variety, OK, so let's go...

(Huge sign: "Those who indulge, bulge.")

WOMAN 2: Cannot cannot... So fat already. I cannot eat buffet tea. I'm not prepared.

MAN: Prepared?

WOMAN 2: Yah-what? Must diet for a week then can go.

MAN: Why bother?

WOMAN 1: Eat first, go to gym and work-out later.

MAN: Where got time?

WOMAN 2: I really wish I didn't have to work. Look at her. *(STELLA leading her charmed life.)* She's got the Good Life. She can go shopping any time she likes, sale or no sale. She can go for teas anywhere she likes and she can spend hours at the health club, working at keeping her figure trim.

WOMAN 1: Cheong doesn't want her to work...

MAN: A rich man would be ashamed to let his wife go to work.

WOMAN 2: Can't stand these ladies of leisure.

MAN: No-what, she's quite busy. Always organising this and that. I always see her in this sports car, going here and there for this charity function or that one.

WOMAN 1: I always see her in the society pages in fashion magazines. Always so beautifully dressed. Always on the arm of her husband. The perfect couple.

WOMAN 2: He must surely love her. He gives her everything.

SCENE: SO TELL ME, ARE YOU REALLY HAPPY?

EDDIE: So tell me, Stella, are you happy?

STELLA *(trace of ennui in voice)*: I am, of course, I am. Why shouldn't I be?

EDDIE: Everything you've always wanted?

STELLA: Let's see. Life is comfortable.

EDDIE: More than comfortable. A semi-dee in Thomson. A Filipino maid. Two cars... You have the Good Life.

STELLA: Isn't there supposed to be something else?

EDDIE: Is there?

STELLA: I don't know. I keep getting this nagging feeling that there's something that's missing.

EDDIE: Cheong?

STELLA: Cheong is too busy. Cheong treats me alright. He gives me everything I ask for, even the things I don't. But...

EDDIE: But what?

STELLA: I don't know. There's a strange restlessness in my soul. I can't put my finger on it and it eludes me. I don't know what's wrong...

Eddie: So tell me, are you really happy?

STELLA: I don't know... All the time, people asking me, asking me, over and over, am I happy?

EDDIE: But you are having a good time...

SCENE: LIFE IN THE FAST LANE III

EDDIE: It's party time! Today we celebrate the birth of three babies, six promotions and several wedding anniversaries.

WOMAN 1: How the years just fly by...

WOMAN 2: Three in a row before I'm twenty-eight, so that I can get my tax rebate.

WOMAN 3: Wait till they all have to go to school. You line up from 4 pm the day before just to get them into a good playschool.

EDDIE: We are going places.

MAN 1: I'm getting a bigger house.

MAN 2: I'm getting a bigger car.

MAN 3: I'm getting a divorce. My wife just left me for another man. Shit!

EDDIE: And you, Stella darling, what are you getting?

STELLA: What can I get except more of what I already have. I'm only getting old.

WOMAN 2: Excuse me, Stella, could you hold her a minute? *(As STELLA holds the baby, it seems like there's a moment of discovery or enlightenment, as if a child might be the thing that could save her.)*

STELLA: A baby, a pretty little baby.

WOMAN 1: You like them don't you?

STELLA: Yes, I do...

WOMAN 2: Then when are you having one?

STELLA: I never thought about it before.

WOMAN 1: Oh, you and Cheong are too busy. Maybe you should take it easy and have a baby. It makes all the difference to a marriage you know.

MAN: You both aren't getting any younger, and what are you going to do with all that money that Cheong is making? You've got to hand it down to the next generation.

WOMAN 2: But first there must be the next generation. Eh-you know, it's true. All those campaigns "Children – your life wouldn't be complete without them."

WOMAN 1: Yes, you and Cheong have everything already. Children would be the cherries and icing on the cake.

STELLA: Children... maybe. I'll think about it.

EDDIE: Government propaganda... It always serves a purpose.

SCENE: DILEMMA TIME

STELLA: What can I say? It's not that we didn't try. It's not something that any woman will admit to. Who talks about these things anyway? Well... How do you go about explaining that for the six years in your married life you've hardly made love because your husband is too tired and can't get it up enough to satisfy you. It's too much of a bother getting it up to a point and not being fulfilled. It's a let-down. Better not to even try than to get frustrated in the attempt.

SCENE: THE QUESTION

(CHEONG is writing at his desk.)

STELLA: Cheong...

CHEONG: Yes, what is it?

STELLA: I was wondering...

CHEONG: Look, I have some important decisions to think about and I need to look through these figures tonight. Is it important?

STELLA: Yes, it is. *(Pause.)* Cheong, I want to have a baby.

CHEONG: Like, now? Stella, you know I can't.

STELLA: I mean, could you just think about it sometime when you're not too busy?

CHEONG: Stella, babies are nice, if they're someone else's... But they don't fit into my scheme of things or my schedule.

STELLA: Cheong, you're always so busy working. I need a diversion, I need something to love, something to keep me occupied. I don't know what.

CHEONG: No, Stella, for more than one reason, we will not have a baby. For the first thing, you know I... we can't. Second, no baby's going to be part of a novel project you begin with and get tired of later.

STELLA: I didn't mean it that way.

CHEONG: What did you mean?

(Silence.)

STELLA: Sometimes I think you hate me.

CHEONG *(laughs)*: Just because this once, I have denied this fancy of yours. *(Sobers.)* My heart will never be a simple little trinket you play with till you get bored and then leave in one of your many jewellery boxes. A child would be no different...

STELLA: If you didn't love me, why did you marry me?

CHEONG: I wanted a fancy woman. I wanted to make her happy.

STELLA: I don't believe this. You've grown colder and harder as the years go by. It's this damned drive to earn and keep earning that's changed you. You're like a machine...

CHEONG: It's become an acquired habit but you'll never know what set the wheels in motion, will you?

SCENE: LEFT OF CENTRE

(CHEONG onstage. EDDIE comes in.)

EDDIE: Do you have a little ... time?

CHEONG: What do you want?

EDDIE: Pretty ugly scene there just now...

CHEONG: Life is full of ugly scenes here and there.

EDDIE: Cold.

CHEONG: Rational.

EDDIE: How do you reconcile your passionate fidelity to one woman with this cold business machine you've become?

Cheong: I don't. It's not necessary.

EDDIE: You don't. Tell me honestly now. Do you still want her? You said you don't love her.

CHEONG: I have always wanted her and I will always want her. If you... love somebody or someone, you have to love them till the very end.

(STELLA is holding a bottle and is steadily drinking out of frustration.)

EDDIE: What are you going to do now?

STELLA: I don't know. What can I do?

EDDIE: Take a lover.

STELLA: I can't.

EDDIE: Why not? *(Pause.)* You haven't gotten rid of your middle-class value system yet, have you?

STELLA: No...

EDDIE: Leave him...

STELLA: I can't...

EDDIE: But you don't love him.

STELLA: I don't know... I don't know.

EDDIE: Do you know what you are... A spoilt petty child whose first request has been thwarted. Cheong has given you everything you have asked for but he can't give you this...

STELLA: He can't or he won't?

EDDIE: How will you ever know?

STELLA: Cheong...

(CHEONG appears. He is impassive, not disgusted at her. She wheels towards him.)

CHEONG: Drunk...

STELLA: Cheong, my husband... my darling... to whom I vowed eternal fidelity... do you know that in the six years we've been married... you never once told me you loved me?

CHEONG: Was it necessary?

STELLA: I just wondered, that's all.

CHEONG: Have I ever denied your every whim and fancy?

STELLA: No.

CHEONG: Have I ever treated you cruelly?

STELLA: No.

CHEONG: Have I ever looked at another woman and given you cause for jealousy?

STELLA: No. Cheong, are you gay?

CHEONG: No.

(STELLA reaches the edge of despair.)

STELLA: What has become of the two of us? What has become of me? What has become of the boy who used to read *The Little Prince*? Where has he gone?

CHEONG: Strange. You never looked for him before.

STELLA: Is he here?

CHEONG: No...

STELLA: Oh, Cheong...

(She flops over him and tries to undo his zip. They struggle. He takes the empty bottle from her and throws it to one side. He pushes her away, slaps her.)

STELLA: Cheong, I love you. I need you.

CHEONG: You're really drunk, you don't know what you're saying.

STELLA: Cheong, do you love me?

(Silence.)

CHEONG: You never wanted to know before.

STELLA: I want to know, do you love me?

(CHEONG does not answer.)

STELLA: You must hate me then...

CHEONG *(quietly to himself)*: You can't hold stars in your hands without your hands becoming cut by their sharp shiny points, nor your fingers frozen by their cold.

STELLA: Cheong, I just want you to hold me tonight. I don't want a baby. I just want you to hold me. Please... Please...

CHEONG: No.

(He exits. She is alone.)

SCENE: THE ULTIMATE SEDUCTION

(Scene reopens. STELLA is smoking coolly.)

EDDIE: So what now, pretty lady?

STELLA: What? You're going to ask me if I'm happy. Yes, of course I am. Ever since I stopped asking myself if I was really happy... I'm just going to live the life I want.

EDDIE: What about Cheong?

STELLA: What about him? He doesn't love me. But what does that matter? I never wanted his love in the first place.

EDDIE: And babies?

STELLA: Stupid crying little things. Besides, If I really want one, I can adopt, right? Because of our status in society and my charity work, which adoption agency would refuse me?

EDDIE: Is this what you always wanted?

STELLA: Try to imagine me. Happy little housewife in a five-room HDB flat with two or three little darlings in tow. It is evening. My husband comes home after a long day's work. I greet him at the door with a kiss and a cup of hot tea. We have our dinner. We put the darlings to bed. He watches TV and when the day is done, we'll go to bed. *(Laughs)* Domestic heaven. How middle-class!

One day, I will get a house in Queen Astrid Park, three servants to do my bidding and a chauffeur. Swimming pool with attached sauna. I'll do my charity work. Meet up with friends and maybe set up a shop which I will run for the sheer fun of it. A Happy Life... a happy, happy life.

EDDIE: What about love, Stella, what about love?

STELLA: Love is for those who have little else to divert them. Love

is for the pitiful... I'm just going to live my life the way I please.
I'm always going to get what I want.

EDDIE: But what about your vague restless feeling?

STELLA: What about it? We all have vague restless feelings. They
pass.

EDDIE: Aren't there any other choices in life?

STELLA: There are none. I have chosen the path I walk. There is
no turning back.

EDDIE: But are you sure?

STELLA: Look, the road ahead is rosy, tree-lined, wide. The streets
are paved with gold... I can live with it. I can live with anything.
I have everything I want.

(EDDIE laughs, very amused.)

STELLA: Last night I had a dream. I dreamt that I went driving
with Daddy again. Again, I was sitting on two cushions on that
white towelling that he spread over the seat. But this time the
beautiful silver car is mine. There was no uncle to tell Daddy to
stop the car and the lady with the wings turned and smiled at
me. She asked me where I wanted to go. I told her I wanted to
take the fast lane. Anywhere. She took me to a big beautiful
room. The music tinkled like the song from a music box. There
were stars hanging from the ceiling and fancy women with stars
on their hands and in their ears and they were calling me to
dance. To spin and to keep spinning.

(There is a pause and a moment of recognition.)

STELLA: And I saw you there. You were always there waiting for
me, weren't you? Waiting for me to be done, dancing with the
others... I am here now waiting...

(Eddie stands taller and larger. He moves to a kind of a raised

platform or pedestal. MOTHER comes in with her basket. The EN-
SEMBLE moves in. MOTHER hands them a dark shroud-like robe
which they place upon her shoulders. They drape her with jewels
and pearls. There is the low moan of chanting and the ching of
temple bells. She walks slowly towards him and lights the candles
on the altar that resembles a kind of car. An atmosphere of wor-
ship.)

STELLA: I am here, and I await your further blessing.

EDDIE: At last... at last. And soon... many more.

EPILOGUE

(The stage is dark again. Single spotlight on EDDIE GOODTIME.
The mood is sombre. He plays the hypocrite.)

EDDIE: If you've gotta dream, dream big. Dreams are free. Don't
you be afraid of dreaming.

Life in the fast lane – where does the fast lane take you? Where
does it end?

The dream comes with a little price-tag. Just a little one. It's not
much considering what you gain in return.

You can have it all.

Hey, isn't it worth it? You have a choice to make it happen.
Anybody wanna buy a brand-new dream?

–END–

Absence Makes
The Heart Grow Fonder

by Robin Loon

The D'Cruz family is the typical happy three-tier family. Beneath the spectacle is a brittle bond held together by the mother, Dorothy. The daughter, Vanessa, is estranged from the family. The son, Henry, his wife, Peck Yah and their son, Peter, construct the realities of everyday domestic life. Dorothy dies and soon after, Raymond the patriarch suffers from Alzheimer's disease. The family breaks down in the face of this domestic crisis.

The son, Henry, is unable to cope with the disintegration of the perfect family. He escapes from the fear of losing his father into his work. Peck Yah, his wife, struggles to hold the family together, fulfilling a promise she made to her mother-in-law. Raymond's condition deteriorates while domestic values and responsibilities are neglected.

The play looks at how relationships are tenuous and how our reality can deconstruct before our eyes if we do not value or confront it. The play looks at how people we love will forget about us if we forget about them.

CHARACTERS:

RAYMOND D'CRUZ

DOROTHY D'CRUZ

HENRY, their son

PECK YAH, their daughter-in-law

VANESSA, their daughter

PETER, their grandson

DOCTOR TAN

ABSENCE MAKES THE HEART GROW FONDER premiered at the Drama Centre on 7 April 1992. It was directed by Alec Tok, with settings by Michael Lim, lights by Thio Lay Hoon, and music by Babes Conde. It was produced by Theatreworks and featured the following cast:

RAYMOND	Alex Abisheganaden
DOROTHY	Rosaly Puthucheary
HENRY	K. Rajagopal
PECK YAH	Nora Samosir
VANESSA	Noraizah Nordin
PETER	Yolande Goh
DOCTOR	Diong Chae Lian

It was given a rehearsed reading by Theatreworks on 18 Sept. 1991. The reading featured Alex Abisheganaden, Lok Meng Chue, William Grosse, Claire Wong, Cindy Sim, Noraizah Nordin and Koh Chieng Mun. It was directed by Ong Keng Sen.

ACT ONE

SCENE ONE

(In a photo salon. The D'Cruz family is having a family photo taken. DOROTHY and RAYMOND seated, PECK YAH and HENRY standing behind them. Their son, PETER, sits on the floor in front of DOROTHY and RAYMOND, and they seem very happy.)

Voice: OK! All look to the camera. Smile! Ready?

(A flash.)

Voice: OK, perfect!

SCENE TWO

(In a classroom. PETER is about to do a presentation on the people he loves.)

PETER: Yes, Ms Teo? I'm ready. *(Clears his throat.)* "My Grand-parents" by Peter D'Cruz. I have two grandparents, a Grandpah and a Grandmah. They are both very old. They are my father's parents. My Grandmah is Chinese. Grandmah always says that Daddy was a difficult child and it was like carrying an atomic bomb in her stomach for nine months. But every time I ask Daddy why, he always tells me to shut up. My Grandpah used to be a navy captain and is now retired. He lives with my Daddy, Mummy and me… oh sorry, and I. Grandpah doesn't do very much except comb his hair. I don't understand why because he doesn't have that much hair to comb in the first place. Grandmah always says he's full of macho-shit. When I ask my Grandpah what is macho-shit, he always tells me to shut up. I spend a lot of time with my grandparents. My Grandmah is very sweet and she cooks very well; she always cooks my favourite which is marshmallow with *chingchow*. Mummy says it's not good for me but Grandmah says it's alright because I am a growing boy. As for Grandpah, he's very forgetful. Just the other day, he was shouting across the room for his glasses so Grandmah and me... and I look high and low for it but we still couldn't find it. In the end, we found out that it had been on his head all the time. It was very funny. Grandpah is very gung-ho and tries to command the house as though he was on one of his ships. Even Daddy say he's full of macho-shit. I love him very much although everyone thinks he's full of macho-shit. Thank you... excuse me, Ms Teo, what is macho-shit?

SCENE THREE

(Dining room. PECK YAH and DOROTHY are preparing for dinner.)

PECK YAH: Let me do it, Mah. Why don't you sit down and rest for a while?

DOROTHY: Don't be silly, Peck. I can do this very well. It's no problem at all.

PECK YAH: Don't strain yourself, Mah. Doctor says your heart is not very strong.

DOROTHY: Will you stop treating me like an old woman. What do doctors know? All they want to do is scare you into going back to them. I'm as strong as an ox.

PECK YAH: Anything you say, Mah. If you get tired, just tell me, OK?

DOROTHY: Eh, Peck? Where is the soup bowl?

PECK YAH: It's right in front of you, Mah!

DOROTHY: So it is. Silly me!

(Pause.)

DOROTHY: You know, Peck. Your Pah and I have been married for thirty-five years. Quite amazing. After the fifth year, I honestly thought I wouldn't last. Your Pah is not the easiest man to live with, you know. He may be twelve years older than me, but I tell you the man can get so horny.

PECK YAH: Mah! Please!

DOROTHY: What? You're not an outsider, we can discuss this openly, we're women of the nineties.

PECK YAH: Of course, Mah. But I never thought about it. It just hasn't crossed my mind that you and Pah... you know... you know...

DOROTHY: What? Make out? Of course we do.

PECK YAH: I know you do, but I just...

DOROTHY: If we didn't do it, how do you think your husband came about? We didn't have artificial insemination back then.

PECK YAH: I know... I just never thought about it.

DOROTHY: I tell you, Peck, every time he comes home from one of his one to three month duties, he's like one of those 4 cylinder, 5 speed cars on over-drive! I have to work out while he's away to keep up with him! I married your Pah when I finished my secondary school. I tell you the first time I saw him, I knew he was my man. So I just packed up and married a sailor.

PECK YAH: I didn't know that.

DOROTHY: You never ask me! Now tell me about my son, what is he like?

PECK YAH: He's alright.

DOROTHY: Oh come on, Peck, tell me all about it!

PECK YAH (*very shy*): Well... he can get quite horny too.

DOROTHY: I knew it, just like his father.

PECK YAH: Mah!

DOROTHY: I bet he doesn't use any contraceptive either?

(PECK YAH very coyly nods.)

DOROTHY: The D'Cruz men are all full of macho-shit.

PECK YAH: Mah?

DOROTHY: What now?

PECK YAH: I don't know... but Henry and I... Henry doesn't...

DOROTHY: He doesn't seem to want to do it, right?

PECK YAH: Something like that.

DOROTHY: I can tell, you have the makings of a repressed house-wife. OK! Peck! You and I are going to Thailand for a dirty weekend. We're going to let our hair down and cross legs at singles bars. It's on me.

PECK YAH: Mah, be serious!

DOROTHY: I am! I've got more steam in me than a pressure cooker.

PECK YAH: You know I can't, Mah! I've got Henry and Peter.

DOROTHY: Yah, I've got Raymond.

(Discussion stops for a minute.)

PECK YAH: Mah? Do you and Pah still... you know...

DOROTHY: Do we still make out – of course. Every Wednesday, without fail...

(HENRY enters.)

HENRY: Hi Mah! Peck, can we eat?

DOROTHY: How about telling your wife she looks good for a change. She's your wife, not your Sri Lankan maid!

PECK YAH: Mah!

DOROTHY: I just want to remind you that your wife is a very pretty woman and you are very lucky to have two beautiful women taking care of you.

HENRY: I'm hungry, Mah!

DOROTHY: Be a good boy and wait outside for us.

(HENRY exits. PECK YAH and DOROTHY begin to laugh.)

DOROTHY: Now... where was I? Oh yes! Every Wednesday, your Pah will give me his standard come-on line. He'll come out of the bathroom and say in his best sexy voice: "Dot? Have you seen my underwear?" That's my cue to ram the engine. Isn't it the funniest thing? To think that it has been going on for twenty years!!

PECK YAH *(giggling)*: I never knew, Mah!

(Both women laugh even louder. RAYMOND enters.)

RAYMOND: Dot? There you are. Dot? Have you seen my underwear?

(Both women look at each other and laugh heartily.)

SCENE FOUR

(Living room. RAYMOND enters with his model ship and admires it. HENRY enters.)

HENRY: Hi, Pah! Where did you find the ship?

RAYMOND: Found it in the store room. I thought I lost it.

HENRY: This is the model of that ship you saved in '64?

RAYMOND: Yah! My CO gave this to me in appreciation of my valiant effort. Not bad, right?

HENRY: Yah, Pah! Very nice.

RAYMOND: Eh, Henry? You got a cigarette?

HENRY: Yes, Pah! Why?

RAYMOND: Give me one.

HENRY: Cannot lah, Pah! Mah will kill me if she finds out.

RAYMOND: She won't. Just give me one, quick, before she comes.

(HENRY gives RAYMOND a cigarette. They smoke.)

RAYMOND: Shiok! Nothing like a cigarette after a meal.

HENRY: Yah.

RAYMOND: Not those stupid menthol lights. Must be Marlboro then shiok, right?

HENRY: That's right, Pah! A real cigarette.

RAYMOND: Henry, what's this I hear you're very busy.

HENRY: No lah, just trying to earn more money.

RAYMOND: You need money, tell me. I've got enough pension to feed us all.

HENRY: It's alright, Pah! I can make enough. I'm the man of the family now.

RAYMOND: Eh, your old man can still take on a whole ship.

HENRY: I know Pah, now it's my turn.

RAYMOND: So, you think you're all grown up, can take over your father?

HENRY: No problem, Pah, I can do better.

RAYMOND: Good, that's my son! A chip off the old block.

(Both laugh.)

DOROTHY *(offstage)*: Are you two smoking again?

(Both quickly stub out their cigarettes.)

SCENE FIVE

(Chinese New Year. The D'Cruz family are preparing for the traditional tea ceremony. RAYMOND and DOROTHY are sitting on the chair. PECK YAH enters with tea tray. HENRY and PETER follow behind.)

RAYMOND: What's all this? There is no need to be so formal, we're family.

DOROTHY: That's right, Peck. We don't expect you all to do this. Let's just all go out and have brunch.

PECK YAH: No, Mah! We must pay our respects.

HENRY: Yah, Mah! You used to do it every year with Grandpah and Grandmah.

DOROTHY: That was because they were old-fashioned. I never enjoyed it, not a single bit. So *lay-chey.*

RAYMOND: Let them have their fun. We just sit back and enjoy this attention.

(PECK YAH and HENRY, holding a cup of tea each, kneel before DOROTHY and RAYMOND.)

HENRY and PECK YAH: We wish Pah and Mah a Happy New Year and many more long and healthy years to come.

(DOROTHY and RAYMOND both receive the tea and drink up. There is an awkward pause after that.)

DOROTHY *(softly)*: Raymond. Raymond, give them the *ang-pow.*

(RAYMOND can't hear. DOROTHY tries again.)

DOROTHY: Raymond! The *ang-pow.*

(RAYMOND finally remembers.)

RAYMOND: Oh yes! Here. *(Hands the* ang-pow*)* And this is for a happy and long life also to you too.

HENRY and PECK YAH: Thanks, Pah!

(PETER's turn.)

PETER: Happy New Year to Grandpah and Grandmah and may Grandpah grow more handsome and Grandmah grow more pretty.

(Everyone laughs. Pause. DOROTHY looks at RAYMOND, gesturing him for the ang-pow*. RAYMOND suddenly remembers.)*

RAYMOND: Here you go, Henry! Happy New Year and you grow up to be a smart and strong boy.

DOROTHY: Raymond, it's Peter your grandson. Henry is over there.

RAYMOND: Of course, Peter. Happy New Year.

PETER: Thank you, Grandpah!

DOROTHY: Can we go now?

HENRY: Let's wait for Van. She says she's coming to visit. She promised she'll try.

DOROTHY: Oh good! I haven't seen her for so long.

RAYMOND: Is she really coming?

PECK YAH: She said so.

RAYMOND: Let's go, she won't come.

DOROTHY: Raymond, let's wait for her.

RAYMOND: She's never come and she won't this time. Let's not waste time.

(Phone rings. PETER answers offstage and comes back.)

PETER: Aunt Vanessa said she can't come.

(RAYMOND stands up and walks on.)

RAYMOND: What are you all waiting for? I told you she wouldn't come.

SCENE SIX

(House. DOROTHY is sitting on her rocking chair. She has a visitor, her daughter VANESSA.)

VANESSA: Hi, Mah! Happy New Year.

DOROTHY: Hello, Vanessa.

VANESSA: I've come to visit you and Pah. Where is he?

DOROTHY: He's gone out. What is it this time?

VANESSA: Whatever do you mean, Mah?

DOROTHY: I may be old but I'm not stupid. What do you want this time?

VANESSA: Well... Mah, you remember that boutique I was telling you about, the one I'm setting up with Mrs Wee? Well every-thing is just about set except for the money. I need some money for the partnership and so I thought you and Pah could, you know...

DOROTHY: Give it to you. How much?

VANESSA: Think of it as an investment, Mah. By the way did you see me in this month's issue of *The Singapore Tatler?*

DOROTHY: How much do you need, Vanessa?

VANESSA: Mah, this boutique is just what I need. I have all the connections and in no time, I will have the most glitzy clientele in Singapore.

DOROTHY: $50,000?

VANESSA: Actually, I need 100 K.

DOROTHY: That's a lot of money Van, I haven't got that much with me. I'll have to talk to your Pah about it.

VANESSA: Don't, Mah! Pah is forever against anything I do. He's so stubborn and he never helps me in anything.

DOROTHY: Your Pah wants you to be independent, Van. You have your own life now. You can't keep coming back to us when you need something.

VANESSA: Mah, don't make it sound as though I am sponging off you and Pah. If asking for a little money is too much, then forget I said anything.

DOROTHY: Don't get upset, Van. I'll have to think about it. If only you were more like Peck.

VANESSA: So that's it. Mah, I'm your flesh and blood, she's an outsider. How can you compare?

DOROTHY: She's a part of the family.

VANESSA: And I'm not, is that what you're trying to say? Fine. I'm married off after all, why should anyone bother?

DOROTHY: Stop it, Van, you're giving me a headache. I said I'd think about it and I will. Even if I give you the money, it will have to take some time. I 'll tell you when.

VANESSA: That's a yes? Thanks, Mah! You won't regret it.

DOROTHY *(to herself)*: I won't live to regret it.

VANESSA: I'll call you soon, Mah. *(Kisses DOROTHY.)* Have to go, tell Pah I said hello. Bye.

(VANESSA exits.)

SCENE SEVEN

(Dining room. RAYMOND is teaching PETER Maths.)

PETER: How, Grandpah? I don't know how to do this sum.

RAYMOND: Aiyah, boy! Simple multiplication also don't know.

PETER: I know but they always put the problems sums in strange ways. I never know what they really want.

RAYMOND: Very easy. When they say "the sum," it's plus. When it's subtract, that means minus. When it is product, it's times, and quotient means divide.

PETER: Then how come they don't say so, everything is so difficult.

RAYMOND: If everything is simple, where's the challenge? Back in 1964, your Grandpah singlehandedly saved a sinking ship. The waves were ten times taller than me and everyone on the ship was scared. But your Grandpah ran to the deck and commanded the sailors to their stations. If it weren't for me, everyone would have died.

PETER: Wah, Grandpah, you're so super!

RAYMOND: Of course I was.

PETER: But Grandpah, I still don't know how to answer this question.

RAYMOND: Let's see. If Kim Chuan had 5 apples and his mother gave him two times as much, how many apples would he have? Simple, boy; it's times.

PETER: But there isn't the word "product," I thought you said...

RAYMOND: Never mind, boy, trust me. It's times.

PETER: How many times how many?

RAYMOND: It's 5 x 2, boy.

PETER: 5 x 2 is how much?

RAYMOND: Grandpah'll teach you. 1 and 2 is 2; 2 and 2 is 4; 2 and 3 is 6; 2 and... 2 and... 2 and...

PETER: 2 and 4, Grandpah!

RAYMOND: Yah! 2 and 4 is... is... 8; 2 and... 2 and... 2 and what, boy?

PETER: 2 and 5, Grandpah!

RAYMOND: That's right! 2 and 5 is... is... is...

PETER *(whispering into his ear)*: 2 and 5 is 10.

RAYMOND: That's right! 2 and 5 is 10.

PETER: So Kim Chuan has 10 apples.

RAYMOND: Apples? What apples?

PETER: Kim Chuan has 12 apples altogether.

RAYMOND: Who's Kim Chuan? Boy, what are you talking about? Do your problem sum.

PETER: I am, Grandpah! Kim Chuan has 10 more apples.

RAYMOND: Kim Chuan has 10 more apples than what?

PETER: Grandpah, the problem sum!

RAYMOND: Problem sum?

SCENE EIGHT

(RAYMOND and DOROTHY's bedroom. RAYMOND enters.)

RAYMOND: Dot! Dot! Where are you?

(RAYMOND looks around for DOROTHY but doesn't find her.)

RAYMOND: Dot! Where are you!? Dot! Where are you?

(RAYMOND gets hysterical and shouts for DOROTHY. DOROTHY rushes into the room.)

DOROTHY: What's the matter, Raymond?

RAYMOND: Dot! Where were you? Couldn't you hear me?

DOROTHY: I was downstairs with Peck. Why were you screaming?

RAYMOND: I couldn't find you!

DOROTHY: Don't be silly! I'm here!

(PECK YAH enters.)

PECK YAH: Mah, is everything alright?

DOROTHY: Everything is fine, Peck! Go downstairs and watch the stew. I'll handle this!

(PECK YAH exits.)

RAYMOND: Who was that?

DOROTHY: Peck Yah, you stupid old man, your daughter-in-law.

RAYMOND: That's right.

(DOROTHY wants to leave.)

RAYMOND: Where are you going?

DOROTHY: I'm going downstairs to cook.

RAYMOND: Don't go, please, Dot!

DOROTHY: Raymond, I've got work to do.

RAYMOND: Let that woman work, you stay with me!

DOROTHY: OK! OK!

RAYMOND: I hate being alone, Dot! This house is so big, not like our house in Ang Sa Lee. Now *that* is a house.

DOROTHY: What are you talking about, Raymond? We haven't been living there since 1981. This is our house.

RAYMOND: I don't like this place.

DOROTHY: Well, it's a bit too late to complain.

RAYMOND: I just don't like it, I want to live in Ang Sa Lee.

DOROTHY: Don't be silly, Raymond. We're very happy here.

(DOROTHY wants to leave again.)

RAYMOND: Dot! Where are you going?

DOROTHY: I have to work, Raymond.

RAYMOND: Don't go, please!

DOROTHY: OK, but promise me you'll rest before dinner.

RAYMOND: Anything.

(DOROTHY strokes RAYMOND's hair.)

DOROTHY: You know, Raymond! I like the way your hair curls upwards.

RAYMOND: You do?

DOROTHY: Yes! I think that's why I married you.

RAYMOND: Really? But now I don't have that much hair left.

DOROTHY: This is true. Actually, your curly hair used to irritate me, it was so inconvenient.

RAYMOND: But you said you liked it.

DOROTHY: Yah, but I didn't say I liked living with it.

RAYMOND: Should I shave it off, then?

DOROTHY: No, dear. At your age, you won't know whether it'll grow back.

RAYMOND: So what can we do?

DOROTHY: Nothing, dear. I guess I'll have to get irritated with it. But now since there is less, maybe I'll get less irritated.

RAYMOND: I'm sorry, dear!

DOROTHY: Don't be stupid, Raymond.

RAYMOND: Dot, I'm old!

DOROTHY: So am I, dear, so am I.

RAYMOND: What will happen to us?

DOROTHY: I don't know, Raymond.

RAYMOND: Dot, I...

DOROTHY: What?

RAYMOND: Never mind.

(Pause.)

DOROTHY: Raymond, I still love you, even if your hair curls upwards.

RAYMOND: You do?

DOROTHY: So long as you love me when mine starts to curl upwards.

RAYMOND: I will, you know I will.

DOROTHY: And our children love us too.

RAYMOND: Even Vanessa.

DOROTHY: Even Vanessa.

(Pause.)

DOROTHY *(To herself)*: Oh Raymond, what is happening to you?

SCENE NINE

(PECK YAH and HENRY's bedroom. HENRY is lying on the bed and PETER is lying on HENRY's lap, fast asleep. PECK YAH enters.)

PECK YAH: Peter? Are you...

HENRY: Sh...! *(Whispers)* He's asleep!

PECK YAH: Stupid boy! I'll bring him back to his room.

HENRY: Let him sleep here for a while!

PECK YAH: OK.

(PECK YAH gets on the bed beside HENRY. Both look at PETER fondly.)

HENRY: You know, Peck! I used to do this all the time when I was young! I used to climb into my parents' bed and refuse to leave. Pah would pat my head and stroke my hair lightly. Just like this...

(HENRY strokes PETER's hair.)

PECK YAH: Henry. I have something to tell you about Pah!

HENRY *(apparently not hearing PECK YAH)*: You know, Peck! Pah is a really fine man! Ever since I was young, he was always the person I wanted to be, even now. You should have seen him at his prime.

PECK YAH: Henry, about Pah...

HENRY: Yah? You were saying about Pah?

PECK YAH *(hesitates)*: Never mind, Henry!

HENRY: Peck, I'm sorry that we haven't spent enough time together. I want to but I just never seem to have the time.

PECK YAH: It's alright, Henry.

HENRY: I knew you would understand.

PECK YAH: I'll bring Peter to his room.

(PECK YAH carries Peter. Exits. HENRY falls asleep. PECK YAH enters.)

PECK YAH: Henry. I think there's something wrong with Pah! He forgets too easily. And Mah is also quite ill. Why don't we bring them to the doctor tomorrow. I know you're busy but I'm sure you'll...

(PECK YAH doesn't get a reply. She turns to the bed and finds

HENRY *sleeping.* PECK YAH *smiles and walks to the bed. She kisses* HENRY *on the forehead.)*

HENRY *(murmuring in his sleep)*: We'll talk about it tomorrow.

SCENE TEN

(Living room. PETER *is eating his marshmallow with* chingchow. VANESSA *enters.)*

PETER: Hi, Aunt Vanessa!

VANESSA: Hello, boy! Where's everyone?

PETER: Grandpah and Grandmah are in the room. Daddy and Mummy went out. Who are you looking for?

VANESSA: I'm looking for Grandmah! Boy, what are you eating?

PETER: Marshmallow and *chingchow*. Grandmah made it specially for me! You want some!?

VANESSA: No thank you, dear! Aunt Vanessa doesn't like marshmellow and *chingchow*!

PETER: What do you like, Aunt Vanessa?

VANESSA: Well! *(She sits down with* PETER.*)* When your Aunt Vanessa was a little girl, your Grandmah used to make the best coconut candy in the world and I would eat and eat so much until all my teeth nearly fell off.

PETER: Aunt Vanessa was a greedy girl!

VANESSA: Yah! When my teeth hurt very badly, I would run to Mah and she would give me an ice cube to suck on. It was OK for a while but then it started to hurt again! Pah just sat there reading his stupid newspaper! I bet he would have jumped if it was Henry!

PETER: Oh?

(Pause.)

PETER: Aunt Vanessa? Why don't you visit us more often?

VANESSA: Because Grandpah doesn't like Aunt Vanessa!

PETER: But why?

VANESSA *(somewhat resignedly)*: Because I wasn't a son! Because
  I wasn't the daughter he wanted me to be! Because he always
  wanted me to...

(VANESSA stops and looks at a confused PETER.)

VANESSA *(laughs)*: How could you understand? You're a son! Let
  me put it to you simply boy, nobody wants Aunt Vanessa, no
  one loves Aunt Vanessa!

PETER: But I do! I love you very much, Aunt Vanessa!

VANESSA *(pleased)*: Really? Thank you, boy!

PETER: And I think Grandpah, Grandmah, Daddy and Mummy
  love Aunt Vanessa too! They really do!

VANESSA: I don't think so, boy!

(HENRY enters.)

HENRY: Hello, Van!

VANESSA: Hi, Henry!

HENRY: Did you want something?

VANESSA: I came to give Mah some papers. She's asleep?

PETER: Daddy, Daddy! Did you eat coconut candy until all your
  teeth fell out when you were a boy?

(HENRY looks at VANESSA. They both laugh.)

PETER: What's so funny?

HENRY: Never mind, boy! Go out and help your mummy with the shopping!

PETER: OK!

(PETER exits.)

VANESSA: He's grown so much!

HENRY: Yah! Reminds me of me when I was a boy!

VANESSA: Yah! You used to bully me, Henry!

HENRY: What? I never did!

VANESSA: Of course you did! I still remember that time when we fought over that stupid sugar-cane. You gave me a black eye and Pah gave you the sugar-cane!

HENRY: Come on, Van, we were only kids!

VANESSA: It's alright! I don't mind! It's all in the past! I have my own life now and I'm happy!

HENRY: If you say so, Van!

VANESSA *(looks at her watch)*: Oh my goodness! It's five already! I have to go! I have another appointment!

HENRY: Cancel the appointment, Van! Have dinner with us, the whole family!

VANESSA: I don't think so, Henry! Anyway, Pah may get indigestion with me around!

HENRY: Come on Van, just...

VANESSA: Look, Henry! I really don't have the time! Maybe next time. Will you please give Mah these papers and tell her that she has to give me the answer as soon as possible.

HENRY: OK. But are you sure...

VANESSA: Stop being a nag, Henry! I really have to go! Don't forget to give these papers to Mah! I'll call you. Tell Mah and Pah I was here! Bye!

SCENE ELEVEN

(Sitting room. DOROTHY is resting. She appears tired. She shuts her eyes for a while. PECK YAH enters.)

PECK YAH: Mah?

DOROTHY: What is it, dear?

PECK YAH: Vanessa just called. She wants to know whether you have made up your mind, and when.

DOROTHY: Vanessa. My daughter. If she calls again, tell her... never mind, I'll tell her myself. Where's your Pah?

PECK YAH: He's outside playing with Peter. They're having so much fun.

DOROTHY: I'm glad he's having fun. He deserves it.

PECK YAH: Mah, are you alright?

DOROTHY: I'm fine.

PECK YAH: Alright, Mah.

(PECK YAH is about to leave.)

DOROTHY: Peck, where did I go wrong?

PECK YAH: Sorry, Mah?

DOROTHY: Every time Vanessa comes to me, it's money. It's been like this since she was a little girl. I was always the doting mother and I just kept giving it to her. Now, she doesn't know how to stop.

PECK YAH: No lah, Mah – she's not that bad.

DOROTHY: Don't console me, Peck. I'm tired, so tired. I'm tired of looking out for my children after they have all grown up.

PECK YAH: Stop it, Mah. You're beginning to sound like an old woman.

DOROTHY: Old woman?! Nonsense. Peck, so are we still going to Thailand? I haven't forgotten, you know.

PECK YAH: Thailand? I thought you were joking, Mah!

DOROTHY: Joking? We're taking the next flight there. Let me call my travel agent.

(DOROTHY gets up but suddenly feels faint and collapses back into the chair. PECK YAH panics.)

PECK YAH: Mah! are you OK?

DOROTHY: Don't be silly, of course I'm alright.

PECK YAH: Mah, I think you'd better rest. I'll make an appointment with the doctor.

DOROTHY: Don't panic, Peck. I'm OK.

PECK YAH: I still think you should rest.

DOROTHY: Yah. I think so too. *(Pause.)* I think I'm really old.

SCENE TWELVE

(Classroom. PETER is daydreaming.)

PETER: Yes, Ms Teo? The island north of Singapore? What is the question? What is the island north of Singapore? I... I... no, I know! The island north of Singapore is Sentosa! No, Ms Teo, I wasn't daydreaming. I was paying attention. My homework? Oh I forgot to bring! Actually I didn't forget, I didn't do it... not because I was lazy or anything but because I didn't know how to do. *(To another child)* I'm not stupid!! I just don't know how to do. I don't know who to ask. Grandpah can't help me any more because he forgets very easily and doesn't make any sense. Mummy? She's always at the hospital. Yes, Ms Teo, my Grandmah is in hospital; she's not well. Nobody can tell me what's wrong with her. When I visit her at the hospital, she just lies there not doing anything. I talk to her but she never answers. She looks at me and moves her mouth but nothing comes out. She didn't eat the marshmallow and *chingchow* I made for her. Daddy says she cannot eat because she is sick, but I only get sick after I eat it and not before. I don't understand what's happening. All I know is that Mummy gets angry very often and yells at Daddy and me... and I. Daddy yells back and everyone is so upset. Grandpah is the best, he just sits at home and plays with me, he's not upset at all. But shouldn't he be?

SCENE THIRTEEN

(The family car. HENRY and PECK YAH are driving to the hospital.)

PECK YAH: She's not getting any better, Henry. Do you know that?

HENRY: Yes.

PECK YAH: Well?

HENRY: I don't know.

PECK YAH: Is that all you can say? Don't know?

HENRY: What else do you want me to say? It's too early to cry.

PECK YAH: Henry! Your mother is dying!!

HENRY: We don't know that for sure.

PECK YAH: So?

HENRY: So? So what do you want me to do about it?

PECK YAH: Henry, I'm glad you're so upset over it. For a moment there, I thought you weren't very bothered about it. Now I can see how worried you would be when I die.

HENRY: Please, Peck! I'm not in the mood to argue with you. Sime Darby just dropped another two points and I have just now lost my promotion. Five years and they decide to promote some new Harvard MBA. Is that fair?

PECK YAH: How can you talk about work at a time like this!?

HENRY: What else can I talk about? Look, my mother is dying, that's the truth and fact. Nothing we say or do will stop it. All you can do is sit there all day and talk and talk.

PECK YAH: Well, it's better than not doing anything.

HENRY: I don't want to discuss it now.

PECK YAH: Why not?

HENRY: I'm not in the mood.

PECK YAH: When are you ever in the mood?!

HENRY: Oh, shut up! I don't need a lecture now.

PECK YAH: Yah, you probably don't need anything!

HENRY: What do you want me to do?

PECK YAH: Nothing! Nothing at all. Just drive the car.

(Awkward pause.)

PECK YAH: Did you call Vanessa?

HENRY: Yes. She's busy. She's got to fly to Japan. She can't cancel it because she made an appointment with the Tokyo designer tonight.

PECK YAH: I suppose she'll be here in spirit.

HENRY: Van is like that. Mah will understand.

PECK YAH: That's the problem. Both of you expect people to understand and you take too many things for granted. Your sister hasn't lifted a finger to help when Mah is in hospital. She visited, once. She can accuse me of currying favour. Sometimes I don't know what to do with your family!

HENRY: Shut up, Peck! I'm sick and tired of listening to you telling me how horrible we are!

PECK YAH: It's the truth.

HENRY: I don't want to hear it!!

(The handphone rings.)

PECK YAH: Hello? My God, the hospital? Yes, Dr Tan! Yes, my husband and I are on our way! What? She's started to talk again! That's great! Does that mean she's…? No? But she's able to talk now, surely that must mean… oh, I see. We'll be there in ten minutes. Thank you for the call. Good-bye.

HENRY: I told you there was nothing to worry about. She will be fine! She can talk now and that's a definite sign of recovery.

(PECK YAH is silent.)

HENRY: Peck? What's the matter now? She is going to be fine! What's wrong with you? One minute you want her to recover and now she has, you keep quiet. The doctor said she'll be fine, right? Right? Peck! Don't just sit there, she is going to be alright, isn't she? Peck, talk to me!!

SCENE FOURTEEN

(Hospital. DOROTHY lies on the bed. The family visits her.)

HENRY: Mah, are you alright?

DOROTHY: Never felt better, dear. Do I look sick to you?

HENRY: I'm serious, Mah.

DOROTHY: So am I. I know I'm dying.

PECK YAH: Don't say that, Mah. You'll recover. The doctors said so.

DOROTHY: What do the doctors know?

PECK YAH: Look, Mah. We're taking the next flight to Thailand after they discharge you.

DOROTHY *(laughs)*: Our dirty weekend!

(DOROTHY and PECK YAH laugh.)

HENRY: What's so funny?

DOROTHY: It's a secret your wife and I share.

(Pause.)

DOROTHY: Where's my husband?

HENRY: We've sent for him and Peter.

DOROTHY: And Van?

PECK YAH: Er... she's on her way.

DOROTHY: It's alright. I didn't expect her to come. *(Pause.)* Peck! I want to talk to my son.

(Spot on HENRY and DOROTHY.)

DOROTHY: Have I been a good mother?

HENRY: Of course, Mah. The best.

DOROTHY: You never told me.

HENRY: Of course I did.

DOROTHY: I don't mind it, but it would have been nice to hear you say it.

HENRY: I'm sorry, Mah. There were times I wanted to but I... just never got round to saying it.

DOROTHY: It's OK, dear! Just tell me now.

HENRY: You're the best, Mah. I love you.

DOROTHY: It's funny. Your sister tells me all the time but it's become a habit. At least you mean what you say.

(Spot on PECK and DOROTHY.)

PECK YAH: Van loves you, Mah! I know she does.

DOROTHY: I know she does, Peck. I've spoilt her. I've made her the princess and now her royal highness no longer needs her queen, just the crown.

PECK YAH: Don't say that. It's not your fault...

DOROTHY: But, Henry. I always knew Henry was different.

PECK YAH: I hope so, Mah. I really hope so.

(Spot on HENRY and DOROTHY.)

DOROTHY: Henry. Whatever money I have left, give Van her 100 K. I guess it's the only thing she'll remember me for. At least she'll remember me.

HENRY: I will, Mah.

DOROTHY: Promise me you'll take care of Pah when I'm not around.

HENRY: Mah, please don't...

DOROTHY: Let me finish, Henry. Like it or not your Pah is old and he's sick. You must take care of him. He needs the family more than anything now.

HENRY: I will, Mah!

DOROTHY: Take care of yourself, and your wife. She's your wife and she deserves a bit of attention now and then. Don't wait till the last minute.

(Spot on PECK YAH and DOROTHY.)

DOROTHY: Peck, you're a good daughter-in-law. I'm very thankful and grateful.

PECK YAH: Thanks Mah.

DOROTHY: Your husband's not so bad. Give him some time. He's like his father.

PECK YAH: I know, Mah.

DOROTHY: Peck, I must ask a favour.

PECK YAH: Of course, Mah.

DOROTHY: Please look after your Pah for me. And I don't mean an old folks' home or a hospital. Keep him at home, please.

PECK YAH: I will. I promise.

DOROTHY: I can't depend on Vanessa and Henry... he's too much his father's son to accept that he's old and useless. My hope is with you.

PECK YAH: No, Mah. Henry and Vanessa will take good care of Pah. I'll make sure of it.

DOROTHY: Thank you, Peck. *(Pause.)* Oh, Peck!

PECK YAH: You're a good wife and a devoted mother, Mah. You did a great job.

DOROTHY: Really? I must have gone wrong along the way then. I must have set my children on the right path but they detoured. I've lost Vanessa and I pray to God I still have Henry. He's a good man, Peck. He's just too much like his father: proud, bull-headed and full of macho-shit. How did we get mixed up with these men?

(Spot on RAYMOND and DOROTHY.)

RAYMOND: Woman. What are you doing lying in bed?

DOROTHY: You want to join me?

RAYMOND: What are you doing here?

DOROTHY: I'm sick, you stupid old man.

RAYMOND: Old? Who's old?

DOROTHY: We are, Raymond.

RAYMOND: Rubbish. I'm as young as I was in '64 when I single-handedly saved...

DOROTHY: Saved a ship from sinking. I know Mr Macho. Tell me, can you save this ship from sinking?

RAYMOND: Ship? Where?

DOROTHY: Nothing, Raymond. Come sit beside me.

RAYMOND: You pack your stuff and we go home to Ang Sa Lee now.

DOROTHY: Raymond. We moved out of Ang Sa Lee years ago.

RAYMOND: Our house is in a mess. You must come home with me.

(Spot on PECK YAH and DOROTHY.)

PECK YAH: I don't know whether I can do it, Mah.

DOROTHY: I know I'm asking a lot but he's the only person I worry about. He's old, Peck. You must help him. I want him to be happy.

PECK YAH: But Mah, I really...

DOROTHY: Please? Peck, you're my last hope.

PECK YAH: I'll try, Mah. I promise I'll try.

(Spot on DOROTHY and RAYMOND.)

RAYMOND: Guess what I found?

(RAYMOND digs into his pocket and pulls out a butterfly bow.)

DOROTHY *(giggles)*: My goodness! Where did you find it?

RAYMOND: Remember our tenth anniversary.

DOROTHY: Of course. I sat in the study stark naked with this butterfly bow on my head, waiting for you to walk through that door. I nearly froze to death.

RAYMOND: I kept you warm, didn't I, Dot? *(Growls.)*

DOROTHY *(giggles)*: Stop it, Raymond. You're being stupid again.

RAYMOND: Who's stupid?

DOROTHY: Not you, Captain!

(DOROTHY coughs.)

RAYMOND: Are you alright, Dot?

DOROTHY: I'm alright, dear. Now put that bow on me.

(RAYMOND puts the bow on DOROTHY.)

DOROTHY: Now kiss me.

(RAYMOND kisses DOROTHY.)

DOROTHY *(looks fondly at RAYMOND)*: Thank you, Raymond.

RAYMOND: For what?

DOROTHY: For spending thirty-five years with me. For loving me thirty-five years.

RAYMOND: You're most welcome.

DOROTHY: Promise me you'll behave yourself.

RAYMOND: I promise.

DOROTHY: I love you, Raymond.

(Spot on PETER and DOROTHY.)

PETER: Hi, Grandmah. I brought you *chingchow* and marshmallow. I made it myself.

DOROTHY: Thank you, boy! It must be good, better than Grandmah's.

PETER *(shyly)*: No lah.

DOROTHY: How did you get in here? Where's everyone?

PETER: Daddy and Mummy both outside but they're very quiet. Grandpah has gone off to the canteen to play with the vending machine. He's more naughtier than me... than I.

DOROTHY: You must look after Grandpah for me, boy.

PETER: When are you coming home, Grandmah?

DOROTHY: Soon, boy. Soon.

PETER: Then you can teach me how to make *chingchow* and marshmallow without messing up the kitchen.

DOROTHY: You must stop drinking that, boy, or you won't grow.

PETER: What about you, Grandmah?

DOROTHY: It's OK for Grandmah. Grandmah won't grow any more.

PETER: I want to grow up so I can go on one of Grandpah's ships and travel around the world.

DOROTHY: Don't forget to bring Grandpah with you, boy.

PETER *(yawns)*: I won't.

DOROTHY: Go home boy, you must rest for school tomorrow, Grandmah must sleep.

PETER: Goodnight, Grandmah! *(Kisses her.)*

HENRY: Goodnight, Mah! *(Kisses her.)*

RAYMOND: Goodnight, Dot! *(Kisses her.)*

(Spot on PECK YAH.)

PECK YAH: I cried at the funeral. Mah's not here any more. She's always been here for me but now she's gone. Everyone acts as though nothing happened. *(Pause.)* Me? Life goes on I guess. I promised Mah I'd take care of Pah and I will. Mah? I just don't know.

END OF FIRST ACT

ACT TWO

SCENE ONE

(Living room. RAYMOND sits alone playing with DOROTHY's butterfly bow.)

PECK YAH *(offstage)*: Pah, time for dinner.

HENRY *(offstage)*: Pah, time to eat.

PETER *(offstage)*: Grandpah, come and eat with us?

HENRY *(offstage)*: Pah, you're using your chopsticks all wrong.

PECK YAH *(offstage)*: Peter, get your Grandpah a spoon and fork.

PETER *(offstage)*: Grandpah, you're making a mess of your dinner.

HENRY *(offstage)*: Are you hungry, Pah? Did you have lunch?

PECK YAH *(offstage)*: Do you want me to feed you, Pah?

PETER *(offstage)*: Where are you going, Grandpah?

SCENE TWO

(DR TAN's office. DR TAN has examined RAYMOND and is now presenting his diagnosis.)

DOCTOR TAN: Mr and Mrs D'Cruz. Your father has Alzheimer's disease. In layman terms, it's a sort of senility but it's more serious than that. It's a kind of dementia where the victim suffers from a loss of intellectual power. The patient will have difficulty remembering, making decisions, thinking through complex ideas. Slowly, the patient will also have problems performing practical activities, retaining new information or acquiring new skills.

(Family car. PECK YAH and HENRY on their way home.)

HENRY: Alzheimer's disease? I still don't know what the hell it's all about? Peck? What do you think?

PECK YAH: I don't know. Dementia. He made Pah sound as though he's mad.

HENRY: Maybe he really is demented.

PECK YAH: Stop it, Henry! Pah is not demented. He is sick. We must do our best to take care of him.

HENRY: We're not doctors.

PECK YAH: We're family.

HENRY: Dr Tan said he will get worse...

(DR TAN's office.)

DOCTOR TAN: Unfortunately, this is progressive, meaning that the condition will slowly get worse. At the moment, the diagnosis is multi-facet dementia. It's caused by a series of small strokes in the brain creating areas of dead brain cells. The arteries leading to and from the brain will harden gradually.

(In the family car.)

HENRY: The doctor said Pah needs professional treatment.

PECK YAH: What are you saying, Henry?

HENRY: We must admit him to a geriatric home.

PECK YAH: No!

HENRY: Don't be stubborn, Peck! We must face the fact that Pah is sick and a sick man belongs in a hospital or a nursing home.

PECK YAH: No!

HENRY: He will be hell around the house, you heard what the doctor said...

(DR TAN's office.)

DOCTOR TAN: Let me put it this way. Your father is slowly losing all awareness of everything. He will not be able to remember half of the things he did or ate the day before and will probably not know where he is most of the time. He will get excessively upset and less adaptable to the environment, and he will gradually withdraw from the people around him; he may or may not be aware of his own condition. Alzheimer's cases vary from case to case.

(In the family car.)

PECK YAH: The doctor also said it is different for different people.

HENRY: Be reasonable, Peck. Pah is not going to recover at home; at the nursing home he may have a better chance. We're doing the right thing.

PECK YAH: The man is not just another Alzheimer's patient! He's your father, for Christ sake.

HENRY: I know he's my father.

PECK YAH: No, Henry! I won't allow it.

HENRY: Look. It's not as though we can't afford it. What the hell is wrong with you?

(DR. TAN's office.)

DOCTOR TAN: I'm afraid there isn't a cure for Alzheimer's, not at present. You must realise that he will slowly cease to be your father as you remember him and he may even develop other related diseases. Parkinson's disease is one possibility. No, Mr D'Cruz. Alzheimer's disease is usually non-hereditary and certainly not contagious. However, there may be some domestic problems if the family decides to keep the patient at home. The patient may consciously or unconsciously do things or say things that may be dangerous to himself and others around him. I would recommend that you admit him to a geriatric home where he can be treated. On the other hand, staying with the family would be beneficial as the patient needs the family's support. Do consider both.

(In the family car.)

PECK YAH: He's not going to a home, Henry! I said no!

HENRY: I say he's going and I mean he's going!!

(PECK pulls the handbrake abruptly. The car screeches to a stop.)

HENRY *(furious)*: What do you think you're doing? You want us all to get killed?

PECK YAH: This is the only way I can get you to listen to me! Your father is not going to spend the rest of his life vegetating in a home. He's staying with us. It's our duty!

HENRY: Don't you put me on a guilt trip!

PECK YAH: I can still bring him for therapy and treatment but he's staying at home, you understand?

HENRY: Fine, you take care of him!

PECK YAH: What?

(DR. TAN's office.)

DOCTOR TAN: Alzheimer's patients are unpredictable and very very difficult to manage. I suggest you seriously consider. There is no shame in admitting him into a home but if he stays with your family, it would give him a sense of belonging and strength the geriatric home can't give him.

(In the family car.)

HENRY: You take care of him. You play Florence Nightingale and you be the martyr. I can't deal with him, not now. I have a lot of work to do.

PECK YAH: Fine. I'll do it. You go ahead and work! I can do it!

HENRY: Stop being stubborn!

PECK YAH: Henry, your own father and you can bear to chuck him in an old folks' home! I really hate you sometimes. Mah was wrong! You're just like Vanessa. Everything in this world must revolve around you, you, you! You don't spare a thought for Pah, me or Peter! All you care about is your stupid Sime Darby! You and your Sime Darby can go to hell!!

(PECK YAH storms out of car. HENRY sits in car, distracted.)

SCENE THREE

(Home. PETER is playing cards with RAYMOND in the living room.)

PETER: Grandpah! You cannot fish. 3 and 8 is not 10. You can only fish when the two numbers add up to 10.

RAYMOND: What do you mean, cannot?

PETER: Cannot lah, Grandpah!

RAYMOND: This is a stupid game. I don't want to play!!

PETER: Finish the game, Grandpah!

RAYMOND: No!!

(RAYMOND flies off the handle and messes up the cards, forcing it to end.)

PETER *(annoyed)*: Grandpah, that's not fair! I was winning! I was winning!

RAYMOND: Win lah, go ahead! See how you win now!

PETER: Grandpah!!

RAYMOND: I don't want to play! I want to go home!

PETER: Home? We are at home, Grandpah!

RAYMOND: No! I live in Ang Sa Lee! This is not Ang Sa Lee. It's just fifteen minutes walk from Kou-Ong-Yah! This is not my house! I want to go home.

(RAYMOND stands up. He reaches into his pocket for his bow but doesn't find it.)

RAYMOND: Where is my bow?

PETER: Grandpah?

RAYMOND: Did you take my bow?

PETER: No, Grandpah. I haven't seen your bow.

RAYMOND *(loudly)*: Then who took my bow?

(PETER gets frightened.)

RAYMOND: Where the hell is my bow?

(RAYMOND searches the room.)

RAYMOND: You! *(Pointing at PETER)* You must have taken it! Give it back to me!

PETER *(frightened)*: I didn't, Grandpah. I didn't!

RAYMOND: Give it back to me. Give it back to me now!

PETER: Please, Grandpah! I didn't take it! I don't know where it is!

RAYMOND: I said give it back to me now!!

PETER: I don't have it, Grandpah!

RAYMOND *(yelling at him)*: Give it back to me!!!

(PETER is terrified. He begins to panic and cry a bit.)

PETER: I'm sorry, Grandpah! I don't have it! I don't have it!

(PECK YAH enters.)

PECK YAH: What's happening here?

PETER: Mummy!

(PETER runs to PECK YAH.)

PECK YAH: What's the matter, boy?

PETER: Grandpah said I took his bow but I didn't! Then, he shouted at me!

PECK YAH: Did he hit you?

PETER: No, but I was very scared!

PECK YAH: Boy, you go upstairs first, Mummy wants to talk to Grandpah!

(PETER leaves.)

PECK YAH: Pah? Pah?

RAYMOND: Oh, Peck! Peck! Have you seen my bow?

PECK YAH: I had it, Pah. You left it outside so I kept it for you. Here it is!

(PECK YAH pulls the bow out of her pocket.)

RAYMOND: Good!

(RAYMOND plays with the bow.)

PECK YAH: Pah? You mustn't be so impatient with Peter!

(RAYMOND doesn't answer.)

PECK YAH: Pah? Pah? Are you alright?

(RAYMOND does not answer her.)

PECK YAH: Pah?

(RAYMOND stands up and leaves. PECK YAH appears distressed.)

SCENE FOUR

(Living room. PECK YAH is tending to RAYMOND's wound.)

PECK YAH: You see, Pah. You must be more careful next time. The railings are not slides, you can get hurt!

RAYMOND: I know!

PECK YAH: Next time, don't go anywhere without me! Remember to let me know where you are, OK?

RAYMOND: OK!

PECK YAH: Good. Does it still hurt?

RAYMOND: A little bit. *(Pause.)* Peck, where's Dot?

PECK YAH: Pah? Mah is dead.

RAYMOND: Dead? When?

PECK YAH: Nine months ago, Pah.

RAYMOND: She didn't say goodbye.

PECK YAH: She wanted to.

RAYMOND: She's not coming back, is she?

PECK YAH: I don't think so, Pah.

RAYMOND: Then where is she?

PECK YAH: She's somewhere up there.

RAYMOND: She left without me.

PECK YAH: She didn't want to.

RAYMOND: She doesn't love me, she left me with all these strangers. I don't know these people. They come in and say hello and I don't know what to say to them.

PECK YAH: Just say hello, Pah.

RAYMOND: Peck. Where did Dot go?

PECK YAH: She died, Pah. It was her time to go.

RAYMOND: When is my time?

PECK YAH: I don't know, Pah. I don't know.

RAYMOND: I want to go. I don't want to stay here.

PECK YAH: You still have me, Pah!

RAYMOND: Yah, I still have Peck.

(Pause.)

RAYMOND: But where is Dot?

PECK YAH: She died, Pah!

RAYMOND: When?

PECK YAH: Nine months ago. I just told you.

RAYMOND: Oh. Where did she go?

PECK YAH: She went to heaven, Pah!

RAYMOND: Is it very near Ang Sa Lee?

PECK YAH: No, Pah! It's very far away.

RAYMOND: She left without me.

PECK YAH: I know, Pah. She left without me too.

RAYMOND: I miss her.

PECK YAH: I miss her too.

RAYMOND: I want her back.

PECK YAH: I want her back too.

RAYMOND: Why are you rubbing your eyes, Peck? Are you cry-ing?

PECK YAH: I've got dust in my eyes.

RAYMOND: Come let me blow out for you! Dot always did this when I had dust in my eyes.

(RAYMOND holds PECK and blows into her eyes.)

SCENE FIVE

(Telephone conversation between VANESSA and HENRY.)

VANESSA: What the hell is that?

HENRY: Pah is losing his memory.

VANESSA: That's normal, isn't it? It's an old folks' disease. Wait! It's not hereditary, is it?

HENRY: No, Van. It is not! It's very complicated. He can't remem-ber anyone very much. The only person he can recognise is Peck.

VANESSA: Your dutiful wife, the martyr of the family.

HENRY: I don't see you visiting very often.

VANESSA: I'm too busy. My business is getting better each day and I need to give it my fullest attention. Just keep me updated on Pah!

HENRY: Van! He's your father too.

VANESSA: And what is that supposed to mean?

HENRY: Can you do something for him, at least this time?

VANESSA: You think of something for me, I'll pay you later.

HENRY: Van?!

VANESSA: Why don't you just send him to a nursing home. We can't do very much with him.

HENRY: I don't know! I don't want to discuss it now!

VANESSA: I'll come around one day! I've got papers for him to sign.

HENRY: I don't care. You just do whatever you want!

SCENE SIX

(Living room. PECK YAH is making a call.)

PECK YAH: Hello, Leng? Hi, it's Peck! I need a favour. Henry is taking me out to dinner tonight! Yah, we haven't been spending much time together so tonight is our first little rendezvous in a long time. Anyway, I need someone to babysit my son and my father-in-law tonight. Can you do it, please?

(HENRY's office. He's also on the line.)

HENRY: Hello? Summertime Florist? This is Henry D'Cruz. I would like to order a bouquet for tonight. I want tiger lilies and lots of baby's breath – it's for my wife. She likes the yellow ones, you know, and make sure it's a big bouquet.

(Home.)

PECK YAH: My father-in-law is no trouble at all. Oh, come on, Leng, don't make it sound as if he's mad or something like that. He's a nice old man. Peter will help you. Look, I really need to go out with Henry tonight, I need a break! Will you call me in a while to confirm?

(HENRY's office.)

HENRY: Yah! Send it to the Latour tonight, please! Yah, and ask for the table under Mr Henry D'Cruz. Card? Just write – "Love always, Henry!" That's right. You'll call me back for a confirmation? No problem!

(Home. The phone rings and PECK YAH rushes to pick up the phone.)

PECK YAH: Yes? So how?

(HENRY's office. The phone rings.)

HENRY: Yes, speaking! Oh? You can't? You're sure? It's alright, it can't be helped. I'll attend the meeting at 7 pm. Why did you have to pick tomorrow morning to fly off to Penang? No problem. I'll cancel my dinner plans. Yah, she'll understand.

(Home.)

PECK YAH: You can't? Why not? Not tonight? But Leng! I have been looking forward to tonight. I can't bring them along, it's for me and Henry! Please Leng, you must do this for me. *(Pause.)* It's alright, who am I trying to kid anyway. It's OK, Leng. I don't mind spending another night with them. Don't worry about it. I'm sure Henry will understand.

(HENRY's office.)

HENRY: Hello, Summertime Florist? Yah, this is Henry D'Cruz. Send the flowers to my house. Yah, send it to 129, Tai Keng Gardens. And change the card to "Sorry, we'll do it some other time. Love, Henry!" Thanks!

SCENE SEVEN

(House. VANESSA comes for a visit.)

VANESSA: Peck? Kor? Is anyone at home?

(Enter RAYMOND with his bow.)

VANESSA: Hello, Pah!

RAYMOND *(not recognising VANESSA)*: Hello?

VANESSA: Are you alone, Pah?

RAYMOND: Eh... yes... eh... no... Peck is in the kitchen.

VANESSA: How can she leave you here alone?

RAYMOND: Hello.

VANESSA: Hello, Pah!

RAYMOND: Hello.

VANESSA *(puzzled)*: Hello. Pah? What's the matter with you?

Raymond: Nothing. Hello. Who are you?

VANESSA: Me? Pah! I'm your daughter. I'm Vanessa!

RAYMOND: Pleased to meet you, Vanessa.

(RAYMOND shakes her hand.)

VANESSA: What's happened to you? What has Peck been feeding you? Have you eaten at all?

RAYMOND: I had... I had... what did I have for lunch?

VANESSA: Where's Peck? I want to talk to her!

RAYMOND: She's in the kitchen.

VANESSA: Peck! Peck!

RAYMOND *(mimics)*: Peck! Peck!

(PECK YAH enters.)

VANESSA: Peck! What is wrong with my father?

PECK YAH: He's not well, can't you tell?

VANESSA: Of course I can tell, but he can't remember me, his own daughter.

PECK YAH: He can't remember very much. He only remembers people he sees more often.

VANESSA: What is that supposed to mean?

PECK YAH: Nothing, Van. Is there anything you want?

VANESSA: I want to talk to my father.

PECK YAH: Be my guest.

(VANESSA turns to RAYMOND.)

VANESSA: Pah! Can you sign these for me?

RAYMOND: OK! *(Pause.)* I don't know how.

VANESSA: What?

PECK YAH: He doesn't remember his signature.

VANESSA: What rubbish! Of course he can. Pah, sign it.

RAYMOND: I don't know how.

VANESSA: Pah!!

RAYMOND: Vanessa?

VANESSA: Yes, Pah! It's Vanessa!

RAYMOND *(abruptly)*: Vanessa! You give me back whatever you took from Mah's room now!

VANESSA: Pah?!

(RAYMOND searches VANESSA.)

RAYMOND: You're not Vanessa! You're too old and ugly. Vanessa is not like that. I will kill her if she grows up to be like you.

VANESSA: Pah? What are you talking about?

RAYMOND: Vanessa! My daughter! She's a terrible girl! Terrible. Always asks for money, always money. Everyday spend money. She stole thirty dollars from her mother once and I gave her such a beating. Dot spoilt her rotten, that's what! Vanessa was such a problem child. If ever there was a problem child, her name is Vanessa!!

VANESSA: Stop it, Pah! Stop it!

RAYMOND: I tell you, Vanessa will grow up to be a stupid woman! I told Dot a million times. She will grow up to become one of those useless women who stand around all day and look pretty. I tell you, you mark my words. Peck! You just watch and see.

PECK YAH: Come, Pah! Let's go to your room.

RAYMOND: I tell you the girl is useless.

(RAYMOND exits.)

VANESSA: I have never been so humiliated in my life.

PECK YAH: He can't help it, Van!

VANESSA: The old bastard! After all these years, he still hates me. He will never change!

PECK YAH: Van, don't say that!

VANESSA: Listen, you think anyone will give a damn for all the things you're doing? Forget it, Peck, you'll just end up like me, unappreciated and unwanted.

PECK YAH: I don't think so, Van.

VANESSA: You just watch and see.

PECK YAH: Vanessa, I think you had better leave.

VANESSA: I will! Look, Peck! Take a look at yourself. You look like shit!

(VANESSA leaves.)

SCENE EIGHT

(HENRY and PECK YAH's bedroom. HENRY is in bed reading the newspaper. PECK YAH enters.)

PECK YAH: Your sister came today.

HENRY: Oh?

PECK YAH: She had something for Pah to sign.

HENRY: What was that?

PECK YAH: I don't know. She didn't say and I didn't ask.

HENRY: Must be the money.

PECK YAH: I suppose so.

(PECK YAH comes to bed.)

HENRY: How's Pah?

PECK YAH: He's OK. he asked for you today.

HENRY: He did?

PECK YAH: Yes. He still remembers you.

HENRY: Oh. Tell him I said hello.

PECK YAH: Don't you want to tell him yourself?

HENRY: Sometime later! You tell him for me.

PECK YAH: Sure, no problem.

HENRY: You look tired.

PECK YAH: Yeah, I look like shit, don't I?

HENRY: Listen, Peck! I'm really sorry about all this, but I...

PECK YAH: Can we talk about this tomorrow? I'm very tired
Henry. Try cleaning up after your father for one day and you'll
know what I mean.

HENRY: I told you to send him to a home.

PECK YAH: Don't start with me, Henry!

HENRY: Fine! Goodnight!!

*(They both sleep. PECK YAH has a nightmare. She is sitting in a
wheelchair. DR TAN appears behind her.)*

DOCTOR TAN: Mrs D'Cruz! You have Alzheimer's disease. You
know what that is? You will not be able to remember a thing,
nothing at all. You will not be aware of anything that is happening to you and consequently you will be a burden to your family.
You belong in a geriatric home where there will be proper
treatment and professionals who will look after you. Strangers
will look after you very well. Your family must be able to afford
it.

PECK YAH: My family will take care of me. They won't send me to a home. They will look after me the way I took care of Pah!

DOCTOR TAN: Definite signs of Alzheimer's disease. She's hallucinating.

PECK YAH: I am not! They love me and they will take care of me!

DOCTOR TAN: My professional opinion is that you will be better off in a home.

(DR TAN disappears. HENRY fades out, PETER appears.)

PETER: Mummy! Why are you sitting in the chair!?

PECK YAH: I'm not well! You must help me!

PETER: I don't understand all this! You are not sick!

PECK YAH: But I am! I'm in a wheelchair, for heaven's sake!!

PETER: I can't help you. I don't know how! You helped Grandpah and Grandmah and they all died! If I take care of you, you will die too! I can't help you because I don't want you to die. I don't want you to die!

PECK YAH: Peter!!

PETER: You took care of Grandpah and he died. You killed him, didn't you! You killed Grandpah!

PECK YAH: No! I was only trying to help!!

PETER: You took care of Grandmah, she died. You took care of Grandpah, he died. I can't take care of you because if I do, you will die. I love you and I don't want you to die. I can't do anything because I love you and I don't want you to die!!

PECK YAH: Peter! You don't understand! I need your support. I need your help!

PETER: Sorry, Mummy! I can't help you because I love you!

(DR TAN reappears with PETER.)

PECK YAH: Help me!

PETER: Shit! Sime Darby is down another five.

PECK YAH: Peter?

PETER: Sorry, Mummy. I love you but I can't help you.

DOCTOR TAN: I recommend a geriatric home with proper treatment!

PECK YAH: Help me, please!

DOCTOR TAN: Sime Darby down another five!

PETER: I love you but I can't help you.

DOCTOR TAN: I recommend a geriatric home.

PETER: Sime Darby!

DOCTOR TAN: I love you!

PETER: Geriatric home.

DOCTOR TAN: I love you!

DOCTOR TAN and PETER: Geriatric home!

DOCTOR TAN: Sime Darby!

PETER: I love you!

DOCTOR TAN: Geriatric home.

PETER: Sime Darby!!

(All characters hover around PECK YAH, chanting louder and more rapidly. The scene becomes chaotic.)

PECK YAH: No!!! Please, someone please help me!

SCENE NINE

(Living room. PETER is studying. HENRY enters.)

HENRY: Hi, boy!

PETER: Hi, Daddy!

HENRY: Maths?

PETER: Yah!

HENRY: Do you know that when they say subtract it's...

PETER: It's minus, right? Grandpah taught me all this. I also know product, quotient and sum.

HENRY: Very good, boy!

PETER: Did you have problems with Maths when you were in primary school, Daddy?

HENRY: I did. But your Grandpah taught me all I knew!

PETER: But Grandpah isn't very smart now! He can't even do addition.

HENRY: He's old, boy! He's sick!

PETER: Do all old people fall sick like this?

HENRY: Some of them do!

PETER: Will you?

HENRY: I don't know, boy!

PETER: I will still love you if you do, Daddy, just like how I love Grandpah now!

HENRY: Sure, boy?

PETER: Daddy, do you love Grandpah?

HENRY: Yes, boy. I do!

PETER: Good, Daddy! I love him too.

HENRY: We all do!

PETER: Do you still love Mummy?

HENRY: Of course I do. Why?

PETER: Mummy said you don't care for anything any more.

HENRY: That's rubbish, boy! Daddy still loves you and Mummy!

PETER: Then why do you shout at Mummy so much?

HENRY: Because Mummy shouts at me.

SCENE TEN

(The hospital. PECK YAH brings RAYMOND for a routine check up.)

RAYMOND: Peck! Why are we here?

PECK YAH: We're here to see the doctor.

RAYMOND: Are you sick?

PECK YAH: No, Pah! You're here for your check-up.

RAYMOND: Oh, I'm sick!

PECK YAH: Wait here for me while I get the doctor.

RAYMOND: Will you bring me home to Ang Sa Lee afterwards?

PECK YAH: Sure thing, Pah! Just don't leave this place before I come back. Don't go away!

(PECK YAH exits. RAYMOND has a nature call. He unzips and pees. PECK YAH returns.)

PECK YAH: Pah! What are you doing?

RAYMOND: I want to pee-wee-wee.

PECK YAH: Why didn't you go to the toilet?

RAYMOND: You said don't go away.

PECK YAH: But Pah, you can't pee here!

RAYMOND: I had to, or I'll wet my pants.

PECK YAH *(to others around)*: I'm sorry! I'm sorry!

RAYMOND: Why are you apologising? Did you do something wrong?

PECK YAH: Pah! Next time don't pee in public!

RAYMOND: Why?

PECK YAH: Don't ask! Listen to me properly! Don't ever do that again! You understand?

(RAYMOND looks blank.)

PECK YAH: What's the point! Let's go!

(HENRY's office. PECK YAH brings RAYMOND.)

PECK YAH: Henry?

HENRY: Peck?! What are you doing here?

PECK YAH: I just brought Pah to the doctors and I thought we'd come over for lunch.

HENRY: Did you have to bring him?

PECK YAH: What do you mean?

HENRY: He should be at home, not wandering around Singapore with you.

PECK YAH: The man is sick, not retarded!

HENRY: Don't shout, Peck.

(All this time, RAYMOND sits quietly on a chair.)

PECK YAH: Look, Henry, if you don't want to have lunch, that's fine. If you want me to go, that's fine too.

HENRY: I didn't say that.

PECK YAH: Then what do you expect me to do? I'm not superwoman, Henry!

HENRY: I know!

PECK YAH: Then do something, for heaven's sake!

HENRY: I don't see the point of this.

PECK YAH: You probably don't see anything! You think it's easy, don't you? Why don't you take care of him – you do it!

(PECK YAH storms out of the office, leaving HENRY with RAYMOND. HENRY looks at RAYMOND. RAYMOND stares back blankly. HENRY runs after PECK.)

HENRY: Peck, for heaven's sake come back! I don't know what to do!!

SCENE ELEVEN

(VANESSA's office. HENRY is complaining.)

HENRY: She just left him there! She just fucking left Pah in my office and took off! Can you believe that?

(VANESSA keeps very quiet while doing her paperwork.)

HENRY: And what does she mean, I don't do anything!? I work my butt off every day for the money! Who do you think pays for the treatment!? She's too much! Don't you think she's too much? *(Gets no reply.)* Van! Have you been listening to me?

VANESSA *(uninterested)*: Yes! Your wife had enough of our father and you're complaining to your sister about it? What do you want, Henry?

HENRY: Don't tell me you think she's right?

VANESSA: I don't think anything! Look, Henry. What exactly do you want me to say?

HENRY: Come on, Van. He's your father too!

VANESSA: Don't you give me any of that shit! As far as I am concerned, I am no longer a part of that family, so stop pouring out all your domestic trouble in my office.

HENRY: Are you trying to push it all onto me?

VANESSA: I have nothing to push in the first place! Go home, Henry! There's nothing I can do for you!

HENRY: Fine! But don't expect anything from me!

VANESSA: Fuck off, Henry, get out of my office! I don't need anything from you! You can keep your money and whatever's in the will! Do whatever you want, I don't care any more!

HENRY: OK! I won't bother you any more! Goodbye!!

(HENRY storms out of the office. VANESSA covers her face, she appears upset.)

SCENE TWELVE

(Home. RAYMOND enters with a suitcase. PETER follows behind.)

PETER: Grandpah. Are you going anywhere?

RAYMOND: I'm going home to Ang Sa Lee.

PETER: Why?

RAYMOND: Because Dot is waiting for me!

PETER: Dot! You mean Grandmah is there?! Can I come too?

RAYMOND: No.

PETER: Please? I want to see Grandmah!

RAYMOND: No!

PETER: If you don't let me go, I'll tell Mummy!

RAYMOND: OK.

PETER: Let's go! Do you know the way?

RAYMOND: Of course!

(On the streets.)

PETER: Grandpah, do you know where we are?

RAYMOND: Of course. I live here.

PETER: But we've been to this place before, this is the third time.

RAYMOND: No!

PETER: Is this place Ang Sa Lee yet?

RAYMOND: Of course! But I don't remember this building. It wasn't here before! I don't see my house.

(One and a half hours later.)

PETER: Grandpah! I'm tired! I don't want to walk any more!

RAYMOND: Don't give up. It must be here somewhere!

PETER: That's what you said one hour ago! I'm tired!

RAYMOND: We will find it sooner or later. Come.

PETER: No!

RAYMOND: You stay here and I will go out there, OK?

PETER: No!

RAYMOND: Just stay here and don't move!!

(RAYMOND exits. PETER sits by himself. He gets attracted by something and moves off. Sound of car brakes screeching.)

SCENE THIRTEEN

(Hospital. RAYMOND is sitting alone with his suitcase. PECK YAH enters in a frenzy.)

PECK YAH: Pah!! What happened? What did you do to Peter? Where did you two go? How could you do this to me?

RAYMOND: I wanted to go home to Ang Sa Lee.

PECK YAH: What do you mean, "go home?"

RAYMOND: Ang Sa Lee!!

PECK YAH: Ang Sa Lee!? Do you know you could have got killed? Do you know that Peter is hurt? Do you know that Peter may die!? Do you know anything at all?

RAYMOND: I don't know!

PECK YAH: You don't know!? You stupid old man. You can't even remember who you are! If my son dies, I will kill you. I will never forgive you. I took care of you when no one, not even your own children, would bother about you. If it weren't for me, you would have been locked up in a nut-house long ago. Do you know what I'm saying, you idiot? My only son is dying in there! Do you know what I'm saying? Say something, old man!!!

(RAYMOND is very frightened and covers his face. HENRY enters.)

HENRY: Peck! What are you doing? Stop it!

PECK YAH: You!? Where the fuck were you? Do you know your son is dying?

HENRY: Keep quiet, Peck! This is a hospital!

PECK YAH: I don't fucking care! I don't care any more! I only know that your father brought my son out to the streets and he got knocked down by a car. He may die, Henry! And you, Henry, you are never around when I need you. You expect me to understand but you never tried understanding me!! Your father is sick and all you can think of is your Sime Darby and sending him away!! I've had enough! I have had it with all of you! Henry D'Cruz, if my son dies today, I'll never forgive you, you and your father!!

(PECK YAH storms out of the hospital.)

HENRY: What happened, Pah?

RAYMOND: I only wanted to go home.

HENRY: Why?

RAYMOND: I want to go to Ang Sa Lee. Who are you?

HENRY: I'm Henry, your son.

RAYMOND: Hello, Henry-your-son, pleased to meet you.

HENRY: No, Pah! Don't!

RAYMOND: So, Henry-your-son, what are you doing here?

HENRY: I'm Henry, your son!

RAYMOND: I know you're Henry-your-son!

HENRY: Pah! I'm Henry, your only son. You must remember me, you must!

RAYMOND: Of course I remember. Where did we meet?

HENRY: Pah! Do you remember how you taught me Maths when I was young? When they say sum, they mean plus. When it's subtract, it's minus. when they say product it's times, and quotient means divide. Do you remember? My Primary 5 exams! Remember that, you helped me pass that exam and you took me to Chinatown for *cheng-teng*. Do you remember?

RAYMOND: *Cheng-teng*? Yes, that's right? Chinatown? Yes, the *cheng-teng* at Chinatown is very good.

HENRY: What about this? Remember once you scolded me for stealing the buttons from your uniform and you said you would call the police. I was so frightened. Then you came home with a bag full of shining buttons and you asked Mah to sew them onto my pajamas. Remember that one?

(RAYMOND looks blank.)

HENRY: Oh, Pah!

(HENRY breaks down.)

RAYMOND: Why are you crying?

HENRY: I'm sorry, Pah.

RAYMOND: Sorry? Did you do something wrong?

HENRY: Yes, I did! I forgot all about you and now you've forgotten all about me. I always thought that I could put things aside and make up for it later, but I'm really too late! I want to make up for lost time, Pah! Every time Peck complains to me about you, I feel so angry. I was angry because she sees so much of you and I was angry at myself for not seeing! Do you understand? Things can't be that bad, right Pah? Pah, please let me make up. I lost Mah, I can't lose you too. Give me a chance to make things better, please.

RAYMOND: No.

HENRY: No?

RAYMOND: No, I can't remember you.

HENRY: Pah! It's Henry and I love you.

RAYMOND: Thank you.

HENRY: Pah, I love you!

RAYMOND: Thank you.

SCENE FOURTEEN

(House. PECK YAH is packing some clothes for RAYMOND. Enter HENRY.)

HENRY: Are we ready?

PECK YAH: Just about.

HENRY: Peck I want to...

PECK YAH: Hold on...

(PECK YAH exits and returns with DOROTHY's bow.)

PECK YAH: Pah asked for this. Now we're ready.

HENRY: What's that?

PECK YAH: Something Pah gave Mah for their anniversary.

HENRY: It was their tenth anniversary.

PECK YAH: Mah told you?

(HENRY nods. PECK YAH is locking the suitcase.)

HENRY: Do you think we're doing the right thing?

PECK YAH: I don't know. We're doing what we need to do.

HENRY: Can't we try again? I will help take care of Pah.

PECK YAH: No, Henry! I can't. I'm very tired. I need some time for myself and for Peter.

HENRY: Some time for me too?

(PECK YAH does not reply.)

HENRY: Is that all Pah needs?

PECK YAH: The home said he'll be wearing their gowns and we don't have to bring him too many things.

HENRY: I hope we're doing the right thing.

PECK YAH: No use thinking, it's too late to think.

HENRY: Is it really too late?

PECK YAH *(pauses)*: Let's go. We're late!

SCENE FIFTEEN

(Classroom. PETER has a presentation.)

PETER: Yes, Mrs Lim! I'm next. This is a report of what I did for the past week. The whole family visited Grandpah and Grandmah at Mount Vernon. I hope they are happy because they had such a tough time when they were around. Grandpah especially. On Wednesday, Mummy finally moved out the rest of her stuff from the house. Daddy said she's gone for a holiday and won't be back till next month. When I asked him where, he just told me to shut up. Dad told me he was going to share some quality time with me. We went to the Theme Park. It was very interesting although I was quite annoyed by the Goddess of Mercy who spoke with an American accent. Daddy hated it. He said they have bastardised everything and it's just one big travesty. He told me that nothing stays the same any more. He went on and on about remembering the past and heritage and all that. If Mummy was there, she would say that Daddy's full of macho-shit. I think he's full of macho-shit but I still love him very much. Thank you.

Mrs Lim? Yes, Mrs Lim. I know what macho-shit is.

-END-

Three Fat Virgins Unassembled

by Ovidia Yu

What happens when little girls grow up? Everybody knows they fall in love with little boys. What happens when little girls fall in love with little boys? Everybody knows they go dating and become big boys and big girls. But what happens when they become big boys and big girls? Everybody knows they get married and live happily ever after. This is a play about three little girls who didn't do the things that everybody knows little girls do. This is a play about three little girls who grew up to be real women.

for Pat Chan

CHARACTERS:

WOMAN

VIRGIN A

VIRGIN B

VIRGIN C

THREE FAT VIRGINS premiered at the Drama Centre on 14 April 1992. It was produced by Theatreworks and featured the following cast:

WOMAN	Cindy Sim
VIRGIN A	Jacintha Abisheganaden
VIRGIN B	Pang Sze Lin
Virgin C	Valerie D'Costa

It was directed by Ong Keng Sen, with setting by Chan Mun Loon and lights by Kalyani Kausikan.

It was given a rehearsed reading by Theatreworks on 21 Sept. 1991. It was directed by Ong Keng Sen and read by Claire Wong, Jacintha Abisheganaden, Noraizah Nordin and Valerie D'Costa.

WOMAN: Once upon a time, at a National Day Celebrations tea held in the Kebun Istana, three fat virgins met under a red and white tent where tea and refreshments were provided, and there they made polite conversation.

(Three Fat Virgins come on. They all hold cups of tea with pinky fingers stuck out.)

VIRGIN A: Isn't it so hot here?

VIRGIN B: My Louis Feraud shoes are killing me!

VIRGIN C: I love your dress! Where? How much?

WOMAN: And in the course of their tea and polite conversation, these three fat virgins discovered that they knew each other from a long long time ago in school—

Of course, they were not virgins then. They were just school-girls. Women in Singapore do not become virgins until they reach puberty and finish secondary school. And if they do not become virgins then... they never will.

And if they do become virgins then... they tend to stay that way.

VIRGIN B: You look very familiar!

VIRGIN A: Actually, I was just thinking that You looked very familiar!

VIRGIN C: Oh sorry – I thought you were talking to me! I was just thinking that You looked very familiar!

VIRGIN B: Didn't you use to be in CHIJ?

VIRGIN A: Didn't you use to be?

VIRGIN C: Didn't you use to be thin?

VIRGIN B: Mavis Wee!

VIRGIN A: Yes! Choo Beng Kee!

VIRGIN C: Well, now I'm Mrs Chee... and aren't you Lai Fong? My, you've put on weight!

WOMAN: Inside every fat virgin is a thin schoolgirl.

There is no sadness like the inner sadness of fat virgins and skinny schoolgirls.

There is no sadness like the sadness of a dreamy schoolgirl trapped inside the body of a fat virgin. The age of self-consciousness is a difficult one to live through; and if your destiny has it that you are to be a fat virgin, you will be living in the age of self-consciousness all your life. Now matter how others see you, looking at yourself you see only the sadness of a fat virgin. And you wonder: how long before everyone finds out? This is why fat virgins are sad people. There is no sadness that is harder for thin men with balding heads and paunches to understand. This has nothing to do with penis envy. It is usually men that suffer from penis envy.

WOMAN: I am a man.

I am Mavis Wee's boss. My name is T.M. Ong. I used to work in SIA but now I work in a private company. I am a firm man with a sense of humour and a big house. I am strict with my sons but I spoil my daughter.

I don't have affairs in the office so I consider myself a very upright and moral man. I know that a lot of my senior staff play around. I don't mind as long as it does not distract them from their work.

I like to joke around with them to make them realise that I am just one of the boys.

To be fair to Mavis Wee, I also joke around with her, to show her that she is also one of the boys as far as I am concerned.

Mavis! Come into my office for a moment.

VIRGIN A: Do you want me to bring in the quality control report from HDB?

WOMAN: Yes, yes, bring it in, bring it in.

(VIRGIN A brings the report into the office.)

WOMAN: Is this it?

VIRGIN A: Yes. And I think it's quite complete. Will that be all?

WOMAN: Hmm. I see. On your way home?

VIRGIN A: Yes, unless there's something else...

WOMAN: No, no. Nothing else. I think I might go for a massage. What do you think, Mavis?

VIRGIN A: Sounds like a good idea. Well, have a good one, T.M.

WOMAN: Have you ever gone for a professional massage?

VIRGIN A: No...

WOMAN: It's very good you know. Relaxes you... you just lie there... it loosens all the tension out of your body. Out of your shoulders, especially. You should try it. Especially as you are sitting down at your desk all day.

VIRGIN A: Well, I swim off the tension. In fact, I'm off to the pool—

WOMAN: I think you should try it, you know, Mavis. But of course, I don't know how they finish it off for women. You should try it and let me know; you know what I mean?

VIRGIN A: I don't see why it should be any different, Mr Ong. Well, I'll see you—

WOMAN: Let me ask you one question, Mavis. Do you know what is a powder massage?

VIRGIN A: I don't know.

WOMAN: What do you think?

VIRGIN A: I suppose... when you get a massage with powder instead of with oil?

WOMAN: Ha, that's what you think, is it? Well, let me tell you something that you don't know. When the girl has finished your massage she will give you a powder massage... you get the idea? To release the tension from all parts of your body completely she will use her hands and give you a powder massage. You can ask Jack. He introduced me to this health club at the Paramount Hotel—

VIRGIN A: I don't really talk to Jack that much—

WOMAN: You should you know. You might learn something. He's a very interesting chap. You know what the girl at the Health Club told me? Her name is Soriya.

VIRGIN A: I have no idea.

WOMAN: She told me, your friend Jack comes here quite often.

VIRGIN A: Oh, really?

WOMAN: They all know Jack down there. Do you know what else she told me?

VIRGIN A: I'm sure you'll tell me.

WOMAN: She told me, your one is six and a half inches, not bad, quite average... but your friend's one is six and three quarter inches! These girls I tell you, they know everything!

VIRGIN A *(coldly)*: Why are you telling me this?

WOMAN: Just for your information.

(VIRGIN A leaves the office.)

VIRGIN B: I am a man. I am Mavis Wee's colleague, Jack.

(VIRGIN B/JACK goes into the office.)

VIRGIN B: So, T.M., how's things going!

WOMAN: Today something very funny happened! I told Mavis Wee about the powder massage. You should have seen her face! Ha! Ha! Ha!

VIRGIN B: I am a bit intimidated by Mavis Wee.

But I know how to carry balls in the right places. Ha! Ha! Ha!

WOMAN: She didn't know what to say! I had to explain to her what a powder massage is! Ha! Ha! Ha!

VIRGIN B: Ha! Ha! Ha! These virgins can't take a joke.

WOMAN: This Mavis Wee. She is a joke.

VIRGIN A: A powder massage is when you grind a man into powder.

With a SEA Games gold medal in judo, I can still grind my boss into powder. But I don't. I am not sure about certain things. Virgins can't always tell where the dividing line between a joke and sexual harassment is, exactly.

When it is your boss, it is usually a joke.

VIRGIN B: I think I'm being sexually harassed in the office.

VIRGIN A: Take it. If you can't take it, leave it.

VIRGIN C: Men. You can't live with them and you can't turn them into *sushi*.

VIRGIN A: Or *tempura*.

VIRGIN B: Or *sashimi*.

VIRGIN A: *Sashimi*, maybe can.

ALL: Hmmmm.

VIRGIN C: But how can you eat your man? As it is, I am already always warning my little daughter, don't put strange things in your mouth. And sometimes I wonder, who am I to tell her this?

VIRGIN B: You don't know who you are? No IC?

VIRGIN A: Only got IC but no identity?

VIRGIN C: Of course I have an identity. I am the wife of Mr Wilson Chee. I am the mother of Jonathan Chee and I am the mother of Melissa Chee. In fact, I have three identities. Isn't that better than having just one? What do you mean, who am I?

WOMAN: Think of me as a man. I am the man who is Mrs Chee's husband. I am Mr Wilson Chee. My friends call me Will. At the office my superiors call me Wilson. My subordinates call me Mr Chee. My wife calls me Ah Ba.

VIRGIN C: Where are you going, Ah Ba?

WOMAN: Out.

VIRGIN C: Out where?

WOMAN: Meeting.

VIRGIN C: When will you be back?

WOMAN: Late.

(Theme music from Popular Mandarin Soap.)

Sometimes I think that I will tell my wife who I respect but do not love that I am having a torrid extra-marital love affair with a woman who I love but cannot respect because she is not a graduate... but then the commercial break ends and the chance of a lifetime is lost. Again.

WOMAN: I will buy back supper for you.

VIRGIN C: Ah Ba, you're always such a good husband!

WOMAN: You be Doris.

VIRGIN B/DORIS: Doris is neither fat nor a virgin. She is, however, a woman. (*She strikes a seductive pose.*)

WOMAN: Doris calls me Dahlingk.

VIRGIN B/DORIS: Hello, Dahlingk.

WOMAN: Hello, Doris.

(*Passionate kiss.*)

VIRGIN B/DORIS: Af chew plannt alreaty whats are we goingk chew do tonights?

WOMAN: Tonight as usual we will go to your Taman Serasi flat which is filled with cute, expensive things that you have bought with the money I give you every month. As usual we will have some fucky and some sucky and then as usual we will go to Kreta Ayer Road for some *siew yeh* because as usual I said that I would buy supper back for my wife. Doris, you know I always buy supper back for my wife.

VIRGIN B/DORIS: Of course, Dahlingk. Do chew know whats it is that I liked best abow chew hah, Dahlingk? Thats is thats in spites of everythink you are remaining still a goods husband excepts for being fateful. Sometimes at times I likes to just pretent and imachine that I am marrit to you... really marrit... which chiltren... yours chiltren... and I wonter exakerly whats its wout really be liked.

WOMAN: You really want to know?

(*VIRGIN B/DORIS sits down on the sofa and puts her feet up. Watches TV.*)

VIRGIN A: I'm going to bed now, Ma.

VIRGIN B/DORIS: Goodnight, Jonathan. Have you finished your homework?

VIRGIN C: I'm going to bed now, Ma.

VIRGIN B/DORIS: Goodnight, Melissa. Have you packed your school bag?

WOMAN: I'm going to go out now, Ma.

VIRGIN B/DORIS: Goodnight, Ah Ba.

WOMAN: I will buy back supper for you.

VIRGIN B/DORIS: Ah Ba, you're always such a good husband!

WOMAN: I will always be a good husband. It is easy to always be a good husband. All you need is a good wife. A fat virgin makes a good wife.

WOMAN: Sometimes a woman marries a man who first makes her his wife and then makes her fat and then makes her a virgin.

Once upon a time, three fat virgins on diets met at the buffet tea at Goodwood Hotel.

VIRGIN A: I simply have to lose ten kilos before the annual dinner and dance.

VIRGIN B: I signed up for a slimming course, you know. Carrot juice and watermelon juice, that's all they allow you to take.

VIRGIN C: Does it work?

VIRGIN B: It cost me five hundred dollars! Of course it works!

VIRGIN A: My cycling machine cum rowing machine cum compact disc player cost more than three times that but it didn't do a thing for me.

VIRGIN C: Oh, I hate those D-I-Y machines.

VIRGIN B: I hate to diet.

VIRGIN A: But then why do you diet?

VIRGIN B: My husband makes jokes about me in front of our friends.

WOMAN: My wife is on a seafood diet. When she sees food she eats it...

VIRGIN B: What is so sad is that his jokes are not even funny so no one even laughs at them. At least if they were good jokes and made people laugh, I would not mind so much. After all, I have a good sense of humour.

VIRGIN C: Fat virgins always have a good sense of humour.

VIRGIN A: Or at least they have to give the impression of having a good sense of humour.

VIRGIN B: But no one laughs when my husband jokes about my weight. My husband thinks that he can make his joke funnier by making me fatter.

WOMAN: Here, wife. Eat this. You know that you like satay with lots of satay gravy. Here, wife, eat this. You know that you like *kway pie tie*. Here, wife. Eat this. You know that you like eating a lot at parties. You know that you like eating a lot anywhere.

VIRGIN B: I eat a lot because my husband is always buying more food and putting more food on my plate and I hate to see food to go to waste. When I was a little girl, my mother told me that...

VIRGIN C: If you don't finish all the food you are given, your future husband will have as many pock marks on his face as there are rice grains left in your bowl! Do you want to marry a man with a face covered with pock marks?

(VIRGIN A lifts her bowl to her mouth and pushes food in with chopsticks then stops suddenly.)

VIRGIN A: But Ma!

VIRGIN C: What?

VIRGIN A: What if my future husband doesn't finish all his food? Does that mean that I will be getting pock marks all over my face?

VIRGIN C: Don't talk with your mouth full.

(VIRGIN A swallows hard.)

VIRGIN A: Ma. What if my future husband doesn't finish all his food? Does that mean that I will be getting pock marks all over my face?

VIRGIN C: Here, Girl. Eat some more food.

I hate to see food go to waste because when I was a little girl there was never enough food, especially if you were a small girl with a big hunger. What I remember best about being a little girl is always being hungry and wishing I was a boy because boys got to eat eggs. Now that I have a daughter I make sure that she gets enough to eat. Feeding her helps me to deal with my hunger of long ago. Eat, eat, eat!

VIRGIN B: My husband doesn't know how much I went through to make sure that he had a beautiful complexion. Now he does have a beautiful complexion. Sometimes I think that all the pimples and blackheads and dry skin that should have gone to him ended up on me...

I'm going to do it! I am going to go on a diet until I am beautiful again. I can do it!

VIRGIN A: Of course you can, go for it!

VIRGIN C: Of course you can. You will be a shining example to all fat wives and fat mothers and fat daughters. You will be thin and beautiful!

WOMAN: But you are beautiful now! Who says you have to be thin to be beautiful?

VIRGIN B: I'm going to plan a reasonable diet and stick to it.

I'm going to exercise. I'm going to cut out sugary snacks and fried foods altogether. I know that my husband who loves me and supports me will help me in my efforts to lose weight and be beautiful again!

WOMAN: Darling, I'm home!

VIRGIN B: Darling, I've decided that I'm going to pull my life together!

WOMAN: That's wonderful, Darling. How much money do you need this time?

VIRGIN B: I don't – I didn't...

WOMAN: Here, take this. Buy yourself something nice. No one can say that I am not a generous husband where you are concerned. I am always more than generous. I am more generous than any other husband I know who has a wife as fat as you are.

VIRGIN B: Thank you, Darling. You are always so good to me.

WOMAN: Darling, now let's go out to dinner to celebrate! What do you feel like eating?

VIRGIN B: Oh Darling, the thing is, you see, my diet...

WOMAN: You can start tomorrow!

VIRGIN B: Oh... Darling, tomorrow we're supposed to be going to have dinner with your golfing friends, I was wondering if I could stay home just once...

WOMAN: Darling, since we are always absolutely honest with each other, I must tell you here and now that I don't like this. Are you saying that your appearance is more important to you than our relationship? Are you saying that your appearance is more important to you than spending time with my friends? Have you forgotten how lucky you are that I married you in spite of your fatness?

VIRGIN B: No, no, no, Darling. That's not true. Of course our relationship is important and I want to spend time with your friends. And I will never forget how lucky I am to have married you!

WOMAN: Darling, I'm glad that you have come to your senses. Now, let's go out to celebrate.

VIRGIN B: Yes, Darling.

VIRGIN C: Sometimes I think that the only things my husband and I enjoy doing together are eating and sex. And I'm not even sure I enjoy sex, so that only leaves eating.

VIRGIN B: Since I got fat, my husband doesn't want to have sex with me so much, so he makes up for it by taking me out to eat more. But that only makes me more fat, so that doesn't really solve my problem at all.

VIRGIN A: From watching my parents together, I didn't realise that married people were supposed to do anything together except eat! They were either eating together alone or eating together with friends or getting ready to go out to eat together or shopping for food to bring home to cook to eat together...

VIRGIN C: Can I offer you more tea? More of these little cakes? I got them specially, you know.

VIRGIN A: Thank you, they're very good.

VIRGIN B: Yes they're really very good. I know I shouldn't, but—

VIRGIN A: Go on! Help me finish them off...

VIRGIN B: ...Well, maybe just one...

VIRGIN A: ...So I don't have to keep them. No more room in the fridge! You can start on your diet tomorrow.

VIRGIN B *(sings)*:   *Tomorrow, tomorrow,*
                 I'll diet tomorrow, tonight we will celebrate.

VIRGIN A *(sings)*:   *Tomorrow, tomorrow, I'll diet tomorrow*
                 Aerobics will have to wait.

WOMAN: For a woman to be a fat virgin, it is not necessary for her to be fat. Neither is it necessary for her to be a virgin. It is only necessary for her to be a woman.

To the young Indian security guard who watches Fort Canning between seven at night and seven in the morning, every woman who is loitering alone in the vicinity during those hours is a fat virgin.

VIRGIN A: I am an entomologist engaged in the detailed observation and study of nocturnal insect life in Singapore. I am highly respected in academic circles all over the world.

WOMAN: I am a man. I am a thin, twenty-eight-year-old man who expected nothing from life but who has been disappointed anyway. I am the security guard that watches Fort Canning between seven at night and seven in the morning. To me, every woman who is loitering in the vicinity is a fat virgin. To me, a fat virgin is my chance to get back at life that is unfair.

Hello, you waiting for somebody?

VIRGIN A: Uhmm.

WOMAN: Waiting for somebody is it?

VIRGIN A: Uhm-Hmm.

WOMAN: Just now looking from there I don't know whether you are boy or girl.

VIRGIN A: Hmmm.

WOMAN: I thought at first, boy. Then come closer I see you are girl.

VIRGIN A: Umm.

WOMAN: So late already now.

VIRGIN A: Ummm.

WOMAN: You married already?

VIRGIN A: Uh-Uh.

WOMAN: No-ah. How come?

VIRGIN A: Hmmm?

WOMAN: How come you never marry?

VIRGIN A: Are you married?

WOMAN: No.

VIRGIN A: How come you never marry?

WOMAN: Slowly slowly lah.

VIRGIN A: Then I also slowly slowly lah.

WOMAN: Slowly slowly ah?

VIRGIN A: Yah.

WOMAN: This place very big know. The other side, go all the way down to Hill Street…

VIRGIN A: Uhmm.

WOMAN: You want to go for walk?

(WOMAN moves in a little. VIRGIN A stands up and throws WOMAN over onto her back.)

VIRGIN A: At times it is good to realise that you still have your judo throws under your belt. But then you wonder... was that really necessary? Maybe not. Maybe I was over-reacting. Maybe I was venting frustration on him that really should have been vented on someone else. Like my boss.

WOMAN: Virgins are allowed to over-react. Virgins are expected to be tense, neurotic and paranoid. That is because people expect us to be frustrated.

Unmarried sisters who live with their families, including children, of their married sisters, are not allowed to over-react. They are supposed to be aunts. It is easier to be a virgin than to be an unmarried sister. If you are an unmarried sister you have to earn a lot of money at work before you get any respect from anybody.

VIRGIN A: I am not a spinster aunt. I earn a lot of money. I promised myself that I would be a CEO before I was thirty years old. Now I am thirty-five years old and I am not a CEO but I am a marketing manager and that's pretty good. I know my life is full of compromises. I have a company car and it is a BMW. But I still don't like it when my mother phones me from K.L. and asks me why I am not married. My mother doesn't ask me in precisely those words but she does ask me. My mother beats around the bush. But only in a metaphorical sense – she neither gardens nor masturbates. She is a retired schoolteacher. Retired teachers are noble, an increasingly rare breed. These days, very few teachers stay in the profession long enough to retire.

WOMAN: Singapore statistics show that if you are in a hotel coffee house at tea time and you overhear a woman between twenty-six and thirty-five years old complaining that she is tired of her job, that she hates her job, that she wants to quit her job and that she wants to go on a diet and lose weight, the chances are ten to one that she is teaching in a government or government-aided secondary school.

VIRGIN B: I am a schoolteacher. I always wanted to be a schoolteacher since I was a schoolgirl. I was always good at English
and composition. I sang in the choir. Now I am a schoolteacher.

I hate being a schoolteacher.

Deep down inside me I have a secret yearning to be a striptease
artist and to pose naked for girlie magazines so that hundreds of
men will lust after my soft young body. But I will turn them all
down and instead marry a rich old man who never knew the
meaning of true love and devotion until I surrendered up my
virginity to him.

However, in Singapore this is not really a viable career option.

So I became a schoolteacher.

I am also a Sunday School teacher.

But I have literary aspirations.

I think that I have it in me to express myself in poetry. Or
perhaps I will write a book. It is not difficult to write a book. But
first I think I will try something else. I will try drama.

I am too shy to act, so I will offer my services backstage.

WOMAN: I am a man. I am a director of plays. I am very successful
at my other career at a major bank, so this is just an expression
of some of my many many talents. I like to express myself in
bold images.

But I am also generous. I understand that women are intimidated by me. I am generous because I understand that and I
allow women to be intimidated by me. You!

VIRGIN B: Yes, Drama Director.

WOMAN: Why haven't you called up all hundred and eighty-five people on the list that I asked you to call last night?

VIRGIN B: But I did call them, Drama Director, even though I have to work a full day at school and a full day marking books and I am having menstrual cramps and I am doing this only because I thought it would be a fun and relaxing way to explore new horizons in the Arts.

WOMAN: I am not interested in your menstrual cramps and your interest in the Arts. Now you are working for me you have to work according to my standards! Well, if you called all hundred and eighty-five people on the list that I asked you to call, why haven't they turned up for my auditions? Tell me that?

VIRGIN B: Some said that they would come and didn't come. Some said that they wouldn't come and didn't come. And some just weren't home. But I called all hundred and eighty-five of them.

WOMAN: How incompetent of you! How inept of you! How ignorant of you! Can't you do anything right? Did you even try to leave messages with those who weren't home?

VIRGIN B: I did. But most of these people didn't come for your auditions because they've worked with you before and they don't want to work with you again.

WOMAN: That's such a stupid reason. Why did you accept such a stupid reason? Why did you let them give you such a stupid reason? Why did you call people who have worked with me before? You should have known better than that. You are such a stupid incompetent fat virgin. I don't know why I ask you to do things when you just make a mess of them and I have to go and do them over again myself and I am such a busy important man in my full-time job!

VIRGIN A: Why do you let him treat you like that? And he's not even your boss. That would be different.

VIRGIN C: He doesn't show you any respect as a person. And he's not even your husband. That would be different.

VIRGIN A: Walk out on the production.

VIRGIN C: Walk out on the production.

VIRGIN B: I can't walk out in the middle of a production.

VIRGIN A: I can't walk out on a career but of course you can walk out on a production.

VIRGIN C: I can't walk out on a marriage but of course you can walk out on a production.

VIRGIN B: No I can't.

WOMAN: Very often, fat virgins live for other people who don't deserve them and don't appreciate them.

VIRGIN A: But you are unhappy. You are miserable. You are having trouble sleeping. And when you do manage to get some sleep you have nightmares.

VIRGIN B: My nightmares...

WOMAN: It's time to wake up.

VIRGIN B: Wake up to what?

WOMAN: Wake up to yourself.

VIRGIN A: Look, I'll be you. You be him.

(They change places.)

VIRGIN A: I quit!

VIRGIN B: Damn you!

VIRGIN A: That doesn't change anything.

(VIRGIN A stalks off then returns.)

VIRGIN A: See? Wasn't that easy?

VIRGIN B: I suppose so...

VIRGIN C: No, look, I'll be you. You be him.

(They change places.)

VIRGIN C: I'm sorry I just can't go on.

VIRGIN B: But I'll try to change. Things will be different.

VIRGIN C: Sorry I just can't go on.

(VIRGIN C walks off then returns.)

VIRGIN C: See? Wasn't that easy?

VIRGIN B: I suppose.

VIRGIN A: Try it!

VIRGIN C: Try it!

(VIRGIN B goes back to WOMAN.)

VIRGIN B: I'm sorry... I want to...

WOMAN: Here. This is for you.

(WOMAN hands big bouquet of ugly plastic flowers to VIRGIN B.)

VIRGIN B: Oh...

WOMAN: Call up the one hundred and eighty-five people again. I'll try to be more understanding because I realise that you are slow and not very bright. But please try harder.

VIRGIN B: Yes. I will.

(WOMAN goes off.)

VIRGIN B: Look at my beautiful flowers.

VIRGIN A: Are you having fun? I thought you were doing this for fun?

VIRGIN C: Are you broadening your horizons? I thought you were doing this to broaden your horizons?

VIRGIN B: Well I've learnt more about myself... I've learnt that I am slow and not very bright. Isn't it so good that the Drama Director is patient and willing to give me another chance?

VIRGIN A: But these are plastic flowers.

VIRGIN B: But these are plastic flowers.

WOMAN: Plastic flowers will last longer. Plastic flowers will last forever.

VIRGIN B: But I don't want something that will last forever. I want something that will be truly beautiful and what is truly beautiful lasts for just a moment...

WOMAN: The pure young virgin of seventeen. The unwanted fat virgin of twenty-seven. It's the same condition. Why do we see it so differently?

VIRGIN C: Ma, I want to be a nun.

WOMAN: But Girl, we're not even Catholic. Why do you want to become a nun?

VIRGIN C: Because of Julie Andrews in *The Sound of Music.* The songs she has sung for a thousand years.

WOMAN: You can't be too careful of the influences on young minds.

VIRGIN A: I saw *The Sound of Music* five times.

VIRGIN B: I saw *The Sound of Music* seven times.

VIRGIN C: I saw *The Sound of Music* twelve times. And I wanted to become a nun.

VIRGIN B: I wanted to become a singer.

VIRGIN A: I fell in love with Julie Andrews.

WOMAN: You can't be too careful of the influences on young minds. Cinema has a certain insidious influence on the emotional make-up of young fat virgins. That is why you can only watch an R(A) rated movie if you are over 21 years old. *The Sound of Music* should have been R(A) rated because of the way it influences young minds.

VIRGIN C: I was a mother for five years when I woke up one morning, and I realised somewhat to my surprise that I had become a virgin again. I had become a virgin mother.

VIRGIN A: Being a virgin is a state of mind.

VIRGIN C: Maybe it was because I was putting on weight.

VIRGIN B: Being a virgin is a condition that you get used to.

VIRGIN C: I looked at myself in the mirror and I realised that I was beginning to look like a virgin again. In Singapore, many women are virgins.

VIRGIN B: I think it's catching.

VIRGIN A: I think it's comfortable.

VIRGIN B: No, that's not true. You look around you when you're out. The virgin is always the one in uncomfortable shoes and bright uncomfortable earrings.

VIRGIN C: But it's easy to mistake them for the unhappy wives. Except that unhappy wives wear shoes that are more expensive and less uncomfortable. And unhappy wives tend to wear minimalist artistic earrings instead of bright artistic earrings.

WOMAN: All categories of woman who are uncomfortable with

themselves camouflage themselves in uncomfortable clothing. This is in the hope that if they make themselves uncomfortable enough, others will not make them more so.

VIRGIN A: Successful career women wear discreet stud earrings. It is necessary, if you want to be a successful career woman, to wear discreet stud earrings, especially if you don't have long nails with nail polish. If you don't, the men in your office will think that you are lesbian and feel threatened by you.

VIRGIN C: Don't worry if you feel threatened by them. That is expected.

VIRGIN A: Feeling threatened all the time keeps women on their toes.

VIRGIN C: Or on their backs.

VIRGIN A: I am a fat, fair virgin dyke who is in love with a happily married and pregnant woman who is a high flier at NPB.

She doesn't know that I am in love with her.

She comes in to meetings in the morning looking tired and it almost breaks my heart to look at her. But she is always patient and concerned and asks me if I'm working too hard. We sit and talk in her office. She is the only reason I am still working in NPB. I am afraid that if I leave NPB there will be no one here to appreciate her and feel sorry for her when she is tired. And every woman deserves to be appreciated by someone, some-where, even if they don't realise it. And I have learnt that if you don't have someone who appreciates you, the next best thing is to appreciate someone. If you are totally in love with someone else just for a moment, you are no longer a fat virgin. You are a woman in love.

(VIRGIN C sits in her office and VIRGIN A goes in and sits facing her across a table.)

VIRGIN C: I have this idea for a survey to be carried out among our workers. The results will help us improve their efficiency and team work and in so doing raise the levels of their productivity.

VIRGIN A: That is a brilliant idea. What are we going to study in this survey?

VIRGIN C: The integration of social minorities... a social and psychological minority that under scrutiny might reveal itself to be a silent majority.

VIRGIN A: I see...

VIRGIN C: We are going to survey the absentee rates, income brackets and racial prejudices of virgins.

VIRGIN A: But... why study virgins?

WOMAN: Why? Because it is dangerous having virgins in our midst without understanding them.

Because they are all around us and they are insidious.

Because you can define a virgin as you cannot define a Christian or a cat lover or a drunk driver.

Virginity is not a transient state.

A virgin is like an asthmatic. The condition is not always evident, but the condition is always present. It is not a condition that can be cured, but it is a condition that you need not always suffer from.

Therefore if virgins continue to suffer from virginity they must do it on purpose and enjoy it.

VIRGIN A: This is why I am a fat, fair virgin dyke. As long as I am fat, people may not notice that I am also virgin.

WOMAN: Fat is embarrassing because eating is a sign of lack of self-control in our society. Any lack of self-control is embarrassing in our society. How can you subject yourself gracefully to group control if you do not understand self-control?

VIRGIN C: My problem is that I am too easily controlled.

I was a controlled child and then a controlled wife and then a controlled mother.

I was an unloved child and then an unloved wife and then an unloved mother.

I had children too early. I got married too early. I was born too early.

VIRGIN B: Did you hear the one about the wise virgins and the foolish virgins?

VIRGIN C: Yes, too many times. I was ready and waiting when I was very young. I took the first bridegroom that came along and was available. And now look where I am.

VIRGIN B: You have a beautiful house and two beautiful children and a beautiful husband and a beautiful mother-in-law and a beautiful BMW and many many beautiful clothes.

These are what you get for being a wise virgin.

VIRGIN C: I have been swallowed up by beautiful habits. If I had stayed with one beautiful habit I could have become a nun.

Nuns are virgins and you can't tell if they are fat because of their habits.

Most non-nun virgins are fat because of their habits.

If you are a virgin nun, Christ is your bridegroom.

VIRGIN A: Who wants to wait for the bridegroom anyway? I always wanted to *be* the bridegroom. Anyway, do you really want to end up with a man who dumps on you because you don't have enough oil in your lamp?

VIRGIN B *(sings)*:   *Give me oil in my lamp keep me burning*
A & C: *(burning burning)*
                    Give me oil in my lamp I pray
A & C: *(I pray)*
                    Give me oil in my lamp keep me burning
A & C: *(burning burning)*
                    Keep me burning till the break of day.

WOMAN: In India, we call it *suttee*.

Some women are born to be unhappy. If that is the case, whether or not they are virgins and whether or not they are fat makes no difference at all.

VIRGIN A: I work in the same office as Michelle. Michelle has just walked in.

Michelle's unhappiness is palpable. It is not a wild sort of unhappiness. It is a heavy sort of despair.

You can reach out and stir it with a stick. It is thick and gooey like melted chocolate.

Michelle left her ang mo husband after six years of marriage. Now Michelle is alone with her three-year-old daughter.

Michelle is worried about what happens when her daughter grows up and asks her what happened to her father.

Michelle will tell her that her father was a good person but not as good a person as her mother.

(VIRGIN A becomes Michelle's mother.)

VIRGIN A: Ma ma, what happened to my Ba ba?

VIRGIN B: You mention your Ba ba again I slap your face!

VIRGIN A: Ma ma, what happened to my Ba ba?

VIRGIN B: Your Ba ba was a good man, and he loved us both very much, but he died young. You must always be obedient to his memory.

VIRGIN A: Ma ma, what happened to my Ba ba?

VIRGIN B: Your Ba ba told your Ma ma that she was frigid and he left her. You must always be on the watchout for handsome men. One of them may be your Ba ba. One of them may be your brother. If you marry your Ba ba or your brother you may end up like your Ma ma.

VIRGIN A: No no no no no... don't want!

WOMAN: One way for fat virgin women to make good has always been through education.

That is why mothers and fathers always encourage their little daughters to work hard in school, especially if they wear spectacles and have pimples. You see, the chances of these little girls growing up to be professional virgins is very high.

VIRGIN C: The Science Project of Melissa Chee. Chapter One.

My daughter's science teacher set them an experiment in school.

VIRGIN B: You will take these green beans and grow them in these little glass bottles on cotton wool.

WOMAN: But important as it is for little girls to try to learn in school, it is even more important for little girls to learn not to try too hard.

VIRGIN B: You are to grow them: 1) with water 2) without water 3) with too much water.

VIRGIN A: Chapter Two: Melissa Chee and the Magic Beans.

Melissa Chee, aged seven and a half, embarks on an exciting career as a budding research scientist.

VIRGIN C: My daughter Melissa Chee comes home and grows seedlings:

1) with water 2) without water 3) with too much water 4) with coca-cola 5) with milk 6) with skim milk 7) with royal blue fountain pen ink 8) with cooking oil 9) with 100% natural no-sugar added orange juice 10) with *tou hwey chue* 11) with barley water 12) with tea 13) with coffee 14) with salt water 15) with dark soya sauce 16) with oyster sauce 17) with 100 Plus 18) with washing up detergent 19) with Uhu glue and 20) with saliva.

I don't know what goes into (21). From the way it smells, I don't want to know.

I came home and I found these bottles and cups and jars full of cotton wool and green beans and strange substances.

I called my daughter to me and I asked her, Melissa, what do you think you are doing?

VIRGIN A: My science experiment for school.

VIRGIN C: What science experiment? Let me see your book.

(The science book is handed over.)

VIRGIN C: Where, where in the book does it say that you have to grow seedlings in coca-cola and saliva... where? Are you playing the fool?

VIRGIN A: But Mum, it's an experiment for science, I just wanted to see...

VIRGIN C: I am an understanding mother. I wasn't even angry any more. I wanted to get to the bottom of this strange behaviour in my daughter. So I went to see my daughter's teacher. The teacher is usually responsible. The teacher is often to blame.

WOMAN: The Mother as Anthropologist.

VIRGIN C: Tell me, why is my daughter, who up till now has been quiet and well-behaved and neat and tidy like a girl should be, filling my house with bottles and cups and jars of dying plants that smell bad? She says that it is an experiment that you asked them to do.

VIRGIN B: No, I did not. You can see it quite clearly here in the textbook. They were supposed to grow seedlings 1) with water 2) without water 3) with too much water.

And the seedling that is supposed to do best is the one that is grown 1) with water.

It's all here in the textbook. If your daughter read her textbook she wouldn't even have had to do the experiment. I would not have given them an experiment to do unless the result was to be found in the textbook. We have to stay within the syllabus.

(VIRGIN C leaves in exasperation.)

VIRGIN B: Parents!

VIRGIN C: Teachers!

VIRGIN A: But Mum, I just wanted to find out what would happen, Ma.

VIRGIN C: Look, if it's not in the syllabus you don't have to know.

It can't come out in the exam. If it won't come out in the exam you don't have to know.

And anyway you don't have so much time to waste. What about your homework, your Chinese tuition, your Maths tuition, your ballet lessons, your piano practice...

Come here darling. I'm doing this all for you, you know. I want you to grow up to do lots of interesting things in life. And if you asked me first I could have told you that plants don't grow in coca cola.

VIRGIN A: Ma, have you ever tried growing plants in coca-cola?

VIRGIN C: Don't talk back to me. Are you trying to be funny?

VIRGIN A: All my plants died. Except the one that got 1) some water.

All the others of my plants died. I didn't mean to kill them. I thought I could discover a secret formula that could make them grow better.

VIRGIN C: I am so sorry, baby. I am sorry I was right. I am so sorry that all your plants died. But as your mother it is my duty to teach you what to expect from life.

WOMAN: If little girls don't learn about life from their mothers, where can they learn about it?

For seven years now I have been the Agony Aunty for *Well Known Singapore Women's Magazine*. *Well Known Singapore Women's Magazine* is read by more fat virgins than any other women's magazine in Singapore.

VIRGIN A: Dear Agony Aunty, there is this boy in my class who is always looking at me. Do you think he likes me? Yours Sincerely, Shy Schoolgirl.

WOMAN: Dear Shy Schoolgirl, you should not be noticing boys in class. You should be concentrating on your teacher.

VIRGIN B: Dear Agony Aunty, I think I am falling in love with my History teacher. How can I make him notice me? Yours Desperately, Sagittarius.

WOMAN: Dear Sagittarius, falling in love with History teachers is a phase that all teenagers in the Arts Stream go through. You should concentrate on your studies.

VIRGIN C: Dear Agony Aunty, I am very troubled because I have just seen a boy who I had a crush on in Secondary Three holding hands with a teacher who I had a crush on in Secondary Four. I can't decide which one of them I am jealous of. Is there something wrong with me? Yours Desperately, Torn Between Two Lovers.

WOMAN: Dear Torn Between Two Lovers, don't worry. You are only experiencing what is very common to many fat virgins in Singapore today. You are a fag hag.

If you have something to get off your chest, or if you need a friendly tongue in your ear, write to Dear Agony Aunty, *Well Known Singapore Women's Magazine*, Singapore 0923.

VIRGIN A: I am a dynamic leader. I believe that regardless of sex, if you see a thing that needs doing you go out and do it.

WOMAN: Of course, everyone knows Cory Aquino.

VIRGIN B: I support my husband in all things because I believe that this is the first and most important duty of a woman who is lucky enough to get married. I will stand by my man through everything and I will stand by him with mascara on so that people won't feel sorry for him, married to a woman with no eyelashes.

WOMAN: Of course, many people know Tammy Baker.

VIRGIN C: I am a mother of a twenty-seven-year-old son who wants to go for a sex change operation. My twenty-seven-year-old son says that he is actually a woman trapped in a man's body. A woman trapped in a man's body! He never played with dolls, he is not like those who wear lipstick... My son says that he wants to face the world honestly as a woman. He also says that he needs to borrow money from me for his sex change operation. He has to go for three of these operations. Of course, it is for medical reasons, how can I refuse him? But I'm not even sure if this can be considered medical reasons. I remember when my son was born. I was so happy, so happy that he was a son.

WOMAN: Seet Ai Mee lost her seat in Bukit Gombak.

VIRGIN C: I don't understand. I just don't understand. What did I do wrong?

WOMAN: You know what you did to make this happen to your son, don't you?

VIRGIN C: No, no. I don't know what you are talking about. I wanted a son. I never wanted a daughter. I only wanted sons. It's not my fault. If I had ten children, I would want them all to be sons. I don't want daughters who would live as I have lived, who have suffered as I have suffered...

WOMAN: No. You wanted a daughter but you wanted a strong daughter who would not live like you, who would not suffer like you, a daughter who would grow up straight and strong for herself. This is the only way to have such a daughter – a woman in a man's body.

VIRGIN C: But he is not a real woman.

WOMAN: What do you mean she is not a real woman?

VIRGIN C: A real woman is not given a chance to choose to be a woman.

VIRGIN A: One is not born a woman but becomes one. Excuse me, Simone de Beauvoir. One is not born a fat virgin but is made one. The only real women are those who choose to be real women. Even if they were born men. Even if they were once fat virgins. Every fat virgin can choose to be a real woman. Every man can choose to be a real woman.

VIRGIN B: I thought... I thought that all women are fat virgins.

VIRGIN A: No.

VIRGIN C: All women are fat virgins or sluts. I, by the way, am a devoted wife and mother.

VIRGIN A: No.

WOMAN: What we have here is a matter of potential.

VIRGIN B: Every woman has the potential to be a slut.

ALL: Yes.

VIRGIN C: Just as every woman has the potential to be a fat virgin.

ALL: Yes.

WOMAN: And every fat virgin has the potential to be a real woman.

ALL: The first step is to acknowledge that you are a fat virgin.

WOMAN: What is wrong with being a fat virgin? Who says that there is anything wrong with being a fat virgin?

VIRGIN A: I am a fat virgin. What's wrong with that?

VIRGIN B: I am a fat virgin. If you don't like it, tough.

VIRGIN C: I am a fat virgin and I am proud of it.

WOMAN: Once upon a time, three fat virgins met for tea—

VIRGIN A: —At the Music Room. We had petits four, cucumber sandwiches, fondants, chocolate cake, Earl Grey, Darjeeling, Orange Pekoe, English breakfast...

VIRGIN B *(overlapping one beat later)*: We met for *tim sum* at Lei Garden. We had *siew mai, lor mai fun, bak fun, har kow, chee cheong fun, char siew pao, siew pao wu kok, dan tart*...

VIRGIN C *(overlapping one beat behind VIRGIN B)*: I met my friends at the Suntory Japanese Restaurant at the Delphi. We had *sushi, sashaimi, wasabe, sukiyaki, sake, teriyaki, tempura, shabu shabu*...

WOMAN: Stop, stop, stop. I am sure there are much more fulfilling things in the life of a fat virgin than meeting for tea...

OTHERS: What?

VIRGIN A: Get real, girl. This is Singapore.

WOMAN: Oh. I see.

(All of them assume a tableau tea pose with tea cups and bright smiles.)

ALL: Once upon a time, FOUR fat virgins assembled for tea. And they lived happily ever after.

WOMAN: That is how the play has been developing up until now... but *this* is how we choose to end it from here on.

(Rewind.)

WOMAN: What is wrong with being a fat virgin? Who says that there is anything wrong with being a fat virgin?

VIRGIN A: I am a fat virgin. What's wrong with that?

VIRGIN B: I am a fat virgin. If you don't like it, tough.

VIRGIN C: I am a fat virgin and I am proud of it.

WOMAN: The whole world was once a virgin forest. Take it back and make it your own.

VIRGIN A: This is a virgin forest.

VIRGIN B: This is the virgin forest.

VIRGIN C: This is our virgin forest.

WOMAN: In the virgin forest the trees are—

VIRGIN A: Dark—

VIRGIN B: And damp—

VIRGIN C: And dim—

WOMAN: I can be free—

VIRGIN A: From lies,

VIRGIN B: From life,

VIRGIN C: From him.

WOMAN: The strength here comes—

VIRGIN C: From believing in yourself—

VIRGIN B: From believing in your potential—

VIRGIN A: From believing.

-END-

Home

by Tan Tarn How

Tang is a depressed old man waiting for his turn to die in a nursing home. Goh is a cleaning lady and Tang's only friend. Alex, spirited and witty, becomes Tang's roommate. In a clash of their contrasting personalities, Alex draws Tang out of his shell. In the process, the lives of all three are changed. The play explores friendship, love and life during old age.

CHARACTERS:

TANG: Inmate in old folks' home, 67

GOH: Cleaner and tea lady, 50

ALEX: New inmate, 63

HOME premiered at the Black Box on 15 April 1992, and was produced by Theatreworks, featuring the following cast:

TANG   Benjamin Ng
GOH   Wong Siew Lyn
ALEX   Charles Giang

It was directed by Lee Yew Moon.

It was given two rehearsed readings by Theatreworks at different stages of the play's growth. It was read by Lim Kay Siu, Neo Swee Lin and Alec Tok on 9 June 1991, and by Lee Weng Kee, Lok Meng Chue and Melvyn Chew on 19 Sept. 1991. Both readings were directed by Ong Keng Sen.

ACT ONE

A room in an old folks' home. There is not a trace of decoration. Two beds, one on each side, the one on stage left for TANG and the other one for ALEX. Upstage, at the head of each bed, is a wardrobe. Between the wardrobes is a study table, facing a window, with one chair. On the table, placed nearer to TANG's side of the room, are an old-fashioned radio from fifteen years ago, a tall glass with a set of fork and spoon, a bottle of Sloans and Chinese medicated oil, two tupperware boxes of half-finished biscuits. At stage left, near to the foot of ALEX's bed, is a door leading to the corridor. Another door, at stage right, leads to a toilet.

SCENE ONE

(At curtain rise, TANG is packing his previous roommate's things from the wardrobe into a cardboard box placed on the bed. He picks up various things, and those he decides to throw away, he puts inside the box.

He takes out the following: A book: flips through to see if anything in between pages, finds nothing; throws. A single sock: searches for matching side, finds nothing; throws. A wire clothes hanger: he bends it back into shape, goes to his own wardrobe and hangs it up. A man's brief: he tests the band but the elasticity is gone; throws. A belt: either too long or too short, depending on TANG's size; throws. Another book: throws without looking. And, lastly, lining paper for wardrobe shelf: takes it out and looks at reverse side which is calendar picture of a young movie star; tries to see if it looks nice pasted on the inside of door of his own wardrobe; decides no; throws.

Near the end of this, GOH enters with broom, dustpan, mop and bucket, but keeps quiet as she observes TANG.)

GOH: Lin Tai.

(TANG turns round, surprised. GOH comes in, starts to sweep.)

Hongkong screen goddess, 1960s. "Love Without End," "Eternally Yours," "How Can I Forget You?" and her best film, "Roses are Red, Violets are Blue."

TANG: Lin Tai.

GOH: I was a teenager then. I watched every one of her movies three times and my mother thought I was mad. I dreamed of growing up like her. Like thousands of other girls. To be young again! *(Looks at TANG, but he gives no response.)* 1960s. Remember rock and roll? That's what I call nice music – with melodies – and real dancing – with steps. Not what the kids do nowadays, no tune, no steps, just any old how. How much we danced! I bet you I can still do a triple turn. *(Does a turn with broom as partner.)* If I have the right partner, that is. *(She waits for response from him, but he says nothing.)* Those were the days, eh, Tang?

(TANG looks out of the window. GOH looks at TANG intently. She sweeps round his legs.)

I suppose they were, for some of us. *(Rhetorically)* Got out on the wrong side of bed again, old man? Move.

(TANG steps aside absent-mindedly for the broom. GOH finishes sweeping, gathers dust into the dustpan, goes into the toilet to flush the dirt down. She comes in again.)

TANG: Did you go to his funeral?

GOH: Of course I did.

TANG: How many people?

GOH: Seven. And that includes matron, Mr Loh and me. His four sons went, but not the wives or children. It was a sorry affair as funerals go, and I have been to lots of funerals after working here for so long. Before you really get to know them, pop they go. You know something strange about funerals, Tang? The sadder everyone is, the less sad the funeral is. *(Notices box. Peers inside.)* What's this? I thought they came and took away everything?

TANG: Almost.

(GOH shakes box.)

GOH: Can't say they left much for you to keep, did they? Not that you would want to. People say it's bad luck to keep the things of the dead. You know what? They say the person who keeps a dead man's things will be the next to go.

(TANG looks at his wardrobe, thinking about the clothes hanger.)

But I don't believe any of that superstitious rubbish.

(TANG looks relieved for a while. Goes to bed and lies down, looking forlorn. GOH goes into toilet with pail for water, and starts to mop the floor.)

GOH *(in the following, GOH tries to elicit some response from him)*: Heh, cheer up! Don't tell me you miss him?

TANG: Him!

GOH: No, of course not. You two never got on, did you? Of course, he is a grumpy old man. Like you, only he was about ten times grumpier. Seven people at his funeral. Can't say he was Mr Popular, eh. Old man, how about putting on the radio?

(TANG switches on radio. Waltz music.)

GOH: The waltz! Heh, want to dance?

TANG: No thanks.

GOH: No worry, matron is out so she won't catch us. Come on.

TANG: I can't dance. *(He lies down and closes his eyes.)*

GOH: Can't dance! Pity. Some day I will have to teach you. *(Holds up mop.)* Never mind, I've got my regular partner.

(GOH waltzes round the room with mop. As she gets into the rhythm she closes her eyes.)

GOH: Your new roommate is coming in, isn't he?

(ALEX appears at door. Neither GOH nor TANG notice him.)

TANG: Yes. *(Turns to face the wall.)*

GOH: I hope he is not another old grouch. One a room is enough, as far as I'm concerned. This is fun! Know anything about him?

TANG: No.

GOH: I hear from Mr Loh that this one's actually quite rich. Maybe *he* can dance. *(Dances.)* You know why he wants to come here instead of live in his own house?

TANG: No.

GOH: If he's rich he will have his own house, won't he? This place is for poor old buggers like you. No place to go and wanted by no one.

(TANG snorts – it's an old routine between the two and he doesn't even have to reply.)

GOH: Probably chucked out by his children. Probably the same old story. Poor old rich fart.

ALEX *(knocks softly)*: Er, excuse me.

(GOH stops in her tracks. TANG sits up.)

GOH: Whoooa! You shocked me.

ALEX: Sorry.

GOH: Who are you?

ALEX: I'm new here.

GOH: I can see that. You looking for something?

ALEX: This is my first day here. Mr Loh was too busy to show me the way. He told me the last room, and this looked like the last one. But I think I must have got it wrong. There are already two of you here...

GOH: I don't live here!

ALEX: You don't? Sorry.

GOH: I work here.

ALEX: Oh. I've come to the right room then?

GOH: Must be, since this room has the only empty bed in the whole nursing home.

TANG: Very recently vacated. *(He switches off radio.)*

(GOH glares at TANG.)

GOH: Yes, left rather suddenly. *(Trying to change subject)* Where are your things?

ALEX: Outside. *(To TANG)* Left suddenly? His family got him out? You must wish you are the one who went, don't you?

TANG: Not to where he went.

GOH: Right, he's much happier here. *(Still trying to change subject)* Want me to help bring them in, your things?

ALEX: No thanks, it's alright. I'll do it myself. *(To TANG, jovially)* I thought once you are in here you stay here forever.

GOH: Most people do. *(Still trying to change subject)* Why don't you bring your things in now?

ALEX: Alright. I'll go and fetch them. *(He makes to go out. Turns back and addresses TANG)* Or until they die.

TANG: That's what happened to him actually.

(ALEX stops short.)

GOH: Look what you have done, you old grouch. He's new here, for heaven's sake.

ALEX: It's alright. Don't get angry on my account.

TANG: Yes, might as well face facts.

GOH: Oh, shut up!

ALEX: It's alright, really.

GOH: Ignore him, he's like that all the time.

ALEX: Yes, I mean, no, I mean, never mind... *(Quietly)* I must admit, when you come down to it, that's what I came here for.

TANG *(flatly)*: That's the spirit.

GOH *(indicates TANG and the empty bed)*: He's badly shaken by the death of his friend.

TANG: He was no friend.

GOH: You see, he's so devastated that he has forgotten everything now.

TANG: We didn't care for one another one little bit. No love lost between us.

GOH *(resignedly)*: Damn you old man. The least I had expected of you was to be nice to your new roommate.

ALEX: Er, I suppose I better get my things.

GOH: Need a hand?

ALEX: No worry, I don't have much.

(GOH takes up her mopping where she has left off. ALEX brings one suitcase in, then another, then a third.)

GOH: Well, we'd better introduce ourselves. I'm Mrs Goh, I help clean the place, as you can see by *(indicates broom)* Fred Astaire here. I also bring in the tea.

ALEX: I'm Alex. Nice to meet you.

(ALEX shakes hands with GOH, who is surprised. He goes to TANG to shake his hand, but TANG remains unmoved.)

TANG: Tang.

(ALEX stops short of TANG's bed.)

Alex: Nice to meet you.

(TANG grunts. He lies on the bed and looks at the ceiling.)

GOH: You settle in. I better go and do the toilet now. *(Indicates Tang)* Don't expect to be entertained by him though.

ALEX: Alright. *(Surveys room)* Nice, nice. Kind of spare though. I think a little decoration would cheer up the place eh? You are the way you live, I always say.

(TANG acts like he hasn't heard. ALEX shrugs and hums. ALEX gets ready to sit down on the bed.)

TANG *(without turning head)*: He died on that very same bed.

(ALEX nearly falls onto the bed but manages to pull himself up.)

ALEX: He did?

TANG: Last week.

ALEX: What of?

TANG: Cancer.

ALEX: It's alright then. Cancer's not contagious.

(ALEX almost sits down again.)

TANG: But he also had some skin disease.

(ALEX just manages to stop his bum from touching the bed.)

ALEX: Skin disease?

TANG: He was scratching all the time, day in day out, until I got thoroughly sick of it. *(Beat.)* The last two months were terrible.

ALEX: Must have been trying for you too.

TANG: I meant the last two months were terrible for *me*. I thought I might get it, even though I made sure I avoided him.

(ALEX is astounded.)

ALEX: Yes. Er, did they fumigate it?

TANG: No.

ALEX: No?

TANG: But they turned the mattress over.

(ALEX sits down slowly.)

ALEX: I suppose they know what they had to do. *(Cheerfully)* Besides which, as I said earlier, I came here to die. So it's my funeral, isn't it? *(Laughs, but stops when TANG does not respond.)* That's a joke. *(Beat.)* I think.

(ALEX decides to see to his own things. He opens the first suitcase. Starts to unpack. He hums. He takes out several dozen books, a vase, some framed paintings – which he stacks on the table. GOH emerges from the toilet.)

GOH *(to TANG)*: I'm done. You can do your biggie now.

(TANG enters the toilet.)

GOH: Every morning, he waits until I clean it before he goes in. He stays there for I don't know how long. Constipation. *(She cleans the place up. They are still a little shy with one another.)* You should try not to mind him.

(ALEX starts to take out the things from his other suitcases, which he lays on the floor – occupying part of TANG's half of the floor – the bed and the study table. There are clothes, pictures, more books, all sorts of things. GOH makes TANG's bed. She tidies TANG's wardrobe.)

ALEX: He's, er, very...

GOH: Difficult? Had a difficult life, that's why. I don't know the details though and he's never wanted to tell me.

ALEX: You seem to get on with him.

GOH: Yes. *(Pause.)* In a strange way, I rather like him and I don't know exactly why. Maybe, it's a feeling I always had for the underdog, and is he some underdog! I think I'm the only friend he has left in the world.

ALEX: He looks very fit.

GOH: Yes. Too fit actually. He's outlasted most of the people here. *(Indicates ALEX's bed.)* That guy must be his number three roommate. *(Pause. She continues tidying the wardrobe.)* Is it true that you are...?

ALEX: Rich? I have had a very comfortable life, yes, if that's what you mean.

GOH *(indicating room)*: Not much of an ending, is it?

ALEX: I suppose not. This isn't so bad, actually.

GOH: You're alone?

ALEX: Yes. I mean no. I still have my children. But they are not here. They are in Canada and the States.

GOH: So why are you here?

ALEX: I went to live with my son in Toronto, and my daughter in the US. But I felt as if I didn't belong, to the country I mean. You know the Chinese have this silly idea that a man should be buried where he's born. At my age, it does not seem so silly. I sold the house. Too big.

GOH *(she examines some of the things)*: You sure brought a lot of stuff here. Lots of books.

ALEX: I was an academic.

(GOH picks up a Chinese vase.)

GOH: Really? *(Holds up vase.)* Nice, although I can't tell one from the other.

ALEX: It's not worth anything. I was a collector, but I sold them all. Just kept this cheap one.

(GOH shakes it, and there is a sound.)

GOH: Heh, there's something inside. *(Peers into it.)*

ALEX *(laughs)*: Oh that!

GOH: What is it!?

ALEX: A ping pong ball. When my son was three, he popped it inside. I was mad at him. I tried and tried but could not get it out. The ball was slightly bigger than the hole. I tried chopsticks, the vacuum cleaner, barbecue skewer, everything, but I just couldn't get the darn thing out. Finally I said, heh, why don't I pour some hot water inside. I thought it would make the ball shrink. But you know what happened – instead of shrinking, it expanded! Then I thought, heck, it's just a ball, and if you leave the vase standing there, no one would know there's anything inside. That's more than twenty years ago. Strange, how you remember some things and forget others.

(Pause. GOH gives ALEX the vase.)

GOH: It will look nice with some flowers.

ALEX: Yes. But I haven't put flowers in it for a long long time. *(Pause.)* It was the first birthday present my wife gave to me. I didn't keep more than a couple of things of hers. *(He puts down the vase on the table.)* Well, I ought to get the things sorted out quick.

GOH: And I ought to be going. I will be bringing the tea round. *(GOH exits.)*

(ALEX continues to sort out his things, which are now scattered over the entire floor and almost the whole desk. The place looks a mess now. He moves some of TANG's things – radio, boxes of biscuits, etc. – away from their original positions on TANG's half of the table until they are all bunched up at one end. He takes out a framed photograph of his family – himself, wife and two children – and places it carefully on the table. He takes out two packets of roasted minced pork, opens one and takes out a piece to eat. Then he places the second box on TANG's bed.
Toilet flush is heard, toilet door opens and TANG emerges.)

TANG: What on earth are you doing?

ALEX: Oh, hi. You were in there a long time. Next time bring a book! Just unpacking.

TANG: Of course I know you are unpacking. Why are all the things on the floor?

ALEX: Pretty hard to hang books on the wall, isn't it?

TANG: I mean why are they on my side of the floor?

ALEX: Your side?

TANG: Yes, my side. My half of the room.

Alex: I...

TANG: There are two of us here you know, you and me. So there's your side of the room, and my side of the room, and your side of the floor and my side of the floor.

ALEX: I don't believe this.

(TANG notices things on his half of the table.)

TANG: And the table too. There are two of us and only one table. *(ALEX mimes TANG's words.)* So there is your side of the table and my side of the table.

ALEX: You're not serious, are you?

(TANG stares back at ALEX to show that he is.)

ALEX: You are serious. I don't believe this. Can't I leave them as they are until I finish packing? After that, I promise, I'll respect the integrity of your personal space. Swear, scout's honour, cross my heart and hope to die.

(TANG gives unrelenting stare.)

I suppose you want the integrity of your personal space to be restored right away. OK, I'll move my things to my half of the room. *(Stops as he is about to move to TANG's half to get his things.)* Am I allowed to go over to your side to get my things or will that be trespass?

TANG: You can step across to my side.

ALEX *(sarcastically)*: Gee, thanks a lot, such a privilege.

TANG: But only this time.

(ALEX pushes his things over to his side of the room. TANG stands there and watches.)

ALEX: Don't you want to help me?

TANG: Since I don't believe in you touching my things, I don't want to touch yours either.

ALEX: Very convenient for you, I would say.

(ALEX finishes moving the things on the floor. He goes to the table and moves his things to his half of the table.)

ALEX: Should I put your radio and things back, or should I leave them as they are now?

TANG: Since I don't believe in touching...

ALEX: OK, alright, I get the drift. You put them back yourself. I don't believe this! *(Sits down on his bed, exhausted.)*

TANG: By the way... that's only one of the house rules.

ALEX: House rules?

TANG: First house rule: you keep to your side of the room, I keep to mine.

ALEX: Oh, yes.

TANG: Pretend that there's a wall in the middle of the room, pretend that this is actually two rooms.

ALEX: Two rooms.

TANG: Yes. Second house rule: you keep your hands off my things and I'll keep my hands off yours.

ALEX: Oh, that one.

TANG: Especially my fork and spoon.

ALEX: Your fork and spoon. Doesn't the kitchen give you...

TANG: I prefer to use my own.

ALEX: Yes. Your fork and spoon.

TANG: Third house rule: no conversation.

ALEX: But I can talk, can't I? You don't have to listen you know.

TANG: Talk by all means, but don't address me, and don't expect to get an answer.

ALEX *(shrugs)*: I suppose this rule is not up for discussion?

TANG: Rule four. Lights out at eleven.

ALEX: Eleven! I like to read until late. I'm a night person.

TANG: Go to the common lounge.

ALEX: I suppose I can read in the toilet.

GOH: Rule five. I get to use the toilet after Mrs Goh washes it in the morning.

ALEX: No way! Why should you have the first go?

TANG: I'm the senior person here.

ALEX: That's pulling rank.

TANG: It's always been like that.

ALEX: That's hanging on to tradition.

TANG: I have weak bowels.

ALEX: Alright, alright. You have right of first use of the toilet. Any more?

TANG: No smoking.

ALEX: I don't smoke.

TANG: Just in case you have visitors.

ALEX: No worry, all my friends are now either dead or enemies.

TANG: And – no snoring.

ALEX: What?

TANG: If you snore, I have the right to wake you up.

ALEX: And vice versa?

TANG: Er, yes – and vice versa.

ALEX: But you are not allowed to come to my side of the room, so how can you wake me up?

TANG: Throw something. A slipper, a clothes hanger.

ALEX: Or a book. I don't know if I'm a good shot in the dark... There's a complication though. In the morning, how do I get it back? Remember rule two: You don't touch mine, I don't touch yours?

TANG: Exceptions to the touching rule can be made for the snoring rule.

ALEX: Sensible.

TANG: Well, that's it. Simple, see, we aim to create the minimum amount of distraction to one another.

ALEX: The minimum amount of distraction to one another... I'm a slow learner and I don't know if I can remember everything you said. But I'll try.

(ALEX starts to pack his clothes into the wardrobe. TANG goes to his bed, finds box of bar-qua *ALEX has left there. TANG's long-sighted so he can't see very clearly things at close range.)*

TANG: What's this?

ALEX: Oh, *bar-qua.*

TANG: I know it's *bar-qua*, but what is it doing on my bed?

ALEX: I left it for you, I thought you might like it. Thought it would be a good way to make friends. Making friends – familiar with the concept? You know, it takes two, you scratch my back and I scratch yours?

TANG: I hate *bar-qua*. Besides which, I need no charity from you. And I don't want to have to owe you anything. See you have broken the principle: create as little distraction for one another as possible. Please…

(TANG and ALEX stand facing one another through the imaginary wall. TANG holds out bar-qua *for ALEX. They stare at one another. Finally ALEX takes it.)*

ALEX: No, I didn't put it there. What actually happened was it fell out of my suitcase onto your bed. It's a very lively box of *bar-qua*, see. (Lies down on bed.) I think I'm getting a headache.

(TANG goes to table and rearranges his things, exactly in the original position. He counts the number of biscuits in his tupperware.)

ALEX *(suddenly)*: Heh, I've thought of something. There's this invisible line or wall running down the middle of the room, how do I get to the toilet, and how do you go out at all? See, it doesn't make sense. Hah!

(Just then GOH comes in with the tea on a trolley.)

GOH: Tea, everybody! What doesn't make sense, Alex?

ALEX: Oh, hi, Mrs Goh. I was just discussing with my roommate here some of the house rules.

GOH: House rules?

(In the following, TANG tries to draw subject away from rules. But GOH insists on knowing, while managing to answer TANG's questions.)

TANG *(cutting in)*: What's for tea?

GOH *(to TANG)*: Your favourite snack. *(To ALEX)* Don't tell me he's has been making things unpleasant for you already. And on your first day too. What are the so-called rules he's made up?

ALEX: No worse than working in the university: lights out at a certain time, no smoking. We even have the no snoring rule – it's for students attending lectures. *(To TANG)* You haven't answered my question about how I can go to the toilet yet.

TANG *(quickly)*: Exceptions to the half-half rule can be made for calls of nature and for going in and out. *(To GOH)* What kind of snack for tea?

GOH *(to TANG)*: Your favourite. *(To ALEX)* No snoring?

ALEX: Yes, no snoring. What's for tea?

GOH: Tang's favourite food, but they only give two miserable tiny pieces each – *bar-qua*.

(ALEX and TANG exchange glances.)

TANG: I don't like *bar-qua*.

ALEX: Any more.

GOH: Don't like it any more?

TANG: Yes.

GOH: Since when?

ALEX: Since about five minutes ago when a box jumped onto his bed and he suffered an overdose.

GOH: You brought them in? You boys are up to something I don't know about. Anyway, let's not waste what the kitchen gave.

(GOH pours out the tea for TANG. Gives him a plate with bread and

bar-qua. *Tang takes the cup but pushes away the plate.)*

GOH: Here, don't be stubborn, old man. Eat it.

(She shoves it onto his lap, and he is forced to take the plate.)

GOH *(to ALEX)*: Coffee, tea or Milo for you, Alex?

ALEX: Coffee, white and with two spoons of sugar, please, thank you.

GOH: Sorry, everything's pre-mixed. It's either coffee white with sugar or tea white with sugar or Milo white with sugar. Coffee, tea or Milo?

ALEX: Coffee then.

(GOH pours coffee for him. Hands him the cup, and also a plate with bread and bar-qua. *She pours out something for herself, and goes to the chair at the table. She looks through the paintings on the table.)*

GOH *(to ALEX)*: What are you going to do with the pictures?

ALEX: Oh, hang them up, I suppose. *(Glances at TANG)* On *my* side of the wall.

GOH: Um, nice. I like this one. *(Holds up a watercolour of roses.)* I really really like this one. Put it up there in the centre.

ALEX: Alright, I will. *(Remembers)* Roses are red, violets are blue.

GOH: Lin Tai.

ALEX: You know Lin Tai? There used to be a Lin Tai film of that title.

GOH: Know Lin Tai! I used to be mad over her. You are a Lin Tai fan too!

ALEX: My wife and I fell in love watching her movies.

GOH: God, they are something aren't they? Don't know if they make them like they used too.

ALEX: But there can only be one Lin Tai.

GOH: Yes.

ALEX: We watched every one of her movies.

GOH: Really! Imagine, I could have sat next to you two and not known it.

ALEX: Wouldn't that be something.

(ALEX looks at TANG.)

GOH *(to ALEX, softly)*: He seldom talks much and he never talks about the 60s. *(Shrugs. Puts down painting.)*

GOH: I better get going. I'll be back for the tea things later.

ALEX: OK, bye.

(GOH exits with tea trolley. TANG eats, observing ALEX. ALEX continues to unpack. Slowly he starts humming again. At one point he steps back and knocks onto the vase. He looks back at it. Then he takes out a pair of scissors from a suitcase and exits.

A minute later, he comes in with a bunch of flowers he's cut from the garden. He takes the vase, shakes it to rattle the ping-pong ball inside. TANG looks up, surprised at the noise from the vase. ALEX comes to the middle of the room, stops at invisible middle line, walks gingerly along it, nearly falls once, comes to a point on the line across from the toilet door and stops. He looks at TANG to ask if it is alright for him to cross over to the toilet. TANG nods in affirmation. ALEX, humming, opens an imaginary door in the imaginary wall, and walks across to the toilet. Sound of running water and humming.

ALEX emerges, arms hugging the vase of water, hands damp. He looks at TANG again to ask if it is alright to cross back to his side of the room. TANG nods. He crosses over quickly to the imaginary line, walks along it toward the table, nearly falls over again, places the vase on the table. He sticks flowers inside the vase. Arranges them. Hums.)

ALEX *(he takes a piece of* bar-qua, *nibbles on it as he stands back to appreciate the flowers. To himself)*: You know, sometimes, there's nothing like flowers to cheer one up.

SCENE TWO

(The following happens in the dark, behind the curtain. Only voices can be heard.

Silence. TANG snores, quietly at first, but rising slowly in volume until it reaches a chortling crescendo. Continue for a while. ALEX cannot sleep.)

ALEX: Shit!

(ALEX sighs, turns in the bed. Rustling of pillow and blankets. He gropes for something, his hand hits on what sounds like a book. He pats the book to be sure.)

ALEX: Sorry I have to do this, Tang.

(ALEX throws the book at TANG with an audible effort. There is a loud whack. TANG wakes, startled. He mumbles.)

TANG: What's that!

ALEX: The *Concise Oxford Dictionary,* sixth edition. Hardback. *(Beat.)* You were snoring, Tang.

TANG: I was?

ALEX: Loud enough to wake the dead. So I applied rule six: no snoring, but if roommate snores, exterminate source by extinguishing said roommate's sleep.

TANG: That hurt like hell. You could have thrown something softer.

ALEX: The *Concise Oxford Dictionary* paperback? I don't have that book.

TANG: Or something smaller.

ALEX: The *Pocket Oxford?*

TANG: Or a slipper.

ALEX: I tried to look for my slippers, but couldn't find them. Too dark.

TANG: Switch on the lights!

ALEX: Sorry, rule four. Lights out at eleven, remember?

TANG: Why didn't you come over and wake me then?

ALEX: I can't see in the dark. And even if I can make my way to you, I would be crossing over to your side and contravening rule one: keep to one's own side.

TANG: Shout then!

ALEX: Rule three: no conversation.

TANG: Choose a smaller book next time. *(Silence.)* Alex? Alex!

ALEX: No conversation – rule three now in force, good night.

(Silence. After some time, TANG's snores start to rise again. But ALEX starts to cough, very softly and suppressed at first. It gets louder and louder, drowning out TANG's snores and until his whole body sounds as if it is shaken by it and the whole room reverberates with it.)

TANG *(stops snoring. Wakes)*: What!? Heh, what's happening?

(ALEX continues to cough severely.)

TANG: What's wrong with you?

ALEX *(in between his cough)*: It must be the *bar-qua*. All that oil and burnt stuff.

TANG: Quiet down! You are waking up the dead.

ALEX *(still coughing, but trying to suppress it)*: OK.

(Silence. TANG's snores rise again. Muffled sounds of ALEX's coughing from under a pillow.)

ACT TWO

(Same room. TANG's side of the room is the same. But ALEX's side of the room is almost unrecognisable. His paintings are up. There is a new low bookshelf for his books. On his side of the table, there is a tupperware of bar-qua, a stack of magazines and a mini-component hi-fi set, which dwarfs TANG's radio. His sheets are different too, brightly coloured with bold geometrical designs rather than the old all-white. Next to his bed, there is an armchair with footrest.)

ALEX: I am going for a walk. You coming?

TANG: No.

ALEX: I suppose not. Well, see you.

TANG: You passing by the kitchen by any chance?

ALEX: Er... I suppose I could go by there.

TANG: I thought you might be able to find out if it's fish for lunch today.

ALEX: Fish. You want to know if they are having fish.

TANG: The cook's hopeless with fish.

ALEX: Oh, I thought he is hopeless with everything.

TANG: Yes, but he is particularly hopeless with fish... or anything that swims.

ALEX: You must know... *(Declaiming)* When one becomes old, one becomes specialists in grades of hopelessness, I suppose, experts in degrees of despondency and professors in desperation—

TANG: Alex...

ALEX: Yes?

TANG: Just pop into the kitchen...

ALEX: ...And check out the fish. Alright. Sure you don't want to come?

TANG: Nah.

ALEX: Will do you good, the exercise.

TANG: Nah.

ALEX: Why not?

TANG: Don't want to talk to the cook.

ALEX: Why not?

TANG: He might ask me if I like his food.

ALEX: Figures... or, worse still, make you try the fish!

TANG: Yes.

ALEX: You can say to him: "I can tell your cooking apart from every other cooks'" or "Your fish is one of its kind."

TANG: Or "I remember your food long after I taste it."

(TANG has cracked a joke – both he and ALEX are surprised by the fact.)

ALEX: A joke? *(Digs ears and rubs eyes.)* A joke! After two weeks of saying very little and saying nothing funny, a joke! From Tang! A Tang joke! An oxymoron.

TANG: Huh?

ALEX: Oxymoron, you know, nursing home food. Clean Singapore toilets. Happy old age and golden twilight years. Oh, never mind. How I wish Mrs Goh was here to hear this. How she'll laugh, eh, Tang?

TANG *(deeply embarrassed, therefore overly vehement)*: Stop it. Behave yourself!

ALEX *(pause – stares at TANG)*: Oh, come on, Tang. This is too quick a relapse to your old grumpy self, isn't it? And I thought you were making real progress.

TANG: Don't forget the house rules.

ALEX: Well, I suppose, one robin doesn't make a spring.

TANG: Quiet! *(Slowly)* I know your type. Your fast-talking type. All talk and nothing else.

ALEX: What…? *(Decides this is not the time)* Alright, my walk is long overdue anyway. I'll pop in the kitchen for you.

(As he goes out) A Tang joke! Oh my God! *(ALEX exits.)*

(TANG looks out of door to see that ALEX is gone. He is unruffled, uncertain what to do for some time. He starts examining everything on ALEX's side of the room with care, even touching them but ensuring that he puts them back exactly as they were – the family photograph, the vase and finally the books.

GOH comes in with a clatter of pails, dustpan, mop and broom. TANG gives a start.)

TANG: I was just…

GOH: ...Looking into other people's things.

(GOH starts her sweeping and mopping. TANG continues examining ALEX's things.)

GOH: I passed Alex on his way out. What happened? *(Laughs)* I almost believed for a moment you cracked a joke or something!

TANG: I did.

GOH *(dismissively)*: And I'm eighteen years old. Stop pulling my leg, old man. *(Mops.)* So, how are you two getting along?

TANG: I don't know... He's a strange man.

GOH: Hear who's talking.

TANG: He's hard to understand.

GOH: Hear who's talking again.

TANG: He seems to be enjoying himself. Imagine, here!

GOH: Maybe it's because he chose to come here.

TANG: Maybe. He talks too much.

GOH: You talk too little. *(To TANG, who is in the way of the mop)* Move. What's wrong with talking too much?

(TANG moves aside.)

TANG: He just lets out what he feels. He calls me "pal."

GOH: Some people consider that a compliment, not an insult.

TANG: But I hardly know him!

GOH: He's being friendly, can't you see? And he likes Lin Tai. Say what you will, I like him. And he's more fun than you.

TANG: His fancy way of talking does not necessarily make him better than I am, you know.

GOH: And your constant moodiness does not make you worse off than him, either.

(She does her work.)

GOH: Look, what I mean is, I don't see that doing him any harm. I've known a few people keep everything bottled inside them. Didn't do them any good that I can see. In fact...

TANG *(not sure if he is being referred to)*: Er, what's for lunch?

GOH: What's all this interest in what the cook's up to all of a sudden? Alex asked me the same question just now.

TANG: So what's for lunch?

GOH: Fish.

(GOH goes in to do the toilet. TANG examines one of ALEX's books. He puts it at hand's distance, but still cannot see clearly. He props it against something on the table, and goes a distance away and squints at it. Meanwhile, ALEX has come in. He observes TANG.)

TANG *(with difficulty)*: *The Interpretation of Dreams,* by Sigmund Fraud. Hmmph.

(TANG repeats with another book.)

TANG: *On Sexuality,* by Sigmund Fraud. Fraud...

ALEX: Doctor Sigmund Freud. Lived 1856 to 1939. Austrian Jew. Invented psychoanalysis. Without him 10,000 psychotherapists would be out of work today. He made hating one's father respectable.

TANG: Freud.

ALEX: Yes, Freud. Kingpin of the sexual blues league. He said that masturbation makes you lose your sight – why are you squinting like that, Tang?

TANG: I wasn't.

ALEX: Maybe not. But not many people I know like to read a book from ten feet away.

TANG: I just want to see if my eyesight is alright.

ALEX: Alright, I will help you test it. *(Holds out a hand, but shows no fingers.)* How many fingers am I holding up?

TANG: Huh?

ALEX: Come on, how many? Count them and tell me.

TANG *(squints)*: Don't be silly. I can see them clear as day. *(Edges nearer to ALEX.)*

Alex *(backs away)*: Hold it, don't come any nearer. Besides, keep to your side of the room – house rules, remember. So how many fingers am I holding out, Mr Tang?

TANG: Don't be silly. I have twenty-twenty vision.

ALEX: How many fingers?

TANG *(in desperation)*: Five, of course.

ALEX: Nope.

TANG: Pulling your leg... Four, of course.

ALEX: Nope.

TANG: Three!

ALEX: Nope.

TANG: Definitely two.

ALEX: Nope.

TANG: One?

ALEX: Nope, nope, nope.

TANG: I know, I have got it!

ALEX: After five guesses you should, shouldn't you?

TANG: Six!

ALEX: Nope. *(Shakes his head. Then holds out two hands.)* How many hands?

TANG: How many – of course, I know how many hands!

ALEX: Just joking. But the fact that you saw any number from one to six fingers when I held out none shows either I can't count or you can't count or you have been playing with yourself too much, dirty old man.

(GOH enters.)

GOH: Who's been playing too much and with what?

ALEX: Our friend here has been—

TANG: Trying to mind his own business.

GOH: Tell me something new. *(To TANG)* Time for your biggie, old man.

ALEX: Sure you don't want to bring in a book to read? If you prop it up against the sink, you might be able to make out the words, Mr Eagle-eyes.

TANG: Shut up.

(TANG goes into the toilet.)

GOH: Pulling his leg again?

ALEX: Have been a naughty boy, I'm afraid. I'm trying out friendship by means of hostility, this being the day for oxymorons. Quite reckless really. Too bad old Freud has no advice in this area.

GOH: Freud? Is he a friend of yours? *(Conspiratorially)* Did Tang tell you it's his birthday today?

ALEX: Really? No wonder he's grumpier than usual. He didn't say a word.

GOH: His sixty-eighth. He probably doesn't remember it himself.

ALEX: What shall I get for him?

GOH: Anything, I suppose. What can he have that could possibly make a difference to him? He doesn't care for things anyway. So, what have you been up to with him?

ALEX: You might not believe it, but testing his eyesight. Do you know he's so long-sighted he can't see his fingers if he holds them out in front of him?

GOH: I always suspected he can't see too well.

ALEX: Now I know why he always looks at everything suspiciously – it's not part of his personality. It's because he can't see!

GOH: You mean his eyes are that bad?

ALEX: Yes. Heh! I have a brilliant idea.

(ALEX drags out a suitcase from under his bed. He rifles through it excitedly.)

GOH: What are you up to now?

ALEX: Wait and see... I've them in here somewhere... There! Dah-dah...

(Produces a pair of spectacles – unmistakably feminine, cat-eyes-shaped and horn-rimmed in bright pink.)

ALEX: Great, eh!

GOH: What's that? I mean I know what they are, but where did you get them from?

ALEX: I'm into wearing women's things.

GOH: My God!

ALEX: No. Remember I said I didn't keep many things that were my wife's? Well this is one of the few things besides the vase. And since he's so cock-eyed, why don't we try it on him?

GOH: But, Alex, I don't think the look is him.

ALEX: What's wrong with these? They belonged to my wife – as I said, I never kept more than a few things of hers – this is my first present to her. *(Puts glasses on.)* What do you think? Not bad, eh!

GOH: They are so, er, girlie.

ALEX: A bit on the pinkish side, I admit. But, the degree should be about right. It's 700.

GOH: Heh, Alex, this can be your present for him.

ALEX: That's an idea. Great! Saves me going out to get something for him.

GOH: No, don't let him know it's a birthday present yet. Let's surprise him.

ALEX: OK. I'll keep mum until then.

GOH: Let me have a look at them. *(Tries glasses.)* Heh, remember, Lin Tai used to wear something like that?

ALEX: Of course I do. You really have got to make him wear them.

GOH: Me? I won't be able to.

ALEX: Only you can do that.

GOH: He won't wear them.

ALEX: Try to make him!

(Sounds of flush.)

GOH: You're asking me to do the impossible!

ALEX: He can't go round half-blind for the rest of his life.

(TANG emerges. ALEX and GOH stare at him. He knows they are looking at him. Checks his fly to see if it is up – it is. Inspects the rest of himself to see if all is well.)

ALEX *(hisses to GOH)*: He's all yours.

GOH *(to ALEX)*: No!

ALEX *(to GOH)*: It's his birthday, remember.

GOH *(to ALEX)*: Thanks a lot. *(To TANG)* Well... Er... um. Tang.

TANG: What?

GOH: Had a good time in there?

TANG: What?

GOH: Oh never mind. *(Blurting it out and not quite knowing what's she's saying)* Tang! Why... have you, er, never said... I'm beautiful!?

TANG: What!?

ALEX *(to GOH)*: I feel you're getting somewhere – definitely.

GOH *(to ALEX)*: Shut up. *(To TANG)* Tang!

TANG: What?!

GOH: Listen to me.

TANG: I'm listening.

GOH: Good... you're listening to me, but, but... *(inspired)* don't look at me!

TANG: What?!

GOH: Yes, don't look at me.

TANG: Are you alright, Mrs Goh?

GOH: Close your eyes!

TANG: Why should—

GOH: —This is very important. Quick, close your eyes. Now!

TANG: OK, OK. This is not one of his stupid jokes?

ALEX: Me? I'm just watching, that's all.

GOH *(to ALEX)*: Oh shut up!

TANG: Now you want me to close my mouth too.

GOH *(to TANG)*: No, not you. I mean him.

TANG: Oh.

GOH: Eyes closed now?

TANG: Er, yes...

GOH: OK, good. Keep them closed.

(GOH goes to TANG. Puts on specs for him.)

TANG: Heh, what's this, what's happening? *(Opens his eyes. TANG starts. Sways back and forth. Clutches specs to his face. Stares at GOH, looking at her like for the first time – which may be true.)* My God, Mrs Goh. You look so... so different. *(Looks at ALEX.)*

ALEX: Hi, I'm Alex. Recognise the voice? Long time no see.

TANG *(quietly)*: This is amazing... I don't remember it being like that.

ALEX: They were my wife's. You look good in them. You can have them.

TANG: No, I can't...

ALEX: Come on, don't feel obliged.

GOH: Go on, old man. Take it.

TANG: Alright.

(TANG looks around, still astounded.)

TANG: I didn't realise that my eyesight is so bad.

ALEX *(to GOH)*: And this is the twentieth century we're living in.

TANG: I think I will go out to have a look round the place.

ALEX: Er, Tang...

TANG: Yes?

ALEX: If you see matron or someone else, just tell them this is a temporary pair, alright. I don't want them transferring you to another kind of institution.

(TANG exits.)

ALEX: You should see the way he looked at you.

GOH: Alex!

ALEX: And I don't remember him giving a reply to your question about why he never told you you are beautiful.

GOH: The idea just came to me like that.

ALEX: That was inspired. And very Freudian.

GOH *(now hostile)*: Look, Mr Alex, don't you throw your learning at me. I may not understand the words, but I don't like the tone of that one.

(ALEX opens his mouth to make one of his speeches, but he closes it after second thoughts. ALEX and GOH look at one another. They laugh. ALEX looks hard at GOH.)

ALEX *(softly)*: You know, my wife used to laugh in the same way that you do? No, don't get me wrong, Mrs Goh. I mean it as a compliment.

GOH: Er, thank you.

ALEX: She was some woman.

GOH: I'm sure she was.

ALEX: Some woman, I tell you, Mrs Goh. Just like you.

GOH *(wishing to cut the line of conversation)*: No, Alex... let's don't start...

ALEX: Why?

GOH: Because... because I don't know what you are trying to do. And I don't know if you know what you are trying to do. Look, Alex, what I want to say is: I mean, I like you. But I am not sure where that would lead to. And I'm not sure if it would help either of us.

ALEX: You know, my wife used to look like that when she got worked up.

(Both laugh.)

GOH: Alex... it's too early for us to say these things to one another now.

ALEX: By the time we're ready, it might be too late.

GOH: Alex...

ALEX: After all, this is an old folks' home.

GOH: Alex, stop that.

ALEX: Yes. I'm beginning to sound like Tang.

GOH: Look, there is wisdom in the Chinese way.

ALEX: Take things slowly in matters of the heart?

GOH: Yes.

ALEX: Yes, we have all the time in the world, eh?

GOH: Yes. *(Pause.)* Look, Alex, I better get going.

ALEX: Alright. Er, Mrs Goh... you did great there just now with Tang.

GOH: Thanks. We both did.

ALEX: Yeah.

GOH: Yeah.

ALEX: We're a team, aren't we?

GOH: Now, Alex, don't you start...

ALEX: Just kidding. The Chinese way it is for me.

(Both laugh.)

GOH: I'll be back with the tea.

(GOH exits. TANG enters.)

ALEX: How do the specs feel on you?

TANG *(touching the bridge of his nose)*: Different.

ALEX: How does the world look now?

TANG: Different.

ALEX: Different! Now that we've got your eyesight, maybe we should work on your vocabulary next! *(Coughs.)*

TANG: You talk too much, Alex.

ALEX: And you don't talk enough, Tang.

(Silence.)

ALEX *(awkward)*: Let's have some music.

TANG: Yours or mine?

ALEX: They're the same, to tell the truth.

(TANG switches on his own radio. A waltz comes on.)

TANG *(he says the following very hesitantly with lots of pauses, as if he needs still to find his voice)*: She's always asking me to dance. Mrs Goh, I mean. She's a good dancer – even with a broom, she looks good.

ALEX: You like her, don't you?

TANG: Don't you?

ALEX: I do. *(Pause.)* So why don't you? Dance with her, I mean.

TANG: I cannot. I can't dance. I was going to learn it once, many, many years ago. *(Stops abruptly.)*

ALEX: And...?

TANG: But I didn't. I learned a bit, then I had to stop. And after I stopped, I never picked it up again.

ALEX: Pity.

TANG *(sighs)*: Yes.

ALEX: It's easy.

TANG: Dancing is for happy people.

ALEX: Yes. Come, I'll teach you. It's easy.

(ALEX pulls TANG.)

TANG *(resisting)*: I can't.

ALEX: You can; dancing is a frame of mind. Just get into the flow of it. I'll be the woman, you be the man.

TANG: With my specs, it might be better the other way around.

ALEX: OK, I'll be the man, you the woman. Just follow me. One and two and waltz. One and two and ouch!

TANG: See, I can't.

ALEX: No, you are doing fine. Carry on. One, two, three. Two, two, three. Three, two, three.

(Their feet clash initially. But TANG picks up the steps soon enough.)

ALEX: See, you're getting the hang of it. Just follow the pressure of my palm on your back.

(They dance smoothly.)

ALEX: How does it feel?

TANG: Strange, dancing with a man.

ALEX: How about me, I'm dancing with a man who's supposed to be a woman. Or is it the other way around?

TANG: This is... fun.

ALEX: That's the spirit.

(They dance. They cover the whole stage. They get better. The dance should be energetic yet graceful. Shouts of Whoa! They seem like they are in their twenties. The tempo picks up but they keep time. It gets even faster, yet they whirl around with style. The dancing and music should reach a suitable climax for TANG to open up later. When the dance ends, they fall to the floor.)

ALEX: God, those were the days, eh? I remember we used to dance for hours on end, each couple trying to outdo one another. Ah, if the old bones can only move the same way. Makes you miss being young, doesn't it?

TANG: Why do you and Mrs Goh always talk about being young as if... as if it is something good to look back to?

ALEX *(sure)*: Because it is. Those were the great days.

TANG *(shakes his head)*: The great days. I was young once. *(Pause.)* Stupid thing to say, isn't it? I was young once. But it isn't of days, of dark afternoons in the cinema watching Lin Tai that I remember. Of course, there was Lin Tai and all that. But it is not what I remember. My wife... she gave me two children, two sons. Let's have a daughter, I said. She said, Yes, let's have a daughter, Poon – she calls me Poon. We had so much energy, then. Even took up ballroom dancing.

ALEX: You did!

TANG: Yes. And we loved it. Our boys were four and two then, and we would put them with my mother for the evening when we went to the dancing classes. The studio was at Outram, I think, you know the row of five-foot-way shops opposite the passport office?

ALEX: Do I know them! I learned most of my stuff there.

TANG: The building is still there, isn't it?

ALEX: Yes, but the studio is gone now.

TANG: Yes. No one wants to learn dancing any more. We had so much energy then, my wife and I. Wanting a daughter. Dancing the waltz. We had three lessons... And then she fell ill. And she got sicker, and sicker, all within two weeks.

ALEX: What happened?

TANG: I don't know. Even the doctors didn't know what happened. They said it was some germ which they didn't know about. And she got thinner and thinner, until her arms were no more than sticks.

(TANG goes to his wardrobe, takes out a box, from which he takes out a photograph. Hands it to ALEX.)

TANG: My wife... I sat by her bed, hours, days and nights. I watched her disappear, Alex.

ALEX: I watched my wife disappear too. Cancer of the cervix. In the end her pain was so great that even I could not stand it. I could not stand to see her suffer. I wished there was a plug I could pull.

TANG: When she died I didn't know what to do! I was completely lost. I worked, I brought up the children without a mother, I tried to make up for what they lacked. But my older son never recovered from the blow of losing her. He saw her death as a betrayal... he never understood. You know how children are.

ALEX: Once, when my boy was three or maybe four, I bought him a lantern, you know one of those many-coloured cellophane types. It was an aeroplane. He was using it to fight with the lantern of his cousin. Then the two strings of the two lanterns got entangled. They tried to sort it out, but I saw that the fire was going to catch on the cellophane. So I rushed to him, "Let Papa help you," I said. He refused, stubborn kid always, he pulled the thing away from me and just then the aeroplane caught fire. And the thing just went up like that. And after a minute all that was left was a black wire frame with some bits of red and green paper dangling from it. And my son thought I had got the thing burning. "You burned it, you burned it," he said. And he cried and cried. And there was no reasoning with him that it was not my fault.

(TANG goes to the table and picks up the radio.)

TANG: Look at this radio. My son gave it to me. No, not the one who sent me here. The idea wouldn't even have entered his head. The younger one it was. A birthday present, I was fifty-one. He had just graduated, law degree. I was so proud of him. That was the first year he worked. He said he wanted to give me something special, something expensive. Here, look. Go on, take a look. Feel the workmanship. General Electric. Still works after sixteen years. Not one of those modern things that you have to throw away after a couple of years.

ALEX: It's older models like us that work best, eh?

TANG: Yes, old models like us. *(Pause.)* It was an accident. Hit and run. I was at work then and by the time I heard, he was already gone. I had to go to the morgue to identify his body. He was all cut up, his face had been dragged along the road, so you can imagine... but it was him, alright. Twenty-three, he was. Twenty-three. Such a long time ago now. When I first moved in here, I had a TV, a colour one too. The son, the older one who lived, the one who sent me here gave it to me. Pa, he said, this will keep you company, will keep your mind off things. As if I need to keep my mind off things. He was good with his words, that one. Like you.

ALEX: So what happened to the TV?

TANG: I sold it. To one of the cleaning ladies for two hundred and twenty dollars. It was a steal for her. No, no more TV for me. What I prefer is this silly little radio from long ago.

ALEX: Like my silly little vase from long ago...

TANG: Sometimes, I wonder how things would have turned out if it was the other son who had died. I know it's a horrible thought, but sometimes I wish that, I wish that it was the elder one that died.

(TANG returns to desk and puts radio down. GOH appears at the door with her tea things, but the two men do not notice her. She listens to TANG.)

My wife died when she was twenty-six. My son died when he was twenty-three. The one who remained behind kicked me out when I became too old and bought me a nice colour TV as a going away present. So those were my good old days.

(Silence.)

ALEX: Tang. Look. I know it's always easy to say "I understand." But really, you might think I don't understand. *(Pause.)* I mean…

(TANG puts up his hand to indicate that there is no need to explain.)

As long as you know.

TANG: Alex?

ALEX: Yes?

TANG: Thank you.

ALEX: You mean for the dance?

TANG: I mean for that too.

(GOH pushes in tea trolley.)

GOH *(flatly. What she heard has affected her)*: Tea.

ALEX: Just in time.

(GOH takes out a small cake.)

GOH: It's your birthday today, Tang?

TANG *(uninterested)*: Oh, is it?

GOH: I got you a cake.

TANG: Er, thank you. Thank you, Mrs Goh.

ALEX: Happy birthday, Tang.

TANG: Thank you, Alex.

ALEX: The glasses are my present to you. They're alright, I hope?

TANG: Yes, thank you.

(GOH lights one candle.)

GOH: I will just use one candle and leave the remaining sixty-seven to the imagination, if you don't mind.

TANG: No.

GOH: OK, it's ready. Let's sing the birthday song?

(ALEX and TANG shrug.)

GOH: Right, one, two, three.

(They sing "Happy Birthday" solemnly. They link arms. Lights come down slowly until the candle is the sole source of light. When they finish, TANG blows out the candle.)

ACT THREE

(One month later. Same room. But now, it is TANG's side of the room that is almost unrecognisable. There are some paintings up. His radio is no longer there. ALEX's hi-fi set occupies the centre of the table. There are books strewn on TANG's side of the table too. His sheets are different too.

At curtain rise, the room is empty. TANG and ALEX enter. They have just come back from a funeral. They are arguing. TANG is wearing a new pair of spectacles. He takes them out and wipes them. It's hot outside; they are mopping their brows. ALEX's tongue is still as sharp, but there is less of his previous energy. He coughs.)

TANG: When I die, I don't want to be cremated. I'd rather... I'd rather... die!

ALEX *(sits down)*: But then, you see, you're already dead.

TANG: Just the body. I'll still be able to feel.

ALEX *(looming teasingly over TANG)*: Feel the flames licking on your toes and flicking on your hair!

TANG: Get off!

ALEX: When you're dead, you're dead. You are not even "are." You don't feel a thing.

TANG: Whatever you say, I'd rather be buried.

ALEX: To each his own, I suppose.

(Silence. TANG puts on the specs.)

TANG: Alex?

ALEX: Yes?

TANG: I've told my son that I want to be buried. And he has agreed.

ALEX: Yes?

TANG: But I don't know if... if he will do as I say. He might just change his mind. *(Pause.)* Alex.

ALEX: I know what you are going to ask me. But what if I go first? And all things considered, this is quite a distinct possibility.

TANG: Maybe the doctor is wrong. Maybe you have more time.

ALEX: Maybe.

TANG: Let's say I go first. Will you do it for me? I have five thousand in the bank. It should be enough. I'll make the arrangements, everything. You have to do nothing. Just see that I get into the coffin, and the coffin gets into the ground.

ALEX: But you have a son. And he has the final say.

TANG: He might not do it.

ALEX: He's supposed to arrange all these things.

TANG: But suppose he doesn't.

ALEX: He's your son.

TANG: He's a bastard!

(Silence.)

> There, I've said it. It took me this long, but I've finally said it. No son would behave like that. No son ought to send his father away with a television as a going-away present, even if it is a colour one. *(Pause.)* Alex, can you do it for me?

(ALEX puts up his arms, he's still reluctant.)

> Can you please?

ALEX: Well, I, er...

TANG: As a friend?

(TANG has struck a chord in ALEX.)

ALEX: Yes, as a friend.

TANG: Thank you, Alex.

ALEX: You know I never bargained for this, Tang. When I came here I thought my life would no longer have any complications. But now you want me to bury you. You ask for too much, you know that, my friend?

TANG: Yes.

ALEX: If I go first, you'll be nice to the old man who comes after me, won't you?

TANG: Yes.

ALEX: No more house rules?

TANG: No more house rules.

(Mrs GOH comes in with tea things. But ALEX and TANG do not notice her.)

ALEX: And you will be nice to Mrs Goh.

TANG: Yes.

ALEX: I like her, you know.

TANG: Yes, me too.

ALEX: Very much.

TANG: Me too.

ALEX: Well at least you will be able to dance with her.

TANG: Yes.

GOH: You two seem cheery today. I don't suppose the funeral did it.

(They wait as GOH serves them tea. She throws them some new Lunar New Year decorations.)

GOH: Here, I brought you two something to put up for the New Year.

ALEX: What a great idea!

TANG: Let's have a look.

(They tear out the things and try them out on the walls. GOH and ALEX come downstage.)

ALEX: This would be a year to remember. Because this would be the last.

GOH: There's the New Year to look forward to.

ALEX: Then the *bah chang* festival after that? Maybe. But certainly not the mooncake festival, eh?

GOH: Alex. I've been thinking about what you said to me on Tang's birthday.

ALEX: Mrs Goh, let's not go into that. That was a moment of foolishness for me. I think, let's leave the whole thing as it is now.

GOH: Alright, if you wish. You know something? I'll—

ALEX: ...Miss me? I'll miss me too. And I'll miss the two of you.

GOH: Alex, are you frightened?

ALEX: On the bad days.

GOH: Some New Year, this.

ALEX: Some New Year.

(TANG comes forward.)

TANG: Heh, how does that look?

GOH: Great!

ALEX: Wonderful. But I think the "Fu" should be upside down.

TANG: Yes, I forget!

ALEX: Let's drink to a happy New Year.

GOH: Yes, happy New Year.

TANG: Happy New Year!

-END-

Blood and Snow

FROM THE 'SNOW WHITE' LEGEND

by Desmond Sim

A beautiful Queen dies and leaves behind her loving husband and an even more beautiful daughter who is on the threshold of womanhood. An enchantress gets into the picture, all glittering, dangerous and beautiful. She wants to be the new Queen. Enter a Prince, all eager to seek a Princess to share his happily-ever-after. The Stepmother ensnares the King, takes over the kingdom and all hell breaks loose.

A potent mix of power, sexuality and treachery results in this dark story of a young girl's turbulent journey into adulthood. A familiar little fairy tale? Perhaps not.

CHARACTERS:

KING RAJA/GRUMPY
SNOW PRINCESS
THE TRUTHSAYER/BASHFUL
MAD COCONUT (COCO)/DOC/SNEEZY
THE DEAD QUEEN
BEAUTIFUL YOUTH/DOPEY
PRINCE CHARMING/HAPPY
THE ENCHANTRESS IXORA/DEATH
CHORUS

BLOOD AND SNOW premiered at the Drama Centre on 22 April 1992. It was produced by Theatreworks and featured the following cast:

IXORA/DEATH	Imogen Smith
SNOW PRINCESS	Lynette Pang
MAD COCO/DOC/SNEEZY	Gerald Chew
PRINCE CHARMING/HAPPY	Darryl David
KING RAJA/GRUMPY	Lim How Ngean
TRUTHSAYER/BASHFUL	Christopher Smith
BEAUTIFUL YOUTH/DOPEY	Peter Zewet
THE DEAD QUEEN	Debra Teng
CHORUS	Peter Zewet, Julian Lim, Abdul Latiff, Lee Chee Keng

It was directed by Verena Tay, with music by Adrian Oh, and lights by Tracie Howitt.

It was given a rehearsed reading by Theatreworks on 22 Sept. 1991. It was directed by Ong Keng Sen and read by Cindy Sim, Tan Kheng Hua, Koh Boon Pin, Remesh Panicker, Melvyn Chew, Daniel Koh and Darryl David.

ACT ONE

SCENE ONE: ON THE ROAD TO NIRWANA (JUST SLIGHTLY OFF NIRVANA)

TO THE BURIAL

(Two women come onto the stage, which is darkened except for a halo of light in the centre. One is tall, riveting – she is in black; the other is pale and beautiful. Both carry white lilies. They walk across the stage slowly and into the circle of light. The white lady is trapped in the circle by an imaginary wall and stops, but the black lady continues till she is at the front of the stage. All this while there is the sound of a solitary girl crying softly. At the front of the stage the black lady speaks. The crying stops immediately.)

DEATH/IXORA: Beginnings are such sensitive matters. They are the start of consequences. A child is born and in the sweep of a statement like , "Once upon a time," she has grown into a fairy tale princess. *(Beat.)* Ah... illusions.

There is a child in each of us that loves a fairy tale – but in spite of what they say, fairy tales do not care about consequences. They prefer happily-ever-afters. Illusions. Nice endings... except that nothing is ever really nice and neat – and things seldom end as and when we want them to. If you think carefully, there are no beginnings. No endings.

Just times that we choose to call them so. *(Beat.)*

And why am I telling you all this? Why am I talking while all others remain mute to your reality? That is because you *know* me. All of you. Every single one of you knows me.

(Casually) I am Death. *(Beat.)*

I am Death and I wear many real faces. I am death of life, death of love, death of childhood, death of innocence... I am death and I am truth because at the end of all illusions, there is only me. Yes, we all live by our illusions but the point at which they falter… that's where the lies and treachery begin.

There is a child in each of us that loves a fairy tale. *(Beat.)*

Tonight, that child… must die.

(The lady in black goes over to the one in white. The solitary sobbing resumes punctuated by a solitary bell or triangle. They dance what seems to be an Elizabethan dance which increases in speed and frenzy till they end up whirling. They exit – the white lady first. Then the black. Once the black lady disappears, the stage is instantly floodlit. There is the sound of glass breaking. Simultaneously loud wailing erupts. The lady in white (now wearing a crown) is borne on the shoulders of six men. They are followed by the KING, PRINCESS and retinue – all in slow procession. All except MAD COCONUT who comes in immediately after the PRINCESS. He seems unaffected and frolics around desperately trying to make merry. The procession ignores him. Finally he goes to the front and speaks… even in his grief he is comic.)

COCO: The Queen is gone.
  She's gone from the cold.
  The cold has no hold upon her,
  She is gone.

(He farts, looks around for someone to blame. Seeing no one, he continues.)

  She wears the earth as her cloak.
  Icicle knives have no way to the heart
  Of one who holds court with worms.
  Yes, they scurry; it is a busy time.
  Warm is the dark earth, silent save
  The quiet gnawing of patient jaws
  On flesh
  Gone from the cold.
  She's dead.

*(He looks distinctly uncomfortable – as if he's going to fart again –
but this time only adjusts his underwear.)*

The icy breast beneath the cold gold chains
Shall heave inwards to a new lover
And she shall moan like the wind
In the hollows; and her passionless ecstasies
Shall hiss like a scythe through air.
There shall be violent mating of flesh
With earth, – her cloak shall collapse
Around her and shall press inwards
At her eyes – and they will yield
With a general stir of sticky, white.
Just-awakened maggots;
And they shall crawl down her face
Like belated tears and hang
Upon her cheek
Where they shall feed
Again.

*(He looks about desperately… finally finding a handkerchief, he
wails into it – and suddenly slips into a real bout of grief, his comic
mask falling away.)*

The wind shall sing its lonely dirge,
The seasons mark time
And her flesh part to show
Bones like teeth when she used to smile
And she shall, after all,
Be a bare, gaping grin.
But for now it is all
There is to say
The Queen is dead,
She's gone.
She's dead.

(The procession ends way before the piece does. Before the last five lines of the piece, the Enchantress [DEATH – now in a high coronet and a gorgeous black robe] appears next to COCO. He finishes the piece. There is silence. She bends over in spasms. COCO, who for the first time notices her, is inexplicably terrified – backs off and runs. The Enchantress throws her head back. She is laughing. It takes a while for her to stop laughing. She gives the audience an even, piercing look and leaves slowly, almost unwillingly – as if she wants to take them with her.)

THE MEETING

(Enter COCO, drinking. He is stark raving drunk.)

COCO: I saw her standing there with the moonlight shining through her sheer silk dress. I loved her the moment I turned my eyes to her. She wore no... underwear. And the night blew winds from all four directions between her legs. I wanted to fly with the wind. She... was... my mother... the whore! No, no, but the other one, she was beautiful... Had cute little titties. She was beautiful and made everything right. But she's dead... my queen's dead... I will never jerk myself off to the thought of another woman as long as I live...

(Starts wailing. Enter PRINCE.)

PRINCE: Who are you and why do you sound like a Greek tragedy?

COCO: Oh shut up, you motherfucker, let me vent my grief!

PRINCE: From the looks of you, I don't think I would have enjoyed your mother. And unfortunately for you I didn't. Because if I did, as you say, fuck your mother, you wouldn't have turned out so ugly and rude. Who are you, loud and wailing one?

COCO: Mad Coconut, the King's Jester. They call me Coco.

PRINCE: How refreshing. A depressed jester. I already like this place.

COCO: Ah, a smart-assed tourist. I already like you too.

PRINCE: What is this place?

COCO: Don't laugh, alright? You're in *Nirwana* – just a little off Nirvana. We had a simple-minded founder who couldn't spell. It's not our fault, we're not responsible for the mistakes of the leaders we inherit.

PRINCE: So why are you wailing with a bottle in your hand?

COCO: Why do butterflies screw butterflies and not grasshoppers? Do you know that when I drink, I can see what life really is? It is shitty you know. Deception upon deception. Decorum masking human impulses – ohhh, just let me be. Stop asking me any more questions or I'll just start saying what you want to hear.

PRINCE: Alright... Nirwana! I hear that this place is famous for its beautiful women.

COCO: Hey, who are you anyway? Coming here with all this bullshit...

PRINCE: Don't laugh, OK?... I'm Prince Charming.

COCO *(laughs)*: Oh, boy that's dumb. That's really dumb. It's like from those stupid stories they tell us. Prince Charming. Who'd believe...

PRINCE: But it is true about the women here? Being beautiful and virtuous. I mean, I'm a prince you know. And I've reached that age where, you know, I'm supposed to... you know...

COCO: Try screwing a sheep? Good heavens, can't you tight-assed noble farts use the correct words when it comes to "it." You need a woman to hump. To bring you sons. To scratch your itch. To quench your fire...

PRINCE: Yes, I'm looking for a wife.

COCO: What, are there no women in your country?

PRINCE: I am a prince, you know. I need a princess...

COCO: Ah yes, I forget. You need fine golden thighs with the bluest of blue veins...

PRINCE: Is there a princess in Nirwana? If so, is she beautiful?

COCO: We have been told of a miracle that falls from the sky. Few here have seen it. They say it is magical. Soft, white and light as a feather. We have never seen snow in this country. Whenever we imagine its beauty we used to think of our kind and beautiful queen. She was so beautiful, we used to say she floated out of our dreams. With skin like snow and lips like blood... we feasted on her beauty. And even if our larders and cupboards were empty, we had beauty to feast on. We were so happy! But she is dead, our queen. And her daughter...

PRINCE: A princess! Is she beautiful?

COCO: Careful, my Prince. Of beauty there are many kinds... What am I saying? I am drunk and confused... of course my princess is beautiful. She is the most beautiful thing in a white dress since...

(Enter IXORA, unseen to COCO.)

PRINCE: Is she really beautiful? I mean like an unopened frangipani at dawn. Like a still pond laced with willows in the twilight...

COCO: God, you're an awful poet. But she is more beautiful than those. She is beyond compare. She is... she is... *(Sees IXORA, recognises her and is terrified.)* Stay away, you! I have seen you before... It was at a wedding... No, a funeral... Anyhow, you have no power over me. I have a cross on me. And a Buddhist charm... and a Hindu talisman...

IXORA: To protect your soul, little man? What about your body? Are clothes enough protection?

(COCO runs off.)

IXORA: Coward. *(To PRINCE)* And who might you be, healthy and well-muscled youth?

PRINCE: Prince Charming. Heir to the kingdom beyond Jade Mountain.

IXORA: And I am already charmed... Would you by chance have the time or inclination to partake of my – hospitality?

PRINCE: Your... hospitality sounds tempting. You know, you are quite beautiful... but there is a princess I have to see.

IXORA: Oh, pity. Just as well. There is a king I have to see too. But what a waste... such a fine, young body.

PRINCE: What did you say?

IXORA: Oh I said... some other time then.

PRINCE: Yes, some other time then.

SCENE TWO: AT THE PALACE

THE RITUAL

TRUTHSAYER: Don't worry, your Majesty. As an old sage used to say, "The flower that has been tended correctly will bloom to face the sun."

KING *(as with a familiar old friend)*: Oh shut up, old man. Wise sayings are for the common people. I am the King. What I want to know is, will my daughter perform the funeral ritual? If she doesn't, I'll have to find a suitable excuse for the people. I'll tell them she's overcome with grief... Will that do?

TRUTHSAYER: She doesn't seem too overcome.

KING: Temporary insanity due to her mother's sudden death?

TRUTHSAYER: She's never appeared more sane...

KING: Oh what do you know!

TRUTHSAYER: The truth. I'm your Truthsayer.

KING: Then tell me, will she or won't she perform the ritual?

TRUTHSAYER *(after a thoughtful pause)*: We'll know in a moment. The truth emerges with time.

KING *(sarcastically)*: I knew that! You're like the bloody weather wizard who guesses there'll be "isolated showers over several parts of the country sometime during the day." You never tell me anything I don't already know! What I want to know is how, what, why, who, when? Give me exact details. Tell me every-thing I *don't* already know...

TRUTHSAYER: If I knew everything there was to know, Sire, I wouldn't be a grovelling Truthsayer. If I knew everything, I'd be up *there*. Then *you* would be working for *me*.

KING *(wryly)*: Do I detect treason, old man?

TRUTHSAYER: No, just truth and a few of its limitations.

KING *(breaking into the first signs of better spirits)*: Hah, you admit defects!

TRUTHSAYER *(good-humoured teasing)*: Alas, it is true. Unlike my Master and his fine country, I am not perfect.

KING: I am too old to succumb to flattery, you decrepit crab! But yes, Nirwana is perfect. However, it is on a balance now that my beautiful, dear wife is… is… gone. That's why I want the Princess… I need her to perform the ritual. Ritual is calming. Traditions soothe uncertainties.

TRUTHSAYER: Maybe, Sire, your country too has grown up and cannot be ruled by rituals and rigid old rules. Maybe it needs new courage…

KING: Nonsense! We have flourished so far on rules and we will maintain our perfection with them.

TRUTHSAYER: That's what the dinosaurs thought too… for a while anyway.

KING: Well, well, not just a Truthsayer but an archaeologist and social reformer too. Looks like I got myself a bargain hiring three persons in one. Are you sure you are really *not* the Holy Trinity travelling incognito…

(COCO enters singing/yelling.)

COCO: She's done it! She's done it! And the crowds packed the courtyard to watch. Eighty thousand, I swear!

TRUTHSAYER: How *do* these officials get their statistics?

COCO: We make them up. No one checks anyway! But the important thing is she's performed the ritual and they loved it! They lapped up every colourful moment.

KING: Tell us, you confused and confounded Coconut, how did they react? Was she beautiful? Was my daughter stunning?

COCO: If only you were allowed to watch! You would have fainted from pride.

KING *(icily)*: Kings don't faint. They collapse. Grandly.

COCO: …She was everything she has been trained to be. Perfect in her splendid white mourning dress! When she lifted the incense urn, they roared out in a wave. Her effect on them was magical. She had them entranced. Almost like her mother...

TRUTHSAYER: I don't understand. She refused last night.

KING: I spoke to her at breakfast.

TRUTHSAYER: Sire! You must not force her. She is a Princess. She must learn to make her own decisions now or she'll never learn to make them for herself. You cannot...

KING: I cannot sit around farting while you second-guess the fate of my kingdom! I had to make her decide...

TRUTHSAYER: One day she may have worse decisions to make on her own and you may not be there to...

KING: By then she would have learnt enough from obeying my decisions.

TRUTHSAYER: By then she would have lost all ability to decide!

COCO: Oh, oh, oh... stop being so ugly, you two! What's important is that they loved her. I loved her. For a moment I joined them in their cheering – "Yay... yay for the Snow Princess! We love you, you beautiful, white, milky vision from our wet dreams!" The men were breathless, the women weeping. And now they can't wait to see her married. They want another spectacle – a wedding bigger than the funeral. More spectacular than our National Days combined. They want...

(*PRINCESS storms into the room.*)

PRINCESS: I want to die!

(*All, consecutively.*)

KING: My dear!

TRUTHSAYER: My Princess.

COCO: My vision!

PRINCESS: No, I want to abdicate!

TRUTHSAYER *(comfortingly)*: You are just upset...

PRINCESS *(ironically)*: I'm not upset. I'm livid with contempt. It's degrading to make a public spectacle of any grief. It's...

KING *(comforting her, pleased that she had obeyed)*: Duty. Duty at your mother's funeral altar. It was necessary for them to see you. It gives them a sense of reassurance. You did it for the Queen, your mother. You did it for your country.

PRINCESS: So do whores who lie back for politicians.

KING: None of that now. You know this is different. *(Beat.)* Now, now don't be cross, my sweet obedient girl. I know it is not easy, but it's small payment for the comfort we live in. I heard you gave offerings. Tell me about it. Tell me what made you angry.

PRINCESS: I gave offerings, Father. But it was awful. They were having a party.

KING: They are shallow everyday people. They are simpletons who don't know what it is that makes life fine and beautiful, what it is that makes existence perfect. The common and coarse people don't know our difficulties.

PRINCESS: They were not there to grieve for Mother, they were there to see my dress, my beauty... I thought they loved her but they just wanted to gawk at me.

COCO: We needed the fantasy and escape. We loved what she stood for.

PRINCESS: Beautiful dresses and perfect skin, you silly dizzyhead?

COCO *(mischievously)*: Among other outstanding points...

KING *(lustfully)*: Oh yes... outstanding points... *(Catching him-*

self) Uh yes, perfection. They loved her perfection.

PRINCESS *(flippantly)*: Perfection? Is that all it takes… Well, was I perfect? *(A bit more seriously, a bit sadly)* Did I do well? Are you proud of me, Father?

KING *(going over to embrace her)*: I am always proud of you, my sweet girl. You chose to do your duty and you will be rewarded. What do you want, dearest child? An heirloom piece from the Crown Jewels? Or shall I commission a new tiara…

PRINCESS: Just one wish.

COCO: Take the tiara. Take the tiara! Then you can give me your old one! I could reset the stones. I'd love new cuff-links. And a matching belt-buckle. You know… the jewel encrusted kind vulgar businessmen wear…?

KING: One wish? Alright, anything you want.

TRUTHSAYER: He who promises you "anything" seldom has that to give.

KING: He who spouts endless diarrhoea streams of counterfeit Confucianisms soon begins to irritate like a flea in a dog's arse-hole. Now shut up while I talk to my daughter. What would you like?

PRINCESS: I just want to be myself – for a few days. A week perhaps.

KING: Is that all? Do you think I am so poor that I cannot afford better?

TRUTHSAYER: It may be more than you can give.

PRINCESS: That is all I ask. To make my own decisions. To be myself for one week.

KING: Alright. It is granted.

PRINCESS: Good.

COCO: Shit, a tiara would have been just what she needed...

(*PRINCESS pulls at a ribbon and the loose white dress falls at her feet. She is in a stunning red gown that shows off her figure.*)

COCO: Shit!

KING: What is this! What the hell is this! Put the mourning dress back on!

PRINCESS: I feel more comfortable in this. You promised me...

KING: Yes, do what you want but you will show some respect for the dead at least!

PRINCESS: I will respect her in my own way...

KING: Alright, but in a white dress!

PRINCESS: In—my—own—way!

KING: No you won't.

PRINCESS: So when can I decide what is good for me?

KING: When I decide you can, my dear child. Now put your white dress back on. People will see you in the red dress and say...

PRINCESS: Which is to say I'll never get to have a say in anything.

KING: You will get to make your fashion statements after the mourning period!

PRINCESS: Then I will stay locked up for the whole 100 days. When the mourning period is over I'll step out in my red dress...

KING: But that would be too obvious. You can't go from mourning to red! Couldn't you at least wear pink first?

PRINCESS: There you see, you will never allow me to decide anything!

KING: That's not true. If you at least explained yourself before you do these silly...

PRINCESS: I had a sign.

TRUTHSAYER: A dream, Princess?

COCO *(mock campy)*: I had a sign once too – but my mother made me get out of *her* red dress. Oo... it was such a lovely red dress too!

KING *(to PRINCESS)*: What sign? Explain to us...

PRINCESS: I don't know how to.

KING: Nonsense. There is no sign. Just wilful stubbornness...

PRINCESS: There was a sign! There was blood...

KING: You dreamt of blood...

PRINCESS: There was blood.

KING: Where?

PRINCESS: There. I was bleeding there the day Mother died. I wanted it to stop but it continued. I was so scared. I was bleeding.

TRUTHSAYER: Oh my dear, dear Princess. There is nothing the matter with you. It's your body telling you that you're a woman now. I thought it had happened to you when you were younger and that your mother would have explained...

PRINCESS: Whatever it is, it is a sign that I must change. I cannot wear white dresses any more, Father. Because if I do, people will know when I bleed.

COCO: There is nothing wrong with bleeding. Bleeding only shows that you're alive...

PRINCESS: Then why don't you bleed, you nuthead? It's easy for you men to talk. No, I know what this bleeding means. It means I am not perfect any more. I cannot wear pure white dresses again because I will always be afraid to dirty them...

KING: You're being dramatic and simplifying things too much...

PRINCESS: Am I Father? Tell me, which prince will marry a princess in a soiled dress? Don't worry Father, this country will *have* its perfect princess. *(Sadly)* If we cannot have a perfect thing, we will have it disguised as perfect, won't we?

KING: Does that mean you'll keep the mourning dress on? Or will you insist on red? *(Beat.)* Come on... will you wear red or white?

(Beat.)

PRINCESS: Black. I will wear black.

(PRINCESS exits.)

KING: But... but black is the colour of our beggars, our outcasts. What is this streak that has gotten in her?

TRUTHSAYER: It is called growing up.

KING: But I did not grow up rebelling like this!

TRUTHSAYER: You grew up in different times than these, Sire.

KING: Then tell me, my smart-aleck wisdom-spouter, where will all this lead her?

TRUTHSAYER: If she is lucky, to a life that she can bear living. If she is unlucky, to a hell she will be forced to endure.

KING: I must help protect her. I can't bear to see her...

TRUTHSAYER: Yes, Sire, you can't bear to see her move away from your will. Become some other thing than what you want her to be.

KING: That is not what I meant.

TRUTHSAYER: But it is what you know. Nevertheless it is something all parents learn when their children grow up. They have to accept differences in even the type of love they have for each other. It is not easy.

KING: It is not acceptable.

TRUTHSAYER: Yet you must accept – even if you are King.

KING: I hate it when you get so pompous and self-righteous – especially when you're right.

TRUTHSAYER: I can't help it. It comes with the training.

COCO *(still gazing after PRINCESS)*: I'll bet she looks sensational in a low black dress. She's got great gazookas like winter melons to fill a low black dress. I'll go see if she needs help with the buttons. Maybe we'll play doctors and nurses like we used to when we were young...

KING: What do you mean, "doctors and nurses?" Come back, here you imp!

(COCO exits, laughing mischievously.)

SCENE THREE: AT THE PALACE

THE GIFT

PRINCESS: There is one who waits
In the dark—
Things glint, obscured by shadows.
Are they teeth or
Are they swords;
But they are crimson
And they glint.

There are eyes that glow
In the dark,
Or are they skulls that turn
Or are they eyes...
Or skulls...
But they are white
And they glow
And they turn.

There are voices
That call in the dark,
Whispers shriek from punctured throats;
Or are they songs
Or are they sighs
But they are voices *(choric echo)* dark voices
That call   call sweetly
And they call   whispering songs
In the night.   and sighs

There is one in the dark
Who waits,
She glints crimson and glows white
And she whispers and she sings
And she weaves her hairy web of illusion
And she calls so sweetly
In the night.
For death as in birth,
After all screaming and whispering,
After clawing in darkness
Is woman.

(IXORA enters.)

IXORA: You are as they say.

PRINCESS: And what is that?

IXORA: Beautiful.

PRINCESS: That is saying very little. Do you have business here?

IXORA: You have a precise tongue. And I thought you stupid because of your beauty.

PRINCESS: Your words twist like beautiful snakes so I *know* you cannot be stupid. Who are you and why are you here?

IXORA: I am Ixora, an emigrant from the Red River Plains. I am here to make your father happy again.

PRINCESS: You are not my mother. Pack up your presumptions... go away.

IXORA: Your father the king has granted me an audience. I have a gift. A condolence gift. He has not been rejecting sympathy has he? Those who were disappointed by the free and just kingdom he promised but couldn't give – they were very forgiving at the funeral weren't they? But it won't last...

PRINCESS: I don't know what you mean...

IXORA: And I thought you intelligent.

PRINCESS: My father wouldn't use a personal grief to...

IXORA: Your father is a politician first. Husband second. That much I understand. But even that little shred of knowledge is all I need.

PRINCESS: I don't understand. What do you mean, witch?

IXORA: Ah, perceptive too. I mean, my dear white, pale and anaemic wench, I could be what your father needs. You see, in spite of his blustering and swaggering, in spite of his protestations of having recovered from grief – I understand him. Thoroughly. *(Beat.)* He kept them charmed with a beautiful wife, didn't he? Charmed with beauty and perfection while he went about locking up those who weren't mesmerised by his vision. He had tied down every limb of protest and only stays king because this, his country, is already his puppet!

PRINCESS: My father loves this country...

IXORA: Love? Oh yes, that. Your father destroys with too much love. Your beautiful country is empty... it is built on the shackled backs of the thinking few...

PRINCESS: ...And he loved my mother. And you will now leave. I will get the guards to...

IXORA: I have an audience.

PRINCESS *(angry and terrified)*: And I don't like you. Get out, vixen. Or I will have you thrown out!

IXORA *(smiling)*: Be polite now, girl. I could be your next mother.

PRINCESS: Over my dead body.

IXORA: Only if you wish hard, my dear. Only if you wish hard...

(Enter TRUTHSAYER.)

TRUTHSAYER *(to PRINCESS)*: Your Highness. *(To IXORA)* It's curious what weeds the winds blow in this season. What do you want, witch?

IXORA: Ah, the Truthsayer. I know you by reputation. So, old mongrel, what evil lies are you protecting the King from now?

TRUTHSAYER: From greedy, middle-aged women who cannot resist powerful widowers.

IXORA: A noble profession. I hope it has a worthwhile pension. Frustrated middle-aged women without men of their own – they are very messy to deal with, you know. Sometimes those who oppose them don't even get to see their retirement fund.

TRUTHSAYER: An interesting warning – but I'm sure the King has nothing to fear from you. A woman of your charms and abilities must have, by now, trapped yourself a... butcher for a husband. So, what can I do for you?

PRINCESS: Send her away. This woman frightens me. I feel that she brings darkness...

IXORA: Quite the opposite. I bring brightness and light. I wish to present the King a mirror. It is a mirror in which he can look into the depths of his desires – past and present. He can see his queen again. He can see any illusion he wants to see – his beautiful perfect country, his perfect love for his people, his family...

PRINCESS: Truthsayer, send her away!

TRUTHSAYER: The King has sent me to accept your gift on his behalf. He sends his regrets but he is engaged...

IXORA: He promised me an audience.

TRUTHSAYER: He is busy. I am sure he will send you a personal word of thanks.

IXORA: Words hold no meaning for me! I will stay till the King keeps his own word.

TRUTHSAYER: You can stay till your breasts droop, ugly one...

IXORA *(dropping her mask suddenly)*: Don't you EVER call me that! You shall pay dearly for this, you dried-up piece of dung...

TRUTHSAYER: As I was saying... you may wait all you want. The King won't be here. Come Princess, I don't think we need to entertain this *ugly* thing...

(They begin to exit.)

PRINCESS: But she's quite beautiful...

TRUTHSAYER: That's why I'm the Truthsayer and you are the Princess.

(IXORA is about to go out in a huff too but then the KING blusters into the room.)

KING: Alright then. Where's the woman? Where's the gift?

IXORA *(delighted)*: Ah, the King. For a Truthsayer, you lie very well.

TRUTHSAYER: Should it surprise you? For the woman you are, you dress very modestly.

KING: So... you... doesn't she look like... My word, Truthsayer, isn't there a striking resemblance?

TRUTHSAYER: Many women in our country try to look like our departed queen.

KING: Yes, but this one... What is your name? I am King Raja.

IXORA: Doesn't "Raja" already mean "king?"

KING *(laughing)*: We kings like repeating of our greatness – but we seldom like repeating our questions. What is your name?

PRINCESS: Father, please, I don't like her. Her words are like dangerous knives... like broken glass...

IXORA *(demurely)*: Ixora, your Majesty. I... have a gift for you. A mirror. To comfort you in your moment of...

PRINCESS: Father, she...

KING: Later, child. I will see the both of you later. Come and sit here, Ixora, and tell me about your mirror.

PRINCESS: Truthsayer, we must do something! She is not what she appears to be. She's pretending.

TRUTHSAYER: That, child, is, unfortunately, the rule of courtship. No one wants to fall in love with reality. There is nothing I can do at the moment. Comfort is a very strong illusion. It won't bring back your mother, it won't solve the problems in this country – but it's what your father wants now. Later. We will see what we can do later.

PRINCESS: I don't want her here.

TRUTHSAYER: Why, because she reminds you of your mother?

PRINCESS: I just don't want her here! And do not speak to me about my mother again. I will ask you this only once... but if you care for me, if you love me, you will remember, won't you...?

TRUTHSAYER: Certainly, my dear Princess.

PRINCESS: Thank you, Uncle Tutu...

TRUTHSAYER *(laughingly)*: Don't call me that. It was alright when you were a child but you are a Princess now...

PRINCESS: If I cannot even hang on to the happy fragments of my childhood, Uncle, the world would indeed be bleak. You, Papa, Coco... why did I think we would always play hide and seek in the fruit garden? No Uncle, I will not play the Princess in front of you. You will always be my Uncle – even when I am queen, even when I am the old queen mother, you will still be my favourite Uncle Tutu.

(She kisses him on the forehead and exits.)

TRUTHSAYER: Poor dear child. Poor, poor child.

SCENE FOUR: TWO ROOMS AND A MIRROR

(Both KING RAJA and PRINCESS's rooms respectively.)

THE MIRROR

(The mirror is wheeled to the exact middle of the stage in such a way that the audience gets only the side view. It is actually an empty box/

frame, full-length and quite elaborate, very much in IXORA's *style. When the lights come on,* KING *and* PRINCESS *are sitting on either side of the mirror, half facing the mirror and half, the audience...)*

KING: She called it the Mirror of Emptiness...

PRINCESS: I feel nothing.

KING: Everything I want to remember, every desire I have...

PRINCESS: There must be something deep inside, some cell where I can share a similar something... squeeze a tear out... but nothing.

(Both get out of their chairs to go near to the mirror.)

KING: Why do I see her still?

PRINCESS: So why do I see her still?

KING: Her long hair twisting to her breast...

PRINCESS: Those eyes looking out at me,

KING: Her lips moving, unsmiling and yet, so soft...

PRINCESS: The fingers at her throat,

KING: Her body warm and yielding,

PRINCESS: The breasts, firm and longing,

KING: Why do you torture me?

PRINCESS: Why didn't you die before I was born?

KING: I would have offered the kingdom for your life.

PRINCESS: I put dogfood at your altar.

KING: I used you poorly but even so, you must have seen I adored you.

PRINCESS: I abhored you, Mother. You left me in the arms of a hundred other people.

KING: Those gentle arms...

PRINCESS: Your baby cried in the arms of every servant in the palace – none of them as beautiful as yours – and your baby grew up wondering how the insides of those ivory smooth arms felt. They felt empty.

KING: They felt wonderful when you held me. But your love was dangerous. It put me in the centre of your world until I had no other existence except when you were with me.

PRINCESS: But you seemed so kind... and they believed you – beauty and kindness. What a combination! Only I knew the deception, the hypocrisy.

KING: But your beauty was also my freedom.

PRINCESS: I live in the prison of your beauty, Mother!

KING: They were kind to us while you were alive. It was the magic of your beauty. I built a city, no... a country in your reflection.

PRINCESS: And when they look at me now, I see the expectation in their eyes. They want me to work your magic with my beauty... somehow... but I am not you and they will be disappointed.

KING: They will hate me because they have been used to looking at the beautiful.

PRINCESS: And there is no desperation like that of the addict who has lost his illusions.

KING: Ultimately, we need some illusions to live by...

PRINCESS: Or else, an illusion to die with.

(Beat.)

KING: I must do something.

PRINCESS: I must get away from this place.

KING: But I am empty.

PRINCESS: But I am afraid.

KING: I wish I had someone.

PRINCESS: I wish I had someone.

(They move to the front of the stage, facing each other.)

KING: She will be beautiful and afraid – and she will need me…

PRINCESS: He will be strong, handsome and firm – and I will lean against his strength, his need for me…

(PRINCESS turns away and KING comes up behind her, embracing her sensuously…)

KING: And I will create another thing of beauty which everyone will bow to again.

PRINCESS: And I will give myself to my hero. Completely. To hell with beauty. To hell with conventions, traditions and morality…

KING: I will look at her face…

PRINCESS: And I will look in his eyes and see…

(They look at each other as if for the first time.)

KING: Oh my God…

PRINCESS: No!

(They run to their respective sides of the mirror to look again.)

PRINCESS *(sadly, almost weeping)*: I… I have to go away from here. I must.

KING: I must do something about this. Before it is too late.

(Lights dim to black. The mirror is whipped away to laughter from a distance. When the lights come on IXORA is centrestage, smiling at the PRINCE.)

SCENE FIVE: AT THE PALACE IN A HALLWAY

PALACE MEETING

IXORA: I do love touching scenes. They are most truthful.

PRINCE: That is a strange thing to say. I thought the children were very mean to the cat. Throwing it into the pond. I daresay it drowned. I was glad to come into the palace grounds. It's so much more civilised here.

IXORA: Never mind. I have a bit of time before my appointment to see the King. In the past months as a guest here, I've found a room below that even the servants don't know about...

PRINCE: I am sorely tempted, beautiful lady...

IXORA: Good God, call me Ixora. You make me sound like a maiden aunt!

PRINCE: ...I am very very tempted, Ixora. But I have to see the royal registration clerk before I can officially apply to become a royal suitor for the Princess's hand in marriage. Then I have an appointment with the Truthsayer – after which the King wants to see all of us. And then...

IXORA: There's something very wrong when one is too busy to be immoral!

PRINCE: That's what's good about being busy! You don't have to think about morality. Just fill your day with happy, beautiful things to do, things to see, things to buy and delicious things to eat. Before you know it, it's already night! And another day has passed without a need to make any moral decisions.

IXORA *(muttering)*: Well, if there's anything to be said for the devil, it is, at least, he bothered to take a stand on morality.

PRINCE: What? Did you say something?

IXORA: No, uh... I think that's the Truthsayer calling for you.

PRINCE: I do believe he's making a rude sign at one of us. I'll go and see what he wants...

(PRINCE exits as COCO enters. COCO sees IXORA and wants to back out but it is too late, she has seen him.)

IXORA: Come back in here, little man. I saw you.

COCO: What do you want, you crotch-grinding bitch-in-heat?

IXORA: I want to know why you are so afraid. Is it because I remind you of her?

COCO: Hated her. Anyway, don't know who you are talking about. I mean, whoever you're referring to I'd hate anyway... so...

IXORA: You never told anyone you loved her, did you?

COCO: Don't know who... don't know what you... shut up. Fuck you!

IXORA: Poor Coco. Poor, poor Coco...

COCO: Don't do that! Please stop saying that... *(weeps)*... I saw her first. I saw her before anyone knew she was beautiful. Way before they brought her to the palace to be chosen from all the most beautiful women in the land. That bloody beauty contest ruined everything. We were children then but I loved her. Brought her fucking beautiful flowers. And she accepted them. But after she became queen, she had a lady-in-waiting in charge of gifts. I'm sure she never saw my flowers! But I saw her first!

It's not fair. It's not fucking fair...

IXORA: Poor Coco. Poor Coco... there's a room downstairs. Why don't we go there. No one will disturb us and you can tell me everything.

(Both exit. Lights dim to darkness.)

SCENE SIX: IN THE THRONE ROOM

THE BETROTHAL

(Lights come on to KING, TRUTHSAYER and PRINCESS.)

KING: My dear, you have been meeting him. What do you think?

PRINCESS: He's a bit too earnest, that makes him seem a bit silly at times...

KING: He's young... earnestness and honesty are virtues, you know.

PRINCESS: And it was not very tactful of him to say that the most beautiful women of his country are dark and tanned.

TRUTHSAYER: He was just careless, your highness. He didn't mean any offence. He's a foreigner, you know.

PRINCESS: All the more reason he should understand *our* sensitivities. After all, he's in *our* country.

KING: Maybe we should take a bit of time. Look for another one...

PRINCESS: It's alright. I'll take this one. At least he has a kingdom and he's not quite a moron.

KING: But I want you to be happy.

PRINCESS: Happiness and wisdom are often incompatible.

TRUTHSAYER: But perhaps your father is right. Such a snap deci-sion... it is not as if anyone is forcing you...

PRINCESS: People do not often base their decisions on belief. They decide quickly because they are afraid they won't get a chance to decide later. So while I appear to have a choice I am actually imprisoned by the fear of taking too long to choose.

TRUTHSAYER: But it is unwise...

PRINCESS: Precisely that! I will learn absolutely nothing from this choice. I just need to learn to know myself. For that, I have to go away first.

TRUTHSAYER: You are becoming too complex. I prefer simple truths.

PRINCESS: That is why I am a Princess and you are only a Truthsayer.

KING: Then it is decided. You will marry him and I, her.

PRINCESS: It is for the best. *(Beat.)* You will be careful, Father...?

KING: Fate ambushes the careful as well as the careless.

PRINCESS: But it helps to keep your eyes open – even as the dart is poised in front of you.

KING: I will keep my eyes open. Politicians who want to continue living often have to do that.

PRINCESS: It is decided then. I shall take my leave soon, Father – but I shall ask two favours. You will send me word every week that you are well, and if I do not hear from you, then I will have your permission to send my husband's troops here to find out what has happened to you. And also, there is a matter of succes-sion. If she doesn't bear you sons...?

KING: Of course you succeed me.

PRINCESS: It is a delicate matter. Not very pleasant. But it is always good to be clear.

KING: You will have it in writing before you leave. It is fine to share a bed with a stranger but an inheritance must go to where the blood connects. That is the way in these parts and thus it will always be. Goodbye, my dear. *(PRINCESS exits.)* Truthsayer, make the announcement.

SHE IS ILLUSION

(Lights come on in the Throne Room to a CHORUS, TRUTHSAYER and KING.)

CHORUS: Sire, do you know what she is doing to you?

KING: She'll be my queen.

CHORUS: Sire, do you know what she is doing to you?

KING: She'll be my wife.

CHORUS: She's an illusion...

KING: No.

CHORUS: Abomination...

KING: No!

CHORUS: An imitation of reality.

KING: She's... my life!

CHORUS: There are times when things seem not what they seem.

KING: There are times when we have to cling to our dreams.

CHORUS: There are times for us to face up to loss.

KING: There are times when we have to cling to a cause.

CHORUS: But not through self-deception.

KING: I'll live with my decision.

CHORUS: Wilful self-destruction...

KING: It's existentialism.

CHORUS: It's your choice.

KING: It's MY choice and I've decided. I have decided.

(Silence.)

TRUTHSAYER: Sire, it is not my place...

KING: Then Truthsayer, hold you peace.

TRUTHSAYER: But I cannot watch you do this.

KING: Truthsayer, please! Your existence here hangs by a thread...

TRUTHSAYER: I may hang yet I must speak.

KING: Must you? And why?

TRUTHSAYER: Because your people love you and they care...

KING: My people, my people. *(Sadly)* What do they know, what do they care? Where are they, late in my nights when I'm up with their troubles, averting a war, or solving a riddle of economy; it gets lonely, very lonely.

What do you know, why should you care? How do you know what it is to carry a kingdom upon a thought, to wish and to hope for your own Camelot; to decide on a plea for the life of one man, to change the lives of a million – and then, and then...

To look by my side where my world used to be... and see nothing, just nothing but a faint memory. So what do you care, what do you know?

TRUTHSAYER: I know she is not real.

KING: But I know too! Yet I've accepted, and so must all of you.

TRUTHSAYER: But Sire...

KING: I cannot do without her – even an imitation must do.

TRUTHSAYER: But you could try.

KING: Truthsayer, I could die.

(Light change.)

TRUTHSAYER: But the fact remains, Sire, that you cannot marry an outsider.

KING: I will change the law. Don't you know I have the power?

TRUTHSAYER: But the morality of it, Sire...?

KING: Morality? Weren't you listening? I—have—the—power. Morality is for the masses. What's the use of power if you can't use it to serve your own survival?

TRUTHSAYER: But this is not survival, Sire. You are choosing a wife.

KING: Do you contradict me, Truthsayer?

TRUTHSAYER: I dare not... your Majesty!

KING: Look, old friend. Do not take such a frosty tone with me. I am sorely in need of comfort.

TRUTHSAYER: I loved her too. We all did – but you must get over her...

KING: But I am! I'm getting married again.

TRUTHSAYER: And the worst part is that you *know* what you're getting into.

KING: A very pretty pair of thighs! *(Laughs.)*

TRUTHSAYER: I meant...

KING: I know what you meant. The problem with Truth is that it's got no sense of humour. But coming to your point...

TRUTHSAYER: I do believe...

KING: No wait, I have a question. Is it better that I marry someone whose faults are less obvious then? Should I marry a seemingly perfect woman to later discover the little cracks... and crevices *(sniggers)* I never knew existed? Your previous queen had no vices – and even while she was beautiful, I knew she had little in terms of humane virtues. You see, it's all about understanding what you are getting into...

TRUTHSAYER: But Sire...

KING: Besides, I will always have my loyal Truthsayer by my side to advise me, won't I?

TRUTHSAYER: I hope to remain...

KING: Won't I?

TRUTHSAYER: Yes, Sire.

SCENE SEVEN: THE BAT IS LOOSE

THE APPLE

(Set in IXORA's secret room below the palace, it is a lavish scene – filled with cartons of red apples. The Mirror of Emptiness is covered with a white drape. A handsome, near-naked youth is apparently asleep on a divan nearby. Ixora contemplates an apple...)

IXORA: And this one... this one will make him want knowledge of all the variations of ecstasies that only I can give him. He will want knowledge – knowledge of every tingling nerve in his pubescent crotch. And while I feed his pleasure I will take over yet another kingdom. That's how I kept Paradise to myself. Adam's wench, Eve, bit into knowledge not knowing that its seeds were illusions. That's why she suffers now. She ate first and fell in love with her own reflection. Then he ate and fell in love with her. That's why she's always been a slave to beauty and he, a slave to her. And so, with the charming boy and his pale princess, they too will fall. She will fall down dead like her mother and he will fall under me. I like the superior position you see. I'm a feminist.

(COCO runs in.)

COCO: I've done it but I won't do it any more, you bitch. Not even if you take away my Tuesday afternoons here.

IXORA: Why... do you tire of me, Coco? Don't I give you enough excitement any more?

COCO: Why don't you give him the wretched apples yourself? He's your fucking husband, not mine!

IXORA: It's a game we play. This way he thinks I'm coy and enjoys his apple even more. Illusions are by their nature sweeter if one believes they are harder to come by.

COCO: Well, I won't play in your stupid games any more. You can play by yourself. Yes. And by the way, I won't be coming for my Tuesday afternoon screw sessions any more. Yes... you can just play on your own. Play with yourself... ha, ha, ha... Forget the apples. Get a carrot or cucumber or... or... a papaya!

IXORA: So you have decided, have you?

COCO: Uh... yes.

IXORA: Alright. Go off then.

COCO: What?

IXORA: I said, you're free... *(Beat)*... though I must admit that I had someone else in training for your role in case you failed me.

COCO: You have? Who's the prick?

IXORA: I'm afraid he was a disappointment too. Had his fuck and refused to pay. *(Gesturing to the divan)* You might as well wake him up and send him on his way too.

(COCO goes gingerly to the couch and nudges the youth on the shoulder.)

COCO: Arhhh ! He's dead. He's fucking dead. What did you do, you bitch!

IXORA: Dead? Oh isn't that interesting. They seem to end up that way, don't they – when they meet strong women...?

COCO: Stay away from me... I've got my crucifix and my charms and...

IXORA: And I will TELL you what you WILL do! You will give the Prince the apple and you will make him eat it!

COCO: No...

IXORA: And then while I am entertaining him here, you will take that pallid Princess to the forest and rip her heart out!

COCO: You are really mad. I refuse... I'll... I'll tell the Truthsayer. We'll tell the King!

IXORA: The King is beyond redemption. Even before eating my apple he already had a love for them. It is too late. There is a bat loose in the Palace – and she's flown out from Hell!

(She unveils the mirror and the TRUTHSAYER with bleeding wounds and in rags – almost a Christ figure – is trapped in the mirror. She laughs in triumph.)

COCO: Truthsayer! Truthsayer! Come out. You must save us. We'll tell the King. Together. Damn it, come out! You are the brave one here. You must save us!

TRUTHSAYER *(whimpering)*: You are beautiful... you are beautiful... you are beautiful... Don't hurt me any more... I can't help it if she's more beautiful than you... Owww! ...No, don't hurt me. You are beautiful... you are beautiful, oh gorgeous one...

COCO: What the fuck have you done to him!

IXORA *(suppressing a smile)*: You might have used that four-letter word correctly for once. He always wanted truth... and there is no harder and more painful truth than that... *(making an obscene gesture)* ...shoved up one's...

COCO: You soulless bitch...

IXORA: That's hardly the point.

COCO: What...

IXORA: The point is that there is just about enough space in the mirror for one more mad fool. Who knows what that old thing may have learnt to love in his madness and pain in there. Perhaps... if you both stay long enough, you might both get mad enough to love each other. Now wouldn't that be a happy picture.

COCO: I won't do it. I won't kill the Princess. I won't deliver your apple. You will have to kill me.

IXORA: That was what the Truthsayer begged me to do – but I thought one dead and contented prick *(gesturing to dead youth)* was enough good luck for the week. No. You have a decision to make.

(Puts apple on the table.)

TRUTHSAYER: You are beautiful, my Queen. Your thighs are splendid like a starry night. I will bask in the perfume of your fart. I will lick your toes like a puppy, my Queen… my beautiful Queen…

IXORA: An apple for the Prince, her bleeding heart for me – or a house in Hell for you.

(Beat. Then COCO grabs the apple and runs out crying.)

THE STORY

(Lights up to same setting as before. The mirror is covered again. The dead youth is removed. IXORA is lying sexily on the divan. PRINCE enters.)

IXORA: At last. It is good to see you.

PRINCE: It is good to see you too.

IXORA: Before we begin…

PRINCE: Begin?

IXORA: Yes, before we begin, I'd like to tell you a story first.

(PRINCE makes to speak but IXORA silences him with a finger…)

Once upon a time, there was a very handsome man in a very

beautiful garden. Now this man was not to eat the apples belonging to the owner of the garden...

PRINCE: I have heard this story before. He was cast out of the garden with his mate, a woman...

IXORA: Except that the woman died before they were made to leave.

PRINCE: Died?

IXORA: Yes. A mad and wild animal tore out her heart. And the man was left with a choice. And do you know what that choice was?

PRINCE: I am sure you will be quite glad to tell me.

IXORA: You see, the snake that had brought on all these complications, she was much misunderstood. In any case, she decided that the man was lonely, and splitting the skin down her back, she stepped out a most beautiful woman...

PRINCE: ...By the name of...

IXORA: ...Dojoji. But since she saw the distress on the man's face, she changed her name as easily as she changed her face and used a simpler name: Lamia.

PRINCE: And what choice did Lamia give the man?

IXORA: To stay in the garden living off sweet, delicious apples... to forget Eve ever existed and to forever relinquish his pleasures to Lamia's capable... abilities.

PRINCE: And if the man refused?

IXORA: There would be no apples, no garden, no pleasures. He would die.

PRINCE: Well, that's a rather interesting story. I wish I had time to chew the fat with you but I have to go now.

IXORA: Go? What do you mean, go? *(Sexily)* Didn't you come here to sample my delicious... fruit?

PRINCE: No. If I wanted fruit I'd go to a market. I just came to say goodbye. I thought I owed you the courtesy...

IXORA: But I thought he gave you the apple... Didn't you eat it?

PRINCE: Coco was rather insistent... I promised but I gave it to the Princess.

IXORA: Arrrhhhh! YOU were supposed to eat it! I made it to charm a man. You stupid fool. You stupid, stupid fool!

PRINCE: I don't understand... what's this fuss over an apple? You women are really strange...

(Enter COCO, weeping, his hands bloody with the heart.)

COCO: Take it! Take it! I don't want to see anyone any more. Take it away from me!

PRINCE: Coco! What's this? What's this mess?

COCO: I'm sorry. I'm a shit. Lower than a fart. She made me do it.

IXORA *(now smiling)*: Remember my story about the man, the garden of apples, the snake and his woman with the ripped out heart? Well, Adam, it is time for you to choose.

PRINCE *(with a growing sense of panic)*: My—name—is—not— Adam.

IXORA: Nonetheless, it is time to choose.

PRINCE *(in anguish)*: Coco, WHAT HAVE YOU DONE! *(To IXORA)* WHAT HAVE YOU DONE TO HER! WHAT HAVE YOU DONE TO HER!

COCO *(keeps whimpering throughout)*: I'm sorry... didn't want to... I'm sorry... so sorry...

(IXORA strolls to the door while the two stare, transfixed – at the heart.)

IXORA: Coco, take it to the kitchen and tell them to cook it. I'd like it for dinner. And you, my young Prince, you still have your decision to make – but perhaps after dinner. You know, we can share two kingdoms together... or you can die alone.

(IXORA exits.)

LIGHTS OUT

ACT TWO

SCENE ONE: THE SEVEN LITTLE MEN OF SUICIDE HOUSE

QUEEN OF SUICIDE HOUSE

(Lights up. The PRINCESS awakens on a throne in a ridiculous throne room. It is furnished with rickety furniture. The throne is a huge piece of scrap art made from newspapers, drink cans and junk. Present are DOC [COCO], HAPPY [PRINCE] and BASHFUL [TRUTHSAYER]. BASHFUL is autistic and comes out once in a while to whisper to HAPPY. Otherwise he rocks in a corner or is involved in his own private world of unfathomable concerns.)

PRINCESS *(awakening)*: Where am I?

DOC: Welcome to Suicide House.

PRINCESS: Suicide House?

HAPPY: It's where the rich and famous get to stay when they bomb out, dear.

DOC: You know, shit hits fan, lives go to pieces, business goes bankrupt, pay a visit to a mental institution – well, one or all of these… it's all here at Suicide House.

PRINCESS: We're not all dead are we? I mean, I just ate an apple and then… and then I don't know what happened. Then I woke up here. We're not all dead are we?

DOC: Good heavens no. You can't commit suicide if you're already dead. I should know, I'm a doctor. You can call me Doc because you're so pretty.

HAPPY: Don't mind him, dear. The rest of us aren't pretty at all but we also get to call him Doc. He's just trying to impress you with flattery. But he's not that smart. He's just a herbalist. Doesn't have a degree to save his life. I'm Happy and this is

Bashful. We're part of the team of the Seven Little Men from Suicide House.

PRINCESS: You seem somehow familiar. Are you sure we haven't met before? Uh... it was really kind of you to save me from the forest but I have to go now. I have a large wedding to organise and a little kingdom to help my husband run...

(BASHFUL whispers urgently to HAPPY.)

HAPPY: Bashful says you can't go, my dear. And I'm afraid I agree with him. You see, sweetheart, the only way out of here is through suicide.

PRINCESS: Nonsense. You brought me in here from out there. If I want to go, I just have to walk out. It's pure and simple logic.

(She starts walking to the door but no one stops her and she is a bit suspicious. She gets to the door, opens it and turns around.)

Very funny. Who put a brick wall there?

DOC: If logic solved all problems, we'd all be in Nirvana by now and the philosophers would be minor gods instead of mouldering corpses. We told you, you can't get out unless you commit suicide. You bombed out, see? From rich, beautiful, sheltered Princess to penniless refugee. Don't be upset, it happens to the best of us. How would you like to die, Miss? Arsenic, razor blades... I've got a bit of rope somewhere...

PRINCESS: Suicide? But I don't want to die – well, not yet anyway.

(BASHFUL whispers to HAPPY.)

HAPPY: Bashful says the only other way out is if you love one of us enough to give him "The True Kiss Of Love." But it's gotta be true love. Real honest to goodness, heart pounding, lip smacking true love.

PRINCESS: This is ridiculous. So stupid.

DOC: Don't make fun of our rules, floozie. YOU'RE the foreigner here. YOU stick to our rules.

PRINCESS: Who made the stupid rules anyway?

DOC: They're not stupid, alright!

PRINCESS: You did. Of course. I should have guessed.

DOC: A few of them anyway. I'm the elected leader but Bashful, he's the main rulemaker. Anyhow, you're stuck here and you just have to cope. No better and no worse than real life. *(Pompously)* Now, I think the high and mighty who have hit the shit and can't accept it – they are the ones who are the most ridiculous. Who agrees with me?

(HAPPY and BASHFUL raise their arms in agreement. HAPPY shouts "Y-a-a-y!" BASHFUL does a weird, silent dance. PRINCESS is sullen, insulted.)

DOC *(tauntingly)*: Everyone agrees. One, two, three. It's three to one. We win. Well?

PRINCESS: Alright, you win. Your rules then. But you certainly won't get the kiss of true love from me.

DOC: Thank heavens. Your loss not mine. To think I flattered a floozie thinking she'd know how to love...

PRINCESS: Just a minute, smug pompous little ass. Happy said there are seven of you "Little Men." Where are the other four? And besides, you don't look little to me.

DOC *(sneeringly)*: She don't know. Father's bloody king and she's as woolly-headed as the next spring lamb... the next dizzy-headed bimbo... Call me a pompous ass, will you?

HAPPY: Give her a break, Doc. *(To Princess)* Listen here, Princess, the other four are tending to the mine now. You see, we common folk – we got no pretensions to speak of, no beauty, no money, no class. We got to work. As for being little men, well that's how the bigshots see us, see...

PRINCESS: There are four others at work. In a mine... That means you can get in and out of here – through the door? How?

HAPPY: That's because we're ordinary folk, dear. We got no education, money and all that crap – and you know, we're always popping in and out of Suicide House cos we live so near it. But we don't succumb to it. We got more bounce-back spirit, see? We're not like the rich and powerful farts. When they get in, they find it tough to get out.

PRINCESS: And "The Kiss Of True Love" solves everything? *(They nod enthusiastically.)* God, this is pathetic. If the rest of them are like the three of you... oh no, it's a nightmare. I didn't go through hours of poetry, music and embroidery classes to deal with this.

DOC *(imitating her snivelling)*: "Poetry... music and embroidery" – HAH! Look here, you're no great shakes yourself alright. White like blooming *tofu*. Well sorry, kiddo. We're all you got. We're reality. So how about throwing yourself into my arms and giving me one on the old smackaroo! We'll have some fun and get you out of here as well...

(He goes up to her and grabs her by the hips and pushes himself onto her. She struggles, he grabs at her breasts. She hits him across the face.)

PRINCESS: Don't you dare! Let go. Get out! Get out of here!

DOC: Are you striking me off? Are you striking me off the list? I dare you to! I dare...

PRINCESS: What the hell is he talking about?

HAPPY: It's your choice, dearie. If you strike him off, he can't come back later.

PRINCESS: Wonderful. I strike you off! Fuck-off, Doc.

DOC: Great! Fine! I hope I see you crawl at the end of all this! You'll go faster than the rest of them – and I'll be there to cheer you on, you rich, beautiful bastard. Cheer you on your way to hell.

(DOC storms out.)

HAPPY *(dismayed)*: Oh no. You really shouldn't have. He was the best among us. Sure, he's opinionated and rough and...

PRINCESS: ...And a molester of women!

HAPPY: ...And even that. I'm not making excuses for him. But if you'd spoken to him first instead of sending him out... well, he was really trying to help. He usually behaves worse, you know. He was trying to help.

PRINCESS: In my country, he would have been thrown in...

HAPPY: You're no longer in your perfectly beautiful country, my dear. I'm afraid you're going to have to cope with imperfection if you want to live somehow.

PRINCESS: Oh Happy, I'm miserable.

HAPPY: Well, that's a start.

PRINCESS: No. You don't understand. Something awful's happened. The apple... it was given to my Prince but I ate it. And when I woke up, I had the strangest feeling. I think there was a spell put on it. I thought I wanted to screw a woman. Then I looked down... and realised that something was horribly wrong. I can't want a woman, I'm a Princess.

HAPPY: Princess, that is how I feel all the time. In a different way of course... no women for me – but you know what I mean, dear. Maybe we can love each other because we're both different. Maybe we'll be really good for each other...

PRINCESS: I'm sorry. I cannot. I really cannot love anyone at...

HAPPY: Nonsense. Anyone can love anyone. It depends on how desperate you are and how much you are willing to give up to survive.

PRINCESS: That's scary.

HAPPY: That's life for you. You're luckier than most though. Excluding Doc, you still have six more to choose from to make your decision.

PRINCESS: What do you mean?

HAPPY: Well, if at the end of meeting each one of us, you haven't decided on, you know, giving the kiss, then you have to die. We get to choose how that happens.

PRINCESS: But that's not fair. What if I decide I like Doc best...

HAPPY: Too late – you sent him off. Those of us who are rejected seldom return – unless they are very stupid. Very, very stupid.

PRINCESS: And if I do kiss someone?

HAPPY: Then both of you get to leave and live happily ever after as loving man and wife.

PRINCESS: But my Prince? What about him?

HAPPY: Too bad about him. I've seen him. He's cute! But hey... you can't have everything.

PRINCESS: But this is terrible. It's so difficult.

HAPPY: Isn't it? And this is only ordinary life. I wonder what hell's like. Listen. Why don't you and I make a go of it...

PRINCESS: I don't know... No, I can't. The apple's effect hasn't worn off yet.

HAPPY: Well... shit. Damn! Piss off. I don't care any more.

PRINCESS: Besides, how can I decide when each of you gets so abusive each time I decline...

HAPPY: Reject. The word is reject...

PRINCESS: Well, I can't love someone I don't know. I can't love someone who is nice one moment then hisses and spits the next because I said something wrong or because I rejected him.

HAPPY: What do you expect? This is the real world. People get hurt. People swear. Besides, you can't know everything about someone, right? Even those you love or are forced to love. Can you stop him from changing? You just handle it. Reality just spits at you in the eye and you—just—handle it. Got it? *(She is sullen and quiet.)* Ahhh piss off. I give up. I'm getting out of here. Try to do better with Bashful. He's really the sweetest of us...

PRINCESS: No. Take him with you. I can't. Not right now.

HAPPY: You're striking us off without trying? *(She nods.)* You are mad. You are not a Princess now. You don't have choices at your feet spread out like dresses to wear in a day. Wake up, girl. Take whatever you can and make whatever you will with it...

PRINCESS: Please. Please leave me alone. Just go, both of you. I just want to be alone. I wanted to leave my country just to be alone. To spend time knowing myself...

BASHFUL *(suddenly speaking – with the voice of an innocent child)*: Let's go, Happy. She wants to be indulgent.

HAPPY: I tried, you know. I really tried.

BASHFUL: She seemed a bit artificial if you asked me.

PRINCESS *(but they don't hear)*: You're a liar! Hah, Bashful is it? You can speak.

You could have talked to me. Why didn't you speak to me? You're no rulemaker, you're a fake!

BASHFUL *(to Happy as they proceed to the door)*: Trouble is, she thinks the world revolves around her.

HAPPY: She thinks she can just sit there and everyone's supposed to reach out and touch her.

BASHFUL: Isn't that a pity. Such a waste of a life, isn't it. Sitting pretty and hoping to be touched... Makes her a bit of a ditz, wouldn't you say?

PRINCESS: Wait, come back. I think I want to know you now. Wait...

BASHFUL: Ah well. Maybe she likes suffering better.

(They go out the door. She tries to follow but runs slap into SNEEZY [COCO], who falls on her in a state of collapse. She staggers back with his weight – both collapsing. DOPEY [BEAUTIFUL YOUTH] comes in and closes the door.

The PRINCESS disentangles herself from SNEEZY and, noticing his unhealthy pallor and sickly sniffles, draws away.)

PRINCESS: What's wrong with the men in this place?

SNEEZY: They're all dying.

DOPEY: Sleepy... uh sent message... uh...

SNEEZY: Shut up, you dope! Retards... they should make them into fertiliser, at least that's good for the plants.

PRINCESS: What do you mean – about the men dying?

SNEEZY: Well, actually it's not just the men. The women, children – they're dying too. Death is an equal opportunity employer. I sneeze on them, they start sneezing and then they die. Men, women, children. But before that, they sneeze on others and...

DOPEY *(insistently)*: I have to say message. Sleepy say he not be able...

SNEEZY: Shut up, you dope!

DOPEY: Name Dopey – not dope. YOU shut up. YOU listen. You sick, sick, sick... make people die. You die now. Stop making Mrs Death come. You sick, sick, sick!

(He goes over and starts roughing SNEEZY up. He tries to strangle him. SNEEZY is weak and unable to defend himself.)

PRINCESS *(breaking them up)*: Stop this. Stop it at once. Dopey, stop... if you stop, I'll let you say your message. OK... let go... alright. If you're scared of him sneezing, we'll put him that side. With the blankets so he won't sneeze on us...

DOPEY: Once I saw. He sneeze. Green stuff. Lots, lots of green stuff come out. Sticky. Like custard. Dopey like to eat custard. But not green custard. Dopey like yellow custard...

SNEEZY: Oh shut up. You're making me feel even sicker.

DOPEY: But you make green sticky custard come out from nose. Cover woman. Green, yellow sticky stuff... all drip, drip, drip... She scream. She die. Three months she scream in bed. Then she die. Green, yellow stuff all on skin.

PRINCESS: Oh... that's terrible.

SNEEZY *(defensively)*: It was an accident. I didn't want to sneeze on her but she was wearing this perfume and I couldn't help myself. Before I knew it – "WHOP!" she was a walking custard pudding. Green custard pudding.

PRINCESS: Ughhh!

SNEEZY: But that's nothing. My lover suffered longer. She didn't scream but her eyes... their silence was worse than the agony in any scream.

PRINCESS: How did you get this way?

SNEEZY: I shared a night of indiscretion with both ignorance and ecstasy. Threesomes are a bit messy, if you know what I mean. You never know what to put where and for how long. Finally ecstasy left in a huff when the novelty wore off, and when I woke up with my nose dripping the next morning, ignorance was gone too. I was ill and I knew what it was and why. I was totally alone too.

DOPEY: I have message from Slee…

SNEEZY: I already told you to shut the hell…

PRINCESS: Let him get it off his chest.

DOPEY: Thank you. Sleepy no come today. He got a good dream. Can't come.

(Beat.)

PRINCESS: That's all?

SNEEZY: Told you it wasn't worth it.

PRINCESS: But wait. That means I have one choice less. That is not fair. I'm supposed to have seven choices. And I wasn't told this till after I sent Doc off. Without Doc and Sleepy I actually have five choices only. Happy and Bashful are gone and now all I get to choose from is…

DOPEY: Still no Grumpy. You no meet Grumpy.

PRINCESS: Oh great. I'm three potential lovers away from a suicide and I have to choose between the terminally ill, a retard and someone called Grumpy. I might as well die…

DOPEY: You want to die? Now? Dopey strong. Dopey squeeze neck. Over in no time. Dopey squeeze you…

PRINCESS *(backing off)*: No, not yet. Stay there!

DOPEY *(sweetly obedient)*: OK. You give word.

PRINCESS *(relieved)*: At least he listens.

SNEEZY: You're not going to make it, are you?

PRINCESS: What?

SNEEZY: You're not going to make it. You're not going to be able to bring yourself to truly love one of us. It's not unusual these days, you know. No one gives themselves over to anything these days. Especially not to another person. You see, we have become so clever we actually realise how imperfect everyone else is and we refuse to allow them to share our own little world of perfect illusions.

PRINCESS: That's very intelligent. I could like you.

SNEEZY: That's very condescending but I forgive you. I could die tomorrow so I have no time to bear grudges.

PRINCESS: I'm sorry, I didn't mean...

SNEEZY: And I don't have time for niceties as well. Will you love me and kiss me?

PRINCESS *(facetiously)*: This is so sudden... *(giggles)* sounds like a proposal too...

SNEEZY: Look, I don't have time. Will you...

DOPEY: No kiss him, Princess. His wife... he sneeze while kissing. She die.

SNEEZY: SHUT UP, YOU DOPE! Princess, will you... oh, no... ah... ah... *(about to sneeze)*.

DOPEY: Arhhh... Arrrhhh... sneeze come... kill him... stop him!

(Rushes over and begins to smother him.)

PRINCESS: Don't kill him! I haven't decided... don't kill him! He's not well. Leave him alone, Dopey... we'll take our chances...

DOPEY: No. Me no die. No die like me mother. Three months yellow-green in bed. He kill Dopey mother. Now he die! Now he die! Now he die!

PRINCESS: Dopey, stop. Please stop it. Then I strike you off! Get out.

DOPEY: No. No strike. I listen. See? No kill already.

PRINCESS: Sorry, Dopey. I can't. Not with you...

DOPEY *(sweetly, innocently)*: But I listen. Listen like puppydog...

(PRINCESS opens the door and DOPEY exits sadly. GRUMPY [KING] barges in. He is dressed like a gentleman. Impeccably groomed.)

GRUMPY: Is it my turn already then? It is time, isn't it?

PRINCESS: Actually I haven't finished with Sneezy yet.

GRUMPY: I'm surprised he hasn't sneezed in all this time. You would have decided immediately if he had. The green stuff's really quite gross...

PRINCESS: You're not really Grumpy, are you?

GRUMPY: Names have a habit of misleading. So have you decided on him then?

PRINCESS: Well, I don't know if I can bear living with someone from day to day worrying if he will sneeze...

SNEEZY: Princess, I beg you – live with imperfections. They, at least, are real. Hope is just the other side of illusion and they are both delusions. There is no perfection – just a more perfect lie.

GRUMPY: He does go on and on, doesn't he. Well look, I haven't got all day. Seems like you're happy here with old sicko and I was just a little too late. That's just...

PRINCESS: No. No, I've decided. Sorry, Sneezy. I really enjoyed talking to you and...

SNEEZY: No, please don't send me off. You enjoyed talking to me. It's companionship after all. Not some grand sunset in the sky. I know I'm less than normal. Don't even look half as good as Grumpy here. But I think with whatever time I have...

GRUMPY: Ho-hum... well, see you lovebirds some other time... Got another appointment...

PRINCESS: I'm sorry, Sneezy. I've got to strike...

SNEEZY: Wait. Before you say that. If you should need me... I don't know if I'll be around but...

(GRUMPY goes and opens the door impatiently.)

PRINCESS: Sorry.

SNEEZY: Goodbye.

(GRUMPY closes the door. It is obvious the PRINCESS is uncomfortable. GRUMPY smiles genially.)

PRINCESS *(a bit reproachfully but obviously glad to have met a charmer like GRUMPY)*: You didn't have to do that, you know.

GRUMPY: He was getting tedious.

PRINCESS: I could have decided on my own without any help.

GRUMPY: You didn't have that much time.

PRINCESS *(coquettishly)*: And who decides that?

(GRUMPY doesn't answer but smiles.)

PRINCESS: And so we begin. Now let's try to get to know each other. It'll be more pleasant this way...

(GRUMPY suddenly rams the PRINCESS against the wall and pulls at her hair cruelly till she gasps in pain.)

GRUMPY: I'm not here to chit-chat, see. YOU are supposed to love me. If you do, you live. If you don't, you die. You might as well know it makes no difference to me whether you live or die, whether I leave this place or not. What I like is available in here or outside...

(He lets go of her. She staggers to a seat.)

PRINCESS *(still stunned)*: ...What is that?

GRUMPY: I thought I'd made it fairly obvious. *(Beat.)* ...Humiliation and pain.

PRINCESS: But what pleasure can that bring you?

GRUMPY: Pleasure? Who's talking about pleasure... I'm just delivering reality to those who are still ignorant.

PRINCESS: That's not reality. That's brutality. Sadism.

GRUMPY: No. this is brutality.

(He throws her bodily towards the throne. She tries to hit him and he armtwists her onto the throne and straps her arms crudely to the armrests. She is whimpering.)

And sadism... You want to know sadism?

(He sits at her feet, takes a broomstick nearby and lifts her skirt slowly. The next few lines are said salaciously, obscenely.)

How you will kiss me after this... Oh yes, suck my lips like the sweetest honey... the kiss of true love... all honesty and passion – when the pain finally ceases. Relief can be so refreshing...

PRINCESS *(whimpering – rising to a scream)*: Sneezy! Help me... Happy please... I'll love you. Come back! Come back! Sneezy, please! Happy... please! No...!

(Blackout. A pool of light. IXORA in death costume [see Act 1 Sc 1] steps in with red apple in hand.)

IXORA: Illusion. Truth. Death. Life. Pain. Ecstasy. Choose.

(Another pool of light comes on. PRINCESS steps in.)

PRINCESS: I choose death. Death. Relief. Letting go. No pain. No choices. Letting go.

SNEEZY *(stepping into the PRINCESS's circle of light and embracing her)*: You should have chosen me. At least there was a probability for some life.

(Princess walks out of circle and into IXORA's circle of light. SNEEZY's circle blacks out.)

Princess: I am tired. Tired of choices. Of uncertainties. Pain is one certainty. Death is another.

(She takes the apple, embraces IXORA and is about to bite into it when the other circle of light comes on with HAPPY in it.)

HAPPY: Belief is another certainty, Princess. Everything... all knowledge, all hope is empty unless you believe in things. I believe you don't want to die, my dear. I believe you are capable of choosing life with all its struggles and all its aches. I believe you can grow to truly love...

(PRINCESS drops apple, turns around and begins to weep silently.)

PRINCESS: Oh Happy...

(She makes a move towards HAPPY but IXORA embraces her tightly from behind.)

IXORA *(meaningfully)*: You were so close to peace.

PRINCESS: Let go of me. Please. I know what I want now.

IXORA: And what might that be, pretty one?

PRINCESS: I want to believe in myself without any pretence. With no illusions.

IXORA: Is it worth the trouble? You are so very close to peace.

PRINCESS: Let go. Please...

(IXORA doesn't let go. The PRINCESS stamps on her feet. She lets go, but before she can regain her composure, the PRINCESS shoves her violently out of the circle and runs into HAPPY's circle.)

PRINCESS *(trembling)*: Oh Happy... Happy... I made my decision. But now I'm so afraid. Hold me, please...

HAPPY *(holding her awkwardly)*: I'm not good at this, you know.

PRINCESS: I'm uncertain myself.

HAPPY: What about the apple...? How do you – feel?

PRINCESS *(with uncertainty)*: Oh that. I don't know any more. It made me scared. I saw things in me I didn't want to see. But you know what's even more frightening?

(HAPPY shakes his head.)

To know that maybe the apple had nothing to do with how I felt. I wasn't afraid of forbidden things, Happy. I was afraid because there are many things in me I don't understand. I was afraid because once I understood the hidden, dark things and believed in myself, there was a chance I would have to become a different person – live a different life. Now isn't that scary?

HAPPY *(unhappily)*: Are you trying to reject me again – in a nice way? You still don't want a man, right?

PRINCESS: It's not just about men and women, Happy. All I'm saying is I'm not afraid of being scared any longer. And not scared of believing in my own decisions. Does that make sense?

HAPPY: In my country it is called courage and honesty.

PRINCESS: In my country, there were no such words.

HAPPY *(nods silently. Then...)*: How about a hug?

PRINCESS: I believe... I would want that very much. *(They hug.)* ...And a kiss?

HAPPY: Uh, not yet, dearest. Don't want to overdo it just yet.

(They laugh, hug again.)

SCENE TWO: THE AWAKENING

(Set in a forest clearing. Lights come on PRINCE and unconscious PRINCESS in a forest clearing. The PRINCE has just kissed the PRINCESS. She awakens.)

PRINCE: You're awake.

PRINCESS: Happy, you kissed me. We got out of the House!

PRINCE *(whiny)*: Happy? Oh God, not again. You're delirious again...

PRINCESS: You're not Happy. You're Charming, aren't you?

(He nods. She slaps him.)

How dare you kiss me! What else have you done to me? Tell me! How have you taken advantage of me...

PRINCE: You're not delirious... This is confusing.

PRINCESS *(coming into full realisation, she turns aside)*: It's you... it's really you. Did you ...?

PRINCE *(sulkily)*: If you apologise and promise not to hit me again, I might be persuaded to join in this conversation. But in any case, I think I'm going home. I'm giving up. All I wanted was a beautiful, dark and well-tanned princess to bring home...

PRINCESS *(stung, then sarcastically)*: Dark and well-tanned! Well, I suppose I could soak myself in tar to please you... An apology indeed!

PRINCE *(flaring up)*: I am in no mood for a marital squabble with a woman who is not my wife, who hasn't an ounce of appreciation for my being by her side one whole week against assorted carnivores, and who I know will never show gratitude for my simple offer of companionship. *(Beat.)* I only kissed you because I was afraid you would die. I am that simple. It was a desperate act.

(She remains sullen and untrusting.)

What the fuck did you want me to do? Tell me, what would have made you happy?

PRINCESS: You could have asked my permission...

(He gets up immediately and starts walking out.)

Wait, where are you going?

PRINCE: I am going back to my father's kingdom – I don't need your permission for that, do I? I am going back to practise becoming a monk or a homosexual – or both. *That* must be easier than trying to marry a goddamned Princess!

(He begins to stalk out but she speaks as he reaches the edge of the stage.)

PRINCESS: I... apologise. I'm sorry. I believe you and I'm sorry.

PRINCE *(without turning around)*: God... *(Beat.)* Something tells me not to stay. Not to listen. I am so... tired. Never expected the journey to be so tedious. So long. And all I wanted was someone...

PRINCESS: Please stay. Please listen. Something tells me that I would be the greatest fool if I didn't at least try to stop you from leaving. My dear – I am also tired. My journey has also been a long one. Forgive me. Stay.

(He turns around, walks to her until he is in front of her. They do not touch.)

I would like your permission to kiss you.

(He does not give an answer for a long while. She turns away in disappointment. She starts to walk away but he speaks.)

PRINCE: I am afraid.

PRINCESS: There's a lot of that going around these days.

(She goes to him. They kiss passionately. Just as they get started, she stops. He is somewhat irritated but not enough to be angry any more.)

PRINCESS: My father! How... is he alive?

PRINCE: He is not dead – yet. She hasn't been able to force him to change his will. He's not well. I myself barely managed to get out with my own life.

(He's about to kiss her again but...)

PRINCESS: I don't remember much... what...?

PRINCE *(giving up romance)*: She threatened Coco. Sent him to rip your heart out for some recipe for eternal youth. Anyway, you know Coco. He couldn't do it. Lost you in the forest and he slaughtered a goat.

(Bursts out laughing.)

She's got horns now, the witch... but poor Coco. She burst his eyes like bubbles with the very horns he had caused.

PRINCESS: We must go back. Now.

PRINCE: No, we must never return. It is too late. Your father is absolutely lost to her. He might not even recognise you now. I don't think he even suffers any more...

PRINCESS: If it were only my father...

PRINCE: Your kingdom then? My father's kingdom is twice the size of yours. I'll give you half.

(She is unconvinced. He speaks soothingly.)

Look, we have a whole new life of happiness before us. Do you know what a happy place my kingdom is? There has been peace there for 200 years. Four generations! In my country, my people work hard – and willingly too. We are rich. We have splendid rules that make everything work perfectly – so long as the peasants never question, we never punish. It is perfect! We spend our weekends picnicking – even the royal family. Come with me, my Princess, and leave all this sordidness behind. Our children can grow up strong and healthy – and happy.

PRINCESS: There was an apple I refused to eat. But now I am tired and it seems so attractive. *(Beat.)* She sent you, didn't she?

PRINCE: Who are you talking about? What's this about apples and...

PRINCESS: She wants my kingdom. She wants to pack me off... well, how much dowry did you make off with, gentle Prince? Enough to pull your flea-bitten plot of a kingdom out of some miserable debt?

PRINCE: Oh, I see. You suspect treachery.

(Pause.)

So what now? Is there to be a test? What, shall I go and bring you her head... her heart, any part you wish...

PRINCESS: There are journeys where the path is narrow enough to allow only one through. Strangely enough, these are the most important journeys in life... It is time for mine.

PRINCE: So you are saying you want to face her alone...?

PRINCESS: You can come with me but I am wondering... what you would be doing behind me as I face her. Would you be holding a sword ready in case I needed it – or would the tip be pointed at my back?

PRINCE: That is assuming I even wanted to go with you. In any case, isn't this the usual worry in the choice of a partner?

(Beat.)

PRINCESS: So, do I go alone?

PRINCE: It is as much your choice as mine.

PRINCESS *(making a decision)*: Alright then. You come.

PRINCE: And my sword? Wouldn't you rather keep...

PRINCESS *(calm)*: You keep it. If you must betray me, then do it with compassion. Make it quick. I will not fear the pain in my body – but you must not look at my face for I shall be crying. And remember... I have decided to trust, to give myself to you...

PRINCE: What do you mean by all this?

PRINCESS: Only this. I have decided to love you.

PRINCE: Decided...?

(She walks over, kisses him on the cheek, caresses his hair briefly and begins to walk out. The light dims to darkness as she exits. The PRINCE is left alone and in awe of her decision.)

SCENE THREE: BACK TO THE PALACE

(Set in IXORA's room. Present are the KING, TRUTHSAYER [still trapped in the mirror], COCO [blinded] and another of IXORA's young men.)

IXORA: Once again.

EVERYONE *(chorusing as if chanting some prayer)*: You are the most beautiful, the most high, the star of our western skies. Show to us your goodness and kindness and beauty, oh wondrous queen so that we may bask in the glory of your benevolence. We will forever humbly kneel before you in wretched servitude and hope to be your servants till such time where you deign to relinquish our services. You are the spring of...

IXORA: Wait. Wait... I don't like the word "beauty" in the second sentence. What kind of second-rated court poet have you hired, Coco? He used the word "beautiful" in the first line. Couldn't he think of another word besides "beauty" in the second? What's the point of holding an Arts Festival if the dedication to me isn't perfect? It's got to be the best piece. Start interviewing for another poet. If you find a better one, get rid of this one. He's served his function. Kill him or something... no one should know that this dedication was... commissioned. We'll get some civil servant to pretend he wrote it for me from the natural wellings of admiration in his simple obedient heart...

COCO: Yes, your majesty.

IXORA: And what's the latest news of the search for the two...?

COCO: Our scouts refuse to go to Suicide Forest.

IXORA: Force them. Threaten them. I don't care what you use.

COCO: I tried.

IXORA: And...

COCO: Three of our best divisions have deserted us.

IXORA: Damn! Then force the worst, lousiest divisions into the forest. Maybe they're more stupid and gullible. Maybe they'll go if we offer them more money. Did you try money?

COCO: Yes, and blackmail, and even bought them women... They won't go. Maybe it's not just the forest. Maybe they just don't want to go after the Prin...

IXORA: If I wanted political commentaries, I would have hired myself a few ministers. Just do as you're told. Your theories bore me. *(Turning to YOUTH)* He's going out to carry out some orders. You need anything?

KING: I need a pisspot.

IXORA: I wasn't addressing you, old fart. You can do it all in your pants. No one's going to mind. *(To COCO)* Go now.

KING: There was an artist who put shit on his head to show the woman he loved what abject misery he felt about his own state when he saw her beauty. I will put shit on my head to make you look more beautiful. Will you love me then?

IXORA: I will despise you just a little bit less if you stop chattering and interrupting me.

KING: Alright, my love. My beauty... *(he continues to mouth meaningless, flattering phrases)*.

YOUTH: Why do you keep him here? You don't even pretend to love him.

IXORA: That is precisely the game. It is not to fall in love but to be loved. He is here so he can see how others desire me and this will drive him wild. How can he not love me more then? He...

YOUTH: But he is decrepit and awful and smelly.

IXORA: These make the best slaves. These will give you everything they own and then offer you their undying adoration. Young ones like you can just suddenly, one morning, find me too old. I, however, will always be younger and more beautiful than him. But you ask too much. I wasn't so much interested in the size of your intellect as...

YOUTH: As the size of my... passion?

IXORA: You have a bad habit of interrupting me. *(Suddenly threatening)* See that it is not repeated. Now come over here...

(She begins undressing him. Notices TRUTHSAYER who is watching balefully from the mirror.)

Ahhh, Truthsayer, what have you to say to this?

TRUTHSAYER *(automatically subservient)*: You are like the unopened rose. You are pure like an untouched stream...

(Suddenly COCO bursts in. There is joy all over his face.)

IXORA *(delighted)*: You have found them!

COCO: No, madame. They have found you.

(He steps aside and the PRINCE and PRINCESS enter. The PRINCE is armed. The KING turns his mumbling flattery to his daughter but doesn't seem to recognise her.)

IXORA: Back from your honeymoon already? Why... was the forest floor an inappropriate place to lose your royal virginity? Too many ants? Alright, enough small talk. What do you want?

PRINCESS: Three things, vixen. One. I have been away one week and have not heard from my father that he is well.

IXORA: He is a little under the weather, so to speak...

PRINCESS: I have an edict here that allows me...

IXORA: I know what that senile old fool...

PRINCESS: You will adopt a more respectful tone when you speak about any person in my family!

IXORA: Ah... new teeth in this puppy. I...

PRINCESS: And the second thing. You will account for this most inhuman treatment of two of our most loyal servants...

IXORA: I—am—Queen. I account for NOTHING!

PRINCESS *(threateningly)*: And the third thing. I have come to take your crown. My father has abdicated in my favour.

IXORA: That's a lie! He was down here with me all this time. There was no new edict. I have his seal...

PRINCESS: You hold the King's seal hostage? That's interesting. I had no idea we were talking treason here.

IXORA: Treason? What nonsense! The King is alive. He adores me. He allows me to keep the seal because I am queen...

PRINCESS: You are *not* the Queen. You are an illegal usurper. You have no sons. My father is now senile and now this is *my* palace.

IXORA: The people know me as queen. They have seen your father's senility and his past deceptions...

PRINCESS: True. They will judge our past mistakes – but do you think, for one moment, they will let you, a foreigner, sit on the throne and judge any of us? Think again, witch. They were cheering for me on my way to the palace.

IXORA: The peasants are bored. When they're not making babies, they enjoy cheering for some celebrity or other. It's in their genes. Nevertheless my army will...

PRINCESS: I met three generals from our best divisions on my way back to the city. They seemed strangely disenchanted with you.

IXORA *(bitterly)*: My, you have changed in a week. *(Beat. Change of tone.)* Alright then, I leave. Coco, it—is—time.

COCO *(fearfully)*: No.

IXORA *(threatening)*: Coco...

(COCO moves towards her. He is whimpering.)

IXORA: Are you mad! She's in the other direction...

COCO: Oh my beautiful queen, my beautiful, beautiful...

(He gets to a confused IXORA and with a sudden strength, throws her to the ground, whipping out a knife. He shouts...)

> She wants to put me in the mirror but I won't do it! I won't betray you! Princess, this is for... *(IXORA twists out of his grasp and turns the knife on him instead)* ...you.

(IXORA makes a move to get to the embedded dagger but the PRINCE is quick and wards her away with his sword. He backs her into a corner. The PRINCESS runs over to a fallen COCO.)

PRINCESS: Coco... oh Coco... my childhood friend. What has she done?

COCO: I would have done it for your mother... if I could have saved her. But my body was no shield for her disease...

PRINCESS: She was not worth your love, Coco.

COCO: Yes. I know ...the pain. Strange how even at the end it is the only real thing I have ever known.

(He dies.)

PRINCE: It seems that a debt is owing here, although I must say the repayment is meagre...

(He is about to stab IXORA when the KING intervenes, almost hysterically.)

KING *(with his hands all over IXORA's body)*: No, no, no, no... not my beauty. My precious beauty. She is the star of the western sky... servitude... her humble servant... lick her toes like puppydog...

IXORA *(repulsed)*: Oh God, kill me!

(The KING continues with his mindless molestation.)

PRINCESS: No. I have suffered in your lies and illusions, now you will suffer my reality. For the rest of your life you will get what you always wanted...

IXORA: Kill me now and get it over with!

PRINCESS *(with a lot of control and strength)*: It's too bad we can't have everything we want in life – or death. But I remember a time when you would have given anything for his adoration. To be his wife. Now here you are. And you will remain. For the rest of your life. You will stay here and feed my father his illusions. Daily. With—a—lot—of—care. If he dies before you, I'll give you to the nearest whorehouse and have your naked body manacled to a bed. And you will have more admirers than you'll ever want... butchers, sailors, labourers... I am sure they would love a sampling of royal... hospitality.

IXORA: I'll kill him. You'll never dare...

PRINCESS: I daresay you'll hate the whorehouse. There are few illusions for you to weave there. *(To PRINCE)* Take them upstairs first. I need to talk to a friend.

(They exit.)

Truthsayer, old friend. Are you suffering? What can I do? Are you in pain?

TRUTHSAYER: It is not too bad now. If only your father had listened...

PRINCESS: Can I get you out?

TRUTHSAYER *(as he speaks it is getting darker and darker...)*: You don't need old truths. You have already found a new one in your heart. But beware, my Princess, at every moment. There is hardly a line between the bitter and the sweet... between honesty and deceit...

PRINCESS: You are suffering. I will get her to...

TRUTHSAYER *(speaks to fading light)*: When one has suffered all the truths life has to offer, he often chooses, finally, to suffer a familiar pain. I am old. I cannot take any more new tortures. I will stay here with what I know. A while back it was dark. But for now there seems to be enough light... We make do with what little illusions we are left to live with at the end... Yes, it is getting brighter...

(Light fades to darkness. There is a sobbing of a woman punctuated by a bell. Then a circular spot comes on. The sobbing woman in the centre is IXORA – bound in ropes. Light, happy dance music drifts in. The PRINCESS and the PRINCE enter with picnic basket, running, playing around IXORA's pool of light as if around a tree. They collapse laughing and in ecstasy on the other side of the stage, away from IXORA. IXORA speaks but they are unaware of her – both of them all the while playing silly, whispering games, eating apples and drinking wine. As IXORA speaks, the rope loosens and eventually falls at her feet.)

IXORA: The child does not die. The kitten did not drown.
Such a pity.
But still,
The child in each of us will love a fairy tale.
And in spite of brittle broken dreams,
Which cut into painful, bloodied feet,
The child will always love
Her apple blood-soaked, red and sweet.

The garden beckons like a long lost dream
With its inviting path of white untrodden snow.
Each season brings different sweet perfections,
The child will never know
How many sets of bloodied footsteps
Have led to the gate of her dreamtime garden
She hopes by turning her eyes to stars…
She hopes she won't awaken.
Such a pity.

(She smiles, re-charged.)

Slowly, I will relearn the strength of my name,
And if patience will not pay, then hatred will.
Slowly my wings stretch and spread again –
Black and leathery like the eternal wind at night
Blowing over lovers their eyes like stars,
I disguise their pain, disguise their scars.
And round and round their lives will spin
Till those who have lost will tomorrow win.
Slowly, slowly I relearn my name,
Slowly , slowly I will rise again.

(During the last four lines, the ropes fall off IXORA and she walks over to the lovers, standing behind them. The lovers laugh at a whispered joke. IXORA joins in their laughter. The lovers stop laughing suddenly, as if hearing her. For a moment there is silence. The lovers suddenly giggle and laugh again. IXORA opens her arms as if in welcome.)

Ah… Paradise again!

(The light fades.)

-END-

Good Asian Values

A MONOLOGUE

by Chng Suan Tze

GOOD ASIAN VALUES is the second in a series of four short monologues that look at events that affect children from the children's perspective. It aims to make you laugh and hopes to make you think – just a little bit !

CHARACTER:

A boy of seven.

GOOD ASIAN VALUES was given a rehearsed reading by Theatreworks on 8 June 1991. It was directed by Ong Keng Sen and read by Alec Tok.

Good Asian Values © **1993 Chng Suan Tze**

(A boy of seven is talking to his mother about what happened in school.)

No mum, today we did not have homework. It's true, our teacher did not give us homework today... I think it's because the teacher need to rest. But we have spelling and dictation today. I got 90 marks only because I have three words wrong. Peter also got 90 marks because he has three words wrong. Guo Wei also got 90 marks... No we didn't copy each other. Actually Fatty Wong also got three words wrong but he got only 88 marks because the teacher minus two marks for oiliness. No, it's not untidiness. The teacher said that Fatty Wong's paper is full of oil... I think Fatty Wong just ate a butter roll and his hands were oily... Only Diana has 100 marks.

Ya, got quite a lot of things happen today. Fatty Wong brought a plastic mask. He look very funny when he put it on. The nose was round and red and it's got two long moustache and the eyes were so long and small and it is smiling all the time. I think his aunty gave it to him. I think the aunty said that it is a Confucius mask. You know, she said that Confucius is a very wise man; he lived in China long long ago. When Fatty Wong puts it on he looks real funny. He looks like a fat, smiling Confucius.

Then Guo Wei want to borrow it and Peter also want to borrow it and Fatty Wong decide to lend to Peter because yesterday Guo Wei did not let Fatty Wong taste his coconut bun, so Guo Wei got angry and he punch the Confucius mask and the nose got dented and Fatty Wong was very angry and he and Peter want to fight Guo Wei and then the bell ring and we have to go to Assembly. No we didn't fight. I already told you the bell ring and we have to line up in twos for Assembly. Every Monday the whole school must go for Assembly.

During Assembly, the Principal was very angry. She said, "Today I want to scold some people." She said yesterday the discipline master caught two girl students from Secondary 2 behaving very badly outside the school.

I don't know exactly what they did. No, they did not steal things. They also did not fight. The Principal say something like they were caught with two school boys from the school next door.

The Principal say it's bad for girl students to play with boy students. She say if we play and play we will not pass our exams. I think I better not play with Laura any more.

The Principal said that the two girls were caught outside the Marina Centre. She said they were wearing school uniforms and playing with the boys. She said its very bad to wear school uniforms and play with boys. She said their behaviour was *tau yan*. What is the meaning of *tau yan*, mum? Oh, *tau yan* means bad also. I thought *huai tan* means bad already. Our Chinese teacher always call us *huai tan*, but she never call us *tau yan*.

Then the Principal says the two girls' behaviour is very bad because they *yao lai yao qu, bao lai bao qu. Yao lai yao qu, bao lai bao qu* means shaking about, right? And hugging also? She said that if they are caught again they will be punished. She said now she will not punish them. She will give them a chance to turn over a new leaf.

Mummy, why people cannot *yao lai yao qu, bao lai bao qu*? Is it because they wear school uniforms or what? If don't wear school uniforms then can *yao lai yao qu, bao lai bao qu* or not?

Then the Principal said that all the bad behaviour is because we all never learn our er, what did she say? Er, ya, she said Asian Values... she said we never learn Asian Values properly. She said that if we had learned it properly during our civics class then we will know how to behave better. In fact she said that good thing the government is going to introduce *shared values* to the students. She said that shared values will be taught in Chinese, so all of us must learn our Chinese properly. She said Chinese is very important if we want to learn to behave well...

Oh, mum, today we have a new "Chinese" teacher. Her name is Wang Lau Si. The other teacher, Chen Lau Si, she resign already. I don't know why she resign. I think its because of her throat. Ya, I think it's because she has a very bad sore throat. Today we also got a new boy in our class. His name is Jonathan Jeffrey Ang. We call him JJ Ang for short. He said his mother sent him to our school because our school, the Chinese is good. He said his mother and father wants him to learn to speak Mandarin well. You know what, JJ Ang doesn't know any Mandarin at all. Only today that he learn that apple is *ping guo,* dog is *xiao gou,* rabbit is *xiao bai tu.*

You know, mummy, during Chinese class something happened. The Chinese teacher was telling us the story of *The Cowherd and the Weaving Maid* but we told her that we already heard that story. Then she tried to tell us the story of *Si Ma Guang* but we said that we also heard that story already, and then JJ Ang got bored and he took out his *Ninja Turtles* comics to read and the Chinese teacher was angry. She scolded JJ Ang and wanted to confiscate his comics. But JJ Ang refuse because he said that the comics belong to his neighbour Sivaraj and he promised Sivaraj that he will return the comics by today. So he refused to let the Chinese teacher confiscate the comics and both he and the teacher were tugging at the comics; the teacher pulled very hard but JJ Ang held on very tight and refused to let go and they pulled like they were playing tug-of-war. Wah, so exciting!

Then Fatty Wong, remember his Confucius mask? Fatty Wong was trying to get the dent out of the nose. He poked and poked but the nose remain dented. Then Peter said that the best is to put the mask on and that's what Fatty Wong did and since Fatty Wong's nose is quite big, his nose pushed the Confucius nose out and there was a loud "pop" sound and everybody look at Fatty Wong and all we saw is a fat Smiling Confucius and we all laugh and laugh again. No, the Chinese teacher didn't laugh. But her face was red and then suddenly we heard JJ Ang start to cry. Remember? They were playing tug-of-war? Nobody win because the *Ninja Turtles* comics was torn into two. Half of it was in his hands and half of it in Wang Lau Si's hands.

Jonathan Jeffrey Ang was crying loudly. He said, "You see lah you see lah, now Sivaraj's comics are torn into two. Next time he won't lend me any more comics and it's all your fault," and he continue crying. And Fatty Wong said to Wang Lau Si, he said, "Actually you are in the wrong, you should not have tore the *Ninja Turtles* comics... if you want to confiscate it, can lah, but why tear it? My father said that tearing up books is an unforgivable crime but it is still not as bad as burning books. Lucky thing you didn't burn the comics..." Ya, he was still wearing his Confucius mask. I think he was also quite excited, that's why he didn't take the mask off.

Then everybody agrees with Fatty Wong, except Guo Wei because Fatty Wong didn't lend him the mask. And everybody start talking and JJ Ang was still crying and there was a lot of noise and then the Principal walk into our class. And Wang Lau Si tried to explain what was happening and we also tried to explain what was happening and the Principal says, "Keep Quiet everybody..." We kept quiet and the Principal ask JJ Ang why he was crying and JJ Ang said: "Wang Lau Si Zhao An tore my neighbour, Sivaraj's *Ninja Turtles* comics." Then the Principal said, "Jonathan Jeffrey Ang, your Chinese teacher's name is not 'Wang Lau Si Zhao An.' *Zhao An* is not a name, it means 'good morning.' Her name is 'Wang Lau Si.'"

Then the Principal look at us angrily and told Fatty Wong to take off his Confucius mask and she told us all to keep very quiet and do our *chau xie* and she told Wang Lau Si and JJ Ang to go to her office.

We were all a bit worried. We don't know who will be punished.

Both of them are new in the class. Fatty Wong said that Wang Lau

Si is more wrong than JJ Ang but Guo Wei disagree...

Then the Principal came back with Wang Lau Si and Jonathan Jeffrey Ang and she did not look so angry any more. The Principal then told us that we must all behave well in class and not read comics in class otherwise we will not pass our exams and she said that Chinese is a very important subject. If we don't study hard and pass our Chinese, we will not be able to get into the university and Chinese is very important because we will learn good Asian Values and she also said that we must not bring toys to class to play because lesson time means that we must study.

And she said that Jonathan Jeffrey Ang has apologised to Wang Lau Si and she has promised to repent and turn over a new leaf. And he said that everybody must repent and turn over a new leaf and promise to be good. And we all said yes and we feel a little bit ashamed of ourselves.

Then we heard the Principal telling Wang Lau Si to try to make our Chinese lesson more interesting. She said that Wang Lau Si should tell us more stories, and she gave examples like *The Cowherd and the Weaving Maid,* or *Si Ma Guang.*

Then the Principal left the class and Peter quickly put up his hand. He said, "Wang Lau Si, I know how to make Chinese lesson more interesting. We must do drama in class." Then Peter took Fatty Wong's Confucius mask from under his desk and put it on and he said, "We must do acting. I will be Si Ma Guang." All of us got very excited and we say, "Ya ya, we want to do acting; we want to do acting with the mask..."

Wang Lau Si look like very angry again and she shouted "KEEP QUIET, KEEP QUIET," and then she went up to Peter and tried to take the mask off his face. She grabbed the mask by the nose and "pop" went the nose and it got dented again. This time the dent was even bigger. Fatty Wong was at that time secretly eating the coconut bun which Guo Wei had given him. When he saw that the mask was dented his face turn red and he looked angrily at Wang Lau Si. He forgot to hide his coconut bun. He look at Wang Lau Si and said, "You, why did you dent my nose? Can't you turn over a new leaf?"

Wang Lau Si at first keep very quiet. Then she started shouting like a bit mad like that. She said, "Everybody sit down and don't move. You all are very naughty. *Huai tan!*" she said. "No wonder Chen Lau Si resign." Guo Wei put up his hand and said, "Chen Lau Si resign because she has a sore throat. I think you better don't shout so much, otherwise you may get a sore throat also, then you have to resign and then we'll have no teacher to teach us Chinese." Wang Lau Si told Guo Wei to keep quiet and sit down. But she was still angry. I think she got a sore throat already. She said, "I am here to teach you good Asian Values. If you all don't behave well, I shall resign and earn more money giving Chinese tuition, just like your Chen Lau Si."

Mummy, "earn more money" – is it a good Asian Value... or is it a Shared Value?

-END-

Bra Sizes

A MONOLOGUE IN FIVE PARTS

by Theresa Tan

Too big, too small, too far apart, too close together. Breasts the assets, breasts the bane. Bra sizes may change over time, but a woman can never run away from the pleasures, the obsession, the pain and the responsibility that comes with being female. Jeannie is a part of every woman; she is one woman's insecurity and another's best friend.

CHARACTER:

JEANNIE

BRA SIZES premiered at the Black Box on 15 April 1992. It was produced by Theatreworks and featured Karen Lim as JEANNIE. It was directed by Dawn Westerhout.

It was given a rehearsed reading by Theatreworks on 8 June 1991. It was directed by Ong Keng Sen and read by Claire Wong.

SCENE ONE: JEANNIE AT SEVEN (1962)

The set: A plush chair, a coffee table with a phone on it, a stack of magazines and books on the table. May have a Christmas tree in the background.

(The character, JEANNIE, is seven, going on eight. She is sitting on the floor, with her back against the chair. There are Barbie dolls and Barbie accessories all over, plus lots of activity books. She is intent on a page of her "Bobo Bunny Annual." She is startled by the phone ringing.)

Hello, Mommy's residence! *(Giggles, then stops, speaking over her shoulder)* Sorry, Mommy, I'm sorry, I won't again, promise. Hello? Angie? Hiiii! Merry Christmas to you also. Eh, what did you get? WAAH! You so lucky! MY Barbie got a new corvettie. Then my father bought me a new watch. And my uncle bought me new books. You got "Magic Faraway Tree" ah? I got for my birthday already, that one. And then my Aunty Mary gave me a new dress, so Mommy let me wear to church and everyone said I so pretty! Huh? No... you also pretty what! But you're not as pretty as me. Never mind one. You can run faster than me... Yeah, but I can swim faster than you.

Eh, don't go. Come here and play with my new Barbie. What? You must go and see your grandmother with your mother, father ah? Oh. When? Not yet, right? OK, talk to me lah. Angie, I got something to give you. Christmas present lor. Never mind, you don't need to give me anything back. You can give me next week.

Oh, yah, last night we open presents after church. Mommy let me stay up late. Then Uncle Peter and Aunty Mary and another Uncle don't-know-what came and they all ate and drank. Then Mommy said I must go to sleep, so I went upstairs. But I couldn't sleep because I thought maybe Santa Claus will come... *(Embarrassed)* I know. Teacher said there is no Santa Claus, but my Aunty Mary said there is. So I could not sleep. Then I went to look for Mommy to ask her to tell me a story, but they all went into my parents' bedroom and they locked it. Then I heard them all laughing, and then Daddy said, "Wah, look at those coconuts!" and then Uncle Peter, I think, said, "Papayas lah, look so big!" and then my Mommy and Aunty Mary laugh and laugh. So I wanted to go inside and see what's happening but when I knocked, they all scolded me and said, "Go and sleep! Children cannot come in!" Then I stood outside the door and pretended to cry, so Mommy opened the door, and I saw them all on the bed, and Daddy was keeping something when I went in. Then my Mommy scolded me for disturbing them, then Aunty Mary brought me back to my room and then I slept! So I didn't see Santa Claus at all! Did you? Oh, you don't believe in Santa Claus *(giggle)*.

What? What were they doing? Oh, last time my cousin Lucy came with Aunty Mary and Uncle Peter, and she said – my cousin is veeeery pretty! She learns ballet and piano and her hair is brownish and long, she is fourteen. Oh, so then she said that they were reading Dirty Magazines. Don't know. Anyway I said, how come they must lock the door and then Lucy said, because inside got pictures of naked woman. *(Giggle)* Yah! *(In a whisper)* Lucy said when we girls grow up we must have big neh-neh in front. You know, like that drawing of Cinderella in my book, when you squeeze your front with your arms *(she demonstrates how)*. YAH! Lucy showed me hers. She said boys like it. She said when we grow up we must have nice big neh-neh, then we will marry a rich man. Oh, then she showed me her bra. *(Giggles)* Yah! Then she said her father always calls neh-neh papayas! My Daddy always say coconuts. He always says Mommy's coconuts are the best in the world. Huh? Your parents call it what? Best? Breast? What's that? Breast. Eeee. Breast.

(She drops the receiver suddenly.)

Sorry, Mommy, I didn't say bad word. It's not my fault. *(Looks at the receiver)* It's Angie. OK. I won't say again. I promise. Promise.

(She picks up the receiver.)

Angie? Sorry, my Mommy said I must put down the phone. *(Brightens)* I'll see you in school next week. You partner me right? Wah, we're in primary two already! OK, bye bye.

SCENE TWO: JEANNIE AT SEVENTEEN (1972)

The set: The same. Except now there are no more Barbie dolls or toys on the floor, but plenty of women's magazines. Christmas tree remains.

(JEANNIE is sitting across the chair, with her legs dangling off the side of the armchair. She is reading "Fanfare." She is pretty, hair in a ponytail. Typical Pre-U girl. Phone rings. She lazily stretches over to pick it up.)

Hello. Oh, hi, Angie! Merry Christmas, my one and only best friend. No, I don't know how many a girl can have. What did you get? Oooh! Gold bracelet some more. So you and Roger can already lah! Don't be shy with me! *(Conspiratorially)* Tell me, have you all done it yet? OK, OK. Don't scream! I won't kaypo... but I sure hope you use protection! *(She holds the receiver away from her ear while she laughs. Suddenly she stops.)*

(Impatiently) YES, MOM! No. Yah, yah, OK! I won't, I swear. I won't swear either. I promise. *(Under her breath)* Like hell.

Angie, you still there? Sorry lah. I was just kidding. It's not my fault. You left yourself open! Hmmm? Oh, dunno. Useless things lah. It's always a gold chain, or a giant teddy bear. Booooring. Why don't guys know how to buy REAL presents? Like what? Like lacy underwear, or Jaguar or something? No lah, my parents will never buy me a car. Over their dead bodies. Oh, they bought me a Bible! Can you believe that? They went and bought their seventeen-year-old daughter a BIBLE, for Christmas! Whoever heard of such a stupid present! I've read that thing over and over and over a million trillion times already! What do you mean, it's not so bad? What did your parents give you? Oh. Yah. Never mind, it's not so fantastic celebrating Christmas either. Actually it's quite boring. *(Laughs)* Yeah, you're right. Better than going to temples. But you always go to church, what. Don't they know? Oh. OK, I won't breathe a word!

Eh, did you like the party last night? Aiya, you so boring! Got Roger already, so we can't even go and pick up guys like last time. What? Are you sure? No lah. I thought my dress was very harmless. Hmm, he said that, really? Oh, I must talk to that Warren more often. He looks quite rich. No lah, of course I don't just fall for rich guys. I fall for RICH, CUTE guys. Joking. Really. That Chee Kiong is very cute, and I like him, AND he's not rich. No, don't change the subject! I want to know what they were saying about me. My bare back very low, meh? No lah! I'm going to kill that Tommy. He has never and will never see my backside! He's a sick pervert. OK, what else? What were they saying? Why don't you want to tell me? Angie, don't—

Shit! *(She is silent for a while, then she starts making funny faces as she is put on hold)* YAH, don't do that again! So quick. Angie, don't pretend. I remember exactly what we were talking about. What did those boys say about me? Tell me, Angie, or I'll tell your parents you go to church. OK, sorry, sorry! Don't torture me lah… Yah… Hmm… *(Suddenly she falls silent.)*

What? No, I'm not angry. No, I'm not mad at you. It's not your fault. Angie, stop it. Stop being so sorry. You agree with them is it? Eh, I'm telling you, my boobs are not too small, OK! I don't care what that Francis Fartface says, or that idiot Kok Weng, or any of those SJI twits! My boobs are just nice! I am a size 34, OK! That's 34 inches, OK! If they want their women with watermelon breasts why don't they all go and screw Dolly Parton?! *(She stops abruptly, holds the receiver away.)*

Sorry, Mom. I'm not swearing! I won't use such language again! I'm just angry. It's not my fault. Mm. Mm. OK. Oh, it's Angie. *(She speaks into the phone)* Yah.

Sorry, Ange. It's my Mom. You know lah. Cannot use foul language in the house, because it's blessed by God. Can't defile the sanctimony or whatever nonsense. No! No, it's OK. Maybe my cleavage isn't very... deep or what. But I have really nice boobs, right? You've seen them what, when we bathed last time at Adventure Camp. *(Suddenly seeking reassurance)* Do you think they are too small? Don't say that just because you're my friend. OK, I believe you. Cup size? Oh, A, but it's a bit small for me. I like it to be a bit small because it makes them look nicer. You're right, it's not important anyway.

Angie, my Mom wants me to eat dinner. Wait, can I tell you something first? Nobody gave me a gold chain. They all gave me books and flowers. Except for Warren, he gave me a mug. I didn't mean to lie or anything. Just felt a bit inferior to your bracelet. You know what my parents gave me? No. Wrong. They're giving me their divorce. Wow, what a merry Christmas! Oh, I don't know how it happened. *(Sarcastically)* I think my Dad was caught fondling some other woman's coconuts. My Mom is really praying for his lost soul now!

OK, I gotta go! No, don't be sorry, Angie! Parents get married so that they can tell their seventeen-year-old children that after eighteen years of marriage other people's bodies seem more interesting.

Hey, I gotta go! Oh, I forgot to give you your present last night! Give you when school reopens, OK? Thanks for the novel. No boobs, but I got brains, right?! Yah! See you. Bye. *(Hangs up, sighs deeply. Then straightens up as if called)* Coming.

SCENE THREE: JEANNIE AT TWENTY-SEVEN (1982)

The set: *The same, but now there is a cot somewhere behind the chair.*

(JEANNIE is sitting on the chair, slouching a little over a book. She looks up, arching her back a little, and gingerly touches her left side with her right hand, under her breast. She picks up the phone and dials.)

Oh, damn! *(She waits for a few seconds, then says brightly)* Hi, Mom! It's me! Merry Christmas! Wanted to read you something from that book you sent. It says here: "The need for the 'bra' has been exaggerated, and it is probably only really necessary when the breast has become fully mature, during pregnancy and lactation. If a woman is more comfortable and attractive without a bra, then she can happily do without."

(She laughs delightedly) See, Mom? Doctor says so. So all the years I never put on a bra I was right and you were wrong! *(Her voice lowers to a hiss)* I HATE talking to your machine; you're my damned mother, why can't you be at home like other people's mothers? I'm in pain, OK, Mom! You never warned me about the pain! My breasts are going to pop! Where are you on Christmas Day anyway? You never come and visit your own daughter... *(Then brusquely)* I'm only twenty-seven, I don't know anything. It's not my fault. Anyway, call me back. Bye. Oh, since I'm lactating I'm wearing a bra, OK? Happy?

(She slams the receiver down, muttering curses. She sighs and picks up the phone again, and dials.)

Hello, Angela please. Angie! Merry Christmas, I need your help. Angie, I must be doing it all wrong. It isn't supposed to hurt like this. Right? *(She continues to skim through her book, reading aloud parts of it.)*

It's my breasts again lah. What did you think? They feel so full, and taut, like balloons. They're going to explode, Angie. How come yours were never like this?

Ah, "Breasts and Breast-feeding," chapter eighteen. I'm reading this manual my mother gave me. Listen: "The primary function of a woman's breasts seems to be that they are a potent attraction to men, although the main function of the mammary gland is to provide nourishment for the infant." Wah, Ange, you should look at this! The breasts of the adolescent are bigger than mine! And I'm lactating! *(She laughs.)*

Where is the breast-feeding bit? Angie, I don't want breasts any more! Take them back!

(Suddenly she laughs) Funny, right? All the years I used to complain, "I got no boobs, I got no boobs." My tits were so small I didn't even need a bra. No chance of them drooping when they hardly protrude, right? Now they are big. I'm a size 36B! Man, I'm not joking, they look like missiles. And it's really painful, Angie!

Yah. I know. You're right, you're always right. I shouldn't have cut those classes. Serves me right. Angie, I'm not kidding. I don't even know how to feed the baby properly! She sucks and sucks until my nipples all crack. Vaseline? For what? You mean I must put on Vaseline?

Then what happens when I have milk and she's not hungry? Pump? Pump what? Into where? Oh, can keep in the fridge ah? Why didn't anyone tell me? My mother? Help me? Please lah. She's too busy helping some charity or what. "Give to God and God will give to you," and all that crap. She doesn't care one lah. She thinks I'm some immoral slut, bane of her life. And SHE was the one who read all those porno magazines. Oww! *(She clutches her breast again.)* Angie, I need help! My breasts are going to burst!

(Baby in background starts to cry.)

Oh, Christ. Now she's woken up. Oh, maybe I can try to get her to feed a bit. I think I'm going to put her on formula. Why cannot? How you know breast milk is better? Really?

No, of course Richard's not around. My husband the party animal. Doing business at some Christmas get-together. Can you come over now? Get me that pump thing? Please? Please? Where to buy a breast pump on Christmas Day? Just try, OK? I'll buy you a great dinner at the Hyatt tomorrow night, I'll baby-sit Pamela whenever you want, promise. I really really need your help. Roger will understand, right? It's Christmas. You're my best friend. I need you. Good! Thankyou-thankyou-thankyou! I'll divorce Richard and marry you, I swear! I'll make you the best wife in the world. Come now! OK? OK? Yes! I love you, Angie! Bye.

(She gets up and goes over to the cot. Baby is wailing.)

I'm not going to pick you up. I don't care if you peed in your bed again. I am not going to feed you until you learn to suck properly. These are nipples, kiddo, not straws. Oh, shit.

(She starts rocking the cot.) Shut up. Shut up.

(The phone rings. She walks over and lifts the receiver, slowly.)

Hello. Oh, it's you. Yes, the little monster is OK. Yes, that's her crying, who do you think it is? Listen, Richard, if you don't like the way I'm treating our baby why don't you come home and take care of her? Yah, right! Business, business. On fucking Christmas Day. Your idea of a public holiday I suppose, getting more money. So if you can't come home, don't complain. No – no, don't you threaten me! You send Janet to your mother's and I'll divorce you. Yah. She'll grow up knowing her father chased her mother out of the house. What do you mean, don't shout! I'm sitting at home, on Christmas Day, all alone with a baby and engorged breasts, my husband is out doing God-knows-what, my mother doesn't give a shit – Richard? Richard! Fuck you! Bloody asshole! *(She slams down the receiver.)*

Yah lah, that kind of father you have lah, Janet Lee!

(The doorbell rings offstage. JEANNIE begins making her way out, stage right.)

Angie, is that you? Oh God, thank you! *(She shouts)* Coming Angie! *(The doorbell rings again and she shouts louder)* Coming already! So impatient! People just gave birth, OK?!

SCENE FOUR: JEANNIE AT THIRTY-TWO (1987)

The set: *Same, more homey, there is a feather duster somewhere in the vicinity.*

(JEANNIE is in a stained apron, with a Coke in her hand and reading a woman's magazine. She looks up now, talking to her daughter.)

Janet! Janet, hurry up! Your grandmother is waiting for you! I told you to get ready earlier, you wouldn't listen to me. You're five years old, what do you mean you don't know how to wear? Hurry up, or she's going to go deaf honking like that.

OK, yah, bye! Don't forget to say Merry Christmas to Grandma for me. No, I don't want to wish her myself, thank you. Tell her your father says Merry Christmas also. OK. Be good, don't spend too much of Grandma's money. Just a few hundred dollars. OK. Bye bye!

(The phone rings.)

Hello. Merry Christmas! Angie, where have you been! I've missed you to death! Aiya, not busy lah. Just lazing around the house. Oh, school holidays. Wow, Australia! How are the kids? Haven't seen your darling Pamela for a while. How old is the other one? Ian, that's right. Six months already! You're not thinking of more, are you?

My mother? No lah, she can't stand my husband, she'll never step into the house, Christmas or not. But she's taken Janet out. Sometimes I think the two of them go out, eat ice-cream and bitch about Richard and me! *(Laughs)* No lah, she's FINE! Healthy as an ox. Stubborn like one too. *(Titters.)*

How's the hubby? Fat? Wait till you see Richard, man. Pale and lumpy like a beached whale. Aiya, still the same lah. How different can he get? Every day, day in day out, year in year out, he's got some business or other. Christmas Day is just one of the 365 working days—

What do you mean? Hear what? From whom? That Pereira woman told you what? *(She falls silent.)* Huh? Nothing. I knew for a long time already lah. But he doesn't want to talk about it. All he does is go and complain to his stupid mother that I do this, or I do that, that I don't take care of Janet. Then at a company dinner or something he makes me wear all these diamonds and sexy clothes so that people will think he treats his family very well. He is so scared I'll divorce him, because his boss likes me.

What? Angie... We've been friends forever. Don't. No, honestly I didn't know he's seeing her. I suspected once or twice but maybe... I didn't really want to know. No, don't say sorry. Why are you always saying sorry? You're not the one who's having affairs behind my back! You're not, right? *(Laughs feebly.)*

Here I am at home every Christmas, waiting like a stupid cow while he goes and humps that stupid cow. I'm thirty-two, Angie, I'm supposed to be peaking sexually and he's missing all the action at home. Not that he's so wonderful lah. I don't believe the cheek of that man! I never suspected, I mean, He's so ugly, right? Must be a damn ugly woman if she wants to sleep with him, right?

What? Got some more? Richard got drunk? When? Oh, yah, and what did he say? Angie. Tell me. What?! Fuck! Fuck him! I... he... *(she is speechless).* You tell me, what has that got to do with having an affair? So what about my breasts? Why, that Teo woman got bigger knockers so he has an affair with her, is it? She's nothing but a silicon valley! What does he mean, I'm cold? He's the one who can only perform once a night, if he's lucky. I'm a very good lover, OK! He's the one who has to watch blue tapes to get it up. *(Close to tears)* I don't believe he said that! I really don't believe—

Oh, you have to go? *(Silence.)* I'm OK, don't worry. Thanks for telling me. No... I don't think it's worth discussing with him. Don't worry, I told you. Angie, shut up and hang up. *(Laughs as best she can)* Yes lah. I'll see you tomorrow. Tell everyone at home I said Merry Christmas! Bye.

(She hangs up and sits back in shock.)

SCENE FIVE: JEANNIE AT THIRTY-SEVEN (1992)

The set: *It's Christmas again. There are toys all over the place.*

(JEANNIE is sitting on the sofa, removing her shoes. She is older, looks tired. She turns now to stare Stage Right.)

Where do you think you're going, Miss Janet Lee? WHERE? Again ah? Her father not tired of seeing you ah? Today Christmas Day, you not shy to go and show your face when you see them everyday ah?

What? Christmas cake? With milk? And what? Pamela's aunty gives everybody presents. Did you buy one for her or not? Pamela lah, who else. What did you get her? What do you mean, "secret"? You make sure you wish everybody, OK? Don't make me ashamed of you. I don't want people telling me I have a rude daughter.

WHAT DID YOU SAY?! You say that again. Called me a naggerpuss, right? You're gonna get it from me. What do you mean Grandma said I'm a naggerpuss. Eh, you got no respect for your mother, huh? Didn't learn your commandments in catechism, is it? Honour your father and mother. Afterwards I'm going to test you on them and you better know.

What lah, Richard? First your daughter now you. What? I know you're late. But you're always late. Married to you for eleven years, it's your only consistent trait. What's so different about today? What is it? More business right? Predictable. What, Naggerpuss? OK lah, encourage your daughter to call her mother names lah, Richard Lee. Next time when I die you'll be left with her, then we'll see.

Go on, Janet, don't be late. Call home when the party is over. Chard, will you be back for dinner? OK. Don't be back late. Mother's coming over. Bye! Bye! Have fun. Don't be too greedy!

(She sits there by herself, flips through "Vogue." Sighs. She picks up her cordless phone and dials. Listens, then she hangs up.)

Angie. After 30 years of friendship and this is the first time you haven't picked up the phone and said "What?" I miss your "What?"

Eh, saw your hubby and that Pamela of yours yesterday. Your daughter is *so* cute! She looks just like you, buck teeth and all! *(Laughs.)* Remember when we were that age? You looked like that. I was pretty, but you were the cute one.

Richard and I... remember what happened? I wanted to get a divorce because he was fooling around with that Teo woman. That cheap slut! You're the one who told me. I was really angry, Angie. I was furious. It came pretty close to a divorce, then I thought, why should I let that silly bimbo have my husband, and besides, Catholics stick by their words. Till death do us part. Boy, did I wish he was dead! *(She laughs.)*

But seriously, I thought about it carefully, for the first time in my life I had to make a decision. I made a mistake marrying Richard, like you keep reminding me. But I wasn't going to make an even bigger one divorcing him like my Mom divorced my father. Why did I marry him ah? What to do, at twenty-six I let him knock me up. Just my luck, it was my first time with him. My parents threatened suicide if I aborted. Amazing isn't it? They were divorced but when they scolded me, they'd do it together. So what to do, marry Richard lah. You were lucky, you got to marry your Roger. I don't have a lot of respect for Richard. But Janet was worth all the trouble.

I love that girl, Ange. Don't tell her, she'll pester me for a Barbie-doll house. She's funny and smart – she makes me laugh like you used to. Remember how we used to talk in Pig Latin? She's picking it up now. She thinks it's a secret language that her mummy doesn't understand. *(Long laugh.)* She called her father a "upidstay olday igpay!" I laughed first, then I walloped her. She and your Pamela are quite thick. God forbid they turn out like us.

What the hell am I doing, talking like this... I miss you, Angela. I guess I should have called you more often but you know...

How many Christmasses have there been? Thirty, can you imagine? Remember the Christmas I told you about my cousin Lucy's cleavage? That was funny wasn't it? Actually, all we ever talked about was breasts, right? Those horrible SJI boys said I got no boobs, remember? They called me "Jeannie the Aircraft Carrier." But I did have. I was a 34A cup.

(Laughs.) Remember my engorged breasts? Wow, they were a real work of God, man. But they hurt like an act of God. I was so proud of them, though.

Oh Angie, what are breasts to us now? More folds of fat, as if we don't have enough already. Remember that stupid book my mother bought for me? It said that after menopause breasts just dry up. So one day Angie, that's what my boobs will be – dried up. Like *seng buay*. After all that fuss, they just shrink and wrinkle. Why did I use to worry about whether they were big enough or not?

Boys lah. All their fault, right? If they didn't care so much, we also couldn't be bothered, right? My father, my husband, those SJI boys. All they cared about was neh-neh, neh-neh. Who said looks don't count.

Angie, I know you've been there for me a lot. I know I didn't give back all the help and attention you gave me. But I also know there were times when I don't know why, but you were jealous of me. Right, Angie? So you liked to tell me that this boy said my boobs were too small. Or that my husband was having an affair because I had no boobs. I thought my secrets were your secrets, but I heard people talking about it even at the club! It had to be you. I never told anyone else.

But never mind, those are small matters. I'm sorry you died of cancer, Angie. It's a really horrible way to die. But isn't it ironic? I'm the one talking about breasts all the time and you go and get breast cancer. It must have been terrible when they cut out your left breast. And after that the cancer still spread. I'm so sorry I didn't come and see you. I was… scared. Angie, you're only thirty-seven. It was so sudden for me. I'm really sorry for all the things I didn't do. I never went to see you at your wedding. Or when you were in hospital. Or even your funeral. I just couldn't. It's all my fault. I didn't try hard enough for you. I'm sorry, Angie.

This is my first Christmas not chatting with you. I'll still talk to you every Christmas, I promise. Maybe if I'm good, when I die, I'll see you in Heaven. It must be wonderful up there. Nobody has breasts in Heaven, right?

-END-

The Playwrights

DANA LAM

Dana Lam worked as a journalist and a book editor between 1976 and 1985. She inflicted herself on Theatreworks as its first PR/ Business Manager in 1986, and began a systematic approach to rally public support for professional Singaporean theatre. She is gainfully married.

Having borne two children who steadfastly refuse to be little geniuses, she now feels it is part of the Big Design that she quits procreation and apply her talents to playwriting. *Bernard's Story*, her first attempt, was written during the first year of the Theatreworks Writers' Laboratory.

RUSSELL HENG HIANG KHNG

Russell Heng was Features Editor of *The Sunday Times* before making a move to academia in February, 1992. He is currently a Fellow with the Institute of Southeast Asian Studies. *Lest The Demons Get To Me* is his first play. It was completed in 1987 for Theatreworks, who could not get a permit to stage it in those years when Singapore was less kind and gentle. It was revived and freshened for the Theatreworks Writers' Laboratory in 1991.

KWUAN LOH

Kwuan Loh's involvement in theatre dates back to her secondary school days when she took on bit roles in church dramas (Kwuan as Mary during Christmas) and a school play (*Twelfth Night*). She returned from a leave of absence when she won the joint Third Prize in the NUS-Shell Short Play Competition in 1988 with her first play *Stage*. *Fast Cars and Fancy Women* is her seventh play written to date and the third to be staged. *Mask*, an adaptation of Arthur Yap's short story, was staged in 1990 as part of Catholic Junior College's annual drama presentation, and *Mistress – The Going* was staged by Speechworks, NTU in 1991.

She wrote the television script for SBC's National Day Celebration 1992 – "Together We Celebrate." She also does freelance writing for magazines purely for interest's sake.

ROBIN LOON

Robin Loon's involvement in drama began when in his secondary school days he wrote and performed skits for school concerts. His first play, *Solitaire*, was written during his army days, and won the special prize in the 1989 NUS-Shell Short Play Competition. He has written two other plays – *Let's Have Dinosaur* (first prize winner in the 1989/90 NUS Drama Festival); and *Rhapsody* (performed by Varsity Playhouse in 1990). Robin joined the Writers' Laboratory in 1991.

Robin is currently doing Honours in English at the NUS. Robin's acting experience includes a role in Entertainment 100 for the ACS centennial, and the role of Malcolm Png in *Army Daze* for the 1990 Theatreworks Retrospective. He has also participated in many school productions. Robin plans to write his best play before he turns forty and aspires to be rich and famous. He is currently working on two new plays, one of which he hopes to improvise with Ong Keng Sen, Artistic Director of Theatreworks.

OVIDIA YU

Ovidia Yu is a thirty-one year-old freelance writer. Eleven of her plays have been performed in Singapore. *Flat Lives* was also performed in Hong Kong, and *Face Values* and *Three Women and a Baby* in Kuala Lumpur. *Round and Round the Dining Table*, which she also directed, was filmed for television after two stage runs.

TAN TARN HOW

Tan Tarn How is a journalist. He joined Theatreworks Writers' Laboratory in 1991, writing two plays: *Home,* and *The Lady of Soul and Her Ultimate 'S' Machine*, which was read in January 1992 at the Black Box. His plays, *In Praise Of The Dentist* and *Two Men, Three Struggles* won merit prizes in the NUS-Shell Short Play Competition in 1986 and 1987 respectively. The latter was staged in 1988 by ST*RS as part of a night of Singapore plays.

DESMOND SIM

Desmond Sim writes poetry, short stories, and plays for the theatre. His poems have been featured in college publications, the Singapore Youth Festival, Singapore and foreign anthologies. His short stories have appeared in an anthology, *MISTRESS and other creative take-offs!* and his story *The Nose* won the top prize for the National Short Story Competition, organised by the National Book Development Council. Desmond has also won a Merit Prize in the 1989/90 NUS-Shell Short Play Competition, and the First and Second Prizes in the same competition in 1991. In 1992, he was invited to participate in a Fulbright Professional Program (for research) in New York and Washington.

CHNG SUAN TZE

Chng Suan Tze is at present teaching Language and Communication at the Temasek Polytechnic. Prior to this she has taught in several government schools as well as a private school (The Singapore Swiss School). It was while teaching at the Swiss School that she began adapting and writing children's stories into plays for the children to act in their end-of-the-year concert.

In 1984, she and a group of drama enthusiasts formed the drama society, Third Stage. To date, she has written and directed five plays (*Oh! Singapore, Corabela, Oh Singapore II, Once Upon a Little Forest,* and *Kevin's Birthday Party*) for Third Stage.

THERESA TAN

Theresa Tan keeps busy as a reporter for *8 Days* magazine. Her first play, *Pistachios and Whipped Cream,* won first prize in the 1987 NUS-Shell Short Play Competition. *Bra Sizes* is her second play officially staged for a public audience. Women liked it, men didn't. She plans to write more plays about women and body parts, R(A) rating notwithstanding.

ALSO AVAILABLE

The Coffin Is Too Big For The Hole ...and other plays
by Kuo Pao Kun

Kuo Pao Kun has been a major figure in Singapore theatre for the past two decades. One of the most versatile persons in theatre, he is a director, playwright, drama teacher and theatre critic. His plays, in Mandarin and English, are innovative and incisive. Drawing on past and present theatrical and cultural traditions, he has provided audiences with a unique and stimulating theatre which continues to redefine our cultural identity and to ask questions of ourselves and the society we live in.

The Coffin Is Too Big For The Hole ...and other plays brings together for the first time his more recent work in English. Included are the title play and the groundbreaking multilingual play *Mama Looking For Her Cat*, a highlight in the development of a Singapore theatre expression. With an introduction by Krishen Jit, a leading Malaysian director and theatre critic, this volume is an important publication for anyone who is interested in or working in theatre.
ISBN 981 204 182 6

Abraham's Promise
by Philip Jeyaretnam

Abraham Isaac, teacher of Latin, philosopher and father, has a young pupil. Teaching pulls him back into his memories: of Rose, his first love; Mercy, his stubborn sister; and most of all of Rani, his beloved wife; of days of youth and promise, when he threw himself into the politics of Singapore in the fifties and sixties, when he believed he had a valuable role to play.

But now the burden of his years weighs on him heavily. Distanced from a present devoid of idealism and obsessed with power and money, Abraham is estranged from his strong, successful son. Descending into the past, Abraham is led from the promise of youth, through cynicism born of experience, to an understanding and reconciliation of his life and times hard-won in maturity.

Philip Jeyaretnam, Singapore National Arts Council's Young Artist of the Year for 1993, is also the author of *First Loves* and *Raffles Place Ragtime*, both published by Times Editions.
ISBN 981 204 515 5

ALSO AVAILABLE

People of the Pear Tree
by Rex Shelley

Rex Shelley weaves two love stories of Eurasians – *Serani* – in the torrid tropical heat against the background of Japanese-occupied Singapore and Malaya during World War II, spicing his narrative with humour, intrigue, and the ring of guerrilla gunshots on the fringes of the Malayan jungle. He writes with a straightforward honesty about down-to-earth people, using snappy dialogue and a pace that races one through the pages in tense anticipation.

People of the Pear Tree was highly commended by the National Book Development Council of Singapore in 1994. *The Shrimp People*, by the same author, won the NBDCS's 1993 top fiction award. Rex Shelley has a third *Serani* novel, *Island in the Centre* (1995).
ISBN 981 204 449 3

Saving the Rainforest and other stories
by Claire Tham

"I believe in the sanctity of the ordinariness of everyday life: beyond its charmed boundaries lies confusion." So speaks the voice of conservatism and conformity. But shouldn't one fly, push oneself to the limit and beyond, break all the rules? With humour and intelligence, Claire Tham explores the tensions that arise when the desire for personal fulfilment clashes with societies' norms: the conservative, middle-aged woman lawyer who finds herself inadvertently dating her best friend's son. Leena, the Indian hotel receptionist who marries an expatriate American against her family's wishes, only to discover his mysterious lifestyle seals her isolation.

In her second collection of short stories, Claire Tham continues a number of themes from her first award-winning collection, *Fascist Rock*. Both books deal with the hidden rebellion lying beneath even the most conventional surfaces: it is the desire to break out, to redefine ourselves amidst a world that expects us to conform and cooperate. In describing this hidden rebellion, Claire Tham strikes a universal chord.

Saving the Rainforest was highly commended by the National Book Development Council of Singapore in 1994.
ISBN 981 204 439 6

ALSO AVAILABLE

Scorpion Orchid
by Lloyd Fernando

Sabran, Santi, Guan Kheng and Peter – four young men united by the bonds of friendship, brought together in the uniquely multicultural society of Singapore. About to graduate from university, they are caught in the political unheavals of the fifties. These are uncertain times: still recovering from the Japanese Occupation, Singapore is on the brink of her fight for independence from the British.

As they watch their countrymen confront each other, tearing the country apart, they face up to the reality of their multiracial society. Against a backdrop of violence and hatred, each embarks on an arduous journey of self-discovery, to reconcile deep-seated cultures and traditions with a new emerging society. In their quest for their true selves, the bonds of their friendship are sorely tried.

ISBN 981 204 327 6

Sayang
by Gopal Baratham

"Though I rarely had occasion to use it, I know the word and its implications well. It describes a love bound to sadness, a tenderness trembling on the edge of tears, a passion from which pity could not be detached ... I did not realise how fully I could understand *sayang*. Had I known, I would have given it more thought ..."

Joe Samy suspects his wife, Ri, is cheating on him, and he engages the rough but affable private eye, Sigmund Lee, to shadow her. As he is led on a roundabout ride, Joe succumbs to temptation himself, first with a transsexual, then with his son's girlfriend. Events begin to take a twist for the macabre as Ri falls mysteriously ill and their son, Kris, submits his body to a drug peddlar while Joe himself tangles with a defrocked priest. As his family falls apart, Joe Samy, now vulnerable and not so smug, takes a hard lesson from life on the true meaning of *sayang*.

Gopal Baratham, winner of the Southeast Asia WRITE award, takes us across Singapore, Indonesia and Thailand to deliver his most thought-provoking and shocking novel yet.

ISBN 981 204 291 1

ALSO AVAILABLE

Another Place

by Boey Kim Cheng

"Most of these poems return from a journey into a land which looks like the past, coming home with a backward gaze, as if not quite believing the moments, which seemed so intensely real, are gone," says Boey Kim Cheng of the poems in his second collection. He has been described by literary critics as one of Singapore's most promising poets, whose "mastery of form and technique is admirably competent". Lee Tzu Pheng, a poet well-known to Singaporeans, says of his poems: "There is no denying the power of his poetry, a poetry so often, one feels, energized by its need to break through."

Somewhere Bound, Boey Kim Cheng's first collection of poems, is also published by Times Editions.

ISBN 981 204 402 7

The Woman's Book of Superlatives

by Catherine Lim

"You held out your hand for an egg and fate put into it a scorpion ... close your fingers firmly upon the gift; let it sting through your palm ... in time, after your hand and arm have swelled and quivered long with torture, the squeezed scorpion will die, and you will have learned a great lesson: how to endure without a sob."

Is it the fate of woman to endure? Is she inseparable from her fecundity? Rape, incest, abortion, sexual harassment, wife-battering, marital infidelity, childbearing, prostitution. The stories in this superbly crafted collection represent the superlatives of woman's endurance in a tragi-comic vein. Laced with touches of the sexually macabre, the lives of women across different cultures are drawn tightly upon that axiom.

Catherine Lim beguiles the reader with a startling contrast: the deification of women in ancient myths, against the degradation of ordinary women in modern times. Time and again, an unwonted bond of sisterhood appears, and is affirmed in a final, fateful collision.

Also by the same author: *The Serpent's Tooth*, *They Do Return*, and *O Singapore! Stories in Celebration*, published by Times Editions.

ISBN 981 204 401 9

ALSO AVAILABLE

The Mouse Marathon
by Ovidia Yu

Lee Jaylin, a 31-year-old workaholic advertising executive, wonders just what the point of it all is when her long-time friend and lover departs to travel the world, leaving her with the less than exhilarating task of promoting 'designer condoms'.

With penetration, humour and roller-coaster momentum, Ovidia Yu subtly weaves an intricate web of hidden relationships with a highly comic series of events, in the process questioning the most cherished assumptions of Singapore's high-pressure, breakneck-paced lifestyle. Is it really a rat race? Or just a long and lonely mouse marathon ...

ISBN 981 204 403 9

The Sin-kheh
by Goh Sin Tub

"The coolie's burning eyes blinked and flashed as they focussed on the men clambering down into the boats. With a snort, he cleared his throat and spat his wrath into the sea.

'Wah piang!' he exclaimed in scorn. 'Sin-kheh!' "

And so begins the story of the rambunctious young Sin Kay, newest arrival of the Wee clan in Singapore, expert in the martial arts, irrepressible lover of the sensuous Jade and the gentle Mah Cheng. It is a tender and gripping, often humorous story of courage, resolution, and determination, a story of the early Chinese immigrants to Singapore, their sacrifices, and the penalties paid particularly by their women.

The novel, based on the life and times of his grandfather, is written by one of Singapore's most established authors. Goh Sin Tub's collection of short stories *If You Too Could Do Voodoo, Who Would You Do Voodoo To?* is also published by Times Editions.

ISBN 981 204 467 1

ALSO AVAILABLE

The Stolen Child
by Colin Cheong

Wing discovers that there are many roads to a single dream. He wants to fly, but his dream is suddenly shattered. As he searches for a meaning in life and other dreams to replace his first love, Wing experiences the trials and tribulations of change – in his family, friends, and most of all, himself.

A powerful and moving story about growing up, innocence and love, toughness and courage. A search across time and space: from the wonders of childhood to the strident urges of young manhood; from the landscape of the mind to the realm of the heart.

Colin Cheong's other fiction titles published by Times Editions include *Poets, Priests and Prostitutes* and *Life Cycle of Homo Sapiens, Male*.

ISBN 981 204 133 8

Beneath The Blue Moon
by Len Webster

To Bangkok, Haadyai and Singapore they come, the enterprising girls of the night that trade secretly in sex. Driven by poverty, ambition or just circumstances, they travel far away from home, their bodies their only asset in hunting grounds like *The Blue Moon* bar.

Recreating an underworld only glimpsed by respectable Singaporeans, *Beneath The Blue Moon* is a shocking book, but also a moving one, for inhabiting the twilight world beneath the warped surface are ordinary people with human stories and individual destinies. Len Webster's little gem is painfully honest and uncluttered by gimmickry. It is told in convincing detail, without horror but also without falling into the cliché of the 'innocent harlot'.

Len Webster's *Hell Riders*, a short-story collection, is also published by Times Editions.

ISBN 981 204 328 4